Joining Janjan

Portsmouth Paranormal Romance #2

By

David H. Barnette

Joining Janjan

Copyright © 2016 by David H. Barnette

Published by Piscataqua Press
An imprint of RiverRun Bookstore Inc.
142 Fleet Street | Portsmouth, NH | 03801
www.riverrunbookstore.com
www.piscataquapress.com

ISBN: 978-1-944393-15-1

Printed in the United States of America

Visit https://www.facebook.com/d.h.barnette for more information

The Nextworld Trilogy (eBooks)
The Next World Over
The Next World Under
The Next World Out

From Piscataqua Press
The Portsmouth Paranormal Romances
Loving Leda
Joining Janjan

1

Travelers Wrapped in Light *(This February)*

"Portsmouth has always been a weird little town," Jerry August said. He and Leda told me their story in January. It was hard to believe. Like most people in Portsmouth, I'd been ignoring all the weirdness. Then came February.

We were having a hard winter, scary-cold, tons of snow, and no time between storms. Snowplows battled to keep up. Towering snowbanks squeezed two-lane roads down to a lane and a half. Traveling two miles to work became an adventure.

I tried to embrace the polar vortex. Whenever I got a chance, I went cross-country skiing after work. Sometimes Beth or another friend came along, but today I was alone.

I skied southwest for miles. Up and down rolling hills under humming power lines. I whished over old packed snow. A new layer of light, slippery powder covered my skis. The ski bindings creaked and the old snow crunched under me. I was feeling fit and strong—for me—this winter. I'd dropped a few pounds without even trying. I'd never have a bikini body, but still. I glided along at an easy pace that helped me think.

I thought: *I'm sick of Portsmouth.* Nobody ever admits what a strange place it is. There's a gap between what happens—or *may* have happened—and what people will talk about. What are they afraid of? They don't share family secrets with people like me who weren't born here. Anyway. Sometimes I thought about moving home, speaking of family.

I wasn't sure where *home* was anymore. Buffalo seemed like another country now. I couldn't really afford to move. Jobs were scarce in Upstate New York. I was earning a decent salary in Portsmouth, but money was still tight. I was renting a house I couldn't pay for alone. And Beth, my remaining housemate, was talking about going home to live with her mother in Providence.

Leda, our third housemate, bailed on us last year. No visit, no text, no call, no email, no cards, no letters, no Facebook, Twitter, Instagram, Tumblr, Snapchat, or Flickr.

She'd been in some trouble, and I'd heard things, like that she'd been *kidnapped*, for God's sake. Then all of a sudden she was back in town. She wouldn't say much about where she'd been, except that her skinny-ass boyfriend Jerry had rescued her. *Yeah, right,* I thought, *a likely story.*

Shortly after she came back, Leda disappeared again, and nobody knew a damn thing. I couldn't help worrying.

I didn't see Leda again until January, just last month. She and Jerry were married now, no surprise.

Like I said, they told me everything that happened to them. There were lots of surprises. I'll get to that later.

Beth and I couldn't find a new housemate we both liked, so we split the rent. It was a financial strain, especially this winter. Heating oil prices kept climbing.

Also, if we were going to stay friends and live in the same house, the two of us really needed to talk. Guys think girls talk about everything. Beth and I had to talk around a big conversational no-fly zone; to enter it would be an act of war.

Naturally I flew into ours. I'll get to that later, too.

While I was pondering the meaning of life, but mostly enjoying the sensual, dreamlike feeling of almost-effortless movement, late afternoon got darker and quickly became low-lit evening. You ask: Is it stupid to ski alone in the dark? Yeah, but I didn't think it was going to get pitch dark. Low clouds reflected light from the highway and from distant streetlights. The snow seemed to shine with a light of its own. I could pretty much see where I was going.

I'd skied further out than I'd ever gone before. It was time to head back to my car. In the exhilaration of skiing, I didn't notice how tired I was. Cold acts as a temporary anesthetic. Sometimes what doesn't kill us makes us stupid.

Hoping to cut a couple of miles off the return trip, I headed east into the gentle hills of an old orchard.

I wasn't the first to go this way since the last snowfall. Even in the dusk I could see ski and snowshoe tracks—and a single set of fresh footprints. Huh. Somebody had *hiked* out here today, even though it was a struggle to walk without snowshoes. In several places the hiker had broken through the snow crust, pulled a foot up out of the hole, and kept going.

My girly-sense told me this shortcut was a bad idea and that I should go back the way I came. Probably sound advice. I ignored it.

In the distance I saw a black line of trees. Between the orchard and the railroad tracks that cut through the fields was a towering wall of evergreen hedge.

A path ran along the east side of the field, uphill and down next to the hedgerow. As I'd hoped, snowmobiles had packed the snow down and

3

broken a trail for me to ski on. God bless my redneck gas-burning snow buddies. I lost track of the footprints, couldn't see them in the shadow of the hedges.

As I bounced up the highest hill on this side of the field, my chubby thighs started to burn with fatigue. I may have heard Garbage singing "Stupid Girl." Is it stupid to be nostalgic for the 1990s? I wondered if boys also suffer from self-mocking musical earworms.

At the top of the hill, I paused to catch my breath. Warm as I was from the effort of skiing and hill-climbing, I still felt the cold getting colder. It was *wicked pissah cold*, as they say around here. *Supernatural cold,* she said ominously.

Off to one side of the trail, a man's head and shoulders emerged from a stand of dense low bushes. *Jesus,* I thought, *my girly-sense was right.* Was I going to have to fight or flee? I flexed my leg muscles, getting ready to turn and make a break for it.

But the man wasn't staring at me like a rapist or mugger lying in wait. He wasn't looking at *me* at all.

He was looking up into the air, the way a cat stares intently at something nobody else can see.

I looked up, too. The clouds had parted above the hillock. It wasn't the Son of Man coming in that cloud with power and great glory.

Whoever they were, those aerial travelers, they weren't sons and daughters of men and women. Or not *just* men and women.

I didn't blame the guy in the bushes for gaping at them. I was staring rudely myself. I mean, the *air* is not where you expect to see people—or any humanoid creatures—walking and dancing. What was that faint archaic music? Tambour? Lute? Voices that seemed to sing in counterpoint? How could any of this be real?

Something happened between the travelers and the guy in the bushes, some communication I wasn't privy to. It seemed they called him to themselves, but he said *No, thank you.*

Sadly, it seemed, they turned their attention away from him.

Hopefully, it seemed, they turned their attention to me.

2

Be Not Self-Will'd *(This January)*

Be not self-will'd, for thou art much too fair,
To be Death's conquest and make worms thine heir.

Shakespeare, "Sonnet 6"

Let me back up a bit.

Before I ever saw any mysterious travelers wrapped in light, I learned my friend Leda was an elf.

She hadn't always been an elf. I mean, people *call* them "elves," but that's not really what they are. It's complicated. The elves are just one of those Portsmouth mysteries only drunks talk about. Even other drunks don't listen to drunks.

It hit me how much I'd been missing Leda Clayton when I got home from work and saw her sitting at the kitchen table with Beth. She was taking a tiny sip of beer from the bottle, just like she did when she lived with us. She was never much of a drinker. She smiled at me. I smiled back.

I went to the refrigerator for a beer and set it down on the table.

When she left, a big Leda-shaped hole in the house opened up. I had to *make* myself stop thinking about it. Beth and I worried about Leda separately, but we stopped talking about her. We adopted the Portsmouth Paradigm: *uncomfortable realities should be denied and never discussed.* Sitting with Leda and Beth in our kitchen again should have felt like old times, but everything was different.

Because *Leda* was so different. Her skin wasn't just suntanned white skin, it had a *golden* color. Her eyes had acquired almost an Asian cast. How is *that* even possible? Her hair had always been dark and shiny, no change there. She looked healthier. I felt a new physical strength when she hugged me. She moved with an unconscious grace I'd never seen before. She sat straight and still in her chair, full of vitality and purpose.

Even her *teeth* had changed, possibly whiter than I remembered, and definitely straighter. She'd had one slightly crooked tooth that she called "my snaggly" and never bothered to fix. I'd always thought that minor imperfection made her even cuter. But our little Leda wasn't just cute anymore.

Thinking about that stupid tooth started me crying in my beer. "Oh my God, Leda, you're so *beautiful.*" *You're perfect* is what I meant. *I miss you* is what I meant.

Before I noticed she was in motion, Leda was standing next to my chair. She put one short-nailed hand on my shoulder and held my head against her hard stomach with the other. Jesus, the kid was all muscle and bone. *What the hell has she been doing?* I wondered.

"I've missed you, too, Janjan," she said. "But you *know* what I've been doing, right?"

Oh, crap. *They* read minds, I'd forgotten.

"I guess. Sort of." I wiped my eyes.

Leda sat back down. "The next world over is pretty great," she said.

"Wanna come home with me?"

By "home" she didn't mean her mother's house in Chicago.

I shook my head No and stared at the floor. "I've got my own problems," I said.

"Tell me," she said.

Beth looked uncomfortable. She fidgeted, worrying I was entering our no-fly zone. Beth thought she was the center of the universe.

Leda looked up at Beth, then looked back at me. Her eyes widened a bit, but she didn't laugh. She wasn't judging.

She did grin at Beth, though. "Relax, sweetie. I promise not to tell the Sisters of No Mercy." Like me, Beth was the victim of a Catholic elementary school, hers in Providence and mine in Buffalo. We'd met in college and been friends ever since. After school, we both got jobs in Portsmouth. When Leda came along, the three of us just *clicked*: instant Grrl Power.

Beth did *not* appreciate having her mind read. She blushed, stood up, and glared at both of us. *"Ugh!"* she said. She flounced off, and we heard her bedroom door slam.

Beth had always been a drama queen. Leda smiled and shook her head: *Beth, huh?* I grinned back at her. For a moment it was like old times when one of us would get hurt feelings and the other two would jolly her out of them. That's what friends do, right?

"Are you guys *a couple* now?" Leda said. She meant Beth and me. She wasn't teasing, just interested.

I drank some beer, trying to think how to answer. I decided to tell my mind-reading friend the truth. "Not exactly. On impulse I climbed into Beth's bed one cold night, and she welcomed me with great enthusiasm—we weren't even drinking. Now she's consumed with Catholic guilt and won't talk about it. So I guess that was a one-time event which will not be repeated."

9

Leda just nodded. She'd always accepted me without conditions.

"So *now* Beth's thinking she should go home to her mother in Providence, go back to church, maybe find a nice cop or firefighter to marry and have his babies."

Leda nodded again. "That wouldn't be the worst thing that ever happened to a human being."

My turn to nod. In the face of Leda's calm, I found myself getting angry. I wasn't sure what I was angry *at*—it wasn't either Leda or Beth.

"I mean, look at me," I said. "What the hell am I *doing* here? I go to work at the Shipyard. I hang out with friends and go out on dates. Sometimes I have sex, like people do. But what's the *point*, you know? What's next? Find some loser who'll settle for marrying the fat girl? Have kids? Divorce the loser when he cheats and have to raise the kids by myself?" I was crying again, and it pissed me off. I wiped my eyes with the heels of my hands. "*Sorry*. Jesus, I'm PMSing big-time here."

Leda smiled at me again. She looked a little melancholy. "I don't have periods anymore," she said.

That stopped my pity-party dead in its tracks. "Sweetie, you mean you went through *menopause?*"

She shook her head. "No, I'm still fertile. It's just that since I moved to the next world over, I won't menstruate or ovulate unless Jerry and I ... are to have a child." She was still looking at me, but part of her attention turned inward. It was like I didn't know her anymore.

"Are you *sad* about that? It sounds great."

She smiled at me, a smile I'd know anywhere, indisputably Leda. I saw how happy she was. "It *is* great. Do I *look* sad to you? It's just that everything's so *different*. Now that I'm back in Portsmouth, I *see* all the differences. I see things I never saw before."

The words were out of my mouth before I could stop them. "If you climbed into *my* bed, *I* would welcome you with great enthusiasm." It was true, and she knew it.

She laughed, and I laughed along with her. "I'm flattered, but I'm also *spoken for*," she said. "Jerry and I are married, you know."

"Wow, congratulations! You *both* can climb into my bed."

Leda smiled; she knew I wasn't entirely serious. "I hate to say no, especially since I came to Portsmouth to ask you to do something for Jerry and me."

"Sure, anything," I said automatically. "What are friends for?"

Leda held up a hand. "Wait till you hear the favor before you say yes."

"Sounds serious," I said.

"What do you know about the Friends?"

"The *Elf* Friends? I know they're not exactly the Quakers."

"Not exactly," she agreed. "When we visit Earth from the next world over, the Friends help us."

I've never had much patience. "For Chrissake, sweetie-darling, what do you want me to *do*?"

Leda looked like she was *assessing* me; she'd never done that before. Her eyes focused on mine. "Jerry and I will tell you what happened to us and what we did about it. You'll write our story down and publish it on the Elf Friends' website. If you agree, I mean." Her eyes flicked up, down, and around my body. It wasn't my body she was looking at.

"So I'll be an Elf Friend?"

"Yup. The Friends will pay you for your time. But they—*we*—don't expect you to give up your day job. You don't have to pay dues or go to meetings."

The light went on. "*That's* where you used to run off to without telling Beth and me where you were going? Elf Friend get-togethers?"

Leda nodded. "I was an Elf Friend the whole time I lived in this house with you."

"Huh," I said. "Beth and I thought you were going to Alcoholics

Anonymous meetings or hooking up with somebody you were ashamed of."

Leda just sat there with an open expression on her face, waiting for my decision. She'd still be my friend whatever I decided.

I shook my head. "Lesson learned," I said. "Never ask an elf *What am I doing here?* They'll *give* you something to do." I looked up at Leda. "Yeah, I'll write your story." It felt like a serious commitment.

Leda murmured something in a language I'd never heard before. Somehow I knew exactly what the words meant: *I thank you for this service, sister Elf Friend.*

The words hung in the air for a moment, brightening the kitchen. I saw some sidelit toast crumbs I'd neglected to sweep off the counter. Tsk, tsk.

What I really saw in that shining language was Leda's *power.*

I wasn't the only one. Beth popped out of her bedroom. "Is everything okay?" she said. "The house shook and I saw a bright light under the door."

"Girl talk," I said. My new part-time job was just between Leda and me.

"Everything's fine, Beth," Leda said. "Come sit down with us, would ya? I've *missed* you."

Leda was very different now, and also very much the same. Even before she went to the elves, she'd kept part of herself to herself. There were things she hadn't gotten around to telling me yet. Was I curious? Yes, dammit. Yes, I was.

Anyone at all could have written Leda and Jerry's story. They could have done it themselves. They both knew their way around computers. Why had Leda come back to ask for *my* help?

I didn't ask. I was afraid she'd tell me something I didn't want to hear.

3

What the Traveler Seemed to Say *(This February)*

...the faeries dance in a place apart,
Shaking their milk-white feet in a ring.
Tossing their milk-white arms in the air;
For they hear the wind laugh and murmur and sing
Of a land where even the old are fair,
And even the wise are merry of tongue...

W.B. Yeats, *The Land of Heart's Desire*

Sadly, it seemed, the travelers wrapped in light looked away from the guy in the bushes. Hopefully, it seemed, they turned their attention to me...

I stood on my skis in the snow, unbelieving. My mouth was open; I closed it. I could see my breath in the freezing air and feel ice prickling my nostrils. I felt the weight of all the travelers' attention as they trooped past. They looked at me with great interest from where they walked the invisible road in the air. The road followed a long unseen hill until it was inches above the frozen field. From there the road gradually began to climb again. I couldn't see where it went. The travelers simply walked out of my sight.

One of the glowing people dismounted from his bright steed at the roadside. He paused to sort-of talk to me while others of his folk, men and women (but no children), went by. As they passed us, several people looked at me and smiled at him with knowing mischief, seemed to say, *Ach, Coran, up to your old tricks with the Earth girls again?*

Okay, I may be using imagination to fill in the bare outlines of our...communication. His name might have been *Coran*. It seemed he called me *Little One*, a sobriquet he had every right to use, being (as I thought) king of the travelers, and being as tall and broad as he was. He looked like the sort of man who takes his heedless pleasure with a woman while she takes her own pleasure with him along the way, if she has the strength. If you know what I mean. Woof.

I say *bare outlines*, because most of what passed between us was suggested and immediately understood in the way we held our bodies, in the expressions on our faces. Only I spoke aloud. I don't know that I said everything I meant to say, but I believe he understood all of it.

I say *immediately understood*, but it might be that I simply *mis*understood everything because of my own desires. Anyway. Here's what I remember:

Who are you?

Us? Your folk call us the Fae. As good a name as any. Come with us and learn who we are.

Where are you going?

Did you think your Earth was the only world? There are many others, some strange and beautiful, some dangerous, others as cold and dull as this one. Come and see!

Interesting, I thought. He says *Come see for yourself*, the same thing Jerry and Leda say. How'd I get to be such a popular girl?

So I asked, *What happens to me if I come with you?*

He shrugged. *What'll happen if you stay here, Little One? You'll grow* old and die—*if not today, then far too soon. Come with us, stay young, and live!*

What will happen to my soul? A Catholic upbringing kicks in before you know it.

He shook his head impatiently. *Soul? There is only body and breath. People on Earth breathe in and out, in and out, for seventy years, more or less. The Fae breathe in for half of forever, then breathe out for the other half.*

And who do you worship?

We fear no one. Why would we do such a thing as worship?

Are you good or evil?

He paused. *Such a lovely lass, so ripe, so full of questions. Is it your moontime?* He looked at me more closely. *Ah! I see that it is.*

Underneath my ski pants, I felt the unmistakable sensation that betokened Aunt Flo's imminent arrival. *How could you know such a thing?*

He shrugged again. *We see much that is hidden from men as we walk the worlds on our ancient path. To answer your question, Little One, such good as we do is done simply by following our own nature. Whatever ills may be are woven into life itself and cannot be unraveled.*

That wasn't exactly true, was it? I've been around enough men to know when they're lying to me. The big, handsome man (he sure *looked* like a man) in the Renaissance Faire clothes was avoiding a subject he didn't want to discuss.

Are you telling me you know nothing about the angels, good and evil?

He didn't recoil from me, not exactly, but his face grew sad. Or: an underlying sadness rose to the surface of his smiling face. *Ah, lass, what have such as we to do with such as they? 'Tis a very old story, indeed, you tell. My people politely said No thank you to those beings you describe, and we went our own way rejoicing. That's no war you want any part of, darlin'. Come with us, then, and none of that good-and-evil business need ever trouble you again, whatever your black-clad virgin priests might tell you.*

My conscience began jabbing me. Or was it simply the cold?

What about that man in the bush over there? Is he one of yours?

Coran looked quickly at the bushes, then back at me. The man had ducked back down into his thicket out of the wind. It struck me that Coran had just seen through thick-woven tangled branches as if they weren't there. As if he saw the life hidden away deep in the roots of things. What did he see when he looked at *me?*

Bobby? He traveled with us a time or two, then left us for Earth again. It seems he's decided to see what's on the other side of death.

You don't know?

We don't need to know, do we? The Fae live forever...for all practical purposes. Why would we want to die?

Well, I can't let him die, can I?

I don't know why not.

I'll say good night to you then, Coran.

I hope to see you again, Little One. In fact, I'm sure I shall.

4

Great Bog Bobby in the 19th, 20th, and 21st Centuries

The wind blows out of the gates of the day,
The wind blows over the lonely heart,
And the lonely of heart is withered away,
While the faeries dance in a place apart...

W.B. Yeats, *The Land of Heart's Desire*

February, Great Bog. Bobby was way ahead of me. He first walked into the
weirdness in 1864—and again in 1945.

Watching the aerial procession took Bobby out of himself and out of the frozen fields and wetlands of Great Bog. He wasn't himself lately.

Why would he want to *be* himself? He was homeless. He stank. He wore every filthy garment he owned on top of filthy long johns. The cold ate into him. The cold penetrated the crappy sleeping bag and the blankets he wrapped around his body. The cold came up through the tarp floor that kept his crappy tent dry inside. There wasn't room to put the tent all the way up in these bushes, so he hung the thin fabric loosely over branches above his head. Although he was out of the wind, he thought he could feel the cold blasting all the way up from the icy core of a frozen Earth. Bobby was not prepared to be homeless in New Hampshire this winter.

He was alone again. He'd hiked through deep snow across the fields until he was miles away from the little encampment of homeless people. Too depressing. Too many mean drunks and desperate drug addicts. Too many people who *wanted* something from him he didn't have to give. Things were getting ugly back in camp. He left before someone tried to fight him over some stupid thing. There had always been fights, even back when the homeless proudly called themselves *hobos*.

From inside his refuge at the center of a dense growth of wild hedge he beheld the Fae and they beheld him. The Fae saw him for whatever he was. They smiled and waved, beckoned to him, seemed to say: *Come back and rejoin the cavalcade, c'mon, we have a great time all the time. Aren't you sick of being merely human, Bobby? Do you want to die? Aren't you tired of being hungry and cold and despised? Aren't you weary of being alone?*

There was, of course, something the fae folk weren't telling him. There was some joke they were wise to that he was not. Bobby wouldn't know what the joke was until he learned the joke was on him and it was too late to do anything about it.

The fae people *wanted* something from him, too. They didn't *need* it, but if he joined them, they'd have to take it from him, whatever it was. Then he'd go a-walking with them down the ancient fae-path up into the sky, around the World Mountain. Then he, too, would be grinning at castoff human beings, beckoning the curious and disenchanted among them to come and join the eternal conga line.

And what would be the point of that? Bobby wondered.

He didn't despair, exactly, but something shifted inside him. A decision arrived.

Time to die, he thought. (Bobby had never seen *Blade Runner*.)

Whoever he'd been, whatever his wanderings had made of him, the decision banished his fear. The power to choose the time of his passing restores a man's dignity.

In their leafy finery, unbothered by cold and snow, unplagued by hunger and thirst, the fae folk perceived Bobby's decision. Their sharp, almost-human faces grew a little sad as they passed through the air above him. Sad for him that he was mortal or sad for themselves that they were not?

❈

This was not Bobby's first experience of the travelers. Twice before, he'd accepted their invitation and gone away with them. There had been singing, but he could recall none of the songs. Music that was both happy and sad in the way of the ancient world. He remembered feasts of food that never surfeited and drink that blurred his wits but never made him sick. There had been many a fae girl to swive with, drawn to his desire and his exotic human solidity. The loveplay had at first meant more to him than it had to the lithe and shining women, who saw such things differently *sub specie aeternitatus.* Finally even to Bobby, fae sex came to mean nothing at all, one almost-sneeze in the loins after another with desire forever undimmed.

When had that happened?

Sitting here in the killing cold of the twenty-first century, Bobby remembered carrying a heavy Sharps rifle back in the nineteenth. He remembered laying that rifle down near the end of the American Civil War, having taken the lives of too many Confederate boys and having no stomach for killing more. Tucked into his uniform pocket was his wife's last letter—and a letter from her sister telling Bobby his first love had died of a fever. When he saw the merry, light-wrapped Fae beckoning to him from the sky above the reeking Pennsylvania battlefield, he joined them and turned his back on death.

But he hadn't stayed with the sky folk. Loath as they were to bid him farewell, they would not hold him against his will. He'd abandoned such happiness as could be found in their perpetual movable feast, their endless celebration (of *what*, exactly?) that was so tinged with sorrow (but *why?*).

He had walked off the fae-road into Portsmouth decades ago, near the end of the Great Depression. The farmer who owned the land hired tramps to harvest his apples. Thinking that Bobby (babbling about magical sky folk) was touched in the head, the farmer took pity on him. The man invited him to live in his barn and work the land full-time in exchange for room and board. The work and the land had been good for Bobby; he asked life for nothing else.

Then the draft board came calling. Bobby found himself called up to fight again. This time he carried a Springfield sniper rifle. He found it easier to kill Germans than it had been to kill his own countrymen. But near the end of the Second World War, Bobby was soul-sick again and soul-weary still.

When the fae folk passed above him that second time (in Belgium it must have been), he heard and understood easily what they seemed to say: *Come back to us, Bobby. There'll always be war down there. Come where you're welcome and study war no more.*

And go with them he had, around and around the worlds on the path that was theirs alone, until he could no longer bear the unrelieved *otherness* of life with the sky travelers.

Once again he'd left the trail near where the farmer's orchard had been. Now the trees bore nothing and the fields had been cut up and sold off. Great Bog had encroached, as bogs will do. Another Depression had swept over the country, although they called it a Recession now, as if that made any difference. Though few Americans starved to death anymore. "Food insecurity" was part of the human condition Bobby grew up with.

There was of course another war, but Bobby wasn't going to volunteer to fight it, not if he had a choice. He was done killing people.

Rejoining the fae folk would be worse than suicide. If he went back to them, he'd be theirs forever, with all the humanity leached out of him. Three strikes and you're out. Maybe the sadness the Fae carried with them was the knowledge that they'd lost something essential and now were making the best of it. Forever.

Dying of the cold tonight, whatever that would mean, wasn't the worst thing that could happen to a man. He was ready to see if anything came next. Bobby sat back down out of the cold wind in the freezing thicket, like Br'er Rabbit in the briar patch, secured his tent flap, and prepared to accept his fate, so long deferred.

5

He Followed Me Home; Can I Keep Him? *(This February)*

We're tenting tonight on the old camp ground,
Give us a song to cheer
Our weary hearts, a song of home
And friends we love so dear.

Walter Kittredge,
"Tenting on the Old Camp Ground," 1864

The Fae went their merry way and took their light with them. I couldn't see the road they walked. I was left standing on my skis in the snow shadows. Not alone, though.

"Um, *Bobby?*" I said to the thicket. I couldn't see the guy's head, but I hadn't seen him go anywhere while I was talking to Coran the Fae. The guy was still in the bushes, wasn't he?

No answer.

I couldn't stay here much longer. My face stung. I could feel the cold radiating right through my lightweight thermal undies. I bounced up and down on my skis impatiently. To generate some heat, I had to *move.*

I tried again. "Bobby, dammit! Dude, c'mon, I'm freezing my ass off here. Unless you're prepared for the Arctic, you'll die of exposure tonight. Is that what you want?"

Finally, a voice from the bush, "How'd...you know...my name ... was *Bobby?*"

The voice sounded slow, like maybe the guy himself was slow. Or drunk. Or drugged. On the other hand, it could be the confusion that happens in the first stage of hypothermia. You learn these things growing up in Buffalo.

I didn't have time to make up a lie. "The Fae told me. This guy Coran, I think his name was? He said you were planning to *die*, Bobby. Not on *my* watch, pal." God, what an idiotic thing to say. More evidence that too much TV was doing bad things to me. I resolved to read a book for a change; that might help me get Leda and Jerry's story written.

A head wearing one of those ridiculous Peruvian drawstring hats hesitantly emerged from the bushes. "You don't *want* me to die?" Bobby said. "Why not?"

"Why would I? You haven't done anything terrible, have you?"

Even in the half-dark he looked confused. "I shot people in the war. *Two* wars."

"I think you're *allowed* to shoot people who are shooting at you, Bobby. You gonna come with me, or not?"

Bobby began climbing out of the thicket. He moved awkwardly; the cold had stiffened his joints. "What's your name?" he said. He reached back into the hole he'd climbed out of. I thought he was falling in again, but he came back out with what looked like a backpack and a tarp. And was that a *tent* he was trying to pull out? Jesus Christ, it was like trying to take a little kid and all his toys home from the beach.

I skied over to help him. "I'm Janjan," I said, as I released my boots from the ski bindings.

"Janjan? Hi, Janjan."

Together we extracted all his gear. We stood facing each other. He was taller than me, but who isn't? Even in the cold I couldn't help noticing that Bobby stank like a Desert Father. Awesome.

But I'd offered, so I was determined to help. He shouldered his pack. I carried his tarp and raggedy tent and shouldered my skis. Thank God the snow on the trail was packed down. Even so, it was hard walking at Bobby's slow pace in my stiff-soled ski boots.

"You homeless?" I said, just to have something to say. We had miles to go, crunch crunch crunching through the snow.

He nodded. "Yeah. It's been a while now. Sorry, I know I stink." He sounded ashamed. In the United States, poverty's the only sin anybody's ashamed of. What, too cynical?

"So you had to shoot people in Iraq? Or was it Afghanistan?"

Bobby shook his head. "Belgium."

Belgium? Who the hell were we shooting in Europe? Was Bobby out of his head, or had I lost track of all the wars my country was fighting?

Back to practical matters. "Tell you what," I said, "I'll drive you to my house, and you can clean up, have some hot food. We've got a spare bedroom you can use tonight. You can figure out your next move tomorrow." I knew Beth would pitch a fit that I was bringing a homeless guy home, but it was an emergency, wasn't it? And it was just for one night. Dirt and stink wash off.

"Thank you, Janjan," Bobby said. He stared at me in the cold uncertain light. It was a quizzical look, not a scary one.

"What?" I said.

"I don't mean to be rude," he said. "You don't seem to *want* anything from me."

"Well, I dunno about that. What can you tell me about the Fae?" I spoke without thinking. As usual.

He stayed silent for long enough that I started to worry. We walked along steadily. Where powdered snow had blown onto the packed trail, it squeaked under our feet. Squeak crunch, squeak crunch. *Janjan's Sense of Snow.*

Finally: "I keep *trying* to remember, but not much comes back to me. Just a flash here and there, like a dream. I mean, I guess they live forever, and they're sort of happy, and they go places you only read about in fairy tales. But they're not *human*, Janjan. That *weighs* on you after a while when you follow along with them. You start missing *people*-people."

"So you...came back to Earth again?"

He nodded vigorously again. Was he a little simple, or just a simple man? Then he laughed and I saw that he was laughing at himself, and at the whole human enterprise. Whatever he was, Bobby wasn't simple so much as *pure.*

"Yeah, I came back because I felt like I was *missing* something." He held his arms out to the sides: empty snow-covered fields, black scraggly trees, thickets, frozen marsh, and high-tension lines on towers that looked like Martian invaders. "Look at all I found!"

I couldn't help laughing along with him.

❋

Beth hissed at me, "What the fuck, Janjan, you brought home a *hobo*?"

Bobby was using the shower. It was going to take him a while to get clean. His ripe aroma lingered in the kitchen, and he'd only walked through it. I'd scrounged up some men's clothes for him to put on. Men seem to leave their stuff any old where—at least the men who take up with Beth and me. We'd have to bag Bobby's old clothes and take them to a laundromat. I didn't think our old washer and dryer could handle that much dirt. Probably smarter to buy him new stuff and put his old clothes out in the trash.

"Bobby's not a hobo *per se*," I whispered. "It's not a lifestyle choice, he's just homeless at the moment. I think if I'd dropped him off at the shelter tonight, he would have just wandered back into the cold and died of exposure. He's temporarily, um, suicidal."

A withering stare. "Great, so he's *crazy?*" Pretty blonde girls do withering better than anybody. "You brought a *suicidal escaped mental patient* into our house?" *Such* a drama goddess.

I held her furious gaze and shook my head No. "You know those things that happen in Portsmouth that nobody wants to talk about?"

Beth dropped her gaze. "Yeah, I guess." She sounded uneasy. She did *not* want to continue this discussion. Just like she didn't want to hear the story Leda and Jerry were telling me. She'd started avoiding the house when they were here.

I didn't have time for nonsense tonight. I put a hand on her forearm. "Beth, sweetie, I *saw* something while I was out skiing. And Bobby saw it, too. If he's crazy, so am I."

Beth smiled. "I've always thought so," she said. "Especially since...*you* know."

God, women are annoying. "By *'you know'*, you mean the night we had sex?"

"Janjan, not so *loud!*" She was blushing bright red.

I felt bad. "I'm sorry that happened, since it seems to have made you so unhappy. I want us to stay friends. That's way more important to me than sex."

She smiled and looked away. "I want us to stay friends, too. It was *good* sex, though. Can you blame me for being confused?"

"Tease," I said. After a pause, "I notice you're not asking me what I saw."

"I'm not sure I want to know," she said.

Before I could get into it, Bobby came out of the bathroom barefoot, wearing clean jeans and no shirt. He was rubbing his hair dry with a towel.

Dude was unexpectedly lean and muscular. Unselfconscious, too, not one of those narcissistic gym rats, ugh.

"I really appreciate you taking me in, Janjan," he said with a big grin. "And thank you, too, ma'am," he said to Beth. He wasn't at all handsome, but his eyes were a shade of very light blue I'd never seen before. Long eyelashes, too, always a grace note on a masculine man.

"*Beth*," said Beth. "Woof." Realizing she was staring at Bobby with her mouth open, she blushed prettily and shook her head. Beth always went for tall, sinewy guys, and she'd been single for quite a while.

"By '*woof*' she means that you clean up good, Bobby," I said. The Girl Code dictates that you help a sister out of a minor awkwardness.

"It's good to be clean," he said, embarrassed.

I put some soup on the stove to heat up for him. I scurried around and found him socks and a sweater. I showed him where to hang his wet towel. I showed him his room. But the way he and Beth were eye-fucking I didn't figure he'd be sleeping there.

❋

"You guys were pretty loud last night," I told Beth in the morning.

"Well, it had been a while for both of us," she said. "Also, he couldn't, um, *finish?* So I stayed with him as long as I could, which was actually pretty wonderful. Finally I just had to call it a night. I felt bad for him, but he didn't seem to feel bad for himself, just happy for me."

"You certainly *sounded* happy."

"Shut *up*, Janjan. *God!*" She was smiling, though.

6

Simon Says (*Last Year*)

Everything living on the Earth, people, animals, plants, is food for the moon... All movements, actions, and manifestations of people, animals, and plants depend upon the moon and are controlled by the moon.... The mechanical part of our life depends upon the moon, is subject to the moon. If we develop in ourselves consciousness and will, and subject our mechanical life and all our mechanical manifestations to them, we shall escape from the power of the moon.

G.I. Gurdjieff

I missed most of last winter's Portsmouth weirdness, lucky me, but Jackson was up to his neck in it. He came back to Portsmouth with a new kind of weirdness inside him.

After his humiliating defeat off the New Hampshire coast, Jackson followed the security protocol. He changed his appearance, stopped practicing magic, made no calls to his MM contacts, ditched his hipster wardrobe, got a buzz cut, and found a crap job. He dressed normcore and hung out with other young working people. No drugs, just a beer after work. He blended right in. Nobody knows what their casual acquaintances are feeling or thinking, anyway. Nobody saw how hurt and frightened Jackson was inside. He didn't hook up with anyone; nobody knew if he was gay or straight or straight edge.

He stayed in Portsmouth and kept his eyes open. His teachers had said opportunity would knock for the Order of Materialist Magicians in the little city on the Piscataqua; *he* was to be ready to open the door. They hadn't told Jackson anything else. He knew better than to question orders.

He did some research; what he learned shocked him. The Order, it turned out, had started wars in Portsmouth and lost all three of them. He didn't talk about the information he acquired, or even think much about it. Some of those above him in the Order had mastered the reading of thoughts. He wouldn't know who until it was too late.

Like all MM disciples, Jackson had an exaggerated view of his own abilities. He was shrewd enough to obey his chain of command. He wanted to be Archmage someday. Nobody knew who the Archmage was these days, or even if the Order had found a new one, but a man can dream.

The elves, whoever and whatever *they* were, had broken the MM leadership. Cut off its head, really. After elves killed two Archmages in short succession, it seemed nobody *believed* in the Order anymore or in its mission to reshape the Earth. It was like how Germans stopped joining the Nazis after Hitler's suicide.

Months passed. Nothing happened in Portsmouth. No elves pursued him. No one from his side contacted him. No new orders came and no opportunities knocked. He saved his money. When he had enough, he abandoned his job and left town without telling anyone where he was going. That, too, was part of the security protocol.

What was *not* part of the protocol was where he went. His MM cell leader in Washington would have taken him in, upbraided him, and redeployed him. But Jackson wanted power. He went seeking power where the Order's secret history began.

❄

It looked like one more abandoned Caucasus cave monastery, which is to say, nothing like the well-preserved desert temple in *Indiana Jones and the Last Crusade*. Built into the side of a cliff, the retreat looked uninhabited. Not at all inviting. Silent, except for water trickling over smooth mossy rocks. There was nothing to attract tourists. Even birds avoided the place.

Standing at the base of the cliff, Jackson looked up at what he thought were windows and maybe a rudimentary balcony or two. All the openings were covered by thick, ancient wood shutters, gray-green with lichen like the rock around them.

It was hard to imagine why anyone would live here, let alone the hidden masters he was seeking. Jackson looked at his guide. "Really?"

The guide pointed forcefully at the rock face. He grinned at Jackson's disappointment. "This it, man." The grin revealed strong, stained teeth and no real amusement.

Jackson unsnapped a pocket to reach for his wallet. American currency, the universal language. "What do I owe you?" There had been some initial confusion about what fee his guide would receive at the end of the long, long trail. Jackson fully expected to have to haggle and still be cheated. Instead the guide surprised him.

"*No*, man! No money!" The guy looked scared. He said a bunch of other things in his own language, a torrent of consonants in Jackson's ear. The guide waved like he was doing panicky jazz hands until he recovered his English. He pointed at the cliff. "You tell *them* this: you say *the words* and I bring you *here*."

"Okay?"

"I leave now," the guide said. "Luck to you." He grinned mirthlessly

31

again, turned around, and walked off.

Jackson was tempted to say *Wait up* and follow the guy, but that would have been stupid. He'd endured a lot of hardship to get here. And he'd said *the words* at the train station, hadn't he? *The words* the Brotherhood had made him memorize back in Washington. Although Jackson understood no local language spoken anywhere he'd traveled in Europe or Asia, *the words* had worked like magic. The ugly sounds backed off muggers and made armed soldiers turn pale and lower their weapons. *The words* took him across borders without incident, but caused mothers to make the sign of the cross and hold their hands over children's ears. *The words* found him poor accommodations, got him weird food, and finally drew this mountain guide to him.

The old ways were well understood in the Caucasus. People didn't understand the Fallen Tongue, but they knew what they were hearing. Certain courtesies were due those who came speaking portentous words of ancient power. *Détente* between religion and Materialist Magic had held for centuries; no priest or mullah dared speak against it.

The Order had more power on Earth than any government; Jackson wanted that power for himself. He stared at the cliff monastery. The sun was sinking on the other side of the mountain. It would be dark in minutes.

It struck him that he wasn't the same soft, cynical boy he'd been when he took ship out of New Jersey. It struck him that his early magical successes (followed by his spectacular metaphysical failure), his emotional breakdown (if he was honest with himself), and his quest to find the monastery had taught him something about the nature of *consciousness and will*, something he understood in his heart, but couldn't put into words.

It also struck him that the smartest thing he could possibly do was hot-foot it away from this place, retrace the long journey, go home, and get another crap job as a Starbucks barista or something. Maybe get a real girlfriend instead of renting prostitutes. Maybe finish college. Hell, maybe join the Marine Corps, fight for his country, and go back to college if he survived whichever war they sent him into. Enduring so much had taught him he was stronger than he'd known. He had his whole life ahead of him.

Jackson didn't do the smartest thing. Instead of acting from his new strength, he let the old weakness reach out from inside him.

He spoke *the words* to the cliff face.

Nothing happened. His voice sounded flat and echoless in the cold, damp air. He felt stupid talking to the rock.

Dark was coming fast. Along with his disappointment, he felt relief. *Well great*, he thought, *it was all a bunch of bullshit. Guess I'll have to camp here. No way I'm going into those caves in the dark with nothing but a flashlight. One more night of sleeping rough won't kill me. I hear good things about Miami...*

A hoarse voice came from somewhere in the darkness inside the monastery, or whatever it was. The voice spoke English with a working-class British accent.

"Your accent's *shit*," said the voice. "Hardly knew what you were saying. *Retarded*, are you? *Damaged* in some way?"

"Um, no?" Jackson said. "Are you, um, the Archmage?"

"*Archmage* he says. Listen to him!" The voice had a wheeze in it like someone old and infirm, but with a dangerous edge of insanity.

Jackson was cold and tired and always quick to take offense. "I spoke *the words* the way I learned them," he said loudly. "Who are *you*, then? *Gollum?*"

"My name's Simon," said the old voice. "You may call me *Master*—if I let you live."

No more words came from the darkness. Instead, something invisible reached into Jackson's mind, took over his will and moved his legs for him, drawing him into the cave face through an angled opening his eyes had not detected.

In the midst of wordless panic, he saw how badly out of his depth he was.

How deep the depths were he'd never even guessed. The depths went down and down and down.

※

The thing about horror is that there's nothing to be done about it. Best to get on with the task at hand and try not to think about who—or what—might have assigned that task to you. Best not to think about *why* you're doing what you're doing.

Jackson was grateful to be alive. It had been touch and go for a while in the Caucasus cave monastery with the horrible old man who made Jackson call him *Master*.

Simon was dressed in ragged layers of clothing against the damp cold. He was filthy. His hair was matted and his teeth were rotten. It looked like his body was falling apart, worse than any Monty Python character. And yet some power in the old Materialist Magician brushed aside young, strong, healthy Jackson's will like it was a spider web.

The old man stared at Jackson in the light of a smoky fire. Stared *into* him, really. Jackson felt his thoughts and memories being picked up, examined, and tossed contemptuously aside. Jackson would have got up and left if he could, but the examination hamstrung him.

Finally the old magician grunted and released his hold on Jackson's will. Jackson would have got up and left, but he didn't trust his legs to hold him.

"They said you'd come," said the old man.

"Me?"

The old man shrugged. "Someone like you. I spoke truer than I knew. You *are* damaged. Been playing at ducks and drakes with Old Gods, have you?"

There was no point denying it. Jackson just nodded his head and looked down at the littered cave floor. "I don't exactly know what you mean by *ducks and drakes*. The god and goddess shared the power of their language with me. They had a whole world of their own. I thought I'd travel to their world, but then they came to Earth and … changed their minds. They just *went away*."

"Left you with nothing, did they?" The ragged magician sounded amused.

"Their language went away with them. I can't remember a word of it. The only power I have left was in the words I spoke outside today."

"*Misspoke*, you mean. Any idea what language you were speaking?"

Jackson shook his head.

"Tsk," said the magician, "you were poorly taught, then." He spoke the words Jackson had used. In the magician's mouth, they sounded altogether different. The firelight in the cave dimmed even further, or perhaps the darkness grew darker. The atmosphere around the two congealed and grew ominous.

Again Jackson knew he should stand up and leave. Again he let his weakness speak for him. If there was real power to be had, Jackson wanted it. He looked up at the old man. "What language was *that*, Master?"

"High Aghartic," said the magician. "The language of the Claimant. You'll learn more of it here. If you survive."

❋

Sometimes time flies, sometimes it crawls. Jackson's successive accelerated initiations into the Brotherhood of Materialist Magicians dragged on agonizingly. Agony was the whole point. That, and learning how to focus attention upon the object of one's desire: *consciousness and will.*

What also seemed endless were the travels master and disciple undertook together, powered by those beings the Brotherhood simply called *the Fallen*. Those journeys took only fractions of real-time seconds; afterwards Jackson fought to forget them. It was clear enough to him, if not to his teacher, that the Fallen *despised* human beings, regarded them as a consumable resource, as *food for the moon*.

Jackson's time under the Old Gods' influence *had* damaged him from the viewpoint of the Fallen. The Old Gods regarded Jackson and all their human devotees with *affection*, the way people see dogs or horses. Intimacy with those nonhuman minds had changed him. Jackson's sense of essential worth, of being *entitled to exist*, went all the way to the core of himself where he never inquired; neither Simon nor those terrifying beings he served could pluck it out without killing the young man.

All Jackson knew is that he wasn't dead yet.

He thought the Brotherhood might be fighting a rearguard action against an enemy who never even bothered to attack them. *The wicked flee when no man pursueth;* no elf ever pursued the MMs, either. Simon provided few details of the Earth's secret history, but Jackson was smart enough to connect what he already knew with the things the old man let slip.

The Brotherhood kept attacking the elves.

The elves defeated the Brotherhood every time.

Ordinary human beings got hurt whenever war broke out. (Only the elves cared about civilian casualties.)

The Brotherhood changed tactics. Rather than attack their mysterious enemy directly (assuming a direct attack was even possible), they'd *redirect* people who sought to reach the world of the elves.

Every year thousands of people quietly passed through Portsmouth on their way to *the next world over*, as the elves called their homeworld, either modestly or ironically. The MMs wanted to divert those people...somewhere else.

If human beings stopped taking refuge with the elves, the elves would get no new recruits. Karmic bonds would weaken naturally over time. Fewer elves would be able to return to Earth.

Eventually, the Brotherhood would again have the whole world as their hunting ground. The Fallen and their leader the Fallen Archangel would again have their way unopposed.

And who would be the key man in this endeavor? *Jackson*, that's who.

Who better? Jackson's first MM teacher, after all, had sent him after the Old Gods, to bring them and their Other World religion to Earth. More people deflected to the service of the god and goddess meant fewer people who could join the elves, gain power in the next world over, and return to oppose the Materialist Magicians.

Jackson's experiences had made him unsuited to a closer walk with the Fallen; despite that, Master Simon saw Jackson as the Order's best new weapon against the elves. The young man was tough and smart; he learned rapidly. The Old Gods were gone now, but there were other beings who'd always welcomed anyone who wanted to leave Earth.

Jackson would help people find those other beings.

7

Curtis "50 Cent" Jackson (no relation)
Performs "In da Club" *(This February)*

I didn't see anything weird about Jackson the night we met. Shows what I know.

Beth and Bobby were having a wonderful time out on the dance floor. She was teaching him some moves. He was doing his best to learn, but his default steps looked like some sort of Appalachian buck dancing, after which he'd try to get Beth to *jitterbug* with him, for God's sake. They kept breaking up laughing. They kept touching each other. Like lovers do.

The DJ was playing the music so loud the bass shook the floorboards. We were all drinking and the lights were flashing. If you were going to have a seizure, now would be the time. Actually, I was doing most of the drinking at the moment, keeping an eye on my stuff and Beth's, not to mention our glasses of light beer. I sipped slowly; you have to pace yourself. I was trying to figure out if I was jealous. And if I *was* jealous, was I jealous of Beth or of Bobby? The joke about bisexuality is how it doubles your chances of getting a date. Nobody mentions that it doubles your potential heartbreak.

I looked around the club, really just a bar with a big dance floor. My girly-sense started tingling. Was that handsome guy (in a nice suit, of all things) looking at *me*? Unlikely. Dude was way out of *my* league. I looked around to see who else he might be looking at. Nothing but guys in my immediate vicinity. The other girls were dancing, or clustered on the other side of the room, or maybe in the bathroom, who knew. Was the handsome man gay? Just my luck, all the good ones are gay or married, blah blah blah.

But no, it *was* me he was looking at. I could tell because he locked eyes with me and stalked toward my table, looking neither right nor left. People moved out of his way.

Oh my God, I thought, *it's Coran.* Of course he wasn't Coran. He wasn't shining, for one thing, wasn't riding a horse, and wasn't as tall or as wide in the shoulders. But like the Fae lord, he did have a premature white streak in his short dark hair.

He also had *Bad Boy* written all over him in letters only I could see.

Like I said, the music was pretty loud. You don't go to the club for conversation, unless you enjoy shouting. But the dude kept staring at me like he was starving and I was a club sandwich. Based on the suit, I figured him for a frat boy from a wealthy family. He looked college age in the dim light.

Here's the thing about being a fat girl with decent legs. Just because they're handsome and maybe rich, asshole frat bros think they're *entitled* to you, especially at the end of the night. But we were still the middle of the evening and the club was full of taller, thinner, prettier girls. *So why me?*

The guy leaned over to speak into my ear, practically the only way to make yourself heard in here. Nice cologne, one I didn't recognize. As he bent toward me, I spoke first.

"Is this one of those fraternity fuck-the-fat-girl contests?" I said. "Because I don't play that. Also, is that white streak in your hair natural?"

That would have scared off an ordinary dumbass. But this guy was just puzzled. He shook his head No. "It's *you* I want," he said into my ear. "I can't explain it. If you're an old-fashioned girl, I'll court you old-school. My hair? I had … *a shock* recently. Long story."

Wanted me, did he? I felt dizzier than two drinks would have made me. I was glad the club was dim; I was afraid the chair might be damp when I got up. He didn't stop looking at me for a minute, and I was feeling all funny in my bad place.

"May I sit down?" he said into my ear. His breath was warm.

I stood up and faced him. "You want to dance?" I said.

He shook his head, refusing to be deflected. "I do *not* want to dance." He held out his right hand. "Jackson," he said loudly. Because of the music: boomp boomp boomp boomp.

I liked the way he took charge. Tentatively, I took his hand and shook it. The old business double-pump. "Pleased to meet you, Jackson. I'm Janjan." I was pretty loud, too. His hand was warm and dry. And big.

He let go of my hand, but I could see he didn't want to. "'Janjan'? Really?"

"My real name's Jadwiga."

"*Janjan* it is, then." He smiled. I smiled back. We both knew what was going to happen tonight.

We ventured onto the dance floor so I could return Beth's bag and tell her not to wait up. Jackson trailed along with one hand on my waist, like he didn't want to let me out of his sight. I was sorry he'd come along, because when guys meet Beth, they figure I'm the Ugly Friend, immediately focus on the Pretty Friend, and start ignoring me. Beth does nothing to encourage that; she's *my* friend.

But Jackson didn't seem interested in Beth or she in him. Instead,

Jackson was looking, and I mean *staring*, at Bobby. I didn't quite know what to make of that.

Uh-oh. Was Jackson gay after all? Or *bi*? There's a lot of that going around these days.

I made quick introductions as best I could. I mean, the club was so loud that I had to read body language and expressions and lips. "My housemates Beth and Bobby," I yelled into Jackson's ear. Sometimes quick is better than accurate.

He nodded like he was politely interested, and his full attention returned to me. Whew.

Beth and I exchanged a series of looks to fulfill the Girl Code requirements:

Are you sure, Janjan? Will you be okay with this guy?

Don't worry, sweetie. I'll be fine. Have fun!

And out the door I went on Jackson's arm.

8

If Thy Whole Body Be Full of Light
(This January and February)

You can observe a lot just by watching.

Yogi Berra

Months after finding Master Simon in the Caucasus, Jackson went back to Portsmouth. Learning true materialist magic had been painful, but gave him power. Meeting the Walloon and the Brotherhood's Washington money managers taught Jackson the *uses* of that power.

But it was the Fae in the cave who'd transformed the way Jackson saw the world and the people in it. The Fae radiated a different wavelength of light than ordinary human beings did; Jackson had seen it.

Speaking the Old Gods' language of dreams had marked Jackson. Fighting elves who spoke the Unfallen Tongue had taught him something, too. Last year when Jerry August was still just a man, Jackson had sneered at his opponent's "elf-stink." It wasn't a bluff, it was inner vision. People who developed close relationships with elves began to reflect glints of clear elf-light.

The god and goddess had laid hands on Jerry August as they had on Jackson, but had left no perceptible mark on August's inner man. Jackson didn't know what otherworldly traces Simon had seen in him. He didn't dare ask.

Materialist Magicians speak a language that embodies the darkness of those they serve. Jackson wondered what he'd absorbed from the Fallen. The Order taught Jackson to conceal himself by keeping to the shadows. Some of those shadows had eyes and claws.

When Jackson returned to Portsmouth, he saw the city's inhabitants by the light they reflected. He knew what to look for even in the deafening music and flashing lights of the dance club. He'd sat here before, nursing a drink and watching. He'd seen nothing unusual until tonight.

He saw that Janjan the hot little redhead was an Elf Friend, but that her tall, thin, beautiful blonde friend Beth was not.

But Bobby, the young man the blonde girl was dancing and laughing with, was something else again. A fitful greenish light shone around Bobby like a will-o'-the-wisp; it was a match to the fae-light that Jackson's inner vision caught in his own shaving mirror. Few people on Earth had ever seen what Jackson saw.

Bobby was fae but not *a* Fae. Jackson looked closer, using his eyes along with his inner vision (he didn't realize how intently he was staring). He saw that the guy wasn't exactly a *young* man, either. Jackson saw no signs of cosmetic surgery or magic; it was more that Bobby wasn't exactly a *twenty-first-century* young man. Something about the way he spoke and moved and carried himself suggested a simpler society or simpler times. Bobby had a working man's hands. Jackson's unconscious mind fed him puzzling images: old daguerreotypes and silent films in black and white; Henry Fonda in *The Grapes of Wrath*.

Holy shit, Jackson thought, *is Bobby a time traveler?* The possibility refuted everything Jackson had been taught about materialist magic. His teachers had omitted any useful information about the elves and the next world over.

How can you fight an enemy you know nothing about? Jackson had studied *the elves'* accounts of the Portsmouth Wars. He spent hours reading the Elf Friends' website, *When Is an Elf Not an Elf?* The MMs said the site was all lies and launched cyber-attacks to shut it down. It didn't read like propaganda to Jackson.

If anything, the elves *understated* their victories over the Brotherhood. They seemed to have no need to exaggerate or to lie. They said that the next world over existed in a different timestream from Earth: leave at 8:00, spend years with the elves, return to Earth at 8:02. The Elf Friends reported what the elves told them, but didn't claim to understand it. Who understands immortality?

He also read how the Order's Archmages attained near-immortality. If the elves were right about *that*... Jackson shuddered and put the thought away.

Jackson figured the Fae also lived in a different timestream and carried it with them. It was a conditional immortality: people remained alive as long as they stayed with the Fae.

Most importantly, those who traveled with the Fae *did not age*. If they left the Fae, Jackson speculated, they'd start aging again like the rest of humankind. But while they walked the fae-road, they remained forever young.

Eternal youth! Quite a selling point.

Would Bobby help Jackson build a bridge in Portsmouth, a detour to the Fae that bypassed the elves? Jackson thought he could persuade him: money talks. The Brotherhood and its financial backers would pay whatever it cost to build the detour. The MM hierarchy needed time to rebuild, recruit, and train.

Jackson had a vague idea of how to carry out his mission. If he worked with Bobby, he thought they could figure out the details.

First things first, though. Janjan seemed to be as interested in Jackson as he was in her. He told her that he'd court her. He didn't tell her he'd be courting Bobby at the same time.

Pleasure before business, Jackson thought. He smiled at Janjan as they walked out of the club together. She smiled back. He wanted her; she wanted him.

She was exactly his type, but Janjan was just a bonus. She'd be his camouflage while he recruited Bobby.

9

Plaisir d'amour *(This February)*

Plaisir d'amour ne dure qu'un moment.
Chagrin d'amour dure toute la vie.

Jean-Pierre Claris de Florian,
"Plaisir d'amour" (1784)

Jackson opened the passenger door of his BMW for me. You don't see much door-opening in the twenty-first century, or maybe that's just the men who are attracted to me. I smiled my thanks, got in, and arranged my dress as modestly as I could. The car was very clean and smelled like new leather. My own car was back at the house because Beth, Bobby, and I had walked into town, planning to take a taxi home. I would have had to fill up a trash bag before anyone could sit in my car's passenger seat. My house is reasonably neat, my body is squeaky-clean, but my car is kind of an archaeological dig site. Maybe two trash bags.

Jackson got behind the wheel. I got out my phone.

"Where are we going?" I said. "I want to let Beth know." He told me. I texted Beth and put the phone away.

We passed the short drive mostly in silence. The BMW was quiet, no engine noise, no music. Jackson drove us into the parking garage below the big-ass hotel overlooking the river. He used a card key in the elevator that took us up to his floor.

If you're thinking *sordid hotel room*, think again. It was an executive suite. I looked around. The man had money and good taste. All his possessions were of good quality and neatly stowed. He felt no need either to show off his wealth or to deny it.

"Would you like a drink?" he said.

"I'd like you to kiss me," I said.

That made him smile. He stepped in, held me close, and kissed me.

It wasn't a bad kiss. His breath was fresh and his mouth tasted good. But he was a little, um, *unpracticed*; we weren't quite in synch. That wasn't a dealbreaker. Most people are teachable, and we hadn't gotten to know each other yet.

Getting to know people is what sex is *for*, right? It's a learning experience. You just don't get continuing education credits.

We got naked and got right into the king size bed. I wanted him. He wanted me. A girl can tell (she said modestly).

I didn't know what Jackson might be learning about me, but I quickly saw that he didn't know a lot about women. Again, not a dealbreaker. There's something about two sexual sophisticates executing polished, unvarying routines together that makes me think *sad robots*.

Here's the thing. When I sleep with a woman, *I* take charge. Bringing a woman to orgasm? Awesome. It's an accomplishment. When I sleep with a man, though, I'd prefer *him* to run the show while I swoon with pleasure as he moves little Janjan into whatever configuration he desires. Bringing a man to orgasm? Also lovely, but not much of a challenge.

Despite my preference, I found myself having to give Jackson clues, subtle and not so subtle, as to what I wanted. He picked up the clues quickly, I'll give him that. We both seemed to be having a wonderful time.

Despite his, um, natural gifts, there were things Jackson was learning for the first time. I wondered who he'd been sleeping with that he didn't know those things. He was no clumsy, ignorant, inhibited virgin. Had he been celibate for a long time? Possible. Divorced? Also possible.

Or had he been sleeping with men? He wasn't at all like any of the practiced, sensual bisexual men I'd bedded. Probably not much hot man-on-man action in his life, then.

A cartoon light bulb lit up above my head. Oh, my God, *prostitutes*. Jackson, the rich executive (I still didn't know what he did for a living. You're such a sloot, Janjan.) had acquired the habit of just *lying there* while a paid professional worked her magic.

Jesus, I thought, *thank God for condoms*. The Catholic Church is *way* off base to oppose them.

The man was a mystery. In my considerable experience, men who frequent prostitutes see women as disposable commodities. I get a creepy vibe from those men that was utterly absent in Jackson. Some guys (usually middle-aged) look at a woman as an assemblage of parts existing solely for their pleasure. No way to treat a lady; no way to treat me, either. Also, those men are able to rent women who are far more beautiful than any woman who would date them in real life. Status markers, ugh.

Again, I didn't see any of that in Jackson. The men (and I *mean* "men," not "boys") who are discerning enough to want to sleep with me know what I am: *hot*. And I say this with no vanity. Little fat ginger girl in the club and on your arm, freaky red-haired tigress in the bedroom or, say, bent over an armchair in the living room and moaning loudly. Jackson really seemed to be *into* me, ho ho.

As our time together wore on, and that's the right word, I came to climax any number of times. Everybody has a unique constellation of skills; orgasms are something I enjoy and do very well. I pride myself on my ability to work with practically any willing man or woman to achieve them. I thank God for this gift every day. I may be lusty and occasionally bitchy, but I'm not selfish in bed; I don't have to be.

It became clear that I would soon be sore from the exertion of attaining all those orgasms, but Jackson wasn't even close to having one. *Antidepressants?* I wondered.

"You've been more than, um, *generous* to me," I said. "What can I do to help you come?" I was sitting on him when I asked the question.

He frowned up at me unhappily and shook his head. "Sorry, I don't think it's gonna happen for me tonight. Weird. I used to have the exact opposite problem to apologize for."

I got off him carefully and lay next to him with my hand on his chest. In the light from the sitting area, I saw again how lean and muscular he was. Yum. "You don't have to apologize, Jackson. Ever hear a *woman* apologize because she couldn't come?"

"Ha! No."

"People aren't machines," I said.

"True enough." Silence.

Oh, dear. When men get all quiet, it usually means they want you to leave. I can take a hint.

"Well, okay. I should use your bathroom and hit the road," I said. "Early meeting tomorrow."

"It's late and the sidewalks are icy. I'll drive you home."

Huh. *That* was unexpected; it made me smile. "Gentlemen of the old school are seldom seen in these parts." I was talking about Portsmouth, not my vagina.

"You have no idea how old that school is." Jackson didn't smile when he said it.

10

Simon's demon carried the two men from the Caucasus to the United States in seconds. Those seconds seemed endless. The hateful creature dwelled in darkness, unable to touch the Earth. Did the demon really dive deep into the blackest shadows as it departed, or did Jackson only imagine that? He shivered miserably and tried to forget the trip.

Jackson found himself standing in the shadow of an enormous house. He couldn't see much of the estate's grounds in the dark.

McLean sounds like a fast food item, but is actually a wealthy Virginia suburb of Washington, D.C. This was Jackson's first visit. Concealed spotlights illuminated the mansion's distant façade, but the two visitors wouldn't be using the main entrance. Two servants were waiting for them in the cold shadows. The servants bowed.

The help whisked Jackson and his master through a side door into the basement of the great house. To his surprise, the cellar was full of ... *cells,* the way he imagined a Christian monastery. In these little rooms transient MMs and their allies rested and prepared for missions in normal American society. He saw no locks on the outside of the doors.

Jackson was instructed to shower and shave off his scruffy beard. When he looked in the mirror to shave, he was dismayed to see a white streak in his hair. What damage had the training in the Caucasus done that he *couldn't* see?

A nervous, muscular young man gave him a hundred-dollar haircut. (Jackson declined to have his white streak colored.) A silent dental technician attended to his teeth and whitened them. Muttering in German, a tailor took his measurements, and quickly brought him new dress shoes and a suit that fit perfectly, along with other clothing in his size. Jackson was not expected to pay for any of these services or to tip those who provided them.

One of the household staff knocked politely on Jackson's door and escorted him to the basement common area. A well-groomed besuited man he didn't recognize was waiting for him. Then the man grinned. There are limits to what even a skilled dentist can do for some mouths in a single visit.

"*Master?*"

"Got it in one," said the old magician. "And look at you—all got up like T.S. Eliot going to work at Lloyds Bank."

"May I ask what we're doing here?"

"Now that we look like the masters of the Earth we are, you and I are going upstairs to meet the Walloon, the master of masters."

Jackson followed the old man and the servant through a maze of passageways and up a staircase. They walked through a full-sized restaurant kitchen where the staff averted their faces.

They're afraid of us, Jackson thought. The thought gave him pleasure.

The servant showed the two guests through a high doorway and closed the oak door behind them.

A slender older man, dressed in a European-cut suit that fit him perfectly, sat next to the fireplace. A small fire was burning. The man held a brandy snifter in one hand (*like a Bond villain*, Jackson thought, *or C. Montgomery Burns*). He waved Jackson and the old magician to nearby chairs.

The magician grabbed Jackson's elbow and pulled him down to kneel next to him on the carpet, heading for a full ritual prostration. Jackson had done plenty of those during his training.

"No, no," said the man in the chair, "no bowing. Please get up. American rules, if you please, Master Simon." Slightly-accented English.

"As you like, Master Louis." Simon gave it the French pronunciation, *Loo-EE*.

Following Simon's example, Jackson got to his feet and sat in the chair.

Their host watched Jackson's face closely, but said nothing. Once again Jackson felt his mind invaded and examined. The examination was brief and clinical.

"So, Mr. Jackson," said the Walloon, "your last...*assignment* ended badly, no?"

Jackson skipped the self-justification. "It did, sir."

The Walloon and Simon shared a glance. They might have been sharing thoughts; Jackson couldn't tell.

"What could you have done differently?" the Walloon said.

"I've given this a lot of thought, Master Louis," Jackson said. "I *could* have gone to the world where the god and goddess lived. But what if they left *that* world the way they left Earth? We'd be no further ahead and I'd be stuck there forever. I think all the gateways to their world are closed now."

The Walloon made an encouraging gesture: *please continue*. The man sat up very straight in his chair. Jackson found himself sitting up straighter, hoping to make a good impression.

"I suppose I could have sacrificed myself to the Old Gods, but I don't know what that would have accomplished besides my death. And they never summoned me."

"Quite right," said the Walloon. "You'd made no agreement with them, had you? If the god and goddess had *incorporated* you, that would have ended your usefulness to the Order."

"As I told Master Simon, the language of the god and goddess gave me some power over, um, our enemies. But now that language is gone. I can't remember a word of it." Jackson shook his head.

"Why did you seek out Master Simon?" said the Walloon. "It can't have been an easy journey."

"No new orders came, sir," Jackson said. "I used my own judgment."

"It's good that you showed initiative. But the fact remains that you have failed the Order. Is there any reason we should not kill you?" The Walloon spoke in kindly, reasonable conversational tones, but his words chilled Jackson; the fireplace was no help.

But the young man who'd traveled here by demon-power wasn't the same callow hipster who'd left the United States on a slow boat.

"I certainly don't want to die, Master Louis," Jackson said, "but killing me seems a waste."

"*That's* the spirit, lad," said Simon. "We live to serve the Order, innit?"

"I swore an oath of obedience, Master Simon," said Jackson. He was looking at Louis when he spoke, though. Simon wouldn't kill Jackson unless the Walloon ordered it.

Inside Jackson's head he heard or felt a *snap*. His vision doubled. Was he having a stroke?

Behind Simon's chair stood a towering dark figure, approximately man-shaped. Behind Louis' chair stood another, larger figure; its head reached the high ceiling of the library. The shadow behind Simon simply watched the old magician like a bailiff or a prison guard. Jackson perceived that neither shadow actually stood on Earth, but manifested through the men who had become instruments in exchange for power. The figure behind Louis mirrored his every movement. Its lips moved, slightly out of synch with the Walloon's.

In fact the shadow moved slightly before Louis moved. It spoke just before he did.

It's moving him, thought Jackson. *It's talking* through *him.* He felt an emotion that was both thrilling and horrible. It was the end of all hope, becoming fear's plaything. Was he repelled by this preternatural possession or did it *draw* him? It was like the depths Simon had shown him; the fear went all the way down to the bottom of everything. Jackson's feelings were as two-sided as his vision. He was careful to keep his gaze on the faces of the two magicians and not stare at the creatures behind them.

The art of disguise was mostly common sense and distraction. If you did the expected thing, you were less likely to be noticed. He pretended not to have seen the creatures who were masters of Masters Louis and Simon.

They see me, he decided. *They don't know I see them.* Simon thought Jackson's time serving the Old Gods had damaged him. Jackson thought that speaking the language of the god and goddess had *sensitized* him to the workings of power. He knew power when he saw it used; he saw whether that power was good, evil, or merely neutral.

"As it happens," Louis was saying, "we plan to send you back to New Hampshire." Jackson heard the shadow's voice before he heard Louis':

"*we* we

plan plan

to to

send send

you you..."

He couldn't tell the real voice from the echo. With a second silent snap his vision returned to normal. He heard only Louis telling him where to go and what to do to prepare for his return to Portsmouth.

Jackson listened carefully, nodding politely like an eager neophyte. Following orders exactly was a matter of survival. Louis calmly, clearly, and kindly explained that another failure would be fatal for Jackson.

Jackson said he understood. He hoped no one would probe his mind and discover his doubts.

He had joined the Brotherhood seeking power. The Brotherhood had sent him to harness the power of the god and goddess, if such a thing was even possible, and to use that power against the elves. But the god and goddess had put themselves beyond all the prayers of their worshipers. *And what's the point of serving the Fallen if you have to give up your own will to do it?* Jackson wondered. *Great power doesn't do you much good if there's no* you *there to wield it.*

"I thank you for this second chance, Master Louis," Jackson said. He sounded completely sincere and was at least half that.

The Walloon watched Jackson in a silence which was doubled by the unblinking shadow looking through the magician's eyes.

11

Working for the elves really *made me wonder what the hell I was doing in Portsmouth.*

"So you and Leda are *married* now?" I said. I was at the little desk in the living room with my laptop, facing one way. Jerry August sat next to the desk, facing the other way, so we could see each other while we talked and I typed.

"Having trouble imagining such a thing?" He was smiling; we both were. I'd always liked him. When we first met, he'd just been a nice guy, good for Leda, but not my type. Actually, I was surprised he turned out to be Leda's type. She'd never dated anybody smart before.

Now, though, umm umm *umm,* I couldn't help wanting him, my type or not. For one thing, he smelled different, by which I mean *very* good. Before, he'd looked like any other wiry medium-sized guy. Now he looked disproportionately *strong* for his frame, like the kind of bad boy who would pull my pants down and bend me over the desk, whether I said I wanted that or not. Ignoring my feeble pretend-protests: *No, you mustn't. Stop, you brute.*

In case you wondered what my type was.

"Did Leda take your last name, or do you use both names and hyphenate?" I said, hoping to derail my lascivious train of thought before he picked up on it.

Jerry paused. "That's a great question. The short answer is *Sometimes.*"

I just *looked* at him. I call that withering look The Boner-Killer.

"You think I'm messing with you," he said. I smiled; he was right. "Okay, here's the long answer. There are no legalities in the next world over. No marriage licenses, no taxes, no *property* to speak of. Everyone has everything they need. We're really all one family. Everybody knows everybody else, so we're *informal,* I guess you could say. A couple uses last names as a form of emphasis, as a way to show what they are to each other. Leda and I belong to each other, and everybody knows we're *spoken for.*"

"So there's no cheating? Sounds like heaven."

"I won't say nobody ever cheats," he said. "People are people. Anyone can make a mistake, especially when they come back to Earth. But is heaven a place you walk through in your own body? You should come over with me and see for yourself."

I shook my head *No, thanks!* and clicked busily away on the keyboard, capturing his words. I felt Jerry looking at me. When I looked up, his face showed only compassion for my fear. He'd go on to tell me how he'd felt what I was feeling—and so had Leda. Wherever the next world over was, they'd walked through their fear to get there.

Jerry put his hand on my chubby little arm. I was tempted to flex the underlying muscles, like men do when we touch them, so he'd know I wasn't just a blob. "Janjan, Leda and I will be married as long as we can be. We're still new to the next world over, as the elves see things. I hope we'll be called upcountry together. We'll always love each other. But if one of us has to leave and the other can't go along, our marriage will be over because we can't be together anymore."

His brief touch was warm. It sparked something in me, creature of impulse and raw desire that I am. I really wanted him to kiss me all of a sudden. Had his sandy hair grown thicker and darker while he and Leda were ... out of town?

He wasn't going to kiss me, of course, and I wasn't going to hit on my friend's husband. My beautiful friend's surprisingly hot husband.

I felt like crying. Don't ask me why.

Jerry *watched* me go through all this with an open expression on his face. I knew—or at least assumed—he could read my mind, but he didn't strike me as someone who'd intrude where he wasn't wanted. He'd never been a bad boy. And what was he now, exactly?

I couldn't imagine a world where everyone could read everyone else's thoughts. Who'd want *that*? I wasn't ready for heaven—or for the next world over, either.

Back to business, then. "You and Leda used to work together out at the airport?" I said.

Jerry nodded. He went on to tell me how he and Leda had met and how they'd finally, um, gotten together. Not that he shared all the dirty details. Neither did Leda, come to think about it, when I asked her the same question. Jerry had always been a gentleman. Unlike me, Leda had always been a lady. Still, they made it clear how deeply they pleased each other. How they *took comfort* together.

What *had* they become? They weren't prudes, that was for sure. Nasty sexual things had happened to them in a world that wasn't Earth and wasn't the world of the elves, either—things that would have driven most people to insanity or suicide. They downplayed their courage when they talked to me.

When it came to sex, Jerry and Leda were skillful, generous, relaxed, and grateful for each other. *And* faithful. Fidelity seemed to be a big deal to the elves. Maybe honorable behavior made life easier, even in paradise. The truth can be so simple it's hard to accept.

Anyway. Jerry and Leda told basically the same story. Jerry smiled when he talked about Leda. I'd kill to have a man smile like that when he talked about me.

It was quite a story. A lot of it was hard to believe, but so what? I kept my doubts to myself and typed it all down like a good little contract employee: everything Jerry told me, everything Leda told me separately, the questions I asked, the answers they gave me.

I did my homework, too. I read up on the Portsmouth Wars, which is what the elves call the battles they won in and around southern New Hampshire. A remarkably consistent picture emerged. I didn't want to think about it. It was all so *weird*. Thinking about what *had* happened made you think about what *could* happen. And what could you do about that?

You could move away and get on with your life, is what. Earth is a small world, but lots of places are safer than Portsmouth. Any of those big square states out in the middle of the country would do.

You could also accept the elves' open invitation to the next world over.

Or you could do what most of us did: stay in Portsmouth and deny its history.

There was another option on the menu, but I wouldn't hear about it until February, when my server Coran the Fae would take my drink order and tell me about the dinner specials.

12

The Fae in the Cave *(This January)*

Jackson thought, *It figures that Master Louis has a fucking dungeon under his fucking castle. Does he have dragons, too?* He remembered the shadow that stood behind the Walloon and spoke through him. He remembered what he'd learned about the Dragon in Bible school. The Walloon didn't have a dragon, the Dragon had him.

Dressed in new hiking gear, Jackson and Master Simon followed along behind the Walloon's security manager, a thirtyish man wearing gray camouflage. The man carried himself like the Materialist Magician who'd taught Jackson small arms, knife work, and unarmed combat. Like Jackson's combatives teacher, their guide had the flat, dead, eyes of a killer. Eyes like that were common in the Brotherhood. Jackson was almost afraid to look closely at his own reflection in the mirror.

They'd been walking for twenty minutes. However big the Walloon's estate was, they couldn't possibly still be under it. The rock corridors were mostly natural but had been widened in places. Dim emergency lights were strung along the walls at long intervals, so they could see to walk. Jackson couldn't help being curious.

"Where are we?" he said. "I mean, what *is* this place? It's pretty cool."

Their guide stopped in his tracks, turned around, and looked at Master Simon for an explanation of Jackson's lapse. The old man simply shrugged: *Kids today, huh?*

The guide glared at Jackson and held a forefinger to his lips: *Shh.*

"*OpSec,*" the old magician whispered to Jackson. As if that explained anything. He meant, basically, that Jackson had no *need to know* and therefore would be told nothing further. Who would overhear their conversation? Jackson would not be told that, either.

Resigned, Jackson nodded to Simon and the guide. "Sorry."

The guide picked up the pace. Old Simon labored to keep up, but didn't complain.

It struck Jackson that the guide might well have killed him for asking a simple question, or for no reason at all. Ruthlessness sounds better in theory than it is in practice, especially when it's you that's the obstacle. Jackson wondered how an organization that showed so little loyalty to its members was able to command loyalty from them.

Oh, right, *the promise of power.* He put his eyes back on the prize and kept walking.

The guide unhesitatingly led them along corridors that branched and branched again. Jackson saw nothing to distinguish the road taken from the road not taken.

After another half hour of trudging along in the featureless half-dark, Jackson saw green light shining from an opening on one side of the tunnel.

The guide stopped and turned to Jackson. "I'm not going anywhere near *them,*" he said. "I'll wait here for exactly one hour. *If* you come out, I'll walk you back." Whoever was in the cave recess scared this stone killer badly.

Jackson had no idea what time it was; he had no watch and he'd had to leave his phone in his basement room.

Simon looked at his watch and nodded. "I'll keep track of the time," he told the security manager.

The guide sat down with his back against the corridor wall. At Simon's urging, Jackson took the lead and walked toward the green-tinted light. It shone out of a living-room-sized natural cave to his right.

Jackson looked into the room. He looked back at Simon. The old man made an impatient two-handed gesture: *Go in.*

Jackson walked through the stone entrance. On the right side of the opening sat an old woman. Another sat on the left. Both wore black robes with cowls that covered their hair. Their eyes flicked up briefly at Jackson, then returned to the crumpled figure at the back of the cave. The old women's lips moved unceasingly, not in High Aghartic, which Jackson would have recognized, but in some newer tongue. The language was full of whispered sibilants that made all the hair on Jackson's body stand on end.

Not black magic like the Brotherhood practiced, then, but magic of another sort, aimed at the creature slumped against the rock wall of the cave. It looked like a man, but what kind of man emits fitful greenish light?

Again Jackson looked back at Simon, who stood in the doorway watching. Simon pointed to Jackson, then emphatically at the creature: *Go to him.*

Jackson went.

As Jackson walked toward him, the shining creature sat up. He smiled at Jackson.

"Look who they've sent," the creature said (or seemed to say). "It's a baby magician." Only part of this communication came out of the man's mouth.

Jackson felt a kind of *pulling* on his inner man when the creature spoke, or seemed to speak. It was quite different from the intoxicating initial effect the Old Gods had had on him. He stopped five feet from the glowing man. "Forgive me," Jackson said, "but are you human?"

The creature's smile was sad. "Maybe once long ago. That's probably a thousand years by now. I hardly remember a time I wasn't with the Fae."

"The ... *Fae?*"

The creature waved his hand. "Just one of the names you people have given us. We walk a path through many, many worlds, a road that touches on your Earth in several places." He looked at the rock walls of the cave. "Ironic. They've called us *the Mound Folk* as well. And here we are, you and I, under the ground. With only witches as companions. Ha!"

Jackson turned around to see what the Fae meant. The two old women continued muttering their spell. Their faces were not good to look at, full of fear and spite. Jackson was relieved to turn back to the captive; he looked more human than the crones.

The Fae examined Jackson closely, looking him up, down, and around. "Been trafficking with gods, have you, young fella?"

"Have they *hurt* me in some way?"

"Well, the older sort of creatures leave their mark on a man, let's say that. For any who know what to look for."

"And the Fae?"

"Ah, I see what you're getting at. A man never *becomes* a god, however long he spends in the company of gods. But a man who travels with the Fae?" The Fae pointed to himself in an elaborate, self-mocking gesture.

"What powers do the Fae have?" Jackson said. "Why would anyone *want* to be one of you?"

"*Power*, is it? Why, only the power to live happily forever. Well, mostly happy and almost forever." He pointed to the two old muttering women. "The Morrigna bid fair to end my long long life—once *you* get whatever it is you came for, young sorcerer's apprentice."

Jackson wanted to deny that, but how could he? He liked the Fae instinctively, but had no power to protect him. So he hardened his heart and asked the question he'd come to ask. "I want people to join the Fae. How can I persuade them to do that?" Then for some reason, he added, "If I fail in this, I'll die." He didn't know why the Fae would care.

The light around the Fae flickered. The creature stared at Jackson from intermittent green shadows and sparks. And now the Fae's face was pure sadness, as much for Jackson as for himself. He beckoned. "Ach, so it's like that? Come closer and I'll show you."

Jackson felt cold from his heart down to his heels. But how could he say no? If he refused his mission, the Walloon would have him killed.

Jackson approached the Fae. The creature got to his feet, painfully and slowly, like all his joints hurt. Jackson heard rustling behind him. The two old women stood up. Their lips still moved. The muttered spell went subvocal, silently potent.

"We inhale for half of eternity and exhale for the other half, as we walk the fae-road wrapped in *the light of other days*," said the Fae with manic gaiety. He moved close to Jackson like he was going to kiss him. "Take my last breath, then, and be damned to you!"

All the green light around the Fae burst into Jackson's face in one sudden strong breath smelling of dry autumn earth: *pah!* Recoiling, Jackson inhaled instinctively in shock. His eyes rolled up into his head as green fae-light filled him up and took his ordinary mind a-roving.

The Fae fell to the cave floor, light and graceful as dry leaves in November wind. Jackson wavered a bit, out on his feet. The slight body of the man, or former man, cushioned Jackson's fall.

13

No Matter Where I Serve My Guests, They Seem to Like My Kitchen Best
(This February)

Jackson drove me home from his hotel. He parked the BMW in the driveway right behind my car. Probably some sexual symbolism there. I decided not to make the obvious joke out loud. We'd *had* sex, but I didn't know how he felt about sex *talk*. You don't want a guy to think you're a whore or something, stupid double standard. Instead I asked if he wanted to come in for a cup of coffee. I was surprised when he said yes. Like maybe *he* didn't want the night to end, either. Eh, who knows?

When we walked through the side mud room into the kitchen, Beth and Bobby were sitting at the table drinking coffee, still in their club clothes.

"Oh, hi, um, Jackson," Beth said. "Would you like some decaf?"

"Love some, thanks, Beth."

I hung up our coats and made a stop in my own bathroom. Jackson was talking to Bobby when I got back to the kitchen. I was amused to see

Beth's pique at having two men in the room but not being the center of their attention, even for a moment. I freely grant you that this was a petty, spiteful, *catty* sort of pleasure, but a pleasure is what it was.

Jackson smiled at me. It was a real smile, if I'm any judge of these things, like he was happy to see *me*, in particular. "Bobby was just telling me how Beth got him a warehouse job," Jackson said. Beth perked up at the mention of her name.

"Temp with a chance for *permanent* if they like me," Bobby said happily. It didn't take much for everything to come up roses in Bobbyland. "I'm a lucky guy. First I'm a hobo and Janjan saves my life, then Beth and Janjan take me in, then Beth finds me a real job. Now I'm paying my share of the rent!" Bobby gave Beth a look no man had ever given me. *The Look of Love*, as the old song has it. Beth smiled back at him. "Once I get my feet under me," Bobby continued, "I'm gonna ask Beth to marry me. If she'll have me, I mean."

Beth's smile faltered. "Whoa, not so fast, cowboy. Let's think about the future ... later!"

Bobby laughed guilelessly. Jackson smiled. I smiled, too, just to make nice. I was thinking that I'd seen Beth do some rapid calculations and conclude that Bobby was fun to dance with and great to sleep with, but not worthy to marry and have children with. *Despite* being the most passionate, skillful lover she'd ever had. That made me think less of her.

It made me think less of *myself*. Are all of us awful? What does it mean to be a woman, anyway? Are we just a support system for the uterus? With great power to carry the next generation comes great responsibility, blah blah blah. But *marrying up*? Ugh, there has to be a better way. Leda seemed to think she'd found one with the elves.

Anyway. What was Jackson saying to Bobby? "You look like you've been around. Military service?"

Bobby looked at Jackson warily, but nodded Yes.

"No pressure or anything," Jackson said, "but I need a part-time assistant. It'd be great to have a competent local guy who could work evenings and weekends. Here's my card. If you're interested, give me a call, okay?"

Bobby took the card (textured ecru, small print) and looked at it carefully like he'd never seen such a thing before. "Sure. Thanks!" he said. His face lit up again. He'd be calling *M. Jackson*, all right. Dude was transparent.

With that, Jackson finished his decaf and said good night to all of us. He leaned over and kissed my cheek. "I'll call you," he said in my ear. I wanted to shiver.

"Yeah, right," I said. "I'll believe *that* when it happens." Guys all *say* they'll call.

I saw Jackson out through the mud room and waved to him as he drove off in the BMW. I think I saw him wave back. I couldn't quite see if he was smiling. What was *up* with that guy? Besides his penis, I mean. Woof. Wouldn't mind some more of it, probably wasn't going to get it. One-night stands aren't my favorite thing or a goal I aim for, but the best of them beat solitary masturbation, skillful as I am at that. Besides, how else do you find out if you're compatible with somebody if you don't sleep with him? Or with her?

When I got back to the kitchen, Beth was sitting at the table alone frowning into her decaf.

"No Bobby?"

"I might have hurt his feelings," Beth said. "He said to say goodnight to you and went off upstairs to bed. In *his* room."

"Oh, dear. Men are *so* fragile." I'm such a bitch.

But she gave me a look of real distress. "Janjan, Bobby and I have had *lots* of sex, but he can't ever *come* with me, no matter *what* I do. I have done *everything* I know—and everything you taught me about. I'm starting to think there's something wrong with *me*."

Great, now she was trying to implicate *me* in her sexual problems, the bitch. "Huh. The same thing happened to Jackson tonight. He couldn't seem to come with me, either. You think there's something going around? I guess it's better for us than a plague of premature ejaculation."

We giggled. Catholic girls have a seriously nasty side. It's all the shaming in childhood and adolescence. "So how *did* it go with Jackson?" she said.

"It was like repeatedly sitting on a well-lubricated beer can."

Beth laughed. "*God*, Janjan, you're *awful!*" Then, more seriously, "Bobby says he feels like he's having orgasms on the *inside*. It's just that ... no semen ever comes out. He thinks it's going to, but it doesn't ever happen. I should quit asking him about it. My bad."

"With Jackson it didn't seem to be deliberate, like that Tantric sex business where the guy learns to control his orgasms consciously." I had actually slept with a guy like that once, and what a self-righteous ass *he* was. Religion, ugh.

"Men are such a mystery," Beth said. She was only half kidding.

"Maybe more of a mystery than I thought," I said.

14

I Find Your Lack of Faith Disturbing *(This January)*

> *The world is too much with us; late and soon,*
> *Getting and spending, we lay waste our powers;—*
> *Little we see in Nature that is ours;*
> *We have given our hearts away, a sordid boon!*

> William Wordsworth,
> "The World Is Too Much With Us"

Before Jackson returned to Portsmouth, the Materialist faction of the Materialist Magician confederacy wanted a word with him.

The exterior of the office building looked familiar; so did the lobby, the elevator, and the carpeted hallways. As he entered the Washington legal firm's luxe conference room, déjà vu made him uneasy. Jackson thought: *We have all been here before.*

He remembered striding into this room in what felt like another life. Last year, one of the law partners had asked the young magician to confirm whose spirit, exactly, was the current occupant of *Jerome* August's body. Jerry had almost convinced the stupid lawyers he was *Quincy August*, his own granduncle, magically embodied in Jerry's flesh by the Old Gods. Jerry told the lawyers things they thought only old Quincy could know. Jackson had exposed the masquerade as elvish trickery.

That episode ended badly for Jackson and even worse for the law firm and its powerful anonymous clients, who eventually lost a fortune— thanks to Jerry August. Jackson had only contempt for those who obsessed about money.

The memory of what had happened to him in this room remained shifting and unreliable. It seemed his mind had been *called up* into the joined minds of the winged god and his goddess as he spoke their magical language of dreams. Then it seemed that Quincy August had taken over Jackson's mind and will from *inside the Old Gods*. Quincy had taunted Jerry in English, breaking Jackson's spell. *Quincy himself* had kept Jackson from capturing Jerry August. Good luck making anybody understand *that*. With Quincy now dead of old age, both MM factions blamed Quincy's spiteful blunder on Jackson—who'd been powerless to prevent it.

He was happy to be the only Magician at today's meeting. He could make no sense of what the dying Fae had done to him in the cave. He felt *different*, somehow; he was anxious to get out of Washington until he could sort it out. Master Simon had returned to the Caucasus. The Walloon remained on his estate like a spider in the middle of its web. Either of his masters could find him in an instant.

Jackson arrived before anyone else. One of the law firm's partners sat waiting with him. This was the man who'd invited Jackson into last year's debacle.

"I'm surprised to see you here again," said the unsmiling lawyer. He looked uneasy.

Jackson didn't smile, either. "Surprised to see me alive, you mean."

"The Brotherhood's not known for giving second chances," the lawyer agreed. "Insofar as I know anything about your side of the organization, I mean to say."

Jackson brought the hireling up short. "You understand that I'm not at liberty to discuss the Order's internal business?" His tone was neutral, but the threat was clear.

"Of course, of course!" said the lawyer quickly. "Er, were you told why my clients wish to meet with you before you undertake your new, er, *assignment*?"

Jackson shook his head. He enjoyed having the whip hand. "Does it matter? I assumed our interests were the same."

"If only," the lawyer said. That was as close to humor as Jackson had ever seen him venture.

Jackson's eyebrows went up. He'd been taught that MMs and their allies were above anything like internal politics. He'd been taught that there was One Will, and that they all served it. That Will was first on the list of things he preferred not to think about.

"Perhaps my clients should speak for themselves in this matter," said the lawyer. "Ah, here they are now."

One conservatively-dressed woman and three conservatively-dressed men entered the conference room through the hallway door. *They'd* all been here before, too, Jackson thought. The Order still commanded enormous wealth through those who served *the prince of this world*, as Saint Paul expressed it. Now, as in Paul's lifetime, most served the prince unwittingly.

The lawyer stood up to acknowledge the presence of a lady or perhaps to genuflect before the altar of wealth. Jackson remained sitting with both palms flat on the gleaming oak table before him. This was *his* meeting, whatever any of these people thought. Having money at stake was one thing; having your ass and your immortal soul on the line was something else. The lawyer looked at Jackson, still sitting, almost frowned at his rudeness, then thought better of it.

The lawyer made the introductions. Jackson nodded but remained silent as each of the new arrivals was introduced and took a place at the table.

To Jackson's surprise, the woman spoke first. Women took a distant second place in Materialist Magician circles. Really, there were fewer women in those circles since the disaster in Tibet decades ago. The Order blamed a woman they called *Magda* or *Himiko* for their defeat—in the same way Christians blamed a woman they called *Eve* for the loss of Eden.

"Mr. Jackson," she said, "do you know why you're here today?"

Jackson hadn't quite caught her name (*Moira*, was it?) He took an instant dislike to her crisp overconfidence, but kept it out of his voice. "I was given an order."

The woman nodded as if she'd expected that reply. "A better question, then. Do you know why you were *ordered* to learn the language of the Old Gods?"

"Something to do with your ... *investment* in the late Quincy August?" Jackson said. If this meeting was about finding a scapegoat for that earlier disaster, there was plenty of blame to go around.

The woman didn't bat an eye. "Money is power, of course. But the god and goddess represented another sort of power, didn't they?" Her tone implied that Jackson's reply was stupid, rather than merely impertinent.

"They represented a power we couldn't control—as we learned to our sorrow," Jackson said. "Where are the Old Gods now? Where's their language?"

"You learned something else, too," one of the men said. "Didn't that language give you power over our enemies?"

The lawyer, Jackson saw, was uncomfortably looking everywhere but at the speakers. He knew *something* had happened to him when the gods descended upon his conference room. He couldn't remember clearly because those powerful beings had temporarily but thoroughly muddled his wits.

"It *neutralized* some of them," Jackson said. "Not all of them, though, and not permanently." Jackson vividly remembered how the elves had finally defeated him out on the cold Atlantic—using nothing but their own magical shining language.

"The point is that we *have* to find a way to sideline the elves permanently if we're going to make any progress toward our long-term strategic goals," the woman said.

"By 'we', she means *you*," said one of the men. The first time he'd spoken. His face was as fat and unlined as a baby's. Before long the rest of him would get fat, too, as self-indulgence took its toll.

Jackson stared at the man and didn't bother to respond to the obvious point. As he was staring, he heard that inner *snap* again and felt his vision double.

Somewhere far behind the rich man wearing the English suit a naked shadow stood. It wasn't standing immediately behind his chair. It wasn't on Earth at all. It was barely visible just above the event horizon of the spirit. The shadow reminded Jackson how he'd seen Quincy August, riding on currents of the Old God's language *inside the god*; how he'd seen face after face behind Quincy's: all the Other-World people whom the god and goddess had incorporated into a temporary, provisional immortality within themselves. And of course he'd seen the god and goddess, who changed the world around them with their language, the language of dreams. The god and goddess watched the activities of mortals with affectionate disinterest, as it were, from across a great gulf. Jackson had felt the warmth of that Olympian affection when the gods—and Quincy— spoke through him.

This shadow, though, had no fondness for the man it surveilled. The man was only a means to its end. To that end, Jackson saw, the shadow had already begun working, even from its current great distance, to influence the man's life, both awake and asleep. After the initial oppression would come obsession in which his life was ruined, followed ultimately by possession like Master Louis', where the man would obey only the One Will.

Jackson saw all that in a flash. He knew not to draw the shadow's attention by staring at it.

After staring rudely at the fat-faced man long enough to make his point, Jackson said, "Having bad dreams lately, asshole?"

"Yes..." the man started to say, too startled to dissemble. "I mean *No!* What the hell do you *mean* by asking such a thing?"

"I *mean*," Jackson said, "that it's easy enough to send somebody off to solve your problems while you sit home and count your money. But you should understand what I am and, more importantly, what I've pledged myself to."

Jackson hadn't quite pledged himself to the Fallen the way Louis and Simon had, not yet, but these people didn't know that. No one could meet Jackson's gaze. The lawyer fought the urge to smile. Schadenfreude is an occupational disease of the legal profession.

Finally the woman looked up at Jackson. "You're right," she said flatly. "I won't answer for my associate here, but *I've* had bad dreams for years now. Ever since the elves started coming to Earth and people started going to their world."

Jackson saw no shadow behind the woman, not at any distance. The mysteries of evil remain mysterious even to its postulants. She'd simply missed his point. "You're having bad dreams?" he prompted.

The woman's expression softened as she searched Jackson's face. "I have two sons in college. You're no older than they are; I didn't see that until just now. People mature rapidly in the Order. But your generation doesn't remember how *simple* life was when Earth was the only world we had to think about. Those were better times."

Better for whom? Jackson thought, surprising himself.

The fat-faced man with the distant shadowy watcher spoke up. "I apologize for my little joke, Mr. Jackson. It was ungrateful under the circumstances. And you're right, all the real risk is on you."

Jackson sat straight and perfectly still, controlling his breathing, watching the other people in the conference room become uneasy. Finally he said, "What do you want from me?" He meant: *What do you people want that's different from what my chain of command wants?*

"What we want—and I'm sure I speak for everyone here—is to cut the elves off from Earth," the woman said. "What we do *not* want is another Portsmouth War."

A second man spoke up, white-haired, distinguished, thin, and wearing a tweed sport coat, for God's sake. He looked like Hollywood's idea of a 1950s college professor. "We had *such* high hopes for the Other World." Jackson could hear the capital letters. "Really, we thought Quincy August was onto something with those Old Gods and their language, something the elves would be powerless against..."

"Whatever you end up having to do, *we* want to limit the *collateral damage*," the woman said. "The Order, if you'll forgive my speaking plainly, is willing to lay the Earth waste to gain it for themselves. We're not."

Jackson sat back, trying not to laugh at the rich idiots in their comfy chairs. "You *do* know what trafficking with the Other World did to the Earth? Does the European Holocaust ring a bell? How about the Cambodian killing fields? The list goes on and on."

The third man finally spoke. "Whatever...*damage* the god and goddess and their offspring did on Earth was delimited by the metaphysical laws in play. We could have lived with that. We'd very much prefer to avoid any further *thermonuclear* unpleasantness, for example. The Third

Portsmouth War could have gone far worse—for all of us."

Nuclear weapons? None of Jackson's surprise showed on his face. He hadn't believed the elves' account of the last war. Until now.

It was maddening. Why did these morons have information Jackson had to go to the Elf Friends' website for? Wait, were they *all* relying on the Elf Friends' account of the Order's history? Now *that* would be ironic. He was careful not to show his frustration. The Materialist Magicians kept their history secret. Only the Archmage knew the whole story. These days there was no Archmage to hoard the Brotherhood's secrets, only Master Louis, whoever and whatever he was.

"Admit it," he finally said, "you have no idea what would have happened if the god and goddess had *stayed* on Earth." Nobody spoke up. Two looked busy taking notes: no OpSec for these people? "Hey, *I was there.* I summoned the Old Gods with their language, *the language of dreams,* we called it. But even I wasn't told what our endgame was." A partial untruth.

"*Distraction,*" the woman said. "We'd hoped to have the Earth to ourselves while the elves were otherwise occupied. A generation or two would do nicely."

"And now?"

"Nothing's changed," said the woman. "What are people looking for when they go to Portsmouth?"

It was a rhetorical question. Jackson gestured impatiently: *Tell me.*

"I'm sure some are just looking for excitement. But a lot of people are looking to find the way to the elves," said one of the men. "I'm told the walls between our worlds are *thinner* in Portsmouth."

Jackson nodded. He'd seen that simple truth for himself.

"What we want," said the woman, "is for people who go seeking the elves to find *something else* instead."

"The Fae?" Jackson said.

"They'll do nicely," said the man with the distant watching shadow. "Instead of going to the world of the elves, people will go walkabout with other creatures out of legend."

"And what do you imagine the elves will do about that?" Jackson said.

"Doesn't matter," the woman said. "If the elves can't recruit on Earth and can't get people to come home with them, they eventually cease to be a problem."

"Like changing the course of a river," said one of the men.

❋

For his assignment, Jackson was given a well-documented new identity in his own name. Along with a company car, he had corporate credit cards, tablet and laptop computers, company phone, memos on company letterhead, and business cards showing him to be an executive with a Massachusetts real estate development company, a firm bankrolled by its Washington silent partners, the Materialists.

Unfortunately, Jackson was also assigned a handler. He was supposed to report his progress up the chain of command every week through a guy named Michael. The man was a vice president in the company that ostensibly employed Jackson. Jackson drove from Washington to his handler's office in a suburb west of Boston.

It was an awkward first meeting. Michael ("Call me Mike"), a thug in a nice suit, had not known Jackson would be coming. Operations security sometimes became so secure that people didn't know they were part of an operation. Or maybe that was just human error.

Michael directed Jackson to sit in a guest chair while he called his own MM contact in Washington. As Michael listened to whoever he'd called, his thick eyebrows went up and stayed there. Jackson noticed because the vice president was staring at him.

Finally the vice president nodded a couple of times at whoever was on the other end of the phone and said, "Got it. Okay. Will do, sir." He hung up the phone and glared at Jackson out of eyes whose whites looked bluish, like hard-boiled eggs. To Jackson he said, "Typical. They didn't tell me to expect you. Nobody wants to tell me what you're gonna be doing. You planning to make my company look bad?"

The whole situation irritated Jackson profoundly. Time to let the ignorant pawn know who was in charge. "I'm planning to do what I was *ordered* to do. Think of it as a recruiting drive. You planning to help me?"

The man's face fell. "Oh, shit," he said, "you're one of *those* guys. You boys with the magic haven't exactly done us proud up in New Hampshire the last few years."

Jackson had an excellent Darth Vader death stare. He deployed it. "And your point?"

"*Here's* my point, pal. *I've* got orders, too. You fuck things up and I'll take a day off, drive up to Portsmouth, and kill you myself."

Jackson could have made Michael's heart stutter or stop, but humiliation was better. Before Michael knew what was happening, Jackson was standing behind him holding the older man's head down to his desk by the left ear while Jackson held the tip of Michael's stainless steel ballpoint pen in the opening of the guy's right ear. The vice president knew enough not to struggle. The pen is mightier than the sword when you jam it through the ear canal into the brain.

"I don't think *you* can kill me," Jackson said. "I suggest you stay *far* away from my operation. Don't call, don't text, don't email, and most of all don't *visit*. Are we clear?"

"*Clear.*" The voice was muffled by the desk.

"I'm not coming down to this shitbox office every month, either. I'll email or call as I see fit when I have something to report, understood?"

"*Understood.*"

"I'm guessing you've got a handgun in your desk. I'd like you to fish it out with two fingers and hand it to me very gently, okay?"

"*Okay*." Gradual, unthreatening movement toward the drawer.

"Atta boy. Nice and slow. Don't make me pith you like a frog."

Jackson took the pistol from the vice president's trembling fingers, stepped back from the desk, ejected the magazine, cleared a round out of the chamber, and threw the weapon into a potted plant in the corner.

The thug surprised Jackson by grinning at him. "That was well done, Mr. Jackson. You may be working on the wrong side of the house."

Jackson was in no mood for banter. "Don't fuck things up for *me*," he said. "You *really* don't want me to come back here."

15

Jerry Loves Leda *(This January)*

I thought I understood men. I couldn't figure Jerry out at all. So that was weird.

"The Old Gods left Earth," Jerry told me. "The good guys won the battle. Mary the former Myrmidon warrior took Leda and me home. We didn't drive back to my house near the cemetery. Instead, we walked to Mary's new home and ours, a place where no cemeteries are needed. We hiked across miles of yielding seawater. We stepped onto solid ground on the gentle foothills of the Invisible Mountain.

"By then we were ready to enter the world of the elves. We were more than ready.

"Once we made landfall, Mary went on ahead. Leda and I walked together, mostly in silence, but always linked in thought in the Unfallen Tongue. We walked for weeks and saw no one else.

"It was so beautiful. Gentle plains, green with grasses. Here and there a stream or a spring. Warm nights. More stars than I ever remember seeing, in constellations we'd never imagined.

"The Other World, home of the god and goddess, had been intimately linked to us in a way Earth was not. The Other World was strange and beautiful, but it wasn't even a faint copy of the place we were made for. Let me say that again, Janjan: *we knew we were part of the next world over.* We knew it immediately.

"When we visit Earth now, we still feel the true sun, warm on our skin. We still hear the thoughts of all our brothers and sisters in our minds, more faintly here. We feel the pull of the next world over in our bodies. Once we've done what we signed up to do on Earth, we'll go home again.

"Like Richard Round a generation ago, Leda and I *needed* the long walk into the world of the elves. A journey of purification, I guess. The unnecessary things of Earth fell away from us. New knowledge came into us from within, from the ground, and from the sky."

Jerry paused and shook his head. "I forgot to tell you about the angel.

"From the Atlantic Ocean outside Portsmouth harbor, we stepped into a place that was shrouded in mist. A mighty being who saw what we were also saw we had every right to enter the world he guarded. His flaming sword remained sheathed. Like the Old Gods, the angel was not made so that human senses could tell what he looked like. If he was made of matter, it was a finer sort than our own bodies.

"And yet the warrior angel, huge, powerful, incomprehensible, bowed to us. *Welcome home, little brother, little sister,* he thought. *How lovely when a bride and groom come here to be wed.*

"We felt the angel's smile. It was his joy to serve.

"I guess it's *our* joy to return to Earth and do what we can." Jerry grinned at me.

I knew he was sincere, but that all sounded kinda highfalutin to me. "I'm writing this down more or less verbatim," I told him as the laptop keys clicked under my fingers. "Maybe I'll understand it later?"

"We get to take all the time we need, Janjan. Hell, Leda and I would still be living in my house across from the cemetery if the bad guys hadn't come after us."

16

Leda Loves Jerry *(This January)*

Nothing Leda told me the next night took any of the weirdness away.

"Jerry and I met when we both worked for Bob's software company in an office out at the Tradeport," Leda said. "I told you and Beth about that, right?" I nodded Yes. Leda had talked our ears off about Jerry before he ever asked her out. She talked about him a lot less after they, um, became *intimate*. Leda went on, "I was the company admin when Bob hired Jerry. Jerry was a bit older than most of the guys Bob hired. He was divorced, with no kids. A girl notices these things, especially a newly-single girl who handles the personnel files. Jerry didn't appear to be dating anybody, or at least he never told dating stories at lunchtime.

"Jerry was friendly, polite, but a little reserved. Formal. I could tell he liked me by the way he listened when I talked. I liked him, too, but there was no way I was going to ask him out, not in a company that small. I liked working for Bob, but I had more than just a financial reason to take a new job downtown.

"*You'll* know what I'm talking about when I tell you this, Janjan. As soon as I met Jerry, I wanted to feel his hands on me. I wanted to touch him. I felt *safe* with him. He was good with people, but never *used* them. He joked that he was a gentleman of the old school, but it turned out to be a code he lived by.

"Imagine that, *me* attracted to a thoroughly decent man. Jerry was nothing like the guys I'd dated in college and afterward, who tended to be pretty boys with big dicks. Big, strong guys who were vain and weak inside and didn't care about me or my pleasure or anything but themselves. Jerry was wiry and kind of average-looking, so what drew me to him? *Strength*, maybe.

"There was something uncompromising in Jerry. Once he'd decided the right thing to do, I was pretty sure he'd do it or die trying. Also he didn't think *he* was special, he thought *I* was. He didn't just want any woman he could get or any supermodel he couldn't get, he wanted *me*. Honestly? He gave me more pleasure than I could handle, Janjan. Nobody has ever responded to me like he did. Like he does. He thinks I'm *beautiful*."

She'd always been beautiful, of course. Why do so many pretty girls *feel* unattractive? Beautiful Leda had found sex *and* love. I felt a painful stab of envy. I hope it didn't show on my face.

Leda said, "So was I settling for less, just because this average-looking guy *wanted* a relationship with me? And how good were his *career prospects?* I heard my mother's anxious voice in my mind. Mom thinks sex is less important than earning power.

"Outside the bedroom Jerry wasn't fearless at all. No macho bullshit with him. He wasn't ashamed to admit what he was afraid of. It scared him even to hear about the elves, but he didn't run away when he found out I was an Elf Friend. Hell, *I* was an Elf Friend because I wanted to be near the elves, but was scared to join them.

"Then the Myrmidons kidnapped me into the Other World away from Jerry. He ignored his fear and his pride. He asked the elves for help, and came into the world of the Old Gods to get me back.

"Did I know the kind of man he was when we were first smiling, flirting, and dating? That's silly. How could I have known?

"Look, you see what I am, Janjan. You see what Jerry is, what we've both become. We're the same people we always were, not perfect, but all grown up now. None of that would have happened if Jerry hadn't stubbornly insisted on finding his own way. We'd still be living in our perpetual selfish American childhoods. Sorry. That came out more judgmental than I intended. I mean *you* no offense.

"But anyway, we were talking about sex. I said that I wanted to feel Jerry's hands on me, to be naked with him, all the usual stuff. I wanted to feel him inside me. What I didn't know until it happened was that I wanted to feel his *mind* inside me, too. You can't *get* more naked than that."

I made a face, and Leda said, "Does that frighten you? I don't blame you. I guess we never would have found that kind of intimacy if our lives hadn't been in danger. We had the Old Gods and the Materialist Magicians trying to kill us in their different ways, for their different reasons.

"But sex teaches you something about the rest of your life that you'd never know otherwise, doesn't it? It's about giving and receiving pleasure, sure, both very good things, but sex points to something I'd never expected. Something I didn't even know I wanted. Tidings of comfort and joy, Janjan. Jerry and I *take comfort* together, as they used to say in the Other World. Only now when we swive, we follow our joy home to its source."

"I like that word *swive*," I said. "Very old fashioned."

Leda laughed at me. "You *would*, you little sloot."

"I'm not sure about sex *pointing* to anything," I said. "Or have I been looking at penises all wrong?"

Leda just smiled. "I wish you'd come home with me, but I understand why you don't want to."

I pretended to scroll back through my laptop notes like I was sitting in a shipyard conference room projecting the record of a meeting onto a screen. "You *did* give me this job to do, remember? And I *did* promise to do it. So tell me what it was like for you in that world where the Myrmidons took you." I looked back up at her, ready to type. My deflection didn't fool her, but she didn't press me.

Leda looked upwards, like people do when they're flipping back through memories, as if those memories are written on the ceiling or in the sky. "Ever dream that you're awake and trying to fall asleep?" she said. "I was a coma, but a light one. They fed me sips of some liquid. It had a mild taste, slightly sweet, and then it was gone. I never felt hungry or thirsty. I knew people were coming and going, servant girls, mostly. I knew when they carried me from an upper room of the temple up an echoing metal staircase to the parapet.

"I knew when the god and goddess began their descent from the sky. And I knew when Jerry showed up because he touched my mind with his."

"You had some kind of *mental sex* together?" I was skeptical. If you can't be honest with your friends, what's the point?

Leda just nodded. "I'd *show* you, but you'd just want to jump my bones right here and now."

"Tease."

She stopped smiling. "You're right, I was teasing. I shouldn't have done that. I apologize."

"Oh, relax," I said. "It's not your fault I have a hair-trigger libido." Even the sex talk we were having in polite generalities was having an effect on me. That's just who I am.

"No, I was taught better. There's a ... *code* we're supposed to follow when we come back to Earth. We're warned not to use anything that looks like a miracle as a spectacle to make people believe us. Earth doesn't need another nutball religion where people worship *'elves'*." Sarcastic Leda made air quotes with her fingers just to be sure I got the point.

I pretended to sulk. "Fine. If that's how you feel, I'll just have to go to bed tonight without all the mental orgasms I so richly deserve."

We laughed together, and for a minute it like it was old times again. Leda looked a bit different now, but she was still my friend. She could still be silly with me even if she was a Serious Person With a Mission.

God, how I hoped *that* wasn't contagious.

17

Where Have All the Hobos Gone? *(This February)*

> *Generations have trod, have trod, have trod;*
> *And all is seared with trade; bleared, smeared with toil;*
> *And wears man's smudge and shares man's smell: the soil*
> *Is bare now, nor can foot feel, being shod.*

Gerard Manley Hopkins, "God's Grandeur"

Hearing Leda's and Jerry's story makes me notice weirdness I'd rather ignore.

If a celebrity baby gets kidnapped or some random dog falls down an old well, boom, the whole country goes nuts. But there are thousands of other disappearances nobody cares about, mysteries nobody bothers trying to solve. God bless America.

It's a severe winter, like I said. One day the temperature briefly climbs almost to the freezing point. A local newspaper reporter snowshoes out to the homeless encampment to see how everyone is getting along. She's trolling for poverty porn feature material. New Hampshire gets a lot of slow news days; human interest stories fill in the white space.

The shacks, tents, and lean-tos are still there, but their occupants aren't.

The reporter asks herself, "Why would people who own so little—and *need* everything they own to survive this winter—leave their pitiful worldly goods behind?"

The reporter scratches her head, takes a bunch of digital photographs, and snowshoes back out of the little lost colony.

The newspaper runs her story in the Sunday edition. (A slow news week, it seems, in which national and international disasters continue rolling along with all deliberate speed.)

Readers post comments on the paper's website. (Don't ask me why they bother with a print edition, but whatever.) Comments like, "Hey, nobody's camping up by the radio station anymore. What's up?" And "There's another empty campsite out back of the high school. Where'd all the homeless people go?"

When asked, the police issue a statement that *says* all the right things, like they were trained to do in media school. But it's clear their spokesman thinks a city without homeless people in the middle of a wicked-pissah-cold winter wouldn't be a bad thing.

To check on people's welfare, pairs of cops visit all the sites where the homeless are known to pitch their tents. They find no people, no notes, and no clues. They see only trash nobody wants to clean up, and whose responsibility is *that*, anyway? The police shrug: *We've got real crimes to solve here. Crimes against real taxpayers who live in real houses and real apartments, not imaginary crimes against transients who come and go with the wind, consuming resources and social services like locusts, dying of overdoses, and getting arrested every damn month.* They don't say it, but that's what they're thinking. Nobody thinks the homeless are real people.

I notice the police spokesman's demeanor because I see his interviews on the TV news. I see video footage of the empty campsites. This story is growing legs.

Some very puzzled advocates for the homeless are interviewed on camera. Even the homeless shelters are emptying out, they say. The advocates wonder aloud where so many of their clients have wandered off to all at once. Did somebody lease a fleet of buses and drive all the vagrants down to Florida to sunburn on the beaches?

Nobody knows. Nobody who gets interviewed, anyway.

But I'm an observant lady. I notice that whenever Beth or I mention the Mystery of the Missing Hobos, Bobby remains silent, changes the subject, or wanders out of the room. When news items come on TV (the story has now spread to the New England cable news), Bobby feigns disinterest rather elaborately.

Poor simple, transparent Bobby is a terrible feigner. Dude couldn't feign to save his life. Being genuine simplifies things, but it's a burden when you have something to hide.

Bobby has something to hide.

Where, I ask myself, might Bobby have acquired guilty knowledge about whoever or whatever is spiriting Portsmouth's derelicts out of town?

From my mysterious bad boy Jackson, that's where.

I inquire innocently (*I* can feign innocence all day long), "So Bobby, what kind of work are you doing for Jackson, anyway?"

Bobby turns red, then turns white, then turns away. Finally he turns back to me. "Oh, *you* know, errands and stuff?"

I hazard a guess. "Bobby, is Jackson, like, *hiring* homeless people and *taking* them somewhere? And are you helping him?"

Bobby gives me such a pained look that I feel bad for him. "Jackson asked me not to talk about his business, okay?"

That sounds a lot to me like an admission. Maybe I should have gone to law school—like so many of the people I went to college with who I still hate.

I have to ask one more question, though, despite Bobby's discomfort. He and I have a bit of history which, I'm guessing, neither of us has shared with Beth. "Bobby," I say softly, "is all this about the Fae? Is that where all those people went?"

Bobby just shakes his head angrily. I've gone too far and pissed him off, yay me. He's not answering that one, but he doesn't have to.

"I've gotta go, Janjan." He heads for the mud room to grab his coat. "I'm working for Jackson tonight. He's picking me up."

Bobby leaves me alone with my dilemma. What happens to Bobby, I wonder, if I tell Leda and Jerry about the hobo exodus?

What happens to *me* if I get the elves involved in this?

18

What It Was Like With the Fae

Come, faeries, take me out of this dull house!
Let me have all the freedom I have lost;
Work when I will and idle when I will!
Faeries, come take me out of this dull world,
For I would ride with you upon the wind,
Run on the top of the dishevelled tide,
And dance upon the mountains like a flame.

W.B. Yeats, *The Land of Heart's Desire*

Bobby didn't like lying to me even by omission, but he remembered more about the Fae than he was able to tell me. He couldn't put his fragile memories, impressions, and feelings into words. And he couldn't bring himself to tell me about the sex stuff.

It was like dreams in a way, Bobby thought. The more you stare at something, the less you see it. The Fae didn't just walk or ride from place to place along the ancient fae-path, they *danced*. A dance of perceiver and perceived in which you make up your own steps as you go along, and the reality (if that's the right word) around you changes and changes again.

On Earth there are so many things it's better not to think about, but on the fae-path you can think whatever you like. Thoughts dance with you. Whatever you look at mutates if you stare too hard; your thoughts are like that. It's scary until you get used to it.

So you walk along with your fellows. You stop to eat and drink and maybe to swive or to fight. Nothing's ever serious enough to carry a grudge about for long. Nobody's ever compelling enough to stay enamored of for more than a week. Bruises of your light body and your light heart vanish like smoke, as if they never were. The things around you (best observed with your peripheral vision, although the fae-light you all carry illuminates the road) are interesting, but never arresting.

You wouldn't mind staying wherever you are, but when it comes time to move on (as it always does), you don't mind mounting a fae-steed and riding off to whatever's next. You're happy just dancing along with the rest.

Wherever you go, you start to remember being there before, but the fae-path is so long and there are so many places along it, so many worlds it passes through, that everything seems almost new when you encounter it again.

Almost new? *Déjà vu.*

And sometimes you walk off the path on purpose because you've found a world that speaks to your heart. Sometimes companions or lovers go exploring with you. Once you enter the other world, you step back into your own mortality.

You start to age and start to die again; you feel it in the marrow of your bones.

Fool! How long have you walked the fae-path that you've forgotten the curse of Adam and Eve? *I'm dying dying dying dying dying,* you think.

Recognizing the inevitable, you step on the path with your breath slowed almost to a stop and loiter near the ancient light-road for the Fae to come walking along again. When they do come back, you join them, though they mock you:

Did you think you wouldn't die, then? But welcome back to the green light of your immortality. We're happy to have you again!

They mock, but you don't mind it much. You don't mind anything much.

In fact, your life with the Fae is a bit like reading a book that passes the time but doesn't fully involve you. The people and things around you are just a bit, well, tenuous in their existence. Or maybe fae life is like watching a movie to ignore your earthly troubles.

The spouse you abandoned, say. Or your foolish, rebellious children. Or the calamitous debts you accumulated. Or the house you were about to lose. Or the lawsuit that was about to ruin you. Or the boss who hated you. Or the dead-end job you saw no way out of. Or the wars you could see no end of. Or your loss of youth, strength, and beauty. Or your fatal illness. Or the crime you'd soon be arrested for. Or all the weight of your griefs and losses. Or the inevitable approach of your own death.

I'll just hide out with the Fae awhile and all my troubles back there will sort themselves out, you think. *I can go home whenever I want.*

And really it's quite lovely here walking or riding along, grandly observing the ever-changing vistas that open up on either side of the road. And the lords and ladies of the Fae are fair to look upon. At night they know their way around the bedroom; all the arts of love are as familiar to them all as driving a car would be to the poor mortals who still live back in Portsmouth.

After all, the Fae have had, what, millennia to perfect their way of life? Some more, some less, of course.

You notice that there are many new recruits (almost all from Earth), but there are a few very old Fae (they don't *look* old) who sadly bid farewell to the road. They never return. You never see them again. Nobody ever talks about the departed and why they might have chosen to depart. Your questions are deflected or ignored. Who really cares?

But your health is excellent. You eat but once a day and drink your fill at night, and yet you never grow fat. As time passes, the fitter and more comely you become. Your real age is impossible to determine from your appearance.

Your oft-suppressed panic at your peculiar existence seems a small price to pay for a surface life that allows you to look so good and feel so well. The question *With whom shall I swive tonight?* becomes more compelling than you could ever have imagined.

19

Jackson Calls a Former Associate *(This February)*

I prefer the personal touch you only get with hired goons.
C. Montgomery Burns from *The Simpsons*

Jackson needed some information. He wasn't about to call the moron who was supposedly his Massachusetts handler.

Last year Jackson had been part of a team operating in Portsmouth. Some of the team members worked in the gray area between the federal law enforcement and intelligence communities. With their worldview, power, and privilege under attack, they joined forces with the MMs. Both groups wanted to prevent elves from coming to Earth and to keep earthlings from going to the next world over. It helped that the Order was generous to its allies in government.

Jackson's trained memory retained all the team's phone numbers. He also remembered the access number that took encrypted phone calls into an inner ring, where the NSA supposedly wasn't listening. Not that

Jackson cared. He answered to a higher power than the American security state, or perhaps a lower one.

The first two numbers he called were out of service. No surprise there. New assignments meant new mobile phones and new numbers for field agents.

The third call went right to a private line on the man's desk in Washington. He picked up on the second ring. "Burke."

"Good morning, Burke," Jackson said. "Joseph here." He used his *nom de guerre* from their joint operation on behalf of the Old Gods and against the elves.

A moment of silence. Burke said, "I'm somewhat surprised to hear from you, Mr. Joseph. Since we last spoke, I've been … *reassigned*."

Burke had thought Jackson was dead. Jackson said only, "I see." Always make your opponent sweat.

Another long pause. Jackson imagined Burke sitting in a sprawling gray-fabric cubicle farm, desperately thinking how to wriggle out of the position he'd put himself in. Finally: "I'm not sure how much help I can be to you. Unfortunately, my new position provides access to *far* less information." Burke was saying that he'd been sidelined and marginalized, all thanks to the elves and the Elf Friends. He was saying that his alliance with the Brotherhood had been a career-limiting move. He sounded bitter, and at the same time he was practically pleading with Jackson not to involve him with MM business again. Pathetic.

"My superiors will be disappointed to hear that you were unwilling to assist me in a simple inquiry," Jackson said.

"Whoa, before you talk to *them*, at least let me *try* to find what you need!" Score.

Jackson gave him the social security and Army serial numbers from Bobby's employment form. To provide further motivation, he stayed on the line while Burke rummaged around in the federal data cupboard.

Burke came back on the line and asked Jackson to confirm the numbers. Jackson did so. He heard keys clicking in the background as Burke repeated the search.

"This is odd, Mr. Joseph, but I'm sure the information is correct. The service number you gave me belonged to a man the Army listed as missing in action in Belgium—in 1945. There are no postwar earnings credited to that SSN. If he *were* still alive, he'd be about 85 years old. So you're probably dealing with an identity thief. Is that what you needed to know?"

Suspicion confirmed, thought Jackson. Like the elves, the Fae had a timestream all their own. Bobby, who looked like a man in his twenties, *was* a sort of time traveler.

Jackson decided to let Burke off the hook for today. "You've been very helpful. The Brotherhood is grateful." Not as grateful as Burke would be that Jackson hadn't had to go over his head.

Another pause. "You're certainly welcome," Burke said. "By the way, your two assistants from our previous New Hampshire, er, *business venture?* Our mutual friends tell me that both men have recovered—as much as they're ever going to. They don't remember much about their last assignment. We got them jobs as *mall security* over at Tyson's Corner." Burke made it sound like a fate worse than death.

He's fishing Jackson thought. *He wants to know what happened in Portsmouth last year. No one's told him. Because knowledge is power.*

Jackson had forgotten about the hired goons who'd been his inept assistants. An elf had defeated all three of them out on the cold Atlantic. Instead of killing them, she'd left their small speedboat moored at a marina—with her enemies still in it. The elf was more powerful than Jackson could have imagined; his defeat was shattering. All three men were stupefied with existential dread. Jackson quickly recovered and escaped before the police arrived. He abandoned his hirelings. They'd been paid, hadn't they? Besides, they knew nothing that would hurt him, not even his real name. To the Order, Materialist mercenaries were as disposable as paper napkins.

"Delighted to hear they're doing so well," Jackson said. "I hate to say more even on a secure phone line. OpSec, you know."

20

Crossed Streams

Don't cross the streams.
Ghostbusters

Jackson dropped me off at my house late. I was pleasantly tired from our time together, but still too wired to sleep. Our late nights were probably hurting my job performance, but I would have had to acquire a methamphetamine habit to become as bad an employee as some of my coworkers. Does that sound unkind? Oh, well.

As usual, Beth had left her stuff all over the place, so I busied myself picking up after her. Leda had been sort of a housemother to me and Beth; the job was mine now. Bobby always picked up after himself, a good habit acquired during the military service he never talked about. He made his own bed, hospital corners and all, and kept the bathroom clean. He never presumed to pick up after Beth, even though they were sleeping together. That task devolved to me as housemother *pro tem*. It didn't piss me off anymore; that's just who Beth was. Beth's mother had spoiled her only daughter.

I turned on the living room light and saw that Beth had left a heavy scarf on the couch. I picked it up and turned to put it back in the mud room.

Leda just *appeared* across the room from me.

It was a shock. I'd read about elves doing that stuff. Jerry and Leda took pains to keep from scaring or startling me. But nobody who's watched as much TV and seen as many movies as I have believes anything she sees. I blinked three times. Leda was still there. Huh.

"Sorry, sweetie," Leda said. "I didn't mean to alarm you." No smile.

I hugged her. God, she *smelled* good, like a warm breeze carrying the essence of open country. It wasn't perfume, it was *her*. "What's wrong?" I said.

"I think you may be in trouble." Still no smile.

"You're kidding, right?" *Now* I was scared.

"I wish. What do you know about your, um, boyfriend?"

Boyfriend? "*Jackson?*" I shrugged. What *did* I know? He was becoming a *very* good lover, and he seemed to be into me. In every possible way. "He's in business, seems to make a lot of money, but he never talks about it. I kinda respect that."

Leda shook her head. "Janjan, he's one of the bad guys. He's a Materialist Magician."

I thought, *Oh, Jesus* and ventured a joke, "Well, I've *always* liked the bad boys."

I always used to be able to make Leda laugh. Not tonight. "*Bad* boys are one thing. *Evil* boys are something else."

I sat down on the couch before my legs quit. "Evil? *Really?* And I thought Beth was the drama queen around here."

Leda watched me calmly out of her new inner silence. She was waiting for me to stop fooling around and accept the truth. Elves make a point of not lying.

I said, "You're *not* kidding, are you?"

"Your Mr. Jackson bears a striking resemblance to the magician who attacked Jerry in Washington. The guy who attacked Jerry *and* me while we were trying to get to the Invisible Mountain. It's no coincidence that he sought *you* out."

"How do you know that?" I said.

Leda pointed to her head. "I was standing in the dark next to your neighbor's house waiting for you to come home. I got a good look at Jackson. Jerry's in the next world over, but he shares my thoughts. If we put our minds to it, we can look through my eyes together to see if our perceptions match. It's the *oddest* thing." She grinned and shook her head. "Hey, my whole *life* is pretty odd now that I think about it. Anyway, Jerry and I agree that Jackson's gotten a conservative haircut, a close shave, and some new clothes. He's stopped wearing mascara, but he's still basically the same person."

I felt sick all of a sudden. "*'Basically'*?"

Leda looked at me, considering what to say. "This stuff is hard to talk about in English, Janjan. And I'm reluctant to speak much Elvish here in Portsmouth. It's like sending up a flare that tells the bad guys I'm here with you."

I swallowed. I was sweating a little, probably not much for a fat girl, and given the evening I'd had, I was not feeling my freshest. "Tell me what you can in English, then. I promise not to give you any more grief."

Leda saw she had my full attention. "Jerry says that back in Washington most of what he saw reflected in Jackson was the power of the Old Gods. I saw the same thing in Jackson out on the ocean when he used magic against the elves who came to help us. That was even before we learned to see things as the elves do." She paused. "Janjan, the man still has the stink of black magic around him, but the god and goddess took all their power away with them when they left the Earth. No, there's a *new* light in Jackson now. It's an energy ... *frequency* we've never seen before."

I'd made a rough draft of Leda's and Jerry's whole story by now. Very rough. It needed editing before it got posted to the Elf Friends' website. Leda was telling me that the guy she and Jerry had called "the hipster magician" had taken off his eye makeup and changed his name. Or, hell, maybe Jackson *was* his real name. My friend was telling me that she now saw things clearly that she used to ignore because they didn't fit her worldview. She was also telling me, the way women do, that she knew *I* knew something about this and that it was up to me to tell her what I knew.

Fine, whatever. I give up, I thought. I was tired of carrying the burden of increasingly-guilty knowledge. My friends weren't going to *hurt* poor Bobby, whatever he might have done in the past—or whatever he might be doing now. And they weren't going to hurt me, either, were they?

"What do you know about the Fae?" I said.

21

Great Bog Bobby Meets Jerry the Elf

Things got weirder. This time it was my fault.

I told Leda how I'd met the Fae out in Great Bog the night I talked Bobby out of freezing to death. I told her about the disappearing homeless people. I told her my suspicions about what Bobby and Jackson might be up to. I said I had no idea *why* they would be doing whatever they were doing. As I talked, Leda nodded, asked a few questions, and took it all in like it was new information. She didn't know what I should do, either. She offered no advice. She also didn't reproach me or say anything to put me on the defensive.

We got to the end of the conversation. What two women would normally do is have the same discussion all over again in slightly different words—maybe two or three times. Not knowing what to do about all this, I would have found the repetition comforting. Leda was still a woman (was she *ever*—woof), but she handled people and information differently since she'd moved to the next world over. She said, "Bye, sweetie." Then she hugged me and kissed me, right cheek, left cheek, and forehead—and just disappeared the way she'd arrived.

✻

The day after I told Leda about the Fae, Jerry dropped by to meet Bobby. Jerry rang the bell and walked in the door like a normal person.

When Bobby came home from work to shower and change before going out again, I popped out of the living room, dragged Bobby in, and introduced the two guys.

Bobby looked guilelessly into Jerry's eyes, shook his hand and said, "I'm pleased to meet you, Mr. August. Are you one of ... *those* Augusts?"

Jerry knew what Bobby meant. Even in Portsmouth where people avoid metaphysical speculation, *financial* speculation is always acceptable. There was a lot of gossip about what might have happened to the August fortune after the August Association quietly ceased operations down on Route One. Lawyers and court employees, state and federal, may *occasionally* let something slip. Yes, that's sarcasm. I knew the whole story because Jerry himself had told it to me.

"*'Jerry'* is fine, okay?" Jerry said. Bobby nodded agreement. "Yeah, Quincy August was my great-uncle, more or less. Turned out he didn't like me much, though. Kind of a long story. Janjan says you're from Connecticut originally?"

Emotions drifted across Bobby's face like clouds in front of the sun. "Yeah, *originally*." It was a loaded word the way he said it.

Jerry hated causing Bobby distress. Elves (both Jerry and Leda, anyway) mirror our feelings like they feel them along with us. That can't be easy, but they don't even try to protect themselves.

I was sitting at the desk. The two men were sitting on opposite ends of the couch. Jerry gestured at himself. "Bobby, do you know what I am?"

At this invitation, Bobby peered at Jerry closely. "There's something *different* about you. I don't know what it is."

"What you see on me is the mark of another world. Know what I'm saying?" Jerry was so gentle with Bobby, who had no defenses. Jerry was already my friend, but his kindness won my heart. I didn't blame Leda for loving him. I wondered what it felt like to love somebody who deserved your love. I wondered what it felt like to be loved by that person. Stupid thought. My eyes stung. Stupid emotion.

"Another world?" Bobby said. "Have *you* traveled with the Fae, too?"

Jerry shook his head. "I think maybe what you've done is travel from world to world *around* the Invisible Mountain. My wife and I have walked a little way *up* the Mountain."

Bobby's lips parted like he was saying *Oh* to himself. I watched him think this through. He wasn't stupid; these were hard things to think about.

Bobby's face got very sad. "All I *did* was go around the damn Mountain. That's all we *all* did. That's all the Fae *can* do—forever. For a while it's a lot of fun, but I just couldn't do it anymore. I thought the only way out of it was to come back to Earth and die."

I couldn't help butting in. "Were you *planning* to die the night we met?" We kept the old house cool to save on the heating bill, but I felt really cold all of a sudden. It had always been winter. It would always be winter. The forecast was for snow again tonight. Portsmouth was worse than freaking Buffalo this year.

Bobby nodded to me. "I gave up." A simple statement of fact.

The three of us sat quietly for a minute. Jerry seemed the most comfortable with that silence. Leda was like that, too. I'd always thought "inner peace" was a cliché or a joke or something.

Bobby looked at his feet in their thick insulated socks. Jerry watched Bobby with real interest. I watched them both.

Jerry finally broke the silence. "Bobby, how do you feel about what you're doing now?"

Bobby looked up. "You're not talking about my warehouse job, are you?" Jerry grinned at him; Bobby was no dummy. "I can't talk about…anything else, Jerry. I signed a non-disclosure agreement. What good is a man who breaks his word?"

I was curious about how Jerry would play this. He and Leda thought that Bobby had gone to work for Jackson, the local sales rep for Transworld Bad Guys, LLC. They didn't think it was mere *human* criminality, either. I almost expected an appeal to Do the Right Thing for the Greater Good of Mankind argument. But Jerry was no dummy, either.

Jerry just shook his head. "I'm not asking you to break a promise or to talk about the conditions of your, um, employment. I'd just like to know how you *feel* about it."

Jerry already knew how Bobby felt. He just wanted Bobby to acknowledge it.

"You think I'm doing wrong," Bobby said.

Jerry shook his head again. "Doesn't matter what *I* think. Given what you know first-hand about the Fae, it matters more what *you* think."

Bobby looked like a kid who was about to burst into tears. He was simply not equipped for a battle of wits. There was no duplicity in him, no strategy, no tactics, only a kind of innocent integrity. "I tell people they're gonna live *forever*," he said. "It's the damn *truth!*"

Jerry regarded Bobby with an open expression. "You know what I tell people?" he said.

"That … the Fae are bad?" Bobby said.

"No. I tell anybody who asks that there's a better way to live. That if they're willing, I'll take them where they can see for themselves."

"I don't get it," Bobby said. He got it, all right, he just didn't like it. I knew exactly how he felt because I felt the same way.

"I tell people there's a better place than Earth," Jerry continued. "You know what I'm saying?"

Bobby got to his feet. His face was closed as tight as he could close it. He knew he'd lost, but he refused to admit it.

"I've gotta get ready to go," he said. "Good meeting you, Jerry. See you later, Janjan."

22

Linkin Park Sings "What I've Done"

Jackson met Bobby a few blocks away from Janjan's house. Bobby climbed into the car, early for work as always. Work brought them together several times a week.

Bobby had a gift that Jackson knew was lacking in himself. Bobby brought his simplicity and decency from a simpler time to twenty-first century Portsmouth. People responded instinctively to him. He didn't *want* anything from them—except maybe to show them something different and interesting out in Great Bog.

Beth and Janjan introduced him to their circle of acquaintance. Those people introduced Bobby to others. Bobby's warehouse coworkers brought him home to eat with their families, took him ice fishing, introduced Bobby to friends and relatives. Everybody liked him.

Bobby was like Peter Pan. When Bobby said, Come with me to Neverland, meet Tinker Bell, and play with the Lost Boys, people found themselves saying Sure, Bobby, why not?

When they saw the Fae, people discovered that fairies were real. That they were beautiful. That they lived forever or close enough. That *you* could join them and be beautiful and live forever, too. Middle-aged Americans found this especially appealing.

The word spread quickly. You have to come see this, people said to their friends. There were Fae-viewing parties out in Great Bog. It snowed and snowed, but people tramped the snow down hard. Hell, they went out to the fields in blizzards. The more people saw, the more they were attracted to the Fae. Who would *not* want to be a traveler wrapped in light? Who would *not* want to sleep with beautiful fae-boys or fae-girls (or with both)? Who would *not* want to go adventuring with the Fae and see all there was to see on the long, long trail a-winding? Hundreds of people wanted to go. Hundreds became a thousand, then more.

Bobby had reservations about exposing others to the Fae, but Jackson pointed out that he, Bobby, wasn't forcing anyone to do anything they didn't want to do. Bobby would just act as a tour guide, wouldn't he?

This'll be our secret, Bobby would say to the young men and women he brought out there. Of course as Jackson intended, it didn't remain a secret.

Portsmouth's young people somehow got the impression that their introduction to the Fae was a one-time offer. That without Bobby as intermediary or guide, they'd have no further access to the fae-path and to those who traveled it. Jackson may have encouraged this misapprehension.

People had doubts, as who would not, but those doubts were easily overcome especially for those who'd been drinking or taking recreational drugs.

For his part, Jackson appeared to do little, to be only Bobby's rich friend, a quiet guy, said to be dating that cute little Janjan Javorski, the smart-mouthed redhead everybody knew. *Any friend of Bobby's...*people said.

But Jackson was actually working magic in the background. Most of his preparation to work with the god and goddess of the Other World was in the *magic of influence*. By the standards of the ancient Brotherhood, Jackson had only a minimal grasp of High Aghartic, the language the elves called *the Fallen Tongue*. The little he knew seemed to be enough.

High Aghartic worked dire magic by shaping the thoughts of those who spoke it, the thoughts of those who heard it, and even the thoughts of anyone nearby. The words embodied what the elves called the Original Mistake. High Aghartic implicated its speakers and hearers in that ancient calamity, insisting that their mere mistakes were unforgivable sins for which the High Enemy had damned them all forever. The magic of influence motivated Bobby's new acquaintances to seek refuge among the Fae, to flee the imaginary divine wrath they believed was pursuing them. In a few weeks, thousands of people walked out into the field with Jackson and Bobby—and disappeared from Earth.

As he whispered High Aghartic night after night, surrounded by fae-light in frozen Great Bog, Jackson learned that the Fallen Tongue worked by drawing the attention of those who think no other thoughts and speak no other words.

He, too, now had a distant watching shadow.

Woeful knowledge. Jackson knew enough not to stare at that high and hateful intelligence. It was at an almost-infinite remove now, but what it wanted was to come closer and closer until finally it possessed him.

23

Where's This Relationship Going?

There's nothing so weird that talking about it can't make it weirder.

Beth had been moody and silent all week. It wasn't a *Look at the Drama Queen* silence, it was a prickly *Leave Me the Hell Alone* silence, very unusual for her. Bobby was working more hours at the warehouse. They'd made him a full-time employee and given him benefits. He paid his share of groceries and rent out of his new bank account with a big smile. Bobby was also gone several nights a week on mysterious errands for Jackson. Was Beth's bad mood connected to Bobby's absences?

By mostly-unspoken agreement, Jackson and I got together on the nights he didn't have business elsewhere. And by "got together" I mean that we were having *all* the sex. I hadn't gone skiing in Great Bog since the night Coran the Fae introduced me to Bobby, but I hadn't regained any weight. Not for nothing is it called "getting busy."

One afternoon I came home from work to find Beth crying into Bobby's open mouth, kissing him like she was about to ravish him. He had tears on his face, too, and was passionately kissing her back like he'd be thrilled to be ravished. They stood locked in each other's arms in the middle of the kitchen. *Like lovers do.* A thunderbolt of envy shot down my left shoulder and burned its painful way out my right foot. Beth's not the only dramatic woman in the house. I just keep all my drama inside.

Even if this dramatic reconciliation was happening in my house, I'd walked in on something that was none of my business. I said, "Oh, sorry," hurried through the kitchen, went to my room, and closed the door.

They hardly registered my presence. I heard muffled voices, but made an effort not to overhear the words. *La la la la, not listening.* The door to the mud room opened, and I heard Beth raise her voice to say "Bobby, wait!" Doors closed, and I was alone in the house.

I wondered what *that* was all about. Were they fighting about marriage or about Bobby's after-hours job? I thought I knew how to begin finding out.

I had Jackson on speed-dial. He picked right up.

"You should come over," I said. "We've got my house to ourselves, hint hint."

A pause. Jackson always thought before he spoke, and I mean *always.* It was either annoying or endearing, depending on how I was feeling that day. "'kay," he finally said. "Be right there." I managed not to be annoyed.

It didn't take him long. Portsmouth doesn't have much traffic even with the streets narrowed by ten-foot snowbanks. My house wasn't far from downtown, assuming downtown was where Jackson had been. If I asked where he was coming from, he might tell me, or he might change the subject. Most of his life outside the bedroom was a conversational no-fly zone. I didn't even know his full name. His business card said "M. Jackson." He said, "Just call me Jackson," and refused to tell me what the "M" stood for.

Jackson rang the bell like always. He was a funny guy that way. One way or another he'd visited every possible Janjan tourist destination, if you follow me, but he never presumed it was okay to walk into my house without knocking. He was passionate, affectionate, attentive, and emotionally *hungry* in a way that touched my heart, if I read him right. He was also oddly formal, like he'd parachuted in from a nineteenth-century novel. That formality was probably the only way Jackson resembled Jerry August, a guy I once thought had a stick up his ass. Beth was right; men *are* a mystery.

Jackson did unbend enough to take off his thick-soled winter boots, a grudging concession to the painful cold, and hang up his black cashmere topcoat. He was wearing a gray pinstriped suit. His subdued necktie probably cost more than the dress I was wearing for his viewing pleasure. Woof. I wanted him to continue undressing for *my* viewing pleasure, but...

"Come into my parlor," I said.

He followed me into the living room.

"No kiss?" he said. "This doesn't look good at all."

I turned back, threw my arms around him and gave him an open-mouthed kiss. He kissed me back the same way. Thanks to my patient teaching he'd become an excellent kisser. He held me tight as we kissed. His strong hands felt their way under my dress to my big, round ass, which he was kind enough to squeeze. I felt *that* all the way from back to front.

We were both getting excited. Before I lost my composure altogether, I stepped back.

"Something's up," I said. "And I don't just mean your penis, fond as I am of that portion of your anatomy."

"It's fond of you, too," he said. "Would you like to see?" Keeping a straight face, he pretended he was about to unbuckle his belt. Such a tease.

I was sorely tempted, but ... Bobby and Beth. Not to mention all the new information Leda had unloaded on me.

"How about if I just sit in this chair for the moment and you go sit on the couch while we talk?" He looked disappointed, but did as I asked. "Look, Jackson, you're a wonderful lover. Before I get completely addicted to you and you break my heart, there are a couple of things I really need to know."

He grinned and tried to make a joke of it. "Is this the where's-our-relationship-going talk?" Such a handsome man. Sometimes you wish you didn't know what you know.

I nodded, but I didn't feel much like smiling. "Yeah, it kind of is. I'm gonna put all my cards on the table. I hope you will, too."

He wasn't smiling anymore. His handsome face fell a bit. Or maybe he put up a wall between us. *"Okay...?"* He wasn't agreeing to anything.

"I have some friends," I said. "They say they know who *you* are ... because a while back you tried to *hurt* them, Jackson."

He sat very still on the couch. All the motion happened in his face. "Aw, *shit*," he said.

❋

We went back and forth for a while, but his heart wasn't in the conversation. His mind wasn't even in the room with me anymore; his thoughts had left the building. A woman knows these things.

He tried to deflect my questions. He tried to change the subject. I wasn't having any of it. So I wasn't surprised when he checked the time on his phone and said, "Look, I've gotta go. We'll talk some more later, okay?"

"Okay...?" I said, sounding as forlorn as I felt. Alone on a wide wide sea, like the Ancient Mariner. Dammit, had I just permanently screwed everything up with him? I let my eyes get wet and sniffled loudly, hoping he'd rush to comfort me.

He didn't take the bait. I considered lying naked with my face on the rug and my considerable ass in the air, but what if I did that and he left anyway? No woman wants to risk having her ladygarden rejected.

Huh. That must be how men feel about their inconstant penises. Anyway.

Jackson rebooted and recoated himself and walked out the door. I watched out the side window as he went out to his car. Dude was in a hurry all of a sudden.

Things were in motion. Well, except for me. I just stood there like a loser, looking at him forlornly. Yeah, my face was wet. So what?

Jackson started to get into his car when he saw one of the old neighbor ladies on her hands and knees on the icy sidewalk. Seriously, what the hell is it with old people that they have to wander out in the winter and fucking injure themselves?

He didn't see me looking out the budget combination window our thrifty Portsmouth landlord had installed. I figured he'd just leave my neighbor on the sidewalk and *I'd* have to go out to help her.

I don't read lips, but I was pretty sure Jackson said *fuck* under his breath. He slammed the BMW's door and stalked over to the lady. They talked briefly.

Then *very* gently, very *carefully* and without yanking on her arm or manhandling her, Jackson slowly and painstakingly helped the lady get her feet under her. He didn't stop with that. He had her lean on him so she wouldn't fall again. Patiently, he escorted her across the icy sidewalk at her hobbling pace, up her icy driveway, and made sure she unlocked her door so she could get into her house, safe and sound.

She got up on tiptoe and kissed him on the cheek. I think he blushed.

That was just about the sweetest thing I'd ever seen. I don't mind admitting that my minimalist underwear was soaking. I felt like throwing off my dress, running to the door, and showing Jackson my naked self. Some impulses a lady simply must resist. Me, too.

Having seen the poor old lady safely back into her house, Jackson got into his car and sped off.

Bad boy? Maybe he'd fallen in with bad companions. Maybe he was leading Bobby astray.

But *evil* boy? I had my doubts.

24

Bryan Ferry Sings "Slave to Love"

I would take the world
And break it into pieces in my hands
To see you smile watching it crumble away.

W.B. Yeats, *The Land of Heart's Desire*

Jackson was addicted to Janjan. He hadn't expected that and he wasn't happy about it. He didn't understand it. For one thing, she wasn't the skinny-actress type he thought an alpha male like him *ought* to aspire to. Sleeping with her conferred no status points. Not only was Janjan not tall and blonde, she didn't feel bad that she wasn't. She had no fear of carbs.

Beth, her housemate, *was* tall and blonde, but to Jackson Beth hardly existed. Pretty, but bland. Beth had yet to figure out who she was. Janjan knew exactly who she was. She thought of herself as fat, but that was just ridiculous white-girl body prejudice. Janjan was *thick* in the best sense of the word. Jackson had seen guys shake their heads appreciatively and say,

"*Damn*, she thick!" Meaning: juicy, healthy, substantial, full of life.

What could possibly be wrong with her hourglass shape, big ass, and strong thighs? What could be wrong with a woman who loved sex, loved everything she did to and with Jackson, and loved everything he did to and with her? *Nothing*, that's what. She rocked his world more than the black magic he knew.

Janjan was sensual, through and through. His social instincts told him he should be ashamed of wanting her, but his time with the MMs had eroded his old conventional thinking. In this case that worked to the Order's detriment.

Hot *and* smart. He should have known she'd eventually figure out what he was doing in Portsmouth. It had been easier to postpone thinking about that possibility.

And now she seemed to *know* that Jackson was part of the Order. That was bad. The "friends" who'd talked to her had to be the fucking elves, like he'd thought when he first saw her. That was worse.

Jerry August and Leda Clayton. He wished he'd killed them last year before they escaped Earth and joined the elves.

Jackson was now supposed to kill Janjan. The Order had rules for dealing with Elf Friends: suborn, recruit, or kill them. OpSec. He didn't *need* her anymore now that he'd recruited Bobby. He knew how to stop Janjan's heart without leaving a mark on her.

He also knew he wasn't going to do it.

Janjan could have had no idea of the effect she had on him. Jackson could find no way to tell her—except to give her orgasm after orgasm, which she certainly seemed to love.

Jackson himself had had any number of orgasms, but since the Fae breathed his last shining breath into Jackson's face, all Jackson's orgasms had been the interior kind, wave after wave of them without release of semen and without loss of desire. It took a while to get used to, but he'd come to like it. So to speak. It felt wonderful, and he loved watching Janjan come to climax as often as she wanted. He stopped trying to control himself and came right along with her.

Janjan was nothing like any of the women whose bodies he'd rented in the past. They'd been pretty enough, by the standards of commercial sex work, but they hadn't wanted Jackson. Why would they?

Janjan *wanted* Jackson. She was completely open about her desire for him. She practically started coming the minute he put his hands on her. He could make her come by kissing her neck and her breasts. Not that he'd ever stopped there.

To the extent his heart was available to be won, she had won it. He wanted more of her.

25

Where the Hell *Is* Everybody?

Finally I couldn't even escape the weirdness at work.

Beth and Bobby came home together and spent the night in Beth's room. They were loudly passionate all night long, like they couldn't get enough of each other. I found their noisy lack of inhibition arousing, which then became annoying. I had to, um, take my own situation in hand before I could fall asleep. *They* might be planning to call in horny the next day, but *I* had to go to work in the morning. Harrumph.

The main reason I didn't want to leave Portsmouth was my job at the Portsmouth Naval Shipyard in Kittery, Maine. In warmer weather I could walk to work across the bridge over the Piscataqua River. I'm no economist, but it looked like something must have happened that destroyed American job security and retirement benefits. Not to mention the forty-hour workweek. But the federal government was still a good employer. Naturally, the rich assholes in Congress were doing their best to contract out the civil service workforce (at increased cost), all while waving a banner that said *What right do you have to exist? Be grateful for your job, worthless federal parasite.*

Hey, I *was* grateful. All the political stuff was safely in the background when I was at work. I arrived at the office on time every day and did whatever the boss asked me to do. It was mostly clerical work, but show me a private company that can get along without that. The government certainly couldn't. Spreadsheets and databases need updating. Status reports need formatting and printing. PCs, printers, and copiers need careful handling, troubleshooting, and service calls. PowerPoint briefings needed to be produced and enhanced. Meetings need to be scheduled and rescheduled and rescheduled again. Office supplies need to be ordered and tracked. Everybody's workday has to be accounted for down to the quarter hour. And don't get me started about budgets. I'd gotten good at all that stuff.

The people I worked with, mostly older married women wearing ginormous engagement and wedding rings and good clothes, were competent, most of them, but their first priority was capital-F *Family*. In practice that meant I had to feign interest in their children or their grandchildren. I'm only exaggerating a little. It's great to have more in your life than your job, but shouldn't your job come first while you're at work? Sorry to get all judgy. I'd also found that Franco-American and Irish-American Catholics looked down on me as a Polish-American Catholic. I can't imagine why, either. Spare me the Polish jokes. Unless you're Polish, I can tell 'em, but you can't. So I felt entitled to judge my judges in return.

Although I was the new kid in the office, I developed more skills than the women I worked with. I'm no genius, but I had more education than most of them and I cared more than they did.

They thought less of me because I was single—like being unmarried was a bad thing. Not wanting to get a reputation as the office sloot, I let it be known that I "had a boyfriend." I never talked about him or said that we'd broken up last year, back when Leda still lived in my house. I never mentioned that there was a mysterious new man in my life. I was happy to add my love life, such as it was, to the list of things people around Portsmouth refuse to discuss.

Men, of course, floated through my busy office, most of them on business, most of them married. Some of the married men flirted with me (fine) or asked me out (gross). I wouldn't consider dating a married guy who worked at the Shipyard. I'd heard merciless gossip about those who strayed. I'd heard about messy divorces, ugly custody battles, and sidelined careers. There were hundreds of buildings spread out over scores of acres of real estate surrounding the dry docks where the Navy overhauled nuclear submarines. There were plenty of national defense secrets on the Shipyard, but there were no human secrets. It was exactly like a small town. I took refuge in my vague relationship status and in the Navy's insistence on protecting people from sexual harassment. Nobody bothers me without my invitation.

I was friendly enough in the office, but I made no close friends there. I avoided everybody's interpersonal drama. It was good just to do my damn job and go home at night. I knew I could probably have a brilliant career if I was willing to move to Washington. I hesitated to apply for a more demanding job. It isn't just men who are commitment-shy.

Today I walked in the door with ten whole minutes to spare, turned on my computer, got a cup of coffee, and set about organizing the things that had to be done *right now*. As the new girl, my desk was on the outer edge of a rat maze of beige modular furniture, the Navy's idea of remodeling a building from the 1960s. Talk about the new wine in old bottles.

I was surprised when Estelle, our fast-track supervisor from somewhere down South (still with a trace of Tidewater accent), sat down in my guest chair.

"Jan," she said without preamble, "where the hell *is* everybody?"

I really don't like being called *Jan*. I'd even rather be called *Jadwiga*. It's been *Janjan*, thank you very much, ever since I was too little to pronounce my own name. Estelle surely knew that. I considered several responses, but finally chose a polite one. "I'm sorry, Stell, I don't know. Did people call in sick?" It had been a tough winter, and some of my colleagues had an irrational fear of flu shots. Anti-vaccination nuts are crazier than anti-abortion nuts.

I was wearing a thick blue sweater over a gray turtleneck and lined black jeans in deference to the cold. The steam heat in our old building was unreliable. Business casual is the ideal winter dress code for employees who don't make big money. Estelle was dressed for success in a nice light gray business suit with a skirt. She looked cold. She'd be attending the afternoon division head meeting. To put on a good show for her peers and for the big boss, she needed reports and suchlike from me and from several of my colleagues. Hence her concern.

Then I saw her face. The lady was *scared*.

"Come with me," she said and stood up.

We took a walking tour of the office. Nobody. Nobody. Nobody. *Nobody*. All the cubies were just as their occupants had left them yesterday.

It was kind of a shock. "Damn, Estelle, what's going on?"

She shook her head. "Nobody even called in, Jan. *Nobody!* I thought..." she paused, and finally continued, "I thought *you* might know?"

I held her gaze and just shook my head. Honestly, I had no idea. She was in a bind. How could she fire everybody all at once and still get anything done?

"Oh, that's right," she said, "I forgot. Even though you're from the Northeast, you're *from away* just as much as I am. With all my southern belle airs and graces."

This was the first trace of cynical humor I'd ever seen in Estelle. It took this crisis to bring it out. Her cynicism made me smile. Sorry, that's just who I am. And she was right that New Englanders can be cold and clannish and unwelcoming until you learn their ways. On the other hand, this was the first time she'd ever bothered to engage *me* in girl talk. People from the South carry around their own kind of cold all wrapped up in the pretensions of class.

"Ugh," she said, "this is more of that *Portsmouth* nonsense, isn't it? All the, er, *local history* nobody from around here will ever talk about?"

I thought about that for a moment. Hmm, missing people (the homeless), mysterious beings (the Fae), elves (my friends Leda and Jerry), and even a Materialist Magician (Jackson my *lover*, for God's sake). I didn't quite see how all these uncomfortable facts connected to each other and to my missing colleagues. Maybe I didn't want to see.

"I guess it is the old Portsmouth nonsense," I said. "I'm probably right in the middle of it. How much do you really want to know?"

It turned out that Estelle didn't want to know much at all. What she really needed, once she thought about it, were inputs from three of the women who hadn't shown up and hadn't called in. Fortunately I'd helped my idiot colleagues manage their files on our shared network, so I knew where they kept their data. We spent the morning scurrying around in a state of barely-restrained hysteria. If that's a sexist comment, it's one I get to make, me being a Vagino-American and so on.

The phones didn't ring all morning. Not once. Out of order? I picked up a handset and heard a dial tone. Huh. Most unusual.

By lunchtime, Estelle had everything she needed for her afternoon meeting. She stuffed her briefbag full of reports for the other meeting victims, um, *participants*. I thought she'd just bustle out of the office, but she turned to me with a big, relieved smile.

"I've never let my boss down once in the twenty years I've worked for the Navy. Well, except the time my appendix exploded and I almost died. You were there for me when I needed you, Jan. Whatever the hell is going on around here, I'll always remember how *you* helped me today. Always."

I grinned. "Yeah, yeah, that's what all the bosses say. You're a fickle lot."

"You'll see," she said. "Just lock the office up while you're out at lunch, okay? And if you happen to take more than a half hour, I'll never know." Off she went to eat some yogurt in a vacant conference room while she studied up to knock 'em dead at her meeting.

I made a quick phone call, hung the *Back By...* sign, locked the office, and walked over to the bowling alley snack bar to meet Mabel. We got grilled cheese sandwiches on whole wheat (for health!) and Diet Cokes (to fight fat!). Mabel was one of those big, busty, loud, dark-haired white girls who are always getting hit on. There was something very 1940s Bad Girl about her that attracted men. And what kind of name was *Mabel* for a modern woman? Even with the double chin you get from drinking too much, she still had had her pick of all the available straight guys. We often saw each other out clubbing. She'd seen me with Jackson. She thought he was hot.

We had lunch together at the Officers' Club restaurant once or twice a week, along with a number of other like-minded young ladies. We called ourselves The Sloots, one of those hilarious internet misspellings of "slut." Our table automatically became The Sloots' Table. You only sat with the Sloots by invitation, and straight men were rarely invited. Naturally we invited some sassy gay men, just to complete the stereotype. If possible, they were bigger sloots than the women. *They* knew what I was. *Gay*dar includes *bi*dar, I suppose. Lesbians avoided us; they tended to be monogamous and discreet. Government employment has that effect on most people. Merciless gossip, remember?

The Sloots' Table was a way of protecting ourselves from the stink-eye all the smug family-values bitches directed at us. People who think it's shameful for an unmarried woman to have an active sex life. People who always have to stop at an ATM because they're too cheap to carry enough cash to go out to lunch. Sorry, am I ranting?

I was glad it was just Mabel and me having lunch today. Come to think of it, there was almost no one in the bowling alley, a few people having lunch and nobody at all bowling. Weird.

"It was just me and Estelle in the office this morning," I said. "It was crazy. Nobody showed up. Apparently nobody even called in sick or whatever." I took a bite of my sandwich. Mmm, grilled cheese.

Mabel looked at me like I was stupid. "You don't know what happened? *What's happening*, I should say."

I stared back. "I guess I don't." I really had no idea what she meant.

I waited while Mabel took a bite of her sandwich. She had very full lips. Such a pretty girl. I wondered what she'd be like to make out with. Even though I thought she was too New-England-straight for that. She gave me her dirty-girl smile. "*That's* kind of funny," she said. "Your friends Jackson and Bobby are, like, the *hosts* of the party."

"A ... *party*?" I'd had a tough morning and I just wasn't tracking.

"Out in Great Bog," she said. "Two or three nights a week. They're not out there snowmobiling."

"Oh, shit," I said.

I saw how all the uncomfortable facts connected. *Beth!* I thought, *Bobby!*

26

Two Roads

When I got home that afternoon, there was no sign of Bobby or Beth. I wandered the empty house to be sure.

The sun set. When Beth didn't call or text (very unusual), I texted her. No response. I called. My call went right to voicemail. I left a plaintive message: *Beth, where are you? Please call me!*

The doorbell rang. It was Leda. I let her in.

"Beth hasn't come home. I don't know where she is," I said. "I'm so *worried*." I started crying because I was scared. And also because Leda had *rung the damn bell* of the house she used to share with me and Beth. *Everything had changed.* There was a barrier between us that hadn't been there until she and Jerry went and joined the elves. She wasn't our housemate anymore. She wasn't an ordinary human being anymore.

Leda just took me in her strong arms and hugged me. Whatever she saw of my thoughts and feelings, she said nothing. That scared me, too.

I finally stopped crying. "Beth's probably gone after Bobby," I said.

"They've been having a lot of drama lately. I have a bad feeling about this."
I'd told her before what I'd guessed about Bobby, the homeless people, and
the Fae. Now I told her about my missing office mates. I told her what
Mabel said about Jackson and Bobby hosting parties out in Great Bog.

Leda just heard me out, nodding occasionally to show she understood.
That scared me worse. She'd known everything I was telling her and kept
quiet about it. The barrier again.

When I ran out of words she said, "What are you going to do?"

✳

I forgot to bring my snowshoes, but it wasn't going to matter. I saw
that the path into Great Bog had been packed down hard as a groomed
snowmobile trail by all the people walking into the snowy fields.

The problem was finding a place to park. The park-and-ride lot was
full of cars. I saw no people. Both shoulders of the road were full of cars
parked bumper to bumper. Again, no people.

I ended up parking at the far end of one of the plowed access roads
through the Catholic cemetery. It was also mostly full of cars. As it
happened, I parked next to Beth's car, blocking her in. No sign of Beth, but
she wouldn't be leaving without me.

Leda said what I was thinking. "Looks like people are leaving their cars,
walking into the field, and not coming back."

"I guess *everyone's* going with the Fae," I said. I was scared all of a
sudden. "*A lot* of people drove here in those cars. What the hell should I
do, Leda?"

Leda stopped walking. I stopped with her at the living fence of bare
trees that marked the edge of the graveyard. Ahead of us a small
embankment led down to the north-south railroad tracks.

Despite the cold, Leda wore only a gray hooded sweatshirt, black jeans,
no hat and no gloves. I was all bundled up for winter adventures, ski
jacket, hat, long johns under ski pants, and wearing warm gloves. Leda

carried her own warmer weather wherever she went. She took hold of my arm. I felt the strength of her grip even through my coat.

"Here's the thing, sweetie," she said. "Long ago when the Earth was shiny-new, those you call *Fae* made one choice. Those you call *elves* made a different choice. Well, let me say it another way. My people chose for our own true home, the next world over. But the Fae simply took to the road around all the human worlds when they *decided not to decide*."

I shook my head. She was giving me a headache. "Um, *what*?"

"Janjan, what I'm telling you is that you can see the Fae and they can see you. If you choose, you can travel with them and share the false immortality they enjoy—or suffer. But *I've* already made my choice. That choice means I can't see the Fae when they're on the path they chose for themselves. They can't see me, either. *Two roads diverged in a yellow wood*, you know what I'm saying?"

I knew what she meant, even if I didn't understand it. I felt sick. "You're saying that if I go with you to the next world over, I won't be able to help Beth. Or Bobby. If they *do* go with the Fae, I mean." Of course I foolishly hoped they wouldn't involve me further in the old Portsmouth weirdness. Like I wasn't already up to my tits in it.

Leda looked at me in that direct, no-bullshit way she and Jerry had developed since they went elf. She nodded. "And if you just go traveling with the Fae all by yourself, you risk getting *stuck* over there forever with Beth and Bobby—because you all forget who you are and where you come from."

"What about Jackson?" I know, I know, stupid question. The angel who stands guard over my lips goes out for cocktails when I'm under pressure.

Leda's look was pure compassion. "Oh, Janjan. Do you *love* him?"

I shook my head No, but we both knew that was an evasion, so I said, "I guess I do kinda love him. As much as that's possible for me. As much as I've ever loved anybody." *Love*, just a word, what does it even mean?

"Does *he* know how you feel?" Her tone was dry as August beach sand. I mean, Materialist Magicians are sworn enemies of the elves. Leda probably wanted to kill Jackson and would do so if he gave her cause. Hadn't he tried to kill her?

"We haven't exactly discussed it. Been kind of busy. What with all the fucking and so on. Pretty sure I love his *diicckk*..." I broke out my vocal fry like a spoiled West Coast girl. I am *such* a bitch.

Leda made a face. "You can't shock *me*. A swan-god tried to get me pregnant, remember? We've been friends long enough for me to know what you're like. What kind of woman you are." She fell silent, thinking for a minute, or meditating, or praying, or communicating telepathically, or whatever people did in the next world over from Earth. Finally, she smiled. "*That's* the answer then."

She was seriously pissing me off. Had I missed part of the conversation? "*What's* the answer, Leda?"

Now she was smiling broadly. "*Love* is the answer. Duh. If you're willing, I can show you something that'll keep you safe if you have to travel with the Fae. *Slightly* safer, anyway. Maybe you can get Bobby off the road to nowhere, too, along with Beth and...*anybody else* that wants to join you. Are you willing?"

Anybody else. She wouldn't even say Jackson's name.

I felt as sulky as a little girl. Compared to Leda I *was* a kid. She'd spent years learning and growing up in the different timestream of her world without aging a day. During the time of Leda's transformation into beautiful adulthood I'd just been fucking around on Earth. As it were.

"I'm willing, I *guess*," I said without much conviction.

Taking me at my sullen word, Leda put her hand on my sternum, insofar as such a thing is possible given the configuration of my boobies. I felt her hot touch all the way from my attic to my basement. I don't mind admitting that I wanted to take her right then and there in the snowbank on the edge of the Catholic cemetery.

But she wasn't putting a sexual move on me. She was *showing* me something essential. In my mind I heard Leda's unmistakable voice:

Do you trust me in your thoughts?

And yes I said yes I do Yes.

27

If You Could Have Whatever You Wanted

I only seem dead.

Note carried by Hans Christian Andersen to keep anyone from burying him alive

Jackson dressed in layers for night operations in the cold. He was both surprised and not surprised at all when Master Simon appeared—*pop*—in his suite. Simon was also dressed for the New Hampshire winter, courtesy of the Order and Master Louis, assuming there was a difference.

Simon wrinkled his nose in a way he must have thought comical. "What is *that* I smell on you? Getting a bit of the old in-and-out, are you?"

Jackson showered regularly. Simon was picking up psychic traces of his disciple's affair. Jackson didn't bother to mention that Simon's own odor had reverted to its full Caucasus bloom. Pick your battles. He didn't mention Janjan, either. Simon would kill her without hesitation if he learned who her friends were and what she knew about Jackson.

Jackson inclined his head in formal greeting. "Good to see you, Master

Simon. The mission's going well. The final stage should happen tonight. Would you … like to come along and see?"

Simon clapped Jackson's shoulder. "Why *else* would I have left my cozy cave and my meditations? Let's see what you've done with this second chance the Order's given you." An unsubtle threat. MMs always had to establish exactly who was in charge. Jackson had begun to find his superiors tiresome.

Jackson turned toward the door. "My car's down in the garage," he said.

"Psh, *cars*." Simon took hold of Jackson's upper arm with a hand like a steel claw. "The Order has a *better* way, remember?" They left the hotel room wrapped in darkness.

Whenever Jackson traveled with Simon, transported instantly by the Fallen, he forgot everything about the trip—until the next time. Once again he found himself cheek by jowl with Simon's cheerfully malevolent thoughts and the burning thoughts of another mind that was far worse. A *non-human* mind. It was like being buried alive in a tiny coffin with Simon and a huge, writhing, sentient poisonous snake.

He wondered what he'd gain from climbing the Materialist Magician chain of command. He wanted power, which in practice meant power over others. The endless aching seconds of black-magical travel reminded Jackson that the demons kept all the real power for themselves.

There was also something intimately degrading about submitting to this agonizing contact with the Fallen. Jackson was glad he'd told Bobby to meet him in Great Bog. He didn't want Bobby to witness his humiliation, or worse, be drawn into the Claimant's embrace.

Jackson began to want something more than power to manipulate the people around him: *life*. Life, liberty, and the pursuit of happiness, things the Order sought to control, ration, or destroy. He hid the thought from Simon and from Simon's master.

The Fallen take a risk by revealing themselves to men. Once you know that evil is real and personal and that it *hates* you for what you are, you might logically assume that somewhere in the universe is something good which still loves you as you were created.

The minds of the nameless god and goddess and the light of the Fae had honed Jackson's intuition. In the flashing instant of transit from the hotel to Great Bog, he saw the form of the demon-shaped shadow within Simon's intention, all burning eyes and talons.

Jackson didn't dare forget what he'd seen this trip. Once he succeeded in diverting enough people to the Fae to generate a continuing riptide, Simon was going to kill his disciple. Jackson had seen too much before the Fallen could possess him fully and make him a Master.

The tool that had served its purpose would be broken before it could cut its maker. Operations Security.

28

Talking Heads Sing "Road to Nowhere"

Back out of all this now too much for us,
Back in a time made simple by the loss
Of detail, burned, dissolved, and broken off
Like graveyard marble sculpture in the weather,
There is a house that is no more a house
Upon a farm that is no more a farm
And in a town that is no more a town.

Robert Frost, "Directive"

This part's gonna hurt, Janjan. Leda's thought appeared right next to mine. I felt Leda's whole mind right next to mine. She never took her hand off my breastbone for a second. I wanted to ravish her right there on the snowbank, and she saw that in my thoughts. I felt her love. Leda loved me like a sister, one I actually liked. She looked me right in the eyes in the weak yellow glow from the street lights. And I thought of cold, of shadows, of finding the exit out of winter, out of Portsmouth, out of Earth. *Back out of all this now too much for us.*

Okay? I thought back.

Leda wasn't kidding around. *You'll need a reminder as you travel with the Fae. Something to remind you who you are, what you are, where you come from, what you want, who your friends are. Jerry and I can't go with you. We don't think we'll be able to speak to your mind with ours. So I'm giving you a riddle to solve and—I'm sorry—I have to paint this mandala into your flesh where no world-to-world transformation can touch it and no one can take it away from you. I'll shield you from any real harm, but the faint memory of this pain is part of what you'll need.*

Holding my gaze, Leda began to whisper in the language of the next world over. Close as she was, the words still danced just out of my hearing. *Magic* is what it was. The magic extracted the silver piercings from my nipples and clitoral hood (I think we've already stipulated that I am something of a sloot) and *etched* metal vapor into the skin over my breastbone and maybe into the bone itself. It went deep.

Leda wasn't kidding about it hurting, but it was no worse than getting the piercings done in the first place. (Asshole ex-boyfriend whose sex slave I was briefly happy to be; long, unhappy story.) Because Leda was in my mind and I was in hers, I felt-and-saw a complex design get hot-cold etched—*painted* as she said—into me. A three-dimensional puzzle for me to solve in case the *New York Times* Sunday crossword was unavailable amongst the Fae. Apparently. I didn't expect I'd have time to be bored.

So my nipples tingled and burned and stood up and the hood of my erected clitoris tingled and burned while my breastbone really fucking *ached*. The pain reached into my heart, which sped up. I would have panicked if it hadn't been Leda working this magic.

Then it was over. Leda kissed me right cheek, left cheek, and forehead. *Brave girl*, she thought.

I saw that the flare of my desire had its answering spark in her mind;

Jerry would get the benefit of it, but I wouldn't.

I tried to imagine being *spoken for*, as the elves say. I couldn't do it.

I have to go now, Janjan. Our enemies are nearby; I can't let them see me, Leda thought. She whispered aloud in Elvish. The sense of the words was exactly *"Go with God, my sister."* The words warmed me up from the inside. My friend loved me as much as I loved her. Maybe I did know what love was.

Leda vanished without much sound at all. I still felt her silent presence in my mind.

I waded down the snowy embankment and walked across the railroad tracks into the field under the power lines.

29

Out Standing in His Field

Early evening. It was below zero under the swaying power lines. It felt even colder. Simon didn't notice the wind. The old man's hate kept him warm, and things were going his way. Jackson was dressed for the weather, but fear froze him.

Decision time was approaching; once again Jackson wasn't ready. He didn't know what to do. He'd been given a glimpse of hell, but couldn't make himself believe in heaven.

The two Materialist Magicians stood in the north wind on the west side of the frozen bog and watched the phenomenon Jackson had set in motion.

In the center of the field stood Bobby, eyes rolled ecstatically up into his head. He held his arms out to the sides to embrace the cosmos. Again tonight innocent Bobby let Jackson help him become a *transformer* of pale green fae-light. A neat bit of magic. Jackson wasn't proud of it. *I am the way and here in Great Bog no one cometh to the Fae but by me*, he thought sourly.

Scores of people walked *through* Bobby and onto the fae-road.

Let's take a walk with the Fae, people thought. C'mon, everybody's doing it.

Men and women, young and old, bored fun-seekers, earnest spiritual seekers, youth-seekers, hedonists, criminals, and their victims shared a thought: *This is the way out. This is the way in.* They meant Bobby. They barely saw him as a person.

The word had gone out up and down the coast: OMG, you have to try this, it's so fun. You get so high, have all the food and drink and sex you want, no diseases, no consequences, no work, just play in *the land of heart's desire.*

Are you talking about Them? people asked, meaning the elves (everybody had heard *those* stories, too). Yeah, no, came the answer, this is the way out of all that good-and-evil bullshit. *This* party never ends.

People asked, You mean I won't get old and die? Stay on the path and you'll stay young forever, came the answer. But what about my children? Well, what about them? They can come, too, now or later.

Seeing all this, picking enraptured thoughts from the ether, Master Simon was pleased. "You've done well, young Jackson," he said. "Very well, indeed. Now how would you go about *standardizing* the process so that people will continue to be diverted to the Fae—and away from our enemies, day after day, night after night—without further input from you?"

Bobby's a sweet guy and has no harm in him, but the world's built on the bones of sweet guys, isn't it; we all die, and what's the point? Jackson thought. That cowardly rationalization made him hate himself.

What Jackson said was, "I was taught to transform a living man into another kind of living thing—to all appearances. My, er, *patient* out there will appear to be a tree. He'll even think of himself as a being whose roots grow down into the Earth. He'll believe his only function is to grow leaves of energy, to stand immobile while people climb his glowing branches to the fae-road. The uninitiated will believe their eyes and see only a tree where the, er, *instrument* stands. The authorities will of course leave that tree in place."

The authorities Jackson was talking about would be bought with the Walloon's money. Simon smiled a smile with many layers and no goodwill. "Make it so," he said.

Jackson nodded respectfully, walked off toward Bobby, into the crowd of seekers and party people.

Jesus Christ, Jackson thought, *am I really going to betray a guy who's done nothing but what I asked him to do? Yeah, yeah, I paid him fifty bucks an hour, but still. Janjan would never forgive me. And 'Make it so'? Really? Is that all power gets you—the power to quote* Star Trek *and fuck people up?*

In his peripheral inner vision Jackson saw that the shadow behind Simon now appeared closer to the old magician; he forced himself not to stare, to keep his eyes moving and pretend not to have seen. A kind of forced intimacy was headed toward Simon. Violence was in the air, an impending violation worse than prison gang rape.

Jackson also managed not to stare at his own shadow. During the time he'd been talking to Simon, the shadow had halved the distance between them.

30

The Land of Heart's Desire

...Until, the breath of this corporeal frame
And even the motion of our human blood
Almost suspended, we are laid asleep
In body, and become a living soul:
While with an eye made quiet by the power
Of harmony, and the deep power of joy,
We see into the life of things.

William Wordsworth,
"Lines Composed a Few Miles Above Tintern Abbey"

A bunch of weird things happened in rapid succession.

Bobby stood wrapped in what I recognized as fae-light; I first saw it the night we met. People passed him by, unheeding. They may have thought Bobby was part of the scenery or part of the phenomenon they were hurrying to become part of themselves. Think of a subway crowd, intent on catching their trains, walking around a befuddled stationary drunk.

Tonight the path the travelers walked was as plainly visible as the emergency-lighted aisle of a commercial jet. The fae-path bent down to touch upon Great Bog *right through Bobby*, continued for a few yards, then rose into the air above the Earth. With great amusement, the Fae thronged along their ancient road, and welcomed earthlings into their merry light-wrapped ranks.

As they stepped into the air and the Fae surrounded them, the Earth people's clothing changed in a swirling dance, became less twenty-first-century-American and more medieval-European. The faces of the newly-minted Fae also underwent a subtle change as their mundane cares turned into … something else again.

As Bobby stood there, Jackson approached him. He put one hand on Bobby's shoulder and began speaking insistently into his ear.

Before Bobby, deep in some altered state of mind, could register whatever it was Jackson had to say, here came Beth, slipping in her stupid slippery leather-sole boots across the snowy field from the main road. After parking her car, she'd gone the long way around so she could walk where the pavement was clear of snow. *That* was Beth being Beth. She ignored Jackson and threw her arms around Bobby. Jackson was unhappy or maybe angry; it was hard to tell in the wan light. Had Bobby told Beth *where* he was working with Jackson every night, had someone else told her, or had she finally guessed?

Beth's embrace woke Bobby from his trance. Slowly, slowly, he put his arms around her, as if she was the place his arms belonged.

Jackson looked like Beth had barged into his high-stakes business meeting to ask Bobby about new window treatments.

And me? I felt jealous. Jackson barely nodded to me as I joined the group.

Beth said, "Bobby, what *is* this? What are you *doing* here? Where are all these people *going*?"

"Beth, you really should leave right now," Jackson said. "That guy over there? He's kind of the *vice president* I report to about my Portsmouth project."

And in fact *that guy over there* began walking toward us. He was old, I could see that, and he looked unhappy. He looked dangerous, too. If you spend enough time with the elves, you start to see who's on your side and who's not. He had Bad Guy written all over him and more shifting shadows around him than anybody else did.

Jackson was *scared,* and not just for himself.

Not knowing enough to be properly frightened, Beth ignored Jackson. She shook Bobby gently. "Bobby? Hel-*lo*? Are you on drugs? I don't know what's going on here, or who those people in the air are, but we really need to talk."

"*Talk?*" Bobby said. It would have been funny, another poor man caught like a deer in an angry woman's headlights, except that Bobby was caught between despair and resignation.

Beth was not interested in listening tonight. "Bobby," she said, "I *missed my period.* I'm *never* late."

And I thought: After all that high drama and make-up sex back at the house, she's only telling him this *now?* Sometimes I don't have much respect for my fellow women.

Slowly, Bobby began to smile. News of his impending fatherhood made him *happy.*

That's when I got it. Bobby might have sounded sort of like one of our American contemporaries, but he was actually from somewhere else. Or *somewhen.* I thought about Leda and the different timestream she'd lived in.

"Oh, Beth," Bobby said, "it's a miracle. I thought I was shooting blanks. I thought I wasn't shooting *anything at all.*"

Jackson asked Beth, "You're pregnant?" Beth nodded vigorously.

Jackson finally sort of greeted me. "Janjan … what…?" His eyes flicked toward the angry man wrapped in shadows who would soon be joining us.

Jackson gave me a look with many levels. I didn't know what to make of it.

Jackson looked at Beth and Bobby. I saw his face change from unhappiness to … what? Determination?

With a nod of his head Jackson indicated the angry old guy. "That's Simon," he told me. "Pretty sure he's going to kill us all if we don't get out of here."

I'd made my decision when Leda put her mark on me. "I guess we should go, then," I said. "With the Fae, you think?"

"Where else?" Jackson said. "C'mon, Bobby. Beth, Janjan, give me a hand here."

The four of us, shining with the fae-light that shone through Bobby, and shone out of Jackson as well, stepped up onto the ancient fae-road.

I imagine we were lost from view as we stepped out of Great Bog.

As we stepped right off the surface of the Earth.

31

The Watchers in Great Bog

Jerry and Leda watched the field from a low hill in what had once been an orchard. They stood close enough to a scraggly, leafless tree to look like part of its trunk. They wrapped themselves in the winter-banked life of the place and remained still. Quiet senses took in coruscating rivers of light. The light that flowed through Bobby. The light that turned solid as scores of people, many of them young, walked into it, walked onto what must have been the fae-path, and walked out of Portsmouth.

Jerry and Leda couldn't see the Fae; the Fae couldn't see them. The elves also went unseen by the heedless human beings who thronged into the field and then, as far as the watchers could discern, joined a party that rose and disappeared.

Fairies? Leda thought, remembering the old stories.

I suppose the Fae are fairies in the same way we're elves, Jerry thought.

They didn't have time to argue about folklore. Upon their tranquil minds two shadow images were reflected, the opposite of the light of the world. They took care to avoid discovery by those other creatures out of legend, shadow-things imperceptible to ordinary human sight.

The dark beings watched over two men who stood to one side of the partygoers. The older man was bound more intimately to shadow than the younger.

The first meeting with evil is always a shock, Daniel Ryun once told Jerry. Ryun had tried to prepare Jerry to meet the evil presented by a young Materialist Magician named Jackson. That felt like another lifetime. Tonight Jerry was worried for Jackson, not for himself.

Jackson left the old magician's side, approached the motionless Bobby, and began speaking to him: some sort of dark magic. Bobby didn't respond or move; magic took the spark of his life and buried it deep within the light that held Bobby between the frozen Earth and the invisible Fae.

Beth and Janjan joined Jackson and Bobby.

This doesn't look good, Jerry thought.

The MMs used Jackson to invoke the Old Gods, Leda thought. *He was expendable.*

Yeah, and the older guy's got discarding Jackson on his mind, Jerry thought. *He's gathering darkness around himself, preparing to kill. I think Jackson was more interested in the power of the god and goddess than he was in serving the Fallen. What power does he expect to get from the Fae?*

I dunno, Jerry. What the hell is Jackson doing to Bobby? And one of the heavies is stalking Jackson, see it? She meant the shadow creature that watched from a distance.

The old magician walked stiffly toward the young magician, like something was pulling his strings. The young magician saw him coming. Beth threw her arms around Bobby. Bobby woke up enough to embrace her. Jackson and Janjan exchanged words.

Beth's pregnant, Jerry thought. *She's scared.*

Bobby loves her, Leda thought. *Beth's not sure how she feels about him.*

And look at Jackson, Jerry thought. *See how he's moving to protect Janjan? He can't admit it to himself, but I think he loves her.*

Leda thought, *How evil can he be, then?*

It was a good question, maybe the critical question.

What could Jerry and Leda do for their friends that they hadn't already done? Evil was at play in Great Bog, but the beings who lived in and for evil had been barred from Earth since the elves returned decades ago.

The Fallen were now limited to spooky action at a distance, which still corroded their victims' humanity. Jerry and Leda saw that the old magician's companion demon had poisoned his will. To their dismay, they saw that preternatural evil had also begun to eat at Jackson. Witnessing human defilement was just one of the things that made Earth painful for the elves.

Jerry and Leda watched the field empty of people. Those who'd come to travel with the Fae stepped up into what the elves saw as thin air—and were lost to view.

Oh, look! Leda thought.

Janjan, Beth, and Jackson broke Bobby's magical paralysis, got him moving, and helped him along. Flames of greenish energy burned up into the air through Bobby and vanished. Before the old Materialist Magician reached them, the four young people had disappeared into the energy.

The old man arrived where the four had been standing. He looked around in angry frustration. Then he, too, disappeared, not by stepping onto the fae-path, but by allowing his watching shadow to enfold him like a cape. The Fallen had deserted the field.

Curses, foiled again, Jerry thought.

Leda smiled in his mind and thought, *Whatever happens is up to Janjan now. Let's go home and talk to people.*

The couple left the field, traveling in an instant from terrible winter to perpetual spring.

32

The Queen of the Fae

> When I remember all
> The friends, so link'd together,
> I've seen around me fall,
> Like leaves in wintry weather;
> I feel like one
> Who treads alone
> Some banquet-hall deserted,
> Whose lights are fled,
> Whose garlands dead,
> And all but he departed!
> Thus, in the stilly night,
> Ere slumber's chain has bound me,
> Sad memory brings the light
> Of other days around me.
>
> Thomas Moore,
> "Oft, in the Stilly Night (Scotch Air)"

I walked into the weirdness of my own free will. The alternatives were worse.

I don't remember clearly what happened next. I felt like Dorothy getting swept up by a tornado in *The Wizard of Oz*. It was like being swirled along in a river of people, a stronger current than you'd feel in a rush-hour subway. Jackson, Beth, and Bobby got whirled off in separate directions, but I was sure they were safe. Well, as sure as I was of anything among these ... people.

It was so *strange. They* were so strange. Stranger than the inhabitants of Oz.

I ended up at the gates of a castle, a roadside palace made of stone, as it seemed to me, in the midst of the queen's retinue.

Her name might have been *Maeve.* I saw the man I'd met before, if man he was, the one called *Coran.* He and Maeve gave each other the side-eye. He smiled at me and galloped off on his gray mare. It seemed to me that Maeve and Coran were a couple, but that they were having a spat. Would Coran be sleeping elsewhere this undark night?

Inside the castle, the queen's handmaidens gracefully stripped away my heavy winter clothes and I stood naked before the queen herself. Maeve studied my naked body. Apparently appropriate clothing was a big deal to the Fae. She made a circling gesture to indicate that I should turn around so she could see my backside. Fine with me, I've never been body shy. So turn I did as Maeve and her attendants discussed my anatomy.

At Maeve's direction, one of the ladies of the court made me hold still while they all perused my lower back tattoo. Have I mentioned that I went through what we might call a slooty period starting in my late teens? I'd acquired a leafy design just above my buttocks in green and black ink. The men who'd been lucky enough to sleep with me had commented favorably on my aesthetic choice. As I may have pointed out, I rather enjoy being taken from behind; so my lovers would have had an opportunity to see my, um, leaves.

No one I'd slept with had ever called my tattoo a "tramp stamp" or a "splat tat" or even "a California license plate." Not in my hearing. Don't insult the lady's skin art if you want the punani. Jackson had stroked the sensitive skin there, gently, gently, with both his strong hands, but never said a thing about the tattoo. He *seemed* to like it, she said modestly.

Anyway. Assuming the tattoo indicated something aesthetically important about my character, Maeve and the others decided I was to be clothed in green and leafy garb with here and there a glimpse of my white white skin. Redheads they understood all about; there were many among the Fae. They didn't understand the little strip of burning bush above my otherwise-hairless ladygarden, but if I'm any judge of these things, Maeve was very much interested in it and also in the rest of me.

Think ill of me if you want, but, being examined like this made my nipples get hard. *Nubbly*, if you must know. The leaves of my labia entered the early stages of erotic sensation, or so I imagined. This continued all during the time the handmaidens were fetching me this and that bit of clothing. Maeve and I were doing some serious eye-fucking. As in *fasten your seat belts, it's going to be a bumpy night.*

But.

I felt another intense sensation, this one higher up, over my breastbone, under it or, hell, *inside* it. Whatever it was that Leda had etched into my poor mortal body was doing what Leda had designed it to do. Maeve and the other Fae girls could see nothing of it.

Huh.

Once I was clothed, Maeve broke her silence. "*I* know what you are, child," she said. "Does anyone from your world?"

Child, huh? Well, who knew how old the queen might be? Was this place like the next world over, where time flowed so differently for Leda and Jerry?

"What do you think I *am*?" I put some attitude into that to camouflage an onset of nerves. I don't like anyone knowing things about me I don't know.

Maeve looked at me with eyes gone huge with dark-dilated pupils, a spooky, unfocused look. "You swive with women like a man and with men like a woman," she said. "*You are the queen who is also a king.*"

Aw, man. Jadwiga, the fourteenth century monarch of Poland whose dorky name I bear, was called a "king" not a "queen" because she was the real ruler and not just a king's wife. I was impressed that Maeve either knew this, or had picked it out of my mind or out of the air. I wasn't at all sure that Polish history had much to do with my current predicament or with the fae condition.

"With all due respect," I said, "I work at Portsmouth Naval Shipyard. I'm not even a supervisor, let alone queen of anything. I won't lie, I do enjoy the company of both men and women, though."

Maeve's eyes returned to normal, blink blink. "I'd prefer that you not enjoy the company of *my* man," she said, "much as he might enjoy a night or two with you."

"Speaking of men," I said, trying to keep the anxiety out of my voice, "have you seen mine? We got separated somehow when we stepped onto the, um, path you walk."

"*Your* man, is he?" Her thick eyebrows went up. Very stagy and exaggerated. Maybe a little drag-queeny, which I find piquant. They were a sight to behold, those eyebrows. My girly-sense told me that Maeve would enjoy it very much if I licked them. Would in fact become putty in my chubby little hands. "And a handsome man he is," she went on. "Here on the fae-path, men tend to stray, my dear. Alas. You shall see the young fellow at dinner, I think. And after that, who knows? We all go our own way."

And off she went in a whirl of silks. *Very* drag-queeny.

I found myself wanting to see what was under Maeve's silks. After all, she'd seen what was under mine.

That curiosity made me wonder if Jackson and I were exclusive; I was starting to think we might be. I may be a bit of a sloot, but I do my best not to hurt my romantic partners.

33

Shall We Gather at the River? *(Nonlinear Time)*

Leda said, "Did *we* put our friends in danger?" She meant Beth and Janjan.

Jerry thought it over as they walked toward Nextworld Portsmouth. The two spoke and thought in Elvish, the Unfallen Tongue in which no misrepresentation is possible. Leda had learned to let him think things through. He was a good thinker, and it was easier to be patient with his silences now that she shared his thoughts.

Leda had asked a tough question. Rather than argue about responsibility and assign blame, elves aim to tell the truth and do the right thing.

Danger wasn't all bad, Jerry thought. Surviving danger had brought him and Leda closer. Danger had finally brought them to the elves. They'd only gone back to Earth Portsmouth because they saw the shadow of some kind of trouble over Janjan. They knew she was going to need their help.

To encourage others to seek them out, new elves left written histories with the Elf Friends on Earth. Janjan *wanted* to know why her friends had suddenly left town; she *agreed* to write their story, however unbelievable she thought it was. While the elves were telling Janjan everything that had happened to them, they found out what had cast its shadow over her. And here they were.

Jerry finally said, "Sometimes danger just finds people on its own. Cause and effect. Janjan stumbled onto the Fae by herself. She found Bobby; without her, he would have died. Bobby and Beth became lovers. Then Jackson found Bobby, maybe because of the fae energy in both of them. So Jackson met Janjan and was drawn to her. I don't know what happened then, but I can guess."

"Swiving," said Leda. She laughed. "Lots and lots of swiving."

Jerry laughed. "Yeah, that, too. Despite Jackson's unfortunate commitment to materialist magic, he and Janjan look like they might be spoken for."

"They do, don't they? God is great," Leda said. She was as happy for her friend as she was for herself.

"Yes, he is." Jerry spoke completely without irony.

Those who live in the next world over, close to the source of all good things, are wise enough to be grateful.

❋

Nextworld Portsmouth looked nothing like Earth Portsmouth. No tall white-steepled church. No snowbanks, ever. No brick buildings or sidewalks. No stores, paved streets, bicycles, cars, or buses. Instead, a constantly-changing collection of reed and straw huts amidst the grass and flowers, houses woven not from any need of shelter, but for the sheer contemplative human pleasure of making things. The tidal river looked much the same as Earth's, though glaciers had never scarred its banks.

An outside observer (had tourists or uncommitted visitors ever found themselves in the next world over) would have seen that the place centered about its people, not its buildings or its geography. The people who lived in the little settlement just called it *the village by the river*. Everybody knew Jerry and Leda were back; many of them walked out to welcome the new kids home.

Between visits to Earth, Jerry and Leda had spent years of time among the elves. They still had a lot to learn. Some of their new friends had lived in that unhurried timestream for so long that Jerry and Leda had to remind themselves not to bow to them. The compassion, strength, and wisdom they saw in the High Elves commanded respect, but not deference.

Beyond certain gradual changes to eyes and skin pigmentation, they couldn't tell much from looking at their brothers' and sisters' physical being. Elves found that their aging process stopped before middle age. Those who came to the next world over near the end of their earthly lives saw their age gradually reverse.

You only know you're talking to an elflady or an elflord by the impact of their presence, Jerry thought.

Yeah, that takes some getting used to, Leda thought back.

Eternity was real enough, but different from anything Jerry and Leda could have imagined. In walking onto the Invisible Mountain, they'd come home safe. But they couldn't just stay here. There was a mission they were uniquely suited to carry out. Some things only new elves can do, partly because it's easy for them to return to Earth. There's a time to every purpose under all the heavens.

The couple hugged everyone who came to greet them. By unspoken agreement, the group strolled down to a grass-covered incline on the bank of the great river to watch the tide come swirling in.

Those who are miscalled "elves" acquire mastery of many arts: healing, fighting, and that ability to work in harmony with natural law that on Earth is miscalled "magic." The foundation of those arts is the Unfallen Tongue, freely given to everyone in their world with no effort of learning;

it has only to be accepted. The original human language shapes accurate thinking and truthful words. Jerry and Leda's meeting with their fellows took place both in speech and in shared thoughts.

Along with words and the flash of thought, a bit of song would float out of the gathering, or perhaps a verse from long ago out of someone's perfect elf memory. Elves had the benefit of both human individuality and freely-shared consciousness. On Earth C.G. Jung had speculated about a human "collective unconscious;" he could hardly have imagined the expanded collective *conscious* mind that only became possible in the next world over.

Jerry and Leda told the others what they'd seen and heard, everything they knew, and what they only suspected. They all talked and thought about it together, expecting to be guided in the right direction.

There was considerable discussion of Bobby and the rediscovery of the Fae. No one present had any personal experience of those who'd stepped out of the human condition so long ago. The elves knew where legends came from, though. They understood how moving from one timestream to another looked like time travel to observers on Earth.

To the elves, finding the Fae was more surprising than stumbling onto the ten lost tribes of ancient Israel. The elves and the Fae had made choices that rendered them invisible to each other. The elves found the Fae more interesting than the Materialist Magicians, their purported enemies. No one was surprised that the MMs would try to use the Fae to keep people from seeking their own true home.

That the MMs would sacrifice the lives of others was also no surprise, given who the Magicians served and where their powers came from.

❋

Daniel and Aimee Ryun looked askance at Leda.

"You *marked* her?" said Daniel. He meant Janjan.

"We don't *do* that," Aimee said. She meant that the elves never force their teaching on anyone.

Leda looked at Jerry and thought, *Have I done the right thing?*

He nodded and thought, *What else could you have done?*

Jerry shrugged and told Daniel, "Janjan didn't come to us for training the way I came to you and Aimee."

"We had to meet her where she was," Leda said. "There was no time to begin teaching her about energy and intuition. Tell me how else I could have prepared her to go to the Fae—where we can't go—with some hope of coming back to Earth."

With joined minds, Jerry and Leda sent their friends and teachers a picture of the symbol Janjan freely consented to have etched into her body.

Daniel looked at Aimee. She looked back at her husband. They smiled.

"The human worlds keep changing," Daniel said. "Even this beautiful world changes. *We* change and the world changes around us."

"I'm surprised you didn't remember that," Aimee teased him. "Of all people."

Jean-Paul Herold had sat silently following the words and thoughts of others, but the elflord's presence rang like a great bronze bell in everyone's mind.

"What you have done is a new thing under the true sun," Jean-Paul said out of his deep silence.

"The last time that happened, it brought the World Mountain to Earth," said Jean-Paul's wife Donita. The elflady smiled at the memory of that day.

"We did what was needed to keep the way open between Earth and our home. And you swived with me naked before all our brothers and sisters," Jean-Paul reminded his wife with a grin.

"It seemed exactly the right thing to do at the time," Donita said. She held Jean-Paul's hand between her small, perfect breasts, covered only by a thin shirt. He felt her love for him in her heartbeat.

"Janjan freely accepted the *mandala* Leda gave her," Jerry pointed out.

"Yes, she did," Leda agreed. "Do *we* have to swive in front of everybody now?" She and Jerry were without body shame, but very private in their physical intimacy.

"What kind of person would *do* such a thing?" said Aimee. She kissed Daniel deeply, deeply and opened her mind so that all present felt their desire. The bliss they lived in.

"I love you so much," Daniel told his wife when he could speak. "God is great."

God is very great, agreed the others in a shared thought. The right direction had become clear to everyone.

34

The King of the Fae

Jackson and Coran came from noncompeting schools of weirdness.

Long ago, Jackson's big sister took him swimming in the warm waters of the Gulf of Mexico. A hurricane had passed by far offshore. The waves were bigger than usual. The kids didn't know enough to be afraid of them.

Melissa held his hand tightly like Mama told her to. It didn't make any difference. The waves had so much invisible power that Jackson was whirled one way and Melissa was carried off another, pulled away from her little brother by a churning rip current. No harm done. They doggy-paddled out of the riptide and body-surfed back to shore with the incoming waves, laughing about it. If Mama ever found out, she would've had Papa beat them. Neither of them ever said a word. It was Jackson's first secret and he savored it.

Boyhood seemed like another life. Now he was a grown-ass man who hadn't seen his sister for ten years. He'd been busy. He'd forgotten her number, or lost it four phones ago. You really didn't want the Order involved with your family. They leveraged your loved ones against you. Jackson lied to his recruiter that he was the only child of now-dead parents. The Order didn't bother to check, and by now that last part might well be true. The 'rents had written their son off, anyway, after a couple of police detectives came looking for him and he decided to skip town.

Jackson grabbed one of Bobby's arms. Janjan and Beth grabbed the other. The four of them stepped out (and up) onto the green-lit fae-path. Green light shone brightly out of Bobby and dimly out of Jackson. Bobby reeled like a drunk from the power flowing through him.

At that point, Jackson found himself whirled away from Janjan, Bobby, and Beth by another riptide of...something. He never knew who, how, or what. It's bigger than both of us, baby, he thought, as his dizzy mind tried to make sense of what his senses reported. He fought against the current at first, whatever it was, then just surrendered to the invisible waves that propelled him, like the Gulf storm waves had carried him and Melissa.

Wherever they were, whatever the hell had just happened, he was sure he and his friends were *safe* from Simon and the Order. Good enough for now.

Friends, though, is that what they were to him? Like when he spoke *the words* at the Caucasus cliff face in poor High Aghartic, Jackson had the piercing sense of having made a decision without considering the consequences. If I do *this*, then *that* follows: nothing will ever be the same again. Whatever Jackson's side was, Janjan, Beth, and Bobby were on it. Did the MMs want to kill Jackson? Well, fuck them and the demon horses they rode in on. Jackson had no friends in the Order. He refused to condemn Bobby to a mindless eternity as the Brotherhood's tree-bridge to fae-land.

His clothes changed around him (he was helped to change by laughing, half-seen others), from winter layers to, what, exactly? He ended up in some kind of *costume*. Medieval? Renaissance? Jackson didn't know the difference. He was even less clear about … this place. His perceptions had become unstable. But at least it was only pleasantly cool here, and not fucking *freezing*, wherever he was, whatever magical wave was pushing him along.

Being Simon's semi-willing apprentice had sensitized Jackson to mental states he'd previously ignored, inner TV channels he'd never watched. He adapted, looking ahead as usual, but also using his peripheral vision. Differences between the fae-path and Earth quickly became obvious.

Never *clear*, though. *Nothing was clear* among the Fae. Nobody was withholding information like the MMs did. Clarity didn't quite pertain here. A different set of laws were in play. Reality was more mutable.

Jackson's interview with Coran (he *thought* the man's name was Coran) was a case study in ambiguity. The Fae seemed to thrive on it, or maybe ambiguity came up out of the ground (if ground was what they were standing on). Hard to tell. Did it matter? The Fae had their ways, and you could either fall in with them or get off their path, your choice. The Fae simply didn't care what you did.

Well, almost.

Coran was travel-stained but dressed like a lord, it seemed to Jackson. They stood face to face in what Jackson's peripheral vision reported to be a stone-floored building. *A castle?* Sure, why not. *Moat? Drawbridge?* No. The Fae seemed to have no enemies: a function of their odd state of being. It was their castle and no one else's; the path they walked belonged to them alone. The castle doors stayed open wide, inviting everyone to enter.

Coran looked Jackson right in the eye for a while. Hoping to intimidate? Jackson, who'd stood face to face with elves, remained unfazed. But Coran was seeking information. He walked slowly around Jackson, *inspecting* him. Peripheral vision reported that Coran was looking Jackson up and down. Mostly, though, he looked *around* Jackson. Simon, or the fallen creature that shadowed the old man, would have looked *into* Jackson, looking for weaknesses in his mind, levers to push.

The Fae was examining the *energy* in him. Jackson had a touch of that gift himself these days.

"What have you done with Eamonn, then, *magician*?" Coran finally said. His words presaged nothing good. "You have his *light of other days* inside you, still."

Jackson's MM apprenticeship required that he master the half-truth and the outright deception, while husbanding the full truth for special occasions, like the *coup de grace*. Jackson decided he was tired of lies.

"We talked," Jackson said. "*I* didn't kill him; he was dying when I met him. Two old women held him prisoner in a cave; their magic weakened him. I didn't even know his name till you spoke it. Eamonn died and breathed his last breath into my face. I thought he was trying to kill me. I passed out."

Coran's affect softened. "Tsk, Eamonn and his ... *adventures*." He sounded amused, a thoughtful man talking aloud to himself.

"Why did he come to Earth?" Jackson said. "He said your folk live forever, or nearly so. I can't imagine why he'd leave *that* behind."

Coran laughed. "A girl, what else?" Seeing Jackson's confusion, he went on, "An Earth girl it was, who talked softhearted Eamonn into coming to her home with her so she could say farewell forever to her dear old ma and pa. He went with her to bring back a new tale to tell us around the fire. Now I think she was no mere girl, but one of *your* lot. I think perhaps she was a magician or beholden to them, as you yourself may be." Coran's voice rose in anger. "I think perhaps she delivered our brother Eamonn into the hands of those cursèd creatures who curse other creatures."

The hags! Jackson thought. "If the girl did that, the magicians have probably killed her. If that makes you feel any better." Coran gave him an appraising look, wondering why a magician would be so candid. "This *light of other days*, as you call it, seems to *offend* those who trained me in the rudiments of their magic. If I return to Earth, the magicians are likely to kill me for it." Jackson held his hands at his sides, palms out: *I'm at your mercy.*

"And speaking of your Earth," said Coran, "why have so many of your folk come to us these past weeks? We're no lack of room; we're pleased to welcome them. But they themselves give no clear account of why they've come to walk with us." He watched Jackson closely, expecting a lie.

'No clear account'? Coming from this guy, that's ironic, Jackson thought. "Of course, you know Bobby, who just came back to you along with my two other friends?"

"Ah, Bobby. I'm surprised to see him again—but happy! There's no harm in the man." Coran shook his head at the idea of harmlessness. It struck Jackson that Coran saw him as dangerous. And fair enough, Jackson *was* dangerous. They both were.

"I … *used* Bobby to bring Earth people to the Fae," Jackson said. His face felt hot, admitting he'd done a bad thing for selfish reasons, or perhaps a good thing for bad reasons. He looked Coran directly in the eye. "I did this as my master bade me."

"Your *master*, is it? Will he come here seeking you?"

"I don't think he *can* come here. His own master will not allow it."

Coran's eyebrows went up. He gestured: *Tell me more.*

"Those who come here are safe from the Fallen," Jackson said. "Surely you know this?" Jackson assumed what he said was true. All sign of his distant stalking shadow vanished the instant he stepped on the fae-path.

"Then your master's master is...?"

"In my mind's eye they look like shadows," said Jackson. "The Fallen ones who rule the Order of Materialist Magicians from afar are also called *demons.*"

Coran spit on the floor in disgust and stalked out of the room.

35

Dinner and Dancing in the Great Hall

Put on my shoes, old mother,
For I would like to dance now I have eaten.
The reeds are dancing by Coolaney lake,
And I would like to dance until the reeds
And the white waves have danced themselves asleep.

W.B. Yeats, *The Land of Heart's Desire*

You worry less about weirdness once you start trying to fit in with it.

Maeve was right. Jackson was waiting for me at the entrance of the great hall. We walked in, looking around the place like awestruck tourists in Grand Central. We sat together at a far corner table during the meal so we could get the lay of the land.

Jesus Christ, I thought, *is this really the first time we've eaten dinner together?* Jackson and I had shared appetizers and we'd raised a glass or two, but mostly we'd had each other. Which is to say that we'd had a lot of very good sex. We'd both wanted that, but thinking about all we *hadn't* done made me sad. Mom would not be happy to know the details. Not that I had much to say to her when she called me (weekly) or I called her (rarely). I hadn't exactly been living the life my mother wanted for me, a thought that didn't make me sad at all. I was *not* ready for serious courtship and marriage, even with Mr. Right, whoever he was, wherever he might be. Hell, at the moment I didn't think I was even living in the same world as my mother. At least she wouldn't be alarmed if she called and got only my voicemail. Janjan, the social butterfly.

Okay, so it wasn't exactly a traditional romance Jackson and I had gotten into. I had more pressing problems than figuring out if he was Mr. Right.

"Have you seen Beth and Bobby?" I said. I put my hand on his face. I loved touching him, spontaneous me. After my interview with the queen, I was horny, not to put too fine a point on it. He looked smokin' hot in his Renaissance Faire outfit.

Jackson stroked my arm. He looked me up and down. Or maybe he was looking through the green and leafy fae-wear Maeve had picked out for me. I got goosebumps, most of which were visible. "I haven't seen them," he said. "Let's ask around after dinner."

"I'm kind of freaking out," I said. "This place is pretty weird."

"No kidding," Jackson said. "Have you noticed that we're not talking like we would if we were breathing the air of Earth?"

I've represented my communication with Maeve and with Jackson as if it was ordinary human Earth speech: *I said, she said, he said*. That's how it seemed in hindsight. But in the moment, it was more like my first very odd meeting with Coran the night I saved Bobby from freezing to death. There was what I *seemed* to say and what Jackson *seemed* to say. The meaning distilled or crystallized in my mind. In our minds. We sort of spoke, but it was more like we each received what the other intended to say to us as soon as the intention to speak was fully formed and moved the muscles in our throats. When other people spoke, I felt something *pulling on me* as I received their meaning.

And this was a good thing, because *we weren't breathing*, not in the usual way. I used the muscles that lower the diaphragm and make it easier for air to enter the lungs. The muscles worked, but there was no way to get more oxygen than was already making its way into me of its own slow accord. Magic?

I started really and truly freaking out. My chest started hitching. I lurched to my feet.

Jackson just laughed and gently pulled me back down. Some of the Fae looked at me. They laughed at the dorky new kid making a fool of herself. My face turned hot pink with embarrassment. I sat.

"Would you *relax?*" he said (or seemed to say). "Breathing works a lot easier here if you just try not to think about it. Hey, it works all by itself."

"Great. Now I can't think about anything else." I could, though. I remembered seeing a House For Sale sign on my way to work; it listed a phone number to call but warned *Do Not Inquire Within*. I'd always thought that was hilarious, like it should be part of the Pledge of Allegiance and written on American money.

Do Not Inquire Within had always been *my* motto. Jerry and Leda gently teased me about how I managed to remain in denial all the while I was recording their improbable stories for them. Stories about how their inner and outer inquiries had led them to elfland. None of *that* had anything to do with *me*, goodness no.

"I met a Fae who was visiting Earth," said Jackson. "He told me the Fae breathe in for half of eternity and breathe out for the other half. I thought that was just … a fairy tale till I got here."

Coran had told me the same thing when I first met him out in Great Bog; I hadn't believed it. I was going to freak out again if I thought about the weirdness of our situation any longer.

Lucky me, there were plenty of distractions to be grateful for. The food was beautiful and beautifully presented. Platters of bread and roasted meats and vegetables, not a grilled cheese sandwich or potato chip in sight. We ate with our hands, which took a little getting used to. Ewers of wine to fill our cups. Finger bowls to clean our fingers before platters of fruit came around for dessert. Cloth napkins to dab our lips.

Going into the meal I felt a little dizzy. The wine enhanced my dizziness, but only slightly. Nausea never showed up. I didn't overeat or overdrink. Neither did Jackson.

My thoughts were all over the place, even more than usual. It was hard to focus on the taste of the food. Afterward I noticed that I *seemed to have eaten* in the same way that we *seemed to say* things when we tried to speak to each other. Hell, the way we *seemed to be breathing*.

We watched the people around us. We all looked like Fae. It was hard to tell who was who. We all wore the same sort of garb, either traditional or designed by the same couturier. But there was something in the manner of those who'd lived here awhile that struck me as devil-may-care and unselfconscious. There was something *extra* in the faces of those longtime Fae, something sharp and slippery that my eyes couldn't fasten on. Voices and laughter almost seemed to echo off the stone walls of the great hall, but that was just my mind confabulating: I picked up scores of trace conversations and filled in missing sounds from my own experience. People seemed happy, or at least glad of each other's company.

Old weapons, darkened by smoke from candles, lanterns, and cooking fires, hung on the walls. Had the Fae once been warlike? There were legends of magical folk erupting from mounds in the earth to aid one human tribe or another. The arms on the walls looked like they'd been there for years. Maybe the Fae had given up such Earthly incursions. I couldn't imagine that spears, broadswords, and longbows would be much use against modern weapons.

I looked around the great hall, but saw no one I recognized. Were our hosts keeping all the new arrivals from Earth separated from each other, or had we all simply been scattered randomly and caught up by different groups of Fae?

Coran and Maeve sat at the head table talking with their companions. They conducted themselves like decent royals everywhere, with dignity and consideration for their subjects. They expected to be obeyed, but not absolutely and not without discussion.

At the moment, judging by the occasional glance the king and queen threw in our direction, the discussion at the head table involved Jackson and me. There was some coolness between the royal couple. Would it be immodest of me to imagine I was the cause? I didn't mention my suspicions to Jackson.

Here's the thing. I might sit at the Sloots' Table during my unpaid thirty-minute Shipyard lunch hour. I might have an active sex life. I might enjoy myself greatly with both ladies and gentlemen who strike my fancy. I might not exactly know what it means to be in love, but during the time I'm sleeping with someone, that person and I are exclusive. I don't sleep with anybody else. *I'm not promiscuous.* Everybody has a line they can't cross without losing their self-respect, and that's mine. I don't do orgies. Okay, maybe an occasional threesome, but that's *it*.

Now I'll freely grant you that in the past I've sometimes been exclusive with someone for only one night. Beth, for example. The door had been open for us to move from brief fling into affair. Awkward though that might have been for our housemate status, I would gladly have taken things to the next level with her. Oh, the things I could have taught her... But she had kindly but firmly shut the door, so to speak. Probably just as well if we were going to stay friends.

Anyway. If Coran and Maeve both wanted me, nothing was going to happen with either of them as long as Jackson and I were together.

"I have a stupid thing to say to you," I said.

He gave me a puzzled look. "Go ahead."

"We're exclusive, right?"

"Yes, we are," he said. He didn't even pause to think about it. Encouraging.

"Not that we can update Facebook from here, but would you agree with me that we are *In a Relationship*?"

"I thought we were *dating*," Jackson said. "Was I wrong about that?"

Dating? I felt like crying, but this was no time for self-indulgence. Back when people had less sexual freedom, life must have been a lot simpler. Childhood, adolescence, formal courtship, marriage, children, old age, grandchildren, death. Jesus Christ, the same yesterday, today, and forever.

Hopeless and depressing, is what that whole program was. And don't get me started about *career*, which ought to be called *work till you die*.

"No, you were right," I said. "I've been making things more complicated in my own head. The way women do."

Jackson smiled. "It's not just women," he said. "Look, I'll admit at first I hit on you partly because you knew Bobby and I thought he could help me do what I came to Portsmouth for. I don't pretend to be a nice guy. I've done bad things and tried to do worse. If you are my girlfriend, I'm glad it's you who's my first."

"I'm your girlfriend, all right," I said. Yeah, I had tears on my face, so what? Tears wipe off. I felt very happy and also deeply sad all at the same time, like the music the Fae began to play. Dinner was over. It was time for dancing in the great hall. Life is a great mystery, but fuck it, let's have fun tonight.

Jackson and I stood at the wall and watched the dancers to get some sense of what they were doing. They moved rhythmically to the music, changed partners, made the rounds slowly, and eventually ended up in another part of the hall with the partners they started with.

I kind of wanted to join the dance, but I also kind of didn't. Whatever it was that Leda had etched into my breastbone had begun to ache. The pain was urgent, impelling me to some kind of action. I just couldn't figure out what I needed to do.

"So Bobby must have got Beth pregnant, huh?" I said.

Jackson watched the dancers, the fae-girls especially. The man had an eye for the ladies. Well, hell, so did I. I thought maybe Maeve would enjoy a dance with me, for her own reasons, and also to piss off Coran.

"You think maybe he didn't use condoms all the time?" he said.

"That'd be my bet," I said. "I mean, from what I understand, neither of you guys, um, ejaculates the regular way."

Jackson gave me the disgusted look men give women who kiss, or whatever, and tell. He had every right. Girls are chronic oversharers, or at least Beth and I are. Then he looked thoughtful again.

"Bobby has a lot of *light* shining out of him," Jackson said. "I guess because of all the years he spent living with the Fae. I've learned how to see it. Coran called it *the light of other days*, whatever that means. I've got some of that light in me. I'm starting to wonder if *the light of other days* can make a woman pregnant all by itself, no sperm required."

I was very glad we'd always used condoms back in Portsmouth. If you're going to sloot around, play safe, says I. I wondered if the morning-after pill would have helped Beth—if she'd even been willing to take it.

"It's just latex," I said. "It would work against any, um, leakage we didn't notice. But what good is latex against this magical light?"

Jackson looked sad and then made a joke of it to cheer himself up, like men do. "What am I, a metaphysician?"

Being a trainee magician, he sort of *was* one of those, but I was too polite to say so. A lady learns not to insult the gentleman she wants to penetrate her later in the evening. Men can be so *sensitive* about their career problems.

187

There came a pause in the dancing. Musicians took a break to drink wine and tune their instruments, plink plank plonk thump ding toot. The first group of dancers sat or stood around the walls while a second group formed up.

Coran took Maeve's hand and led her from the head table, across the floor. The royals were going to lead the next round of dancing. Maeve rested her hand atop Coran's. Her other hand gracefully held the hem of her dress off the stone floor.

And it struck me: *These people have been doing this dance every night since before human history was ever recorded and they haven't aged a day.*

I wanted to ravish both Coran and Maeve, but all beautiful appearances aside, they were really too old for me. And too *alien*, somehow. By which I mean too distant from anything like the human condition.

I had a sudden poignant vision of Beth and me, *both* married to firefighters, living next door to each other in in a working-class Providence neighborhood, surrounded by our packs of screaming kids, wondering where our youth had gone, laughing over coffee about what wild slooty girls we used to be. Now that such a life looked so far out of reach, I almost yearned for it. Almost.

But I'd taken another road altogether when I stepped onto the fae-path, hadn't I? This trip had crystallized around me when I flirted with Coran and talked Bobby out of dying in the bog—and when I started sleeping with Jackson.

Before the second round of dancers could form up around the royal couple, Coran changed course. Maeve looked at him sharply, then fell back into her public persona. The king and queen of the Fae came to Jackson and me where we stood watching the dance.

Coran bowed to me with dignity and great courtesy, a gesture of the body that told me a lot about him. Blushing again, I did an awkward curtsey that made Coran smile. He might also have been smiling at the tops of my boobs. Men are predictable.

Beside me, Jackson was bowing to Maeve. It seemed a far more practiced bow than I would have suspected him capable of. But Jackson wasn't exactly an ordinary American man, was he? Maeve in her turn did a brief curtsey that gave me a glimpse of how she saw herself and shared herself with her people, *noblesse oblige*.

I saw that Maeve would welcome Jackson into her bed this night. From her sly smile I saw that she'd welcome me as well.

Uh-oh, trouble brewing.

Coran grinned at me and held out his big hand. "Come and dance with me, Little One," he said.

I glanced at Jackson to see if he was okay with this. He nodded *Okay, go*. "I'd be happy to dance with you," I said. "Be patient with me, though. We don't dance like this where I come from." I took Coran's hand. "I don't mean to be rude, but what should I call you?"

"Call me Coran," he said. "It is after all my rightful name. We don't stand much on ceremony here."

Again Jackson surprised me. "I'd be honored if you would give me this dance, my queen," he said to Maeve. *My queen*, indeed. God, he was really laying it on thick, but the lady seemed to love it. *Such* a flirt, my hot-eyed dangerous Jackson. Fleetingly I wished I'd talked him into wearing mascara for me, but the time had never seemed quite right for it. Yes, I do have a kink or two.

"I will be happy to teach you," she said. "And you may call me *Maeve*, as do all our folk."

Thus invited, Jackson and I danced with the king and queen of the Fae and with such of the fae folk as joined us on the floor. Dancing's a lot like sex. You don't have to do everything perfectly if your rhythm is good. And really, mistakes become part of the fun. So we whirled and stepped and changed partners to the joyful half-melancholy music. Again and again we danced until the evening was gone.

36

Road Trip

Weirdness quickly becomes the new normal.

How long did that night of dancing in the castle go on? In the happy passing moment I couldn't tell. In hindsight it seemed as long as a Scandinavian winter night on Earth. There was a constant, pleasant blurring of perception not entirely caused by the wine. The old Janjan might have just gone with it and probably ended up lying down with Coran and Maeve—whether Jackson liked the idea of a foursome or not. Call me irresponsible.

The new Janjan had an invisible something etched over (into?) her heart by Leda—out of elvish magic and her love for me. In this world where no trouble and no unsought pain was ever meant to enter, the invisible design *hurt* me. The pain reminded me that I wasn't just here for my own gratification. It reminded me that I was in the middle of a *situation* and that I was the only one of us earthlings so recently arrived among the Fae who had the slightest idea what to *do* about it. Ugh, responsibility.

What the ache did was to nudge me in the direction of Jackson. We'd had that conversation about being exclusive, right? I couldn't very well go sleep with the Fae king and queen—and abandon my half-assed commitment the same night I made it.

From their flirtatious demeanor I could see that Coran and Maeve would have welcomed me, either together or separately. I would've loved to be the center of their erotic attention for the rest of that long, blissful night. Instead, I smiled at them fake-shyly and led Jackson off up a winding stone staircase where we found a vacant room. There we lay down on soft bedding and held each other tight in the midst of the mystery.

We lay together without having sex, something we'd never done before. We were tired; it had been a long, weird day. For a while I lay naked and still, holding Jackson, also naked. Stupidly, I tried to hear him breathing as he dropped quickly off to sleep. My eyes were heavy, but the pain in my heart reminded me of Leda. I reached my mind into the burning sensation, hoping to hear and feel Leda's mind in mine again.

Do not inquire within, my old motto; I set it aside. *Within* I heard no Leda and saw no Jerry, only swirling thoughts and images that wouldn't stay still long enough to be understood. These inconstant reveries were how I saw the world of the Fae: clearer in hindsight than in the moment.

One thought was loud and clear enough to startle me awake: *What about birth control?* I hadn't brought my pills with me; they only work if you take one every day. We had no condoms. There are other sexual options, of course, but still. I nuzzled Jackson. He smiled in his sleep, so I just kissed him and left him to it. No need for both of us to worry about contraception right now.

Finally the whelming weirdness I'd walked into pressed down upon me and took me into the dreamless unconsciousness of exhaustion. There were no bad dreams among the Fae, or so it seemed when I woke up.

✳

What woke us was a sense of clamor and stir in the castle. Jackson and I shared a puzzled look. It was so nice waking up together; why couldn't we just sleep in?

A young Fae man stuck his head in our door. "Up, up, sleepyheads," he said. "Time for all to get on the road. Past time! Hurry, hurry!" He was way too pleased about this.

At the moment, the urgent pressure in my chest was right in synch with the Fae. It felt imperative to throw on my stylish Fae dress and join our hosts wherever they were bound.

Jackson watched me cover up the goodies with that charming male disappointment, like a kid who has to put away his toys and go to school. He got himself dressed quickly. Jackson looked very good naked. Such a shame that we have to cover ourselves up when the weather is warm, I've always thought.

"I guess they only eat one meal a day here," he said. "I'm not even a little hungry. And besides not having to breathe the way we do on Earth, I notice that I don't have to pee, either."

I didn't notice that until he pointed it out. "Weird," I said. "I don't either. Weird, weird, *weird*." Not having to pee (or anything else) made me feel so peculiar that I made myself stop thinking about it. You learn to do that if you live in Portsmouth.

We joined a stream of others clattering down the stone stairs, out the wide-open castle doors. All of us spread ourselves along the Fae road. From the saddle of his white steed, Coran commanded his people with a sweep of his mighty arm: *Forward ho!*

Coran and Maeve led the urgent procession along on horseback. I wondered if they'd reconciled and spent the night together. *Forever* seems an unreasonably long time to stay married, if married is what they were.

The elf-charm in my chest said this was what I was supposed to be doing; wherever we were going was the right destination. I still couldn't help being scared. The Shipyard would probably fire me for abandoning my job, and that was the least of my problems. Jackson walked next to me, content to be in motion. He didn't look scared at all. I took his hand. He looked at me curiously, like he was unfamiliar with hand-holding. Whatever he saw in my face made him smile. He squeezed my hand and held onto it.

"It's okay," he said. "I don't know what's going to happen, but we'll figure it out."

I liked the sound of that *we* business. Exactly what I needed to hear. I hoped he was sincere and not just playing me. Time wounds all heels and karma's a vengeful bitch.

We all walked along and walked along with the wind at our backs. The path seemed to rise to meet us. The lightweight dancing shoes Maeve and the gals had given me were more than equal to the task. They felt better than wearing high heels just to show off my legs, tottering along an icy Portsmouth sidewalk like a penguin.

The Fae sang and joked and teased each other as we walked. Jackson and I listened and learned. I understood about half of what seemed to be said. Remember, most of the Fae were ancient by any human standard, and they'd been nomads a long, long time. Time enough to take English and make it all their own.

I *thought* it was English. If it was pure meaning I was picking up, that meaning still contained experiences the Fae had and I had not, things I knew nothing about. It made me dizzy to think about. *Do not inquire within.*

In the first hour of the journey, we walked past four other castles. Their occupants spilled out and folded themselves into our ranks by ones and twos or else joined the rear of the caravan in big groups. More singing and joking. The path was wide enough for ten people to walk abreast with enough room in between them for acrobats to do cartwheels and backflips without bumping into their fellows. I didn't see any boring jugglers or scary clowns.

As we passed the fourth castle, someone seemed to say, "Janjan! Hey, *Janjan!*"

Mabel elbowed her way across the path past several amused Fae, wriggled between Jackson and me, and side-hugged both of us. She might even have grabbed Jackson's ass. He didn't seem upset.

"Mabel, for God's sake!" I said. "*You* decided to join the party?"

"Live forever and never get old? Drink all you want every night? Fuck every man in sight?" Mabel said. "They can go *all night*, you know. Sign me *up*, baby." She indicated Jackson with a nod of her head. "Who's *this* delicious gentleman?" Like she didn't know who he was or something.

I made the introductions. Mabel was flirtatious, flipped her hair, cast her eyes downwards to check out Jackson's package. When Jackson was merely polite, Mabel got the message. *Plenty of fish in the sea* had always been her motto, and she'd already landed a fae fish or two.

I couldn't remember Jackson *ever* dropping the F-bomb when referring to sex. Mabel had turned him off by doing so. Jackson might have been a bad boy and an apprentice Materialist Magician, but he was also *conservative*. Until he had the good fortune of meeting me, the poor guy had been kinda sexually inexperienced.

We walked on, untiring, glorying in our youth and vigor. Jackson observed the people and the landscape around us closely. Mabel and I chattered excitedly about what we knew about the Fae. She was okay with breathing in this extraordinary way, which is to say breathing so slowly that she couldn't tell it was happening. She thought it was funny that I got freaked out talking or thinking about it. We agreed that it was awesome to be able to eat what we liked and drink (or did we just seem to have drunk and only in hindsight?) without getting sick. She was delighted that whatever it was we were eating and drinking seemed to evaporate out of our bodies without having to pass through bowels and bladder, if you'll forgive the biological details.

And being sloots, we talked about sex, of course we did, and the delights of men who had their orgasms on the inside without blasting sticky semen all over the place.

"*Light* comes out of them instead, you know," Mabel said. "Really lights up a dark room, I can tell you." She looked at Jackson, curious about whether this interesting development also applied to him. I wasn't about to tell her, not with the man himself standing there. He might have been scanning both sides of the road and the horizon, looking for something, but he wasn't deaf and he wasn't stupid.

Mainly, I cared what he thought. I didn't want to offend him.

"*Anyway*," Mabel said when it was clear I wasn't going to share any smutty personal details, "women don't have *periods* here, Janjan. Can you imagine? Best. News. *Ever.*"

I thought of Leda, now period-free among the elves, married and faithful to a man she loved. "How about, um, *infections?*" I said. "How about *pregnancy?*"

"Nope and nope again," Mabel said. "Don't get sick, don't age, don't die, don't have babies. Good thing, too. They're a pre-industrial society, right? Nobody's manufacturing birth control pills or condoms or toothbrushes or any damn thing."

She made me smile. "*Pre-industrial*," was it? Mabel looked like a party girl, but she was smart and educated, something colleagues and lovers forgot at their own risk. I wasn't sure she was right about the no-babies benefit, though. And speaking of pregnancy, where was Beth today?

"You hear all that, Jackson?" I said.

"Ah *did*," he said. "While you and ah were dancin' and flirtin' with the king and queen last night, Miz Mabel here was *gatherin' intelligence* about this strange place we've all ended up in." Was I now hearing a Southern accent I'd never heard from him before? I mean, if I was picking up what he seemed to say the way he intended to say it, he was laying it on pretty thick.

Mabel *blushed*, something I'd never seen her do. It was hilarious. Mabel hated that people judged her by her slooty appearance and underestimated her; Jackson used that to flatter her. He'd made Mabel his to do with as he liked. *That* wasn't funny at all. I wasn't sure I liked this side of him.

Had he also been manipulating *me*? Even if he did help one old lady up off the ice, I wondered if Jackson was actually as evil as Leda thought he was. The trouble with being attracted to bad boys is that they want to deceive me. And maybe I kind of like being deceived.

Jackson continued, "While you ladies were comparing notes, I was observing our surroundings. Very interesting. Take a look and tell me what you see."

Mabel was minding her posture, taking dainty steps to make her butt sway elaborately, and making cow eyes at Jackson, but when she saw he was more interested in her answer than in her assets, she took a look past him at the left side of the road. I busied myself looking at what there was to see on the right.

Mountains in the far distance; they looked gray from where we were. Nearer was a lake, surrounded by reeds. Lake blue, reeds green. Nearer the fae-road the land was flat and covered by brownish grasses and brush with here and there a tree. Okay, fine, got it.

I turned back to Jackson and described the scenery to him.

"Now take another look," he told me.

I looked. The landscape to the right of the road had completely changed. Now it looked like the American desert Southwest, rocks, sand, sparse desert bush that looked all burned out by a hot sun.

"Jesus," I said, "that seems kind of, well, impossible."

"I feel sick to my stomach," Mabel said. Whatever she'd seen on the other side of the road had short-circuited her desire to flirt with Jackson.

"Relax, both of you," Jackson said. "This is just something we have to get used to, like the slow breathing."

Mabel and I recovered quickly. It helped that we were walking along with so many other *people*. I guess they were people; that's what they looked like.

Which reminded me. "Did either of you see any people, or any signs of civilization, buildings or whatever? Anywhere but this road, I mean."

Jackson nodded at me approvingly. "Good eye," he said. "I think maybe the Fae and their habitations are most of the civilization we're going to see."

"I don't think we're in New Hampshire anymore, Toto," Mabel said.

"We're not even on Earth," Jackson said. He wasn't kidding. He wasn't wrong, either.

37

To Travel Hopefully

To travel hopefully is a better thing than to arrive, and the true success is to labour.
Robert Louis Stevenson

There were thousands of people walking along the fae-road together, more travelers than I could count. So it wasn't surprising that we hadn't seen Beth and Bobby. Mabel hadn't seen them; neither had anyone else we asked. The urgent sensation in my chest told me to find my other friends quickly. It worked like this.

I thought: I really should find Beth and Bobby.

I felt: a sudden spike in the burning, like an answer.

Great, everybody but me could have a happy, carefree time among the Fae. Something *within* pushed me toward what I needed to do. I was my own boss here. It wasn't like my day job; nobody was going to give me a performance award or even say Thanks.

"We *have* to find Beth and Bobby," I told Jackson. I might have sounded a little frantic.

"Okay?" he said. The poor guy really did not know how to handle women. Well, except in bed, where he was making great strides. Woof.

Mabel tried to calm me down. "Oh, honey, if they're *here*, they're okay, don't you think?"

Jackson saw Coran and Maeve standing with their horses at a stream next to the road. "Let's ask the king and queen," he said.

He broke trail for Mabel and me across the stream of foot traffic. He had long legs. We hustled to keep up. It was like walking in front of a bunch of people to get to movie theater seats in the center of the row: *excuse me, excuse me, sorry, sorry.* But the Fae were a good-humored lot. They laughed and helped us on our way. This walking they did of their own free will and there was nothing of the rat race about it. They found our haste amusing.

We caught up with Maeve and Coran as the horses bent their heads to drink clear flowing water. It looked clean enough with big smooth stones poking out just above the surface. The stream bottom was dark brown with a mat of old, compressed leaves.

The king and queen stood shoulder to shoulder, like they'd been expecting us. Last night they'd been in a celebratory mood, dancing and happy. Today, burdened by some important business of state, they both looked grave.

"Good morrow, Janjan," said Coran. His smile was kind, but brief.

"Um, hi, Coran," I said. I curtseyed. Last night's formal dancing had made me more graceful.

Coran nodded acknowledgment, accepting the sign of respect as his due. Beside me, Jackson bowed to the royal couple. Always quick to learn, Mabel curtseyed as I had. Maeve nodded to us all, very serious, no smile.

"We still haven't seen our friends Bobby and Beth," I said. "Do you know where they are?"

Maeve's smile was sad, but utterly composed. "We've just been seeing to them," she said. "They're asking after you."

"Follow us," Coran said. "Walk where we walk."

Holding Maeve's hand, the king stepped out on the stones. They crossed the stream deftly without wetting their feet.

Jackson went first. He held out his hand, so I took it. Walking on the dry tops of the stones was harder than it looked. His balance was better than mine. I was glad of his help. I didn't want to get my flimsy fae clothing wet.

We joined Maeve and Coran on the other side of the water. I looked back at the fae-road.

It was gone. No path. No horses. No Mabel; she'd stayed behind. Across the stream where we'd stepped off the road I saw only an empty field.

"Take a good look at those stones in front of us, lass," Coran said. "They're the only way back to the road, the only way back to *us*."

"Where *are* we?" Jackson said.

Coran and Maeve gestured us to follow. We followed.

"See that little copse over there?" Coran said. He pointed to a small stand of trees maybe fifty yards away. "That's where your friends are for the nonce. As to *where* we all are on this side of the road, I think we've stepped into the place where your old friend Cain was sent to wander after he buried his brother. For aught I know, he wanders here East of your Eden still, with a mark on him so no one kills him."

Jackson turned very pale. I thought he might faint. "Cain?" he said. "*Cain?*"

"Aye, the first murderer," said Coran. Seeing Jackson's pallor, he tried to reassure him. "Well, perhaps it's just a story, but it's *your* story, isn't it?"

"Who owns *stories?*" I said. Coran looked annoyed. I've been called a mouthy bitch more than once and gotten a lot of dirty looks, but nobody's punched me yet. I assume it's because I'm short and arguably cute. "And how could Cain be *our* friend?"

Saying no more, Coran walked on ahead of us.

Maeve hung back with Jackson and me. "Go catch up with the king," she ordered Jackson. "Janjan and I have lady business to discuss."

Jackson looked his question at me. I nodded that I'd be okay. Jackson jogged up to where the king was stalking along and fell in step with him.

"Your friend Beth is about to give birth to her child," the queen said without preamble. "She'll want you there to hold her hand and stroke her brow. Don't misunderstand, it won't hurt her a bit, but she'll need your reassurance. Tonight she'll dance with the rest of us and be happy."

"What?!" I didn't care how rude I sounded.

"I know, I know, it doesn't seem possible to you Earth folk, but there it is. Her Bobby was further along to becoming one of us than perhaps he knew. So therefore her child will be ... what the Fae have instead of children." She sounded not sad but *resigned*, and in that resignation I heard how very old—how truly *ancient*—was the queen of the Fae.

For once in my life I was speechless. You think that's funny till it happens to you.

Coran and Jackson disappeared into the grove ahead of us.

38

Tom Petty and the Heartbreakers Sing "Refugee"

Jackson ran and fell into step beside the king. Coran gave him a sidelong glance.

"We've been talking, Maeve and I," said Coran. "We find you and the Lady Janjan interesting."

"Interesting?" Not knowing where his interests lay, Jackson didn't know how to participate in the conversation. Coran's face was mobile and expressive enough, but of what?

"You've no idea what I'm getting at," Coran said. He sounded amused. "But why would you? How'd you and your lady like to be king and queen of the Fae?"

"Why us?" Jackson said. "And why *me*, in particular?" He hoped his total confusion didn't show in his face or in his voice.

"Eamonn was my kinsman. His light is in you because he meant to give it. A bit of time walking the fae-path around the World Mountain will show you what that means. *The light of other days* has made us kin."

"Well, what about you and Maeve?" Jackson said. "What'll you do when you're not king and queen?"

Coran looked around the field, as if the answer to Jackson's question was right in front of them. This world looked pleasant enough to Jackson, but he didn't see what the king was getting at.

"Fae or not, lad," said Coran, "Maeve and I are very old indeed. You've no idea how long we've been walking around the human worlds. How much we've seen. Eternity's longer than we imagined it would be, and we've had enough of it. It's worn us out, see?"

Coran pushed up one sleeve to bare his thick, strong arm. Even in the gentle sunlight, Jackson saw almost all the way through the king's flesh and bone. The hand looked perfectly normal, but the arm did not. He touched the shining forearm with one finger. Coran's body felt solid enough, but looking into the king's arm made Jackson dizzy.

"So, what?" Jackson said, "You'll just *die?* You *want* that?"

Coran simply nodded. There was such a great, deep sadness on him that Jackson felt it, too. "I think perhaps this world will do for that," the king said. "We'll guide your first steps, Maeve and I, then in a year or two when you're ready to ascend the throne, we'll come back here. My love and I will set out a farewell feast in that grove where your friends are. Then we'll invite the angel of death to sup with us."

Jackson had no idea what he should do, but Coran was entitled to an answer. "Janjan and I will talk, sir. I can't tell you what she'll say." Talk about understatement.

Coran grinned. "She's unpredictable, that one. So says Maeve, and I've learned to trust the queen's vision in these matters. Know this, though: she says your Janjan was born to rule."

"Janjan's pretty clear about what she wants," Jackson said.

"As am I, lad," Coran said. "As am I." He recovered his translucent arm and with one broad human hand he stroked Jackson's face.

Jackson cast his eyes downward submissively as the Order had trained him to do. He didn't seek out coupling with other men, but if that was the price of power, he was willing to pay it. He'd paid it before.

——

Numb with information overload, Jackson entered the grove with Coran. The king and queen left quickly.

Jackson gratefully accepted Janjan's suggestion that he patrol the borders of the grove. He needed time to think. Everything was happening too fast. It was like when he'd stood before the forbidding Caucasus cliff face. The same choice was on offer:

Do you want an ordinary happy life, or do you want power over others?

Well, all ordinary life was certainly in abeyance at the moment. Whether you were walking with the Fae or standing in a world that was earthlike but wasn't Earth, you'd stepped out of the ordinary world where most people happily spend their days—and far less happily end those days.

So what power might you grasp? We all die, and what's the point of it, Jackson thought again. Live a long, long, unimaginably long life, like Coran had, and still die at the end of it? Or end up the ventriloquist's dummy of a shadow creature whose language darkens the very air around you, like the Walloon had? And then what?

Jackson sighed to himself. It seemed that he'd made an irrevocable choice back in that freezing Portsmouth field. That he'd chosen *for* his friends and *against* Simon and the Walloon. In doing that, he'd chosen against the Fallen.

He hadn't had real friends before. He'd had sex, but Janjan was his first real lover. She made him laugh. She made him hot with wanting her—because she wanted him and made no excuses for her desire. So confusing.

In his whole life, Jackson had only been free of doubt when the god and goddess of the Other World spoke the language of dreams through him. What power he'd felt! Power that had at first balked even the elves sent against him, half knocked one elf out of his human body.

And what bitterness Jackson felt when elves who'd grown up speaking the language of dreams used Elvish to defeat him. The few High Aghartic spells he knew, all that remained to him when the god and goddess departed, were no match for the Unfallen Tongue.

He'd been taught that the elves were the ancient enemies of the Materialist Magicians, taught that he should kill them on sight. He hadn't even managed to kill Jerry August, who'd been no elf, but only under the elves' protection.

Jackson's painful indecision was interrupted by the sound of all three of his friends gasping at once. He whirled around.

He saw what looked like a newborn child made of nothing but *the light of other days*. The child, if that's what it was, floated across the clearing and out of the grove. He and Janjan and Beth and Bobby watched it go. They watched it—apparently—merge with the fae-road.

Jackson had faced real horrors with Simon and then quickly forgotten them out of self-preservation. None of those horrors saddened him like this. He saw Beth's stricken look. He saw the deep loss in Bobby's face. He saw how Janjan felt her friends' pain along with them.

Janjan was *good*, Jackson thought. He was pretty sure he wasn't. Still...

"Maybe we should give Beth and Bobby a minute here?" he told Janjan.

She nodded and took his hand for comfort. They walked out of the grove and into the field.

39

Mystery School Homecoming Weekend

The bad guys were weird to the bone.

Master Louis looked around the stinking rock chamber that served Simon as both living room and classroom. He was not impressed.

Immediately after Jackson's apparent defection in Portsmouth, Louis had ordered Simon back to the Caucasus. Simon felt quite at home in the cave monastery. He could have lived in a mansion, but material things meant little to him. Now that he could have anything he wanted, he found he wanted almost nothing.

Not being a fool, Simon saw Louis observe that the cave had become a midden. Dirt and disorder were the least of it. Centuries of black magic had eaten invisibly into the rock. The psychic atmosphere was thick with fetor.

"How are the mighty fallen, and the weapons of war perished," said Simon.

If Louis caught the ironic biblical reference, it didn't show on his face.

That face had entered the fixity of full possession, a condition which had also cost him any sense of humor he'd had before the Order recruited him. The perfectly possessed gain great power, but lose most of their humanity. Simon told himself that the Walloon, being only a frog, was ill equipped to appreciate the subtleties of British wit.

"No students?" said Louis.

It was a stupid question, but Simon shook his head politely. "None have sought me out since I finished with Jackson. Are there are any in the pipeline, Master?"

"We have hundreds of postulants in the early stages of their education, but none who will be ready for *you* to teach this year," Louis said.

Magical training normally took years. What happened to MM trainees in the Caucasus was a trial by ordeal, one the Walloon and Simon had passed through long ago. Simon was pleased that young Jackson had survived the short course with his sanity intact.

"Such a shame," said Simon. "The caves above us used to be *full* of likely young fellows." Simon had taken a number of those fellows into his bed, but that sort of dalliance was as long-gone as his own youthful good looks. In recent years, Simon's libido had gone cold, leaving behind baffled resentment and few happy memories.

"Time," said Louis. "*Time* is what we need. The *Materialist* side of the Order can do little without the *Magician* side. *Enfin.* What have you heard from Jackson?"

To give himself a moment to collect his thoughts, Simon sat down on a foul-looking cushion near the fire. He carefully fed a piece of wood to the flames and gestured expansively for Louis to sit on another equally foul old cushion. The fastidious Louis cautiously took a seat, reluctant to soil his spotless new mountaineering gear.

Knowing that lies could get him killed, Simon looked Louis in the eye and began ticking off points with his fingers.

"Jackson did most of what we asked of him," said Simon. "He reported to his contact in Massachusetts. He drove up to Portsmouth..."

"I am *informed*," Louis interrupted, "that Jackson met with certain of our *business associates* in Washington *before* leaving for Portsmouth. Did you order that?"

Alarmed, Simon shook his head. "I didn't know, Master. Perhaps he was acting on his own initiative? I *do* know that young Jackson quickly found someone in Portsmouth who could open a door to the Fae. This man had been a Fae traveler for many Earth years and therefore showed no sign of his real age. I saw Jackson transform him into a *[bridge]*." The single High Aghartic word darkened the cave momentarily, despite the fire.

Louis nodded. "One of our sources in the American government informed Jackson that the *[bridge]* fought in the Second World War, despite appearing to be a young man."

Clearly, Jackson hadn't told Simon everything. Simon was glad he'd told Louis the truth. Louis would have intelligence sources to confirm what he was told. Of course he would. Trust no one, verify everything.

Simon continued, "Jackson used this fellow to send scores of homeless people to the Fae. Having nothing to hope for and nothing to hold them on Earth, they went willingly. They didn't return and no one came looking for them. Jackson then began to work among people of his own generation. Instead of going drinking and dancing every night, scores of young people went to the Fae. They left the Earth on a lark, on the promise of indiscriminate sex, no disease, and a better, safer high than drugs would give them. None of *them* returned, either."

"What of those who come to Portsmouth seeking to join our enemies?"

Simon shook his head. "I have no specific information on elf-seekers, Master Louis. But! In addition to all the young people who left, *their elders* also began going to the Fae to escape their troubles and their duties. A benefit we had not expected."

"And then?" Louis' smooth face remained motionless and his voice was almost kind, but Simon was not fooled.

Simon looked into the fire. "Before Jackson could complete the spell to fix his chosen instrument in place and open our permanent gateway off the Earth, two young women arrived to distract him." He looked up at Louis, thinking: *Could this be the day I die? Where do dead magicians go, I wonder? Is it hotter than this little fire?* "Before I could stop them, they all stepped onto the fae-path and took the *[bridge]* with them."

Louis watched Simon intently for a while. Seeing no sign of deception in the older man, Louis finally nodded. "Sending Jackson to Portsmouth alone was a miscalculation. Jackson's 'handler' was unable to handle him."

Simon shrugged. "Fortunes of war. Our business associates don't really understand magic, do they?" What Simon understood was that he wasn't going to die tonight.

"They don't understand *us*," Louis said. "How could they? They are but our fat cattle. We counted on Jackson to establish a link to the Fae. He came very close to doing that—and without alerting the elves."

"I caught no scent of elf," Simon agreed. "No scent of Jackson, either. He can't travel instantly the way you and I do; he's not been initiated into that magic yet. With my own eyes I saw Jackson step off the Earth, leaving no trace behind." He looked directly at Louis. "It was as if Jackson was *pulled* into that other realm."

"Will he stay among the Fae, do you think?" said Louis.

Simon shook his head. "I think not, Master. He's impatient, like all young men. He's hungry for power and the earthly things power can bring him."

"Did Jackson perhaps *discern* that you planned to kill him and bind his spirit to anchor the *[bridge]* in place?"

Coming out of that inhumanly calm face, the question took Simon by surprise. He'd thought himself in the clear. He desperately wanted to lie, but Louis could commandeer Simon's will and simply *take* whatever information he sought. Simon's obedience was being tested. "Jackson saw me approach him in the field as I was gathering power about me. The Old Gods and our captive Fae *damaged* Jackson; he's no fit vehicle for the Fallen now. But even with the little magic he knows, he may have seen my intent. It's as hard to hide as lightning in a thundercloud." Louis held out his hands and bowed his head: *Do with me what you will.*

Louis fell silent, either tormenting Simon, thinking, communing with his guardian shadow, or all of those things.

Finally Louis shrugged. "I don't know what else you could have done." His voice was mild and comfortless. "We sent Jackson to learn the language of the Old Gods so we could use *them* against the elves. It was not altogether his fault that he failed. If he had succeeded, we would have had to eliminate him, not that he knew that when he took the assignment. There are … *imponderables* at play whenever we deal with creatures outside our order of being. Those who do so encounter energies that make them resistant to deeper initiation into the Order. The only thing for it is to kill them, *faute de mieux,* lest they find the way to our enemies."

Simon again allowed himself to feel relief. "Look at it this way, Master. Jackson's only power lies in the bit of High Aghartic we've taught him; once he uses it, we'll … be notified. We can find him and *make* him finish the task we trained him for."

"Yes," said Louis. "Once his usefulness is at an end, we should end *him* without delay. He knows too much about us." His face went through a slow, mirthless spasm, all that remained of his human smile.

Simon smiled back weakly. Something beneath the Walloon's face had gotten to him. "Excuse me a moment." He bowed to Louis and walked quickly away, hoping to reach the privy before he vomited or soiled himself.

✻

The Walloon not only gave Simon specific instructions but also showed him the surprising courtesy of explaining his reasoning. Simon felt a surge of loyalty for Louis that filled him with helpless self-loathing.

Simon was to return to Portsmouth and keep the field under surveillance. He was to interrogate anyone who left the Fae. At intervals he was to transit the human worlds, scanning for psychic traces of his errant disciple. Once located, Simon was to return Jackson to Portsmouth to complete his task. If Jackson refused or tried to escape, Simon was to destroy him immediately. Jackson's death was inevitable; Simon would use it to the Order's advantage if he could.

Jackson himself would become the Order's eternal gateway to the Fae.

Louis had other resources in reserve. Simon had heard the two old women chanting in the cave below the Walloon's mansion, but feared to look at them. He'd felt the age and depth of their magic. Louis gave Simon the impression that the hags carried some ancient grudge against their own people.

The Order of course had agents inside the American government. If Louis needed leverage against an American citizen, it required only a telephone call to a willing functionary. The authorities were now reluctantly turning their attention to the mystery of all the American citizens who had disappeared from Portsmouth. The government would soon be compelled to respond. The Walloon's agents would shape that response.

For his part, Louis would walk to and fro in the world. He would summon the most useful of the useful idiots from the Order's Materialist side and make them do his will.

Which is to say, the will of the Claimant.

Whether they knew it or not, the Materialists were at Louis' command. Those who needed additional motivation might receive a personal summons to Louis' mansion. People found the Walloon's placid demeanor disturbing; they sensed something terrible lying coiled beneath it and did as they were told.

"Don't worry, Master Simon," the Walloon said, with the sort of kindness that only underscored its threat. "You and I will do our duty to the Claimant. We will soon build our *[bridge]* to the Fae—and away from the elves. The gates of heaven shall not prevail against it."

Louis folded shadow around himself and it enfolded him. He disappeared from Simon's cave.

40

Within a Budding Grove

But clinging mortal hope must fall from you,
For we who ride the winds, run on the waves,
And dance upon the mountains, are more light
Than dewdrops on the banners of the dawn.

W.B. Yeats, *The Land of Heart's Desire*

The day the weirdness showed its sad face.

Bobby sat in the shade on thick dry grass on the far side of the grove, his back against a tree. Beth leaned back against Bobby. His arms held her, and her hands lay on top of his. Her eyes were closed. Beth looked better in her flimsy Fae dress than I did in mine, but what else is new? Her normally flat, gym-toned belly was rounded like I'd never seen before—even yesterday. *Jesus*, that *happened fast*, I thought.

She'd known she was pregnant back in Portsmouth, but she couldn't have been pregnant long. I'd have noticed if she'd missed more than one period.

I also knew that Beth, who had no objection to using birth control or making her lovers do so, would carry her child to term. We'd talked about it: *What would you do if...?* Beth's very Catholic upbringing would kick in, if by some mischance she became pregnant.

Hence all the Beth-drama in our kitchen the day I walked in on them. Hence her conversation with Bobby back in Great Bog before we all joined the Fae to escape scary Simon, whoever he was.

"Right," Coran said to Maeve, "she knows what to do?"

"Aye," said Maeve. "Not that there's much to be done. And young Jackson knows the way back to the path?"

"We've talked, Jackson and I," said Coran. "We'll leave you to it, then," he told us.

"We'll see you all tonight, I hope," Maeve said to me. "Once you're back on the path, you'll find us easy enough. There's no secret to where we go. The wind's always at our back." Her voice was light, but there was that resignation again, as present in her voice as in the music the Fae danced to. Lighthearted sadness.

"Thank you," I said to Maeve and Coran. I didn't know what else to say.

The king and queen nodded and left the grove.

I scurried right over, gave Bobby a quick smile, and kneeled down next to my friend. I put one hand on her arm and the other on her thigh. Beth's eyes opened and she smiled at me. She looked scared.

I spoke softly, so as not to scare her more. "Sweetie, are you okay?"

She shrugged. "It's gonna be *soon*, Janjan. I don't know how I know this, but I'm very sure. I can feel it. It's about to happen."

"I'm not sure what to do for you," I said. "I've never helped anyone have a baby before. My first aid class was back in high school. And even if we had a phone I don't think we could call 911 from here."

Bobby spoke up. His deep voice was calm, resigned to whatever would happen. He rocked Beth in his arms to comfort her and kissed her ear. "*I've* done this before. I helped my wife birth our son. The baby died soon after. My wife died before we had time to have another."

"Was that before you fought in the Second World War, Bobby?" Jackson said.

I thought, *Second World War?*

Bobby looked up at him. "*Way* before that," he said. "It would have been 1860, before the *Civil* War."

That shocked me. Jackson took the information in stride; he already knew Bobby had been in World War II. Given where we were and how we'd gotten here, what difference did a little more time travel make? And I guess it explained how a simple man like Bobby had ended up in complicated twenty-first-century Portsmouth. He'd come to us from a simpler time after spending the intervening years with the Fae, who never age. He'd skipped like a flat stone across the water of time, from the nineteenth century into the twentieth and finally into the twenty-first.

Anyway. Bobby wasn't the problem here. "Does it hurt?" I asked Beth.

She shook her head. "No pain, just...*pressure.*"

I looked up at Jackson. "Do you know *anything* that can help her?" I was hoping for magic, and I didn't care if it was black or white.

Jackson looked lost. He hesitated like he always did. "Nothing I was taught will help Beth," he finally said. "If I try to use the little I do know, it might get us all killed. I don't think we're safe anywhere but among the Fae. Did you notice that we're all breathing and talking to each other like we did on Earth?"

Surprisingly, I had *not* noticed that. Whatever world we'd walked into when we left the fae-path, it was more like Earth than not.

"Okay," I said to Jackson, "in that case, could you watch the field around us and see if anybody's coming?"

"I'm glad to be of use," Jackson said. "I'll stand guard and give Beth some privacy."

Beth and I smiled at Jackson, each of us for our own reasons. Bobby smiled at Beth because he loved her. Looking outward, Jackson began a slow patrol of the grove's perimeter. He'd see any visitors long before they saw us. Once we left the Fae, we'd left sanctuary behind. *Anything* could happen here. *More things in Heaven and Earth*, and all that.

Beth's eyes opened wide, scared. "I feel like I'm gonna have to *push*." She got her feet under her and stood up slowly. Bobby scrambled up behind her and supported her.

All I knew about childbirth was that it was a messy business; Beth's diaphanous outfit would interfere. "Let's get this off you, sweetie," I said. She helped by holding her arms above her head, and I just slid her dress up and off. She was naked underneath.

She was of course beautiful, but I was too fearful for Beth to take the time to admire her. I hung her dress carefully on a low, leafy branch.

Beth grabbed my arm hard enough to hurt. "Oh, my God, Janjan, here it comes!"

I held one of her arms to support her while Bobby held the other arm. She wanted to squat down, so we helped her do that. Everything was happening very quickly, but it felt like time had slowed down.

I smelled sap in the trees and bushes around us. I saw dust motes drift through warm sun and disappear into shadow. I heard insects click and birds chirp. I heard my own heartbeat. From the corner of my eye, I saw Jackson walking with great deliberation around the grove, politely ignoring the beautiful slender naked woman with the little belly. The man had good instincts and good manners. Points for Jackson.

Supported right and left, Beth crouched as if she was about to pee. She breathed deeply. I found myself breathing in time with her.

Beth exhaled. She pushed. Hard. I was prepared for the usual sorts of things that come out of a pregnant female human being.

What emerged instead was *light*.

It wasn't like what comes out of a little flashlight and quickly diffuses. In the daylit grove the light flowed out of Beth's body in the space of three breaths. It *cohered* like thick fluid. It shone bright green on the pale green grass beneath her. Beth inhaled and exhaled convulsively.

Her belly shrank flat in an instant. I saw the abdominal muscles pull closer together. I couldn't see how anything but a miscarriage could happen in such a short time.

The beam of light that had come out of Beth's womb and traveled down her birth canal resolved itself into a human shape. A tiny human baby boy made of light waves and light particles. I could see them because I could see *through* him. He had no navel; there was no placenta. The baby's light further lit up the inside of the grove as he floated just above the ground.

Jackson heard the three of us gasp and turned to look, not at lovely naked Beth, but at the naked child of light.

The child smiled up at his mother. Beth smiled back, but her face was so sad.

Wordless communication passed between flesh mother and energy infant. The newborn turned in the air and floated quickly back out of the grove the way we'd all walked into it.

By the time we all pulled ourselves together and followed the baby out of the grove, the shining child had crossed the field and reached the stream. Without hesitating, he glided across the stream just above the rocks we'd crossed.

The child reached the invisible barrier between this world and the fae-path. His light penetrated the barrier and we saw the road on its other side.

The child of light shined himself into the path. Did the road *absorb* him? The invisible curtain between us and the fae-road fell back in place like it had always been there.

I fetched Beth's fae dress and helped her into it. She was shaking and her face was pale with shock. Who could blame her? She was wondering what had happened. Who could tell her?

Bobby's shoulders slumped. His face was full of grief, old and new. As if he'd looked at a life where children—*his* children—could be so easily lost and judged it not worth living.

Jackson's face was grim and unreadable. He looked ready for war. It struck me that outside the bedroom I never had any idea what he was thinking. Jackson worried me even more than Beth and Bobby. I'd stepped off Earth and then walked away from the Fae into this world that looked like Earth but wasn't. Strange as all that was, Jackson was stranger still.

"Maybe we should give Beth and Bobby a minute here?" he said.

I took his hand. We walked into the field together.

41

Side Trip with Friends and Enemies

Do I not destroy my enemies when I make them my friends?
Abraham Lincoln

Jackson and I walked out of the shade into the sunlit field. I felt terrible for Beth, without quite knowing why. This pregnancy wasn't planned; she wasn't ready to have kids. Hadn't she dodged a bullet today? But *she* felt bad, so I felt bad along with her.

I felt just as bad for Bobby, who'd walked out of fae mystery, back into human misery. He was grieving this loss just as he must have grieved his son's death so long ago.

It didn't matter to either of them that it wasn't a *human* child they'd lost.

And me? I felt guilty that holding Jackson's hand gave me a naughty little thrill. We walked around to the shady side of the grove to keep pale Janjan from sunburn. I thought, *We're dating! He's my boyfriend!*

A stupid thought, given our situation. Without meaning to, Jackson killed the thrill. "Coran, um, offered us a job." He couldn't quite manage a smile. "How'd you like to be queen of the Fae with me as your king?"

"*What?* Maeve didn't say anything about that. She just told me what was going to happen to Beth and said I shouldn't worry about it." But now I thought maybe Maeve *had* told me something about being queen of the Fae, said it with her sadness about the fae condition.

"You don't exactly sound thrilled about the idea," Jackson said. "I don't know what the hell to think about it myself."

Before we could speculate, I spotted a distant human figure strolling toward us. My eyesight's pretty good. In the bright sunlight it should have been easy to see the man clearly. The yellowish grass in the field was no more than knee-high. But it seemed the light was partly deflected away from our visitor.

I had another stupid thought. *Was* it Cain, the first murderer, doomed to wander this world forever, come to kill us for trespassing? Thanks for *that*, Coran.

Jackson had been looking at me as we talked. I pointed to the new arrival. "Company. Anybody you know?"

He looked stricken. Jackson's vision was sharper than mine. Or maybe he had senses I didn't have and saw things I didn't see. "It's Simon. Go get Beth and Bobby and *run* back to the fae-path."

I shook my head. "No, I'm not leaving you. Besides there isn't time."

"You don't get it," Jackson said. "He's going to *kill* us, starting with me. He could do it from a mile away, but he wants to *play* with us first. Like a cat with a mouse." He sounded angry and sad. And *guilty*, for some reason. Believe me, Catholic girls know guilt when we hear it.

"We need help," I said. Why had it taken me so long to think of this?

I put my hand on my breastbone. In my chest I felt where Leda had painted the mysterious burning symbol into my body. Maybe it was something like the Bat-Signal? I put my mind there and closed my eyes.

Leda? I thought. *A little help?*

A long moment of silence. Then Leda's unmistakable mind-voice: *Be right there, sweetie. We've been waiting for your call.*

Her inner voice gave me another naughty little thrill. *Such a bad girl, Janjan,* Leda thought, but I felt her smile.

Up walked the man Jackson had called his vice president. He was dressed for a much colder climate than this world's. There was sweat on his sallow face. Simon was smiling the ugliest smile I'd ever seen. Yeah, what teeth he still had were stained and jagged, but teeth can be repaired and replaced. His real ugliness came from within.

I kept one hand on my chest. It burned. I watched, fascinated, as the burning extended both up and down my insides. I'm sure I looked like a Victorian lady (okay, maybe somewhat *déshabillé,* maybe not exactly a lady) about to swoon, but I was saying the Catholic Act of Contrition that begins *O my God, I am heartily sorry for having offended You...*

If the Church gets you young, they've probably got you for life. Fine with me; I needed protection. I was hoping not to die right now. But if I *was* going to die, I knew which direction I wanted to go; it wasn't with this guy. He stank of evil and it wasn't my nose that was picking that up. Every survival instinct said *Get away from him and don't look back.* Of course I couldn't leave my friends.

Interestingly, the instant I started praying, Simon stopped advancing on us. He stopped grinning, too.

"She's *praying,*" he said to Jackson, like prayer was an obscenity. "Make her *stop it* or I'll kill you both where you stand."

"You're planning to kill us anyway," Jackson said. "The lady can do as she pleases." He gave me a very curious look, though. Surprised that I was praying? I was a little surprised myself.

Heat suffused my whole body from the inside out. I felt like a

Victorian-era Christmas tree with real lighted candles on its branches. I could see each separate light within me just shining away. I wasn't about to catch fire, but I was sweating in a most unladylike fashion.

All the light was pure information. I was an antenna. I was a network. I *knew* things. For example, I knew Leda and Jerry were about to appear just before they showed up. Their minds shone into mine with increasing intensity.

And then—pop!—there they were standing on either side of us, shoulder to shoulder, dressed in black clothes and light boots.

Jerry nodded politely to Jackson and kept most of his attention on Simon.

Jackson gave Jerry the side-eye. Some painful history there. But Jackson surely knew that any threat to him and to the rest of us came from Simon, not from Jerry or Leda.

That's what my physical eyes saw. On the inside I saw something flash between Jerry and Leda quicker than I could grasp it.

Leda nodded. She entered the grove to guard Beth and Bobby.

Also on the inside I *saw* both Jerry and Leda. Or rather, the light in them was mirrored in the light in me. What an odd thing. The light burned me still, but now without pain.

What I now saw in Simon was only shadow. Shadow that roiled like oil smoke. It scared me to look at it closely. I got the idea that looking *into* the shadow would be a very bad idea indeed. I kept praying.

I prayed for Jackson, too. My light showed me that his light was touched by the same kind of shadow that eclipsed Simon's light altogether. A small stain, but still. *Do not inquire within*, I thought. Some things are better left unseen.

Jerry held up one forbidding hand, not that Simon was coming any closer. Simon's face was doing contortions that made it awful to look at, like he was about to puke or something worse. "You should leave now,"

Jerry told Simon. "There's nothing for you here."

Simon said to Jackson, "It's an *elf*. You have your orders. *Kill it!*" He meant Jerry.

Jackson looked at Jerry, then turned back to Simon and shook his head. "*He* doesn't seem to want to kill me. Unlike you." If I'm any judge of men, and I am, this was hard for Jackson to say.

"You can't *leave* the Brotherhood," Simon told Jackson. "You're *ours*, aren't you? Master Louis will be *very* unhappy."

"Louis was pretty clear that if I failed the Order again, I'd be killed," Jackson said. I'd never heard him sound so hopeless. I wanted to hold him tight and tell him everything would be okay, but this probably wasn't the time. "I almost succeeded in doing what you wanted done back in Portsmouth. And you were *still* about to kill me, Simon. I could *see* it." He was so sad, a child whose father had abandoned him.

"Dear boy," said Simon, "nothing could be further from the truth. No, no, not at all! I was coming to *help* you." He may have thought he was smiling, but it looked more like a snarl.

Even I knew Simon was lying. "You guys keep shooting yourselves in the foot," I told Simon. "Don't you even read your own history?"

"*OpSec*," Jackson said. His bitterness was aimed at Simon, not at me. "Operations security. Most of us have no *need to know* our own history."

Balked by my schoolgirl prayers and by Jackson and Jerry, Simon rounded on me. "Is *this* the little whore who's caused all the trouble? Yes, I see that it is. Perhaps a few of us will pay you a visit you when there are no elves around to save you. To teach you some respect for your elders and betters." To be sure I got the point, he made a couple of pelvic thrusts in my general direction. Eww.

As so often before, I regretted opening my mouth. Inner vision saw Simon's shadow reaching out toward me as he talked. I felt sick from the shadow's dark proximity.

Jerry whispered a single word in the shining language of the next world over. The word that meant *whole* or *healing* or *holy* or maybe *wholeness* hung for an impossibly long time in the air of whatever world we were in. The shadow recoiled. My nausea evaporated instantly.

Simon made a strangled *Kh!* sound in his throat. The shadow that kept pace with him furled around him like a flag and he disappeared. The last thing I saw was his pallid, spasming, hate-filled face.

✳

The six of us sat together in the little grove. With Leda and Jerry and their elf perceptions among us, no sentries were needed.

We all told our stories. How we'd come to walk with the Fae. What we'd learned. Who else from Earth we'd seen. (Beth and Bobby had seen and talked to more Portsmouth people than Jackson and I.)

And mostly we talked about Beth. How her human intimacy with Bobby had somehow gotten her with, as Maeve said, *what the Fae have instead of children.* A fae child embodied only in fae-light who, we thought, had now vanished into and maybe become part of the fae-path. Nobody had any idea what that meant. Jerry and Leda exchanged a look, but couldn't tell us anything helpful. Beth looked slightly abashed as she spoke. Poor Bobby looked mortified at our twenty-first-century frankness about sexual matters.

And really, what would help a situation like ours? What *could* help? Maybe Jerry and Leda just weren't telling us all they knew because there was no point.

Then there was the matter of Jackson.

"Mr. Jackson," said Jerry, "you and I last met under unfortunate circumstances." Leave it to Jerry to understate politely.

"I don't think there's any way to apologize for trying to do you harm," Jackson said. "But you're not asking for an apology, are you?"

Jerry shook his head. "I'm more concerned about what you plan to do *now.*"

"I'm sorry, I don't understand."

Jerry looked closely at Jackson, as if he was looking at something in or around his body. "I'm sorry to be so tactless," Jerry finally said, "but your Materialist Magician initiations have put you in danger. And if *you're* in danger, so is our friend Janjan. And our other friends, too." He nodded at Beth and Bobby.

Gulp. That I might be in danger was hard for me to absorb, but not as hard as finding out that Jackson, my lover, *really was* the hipster magician who'd tried to have Old Gods kidnap my friend Jerry into another world. Or maybe had tried to kill him. Or maybe had tried to have him *and* my friend Leda disembodied. Should I *hate* Jackson? I mean, thank God he failed, right?

Jerry and Leda had told me their stories, all right, but those were just *words* for me to take down, put in some kind of order, and post to the Elf Friends' website. It hadn't occurred to me that their little Portsmouth love story had anything to do with little me. Your story stops being just a romantic comedy once the elves get involved.

I caught Jackson's eye. "You wouldn't hurt *me*, would you?"

"Never," he said. He didn't hesitate or even blink when he said it. I believed him.

"Jackson," said Leda, "I know you wouldn't *want* to hurt Janjan. But what would happen here and now if you spoke the words you were muttering to yourself on the ocean outside Portsmouth?" Her tone was gentle. She wasn't challenging Jackson, just asking him to think about things with her.

Jackson started to bristle anyway. *Typical*, I thought. *When men don't know what else to do, they get angry.* He stared at the ground between his knees for a minute. Then he shook his head, disgusted with himself, and looked up at Leda.

"If I speak High Aghartic, it will draw … others to me. To *us*. I didn't dare use the little I know to help Beth give birth today." To me he said, "I'm sorry, Janjan."

He really didn't need to apologize to me. I put a hand on his arm. "So just don't speak that language," I said. "What's the problem?"

Jerry said, "Jackson, I think we've reached the point in our conversation where you and I should speak privately. Would you mind?"

Jackson hesitated, then said, "No. You're right." He got to his feet. To me he said, "Forgive me, Janjan. Maybe if you don't hear this, you won't hate me."

"Don't be silly," I said. "Why would I hate you?" My tone was light, but my heart was not.

Jackson reached down and stroked my face. He knew what that did to me. Bastard, making me feel all gooshy and just walking off.

"I'll be back," he said. "We'll talk."

"That's what they all say. Then they don't call and I never see them again."

My joke fell flat. Jerry and Jackson left the grove. Beth and Bobby, still sort of in their own world, had not been tracking our conversation. Leda had started up a side conversation with them which I had missed. Her voice was gentle, kind, and strong. What she'd suggested caused my friends them to shake their heads: *No thanks.*

I didn't blame them. Going to the next world over with Leda and Jerry wasn't exactly like taking a Caribbean cruise. I watched Leda closely. She wasn't trying to convert the heathens. She didn't care what anybody believed.

All she and Jerry ever said while they were telling me their story was simply, *Come see for yourself. It's pretty great over there.* They weren't selling anything or, God forbid, evangelizing. They just wanted to share the good stuff.

Here in this world we were in danger, just like we would be on Earth. We were in danger *everywhere* except on the road with the Fae or in the next world over with the elves.

Until I looked into Simon's face, I thought danger was perfectly avoidable. Just don't climb Mount Everest, and you won't fall into a crevasse. Just use condoms when you have sex with men. Just don't give creepers a chance to put date-rape drugs in your drink. Just don't text and drive. Just don't drive drunk. Just don't take random pills from random strangers. Just don't leave a good job until you have a better job lined up. And so on. Common-sense stuff.

Common sense wasn't enough. Life had turned out a lot different than I'd expected. Growing up in Buffalo hadn't fully prepared me for the rest of the world. And nothing the Catholic Church taught had prepared me for other worlds. Really, what could?

Back in Portsmouth I'd asked Leda *What am I doing here?* She made her scribe. Then before I stepped onto the fae-path, she basically tattooed an invisible homing device between my breasts, where I couldn't lose it.

Now I'd stepped off the fae-path onto another world, a mostly-empty one that wasn't Earth. It seemed a little stupid to ask Leda again *What am I doing here?* I wasn't sure I wanted to hear her answer. *Do not inquire within.*

Or maybe the *mandala* was the answer, a present that had unwrapped itself. Merry Christmas, Janjan, look at all the pretty lights!

Perhaps following some of my thoughts with me, Leda looked away from Bobby and Beth (he was holding her tenderly and she was savoring being held). Leda looked at me. Expectantly.

"Maeve told me *You are the queen who is also a king,*" I told Leda. Her eyes got all weird before she said it."

"Huh," Leda said. "If you were a bigger girl, I'd say all she meant was that you were bi and large, by and large."

"Bitch."

"Yes, I am."

We were both grinning, though. It was like old times sitting around our house together in Portsmouth, gabbing away and teasing each other. Not a care in the world. Beth caught the mood and smiled at us. My smile faded. Things had changed.

Hey, since last year *everything* had changed.

Leda had been kidnapped into the Other World.

Jerry had gone after her and brought her back to Earth.

The bad guys had gone after Jerry and Leda in Portsmouth to steal their bodies.

They were scared of the next world over, but where else could they go?

Then there was the biggest change of all. They'd become what everybody becomes in that world so close to Portsmouth you can walk there: elves who aren't really elves.

Jerry and Leda could have stayed home with the other elves. They could have traveled almost anywhere in an instant. Instead, they came here to help Beth and Bobby and me.

They were even willing to help Jackson, their enemy.

42

Cherchez la Femme

Even after they were out of earshot of the grove, Jerry and Jackson walked on in silence. Jackson was awestruck by this quiet, empty world. Warm sunlight revealed rich colors unlike anything he'd seen on Earth—or on any other world he'd seen from the fae-road. Jerry found this unnamed world beautiful, but only a shadow of the next world over.

As they walked they got a sense of each other, the way men do. Jackson was taller and heavier, but when he saw how Jerry moved he hoped he'd never have to fight him. Jackson's conflicts with elves had ended badly; they had power he didn't understand. Jerry refrained from prying into the younger man's thoughts, but he didn't have to read minds to see that something was bothering Jackson.

Jerry was first to break the silence. "Is there something you'd like to ask me?"

Jackson stopped walking. "Are you going to kill me?"

Jerry took a step back and held his empty hands at his sides, palms forward: *I mean you no harm.* "Of course not. Why would you think that?"

Jackson looked embarrassed. "I was taught: *Kill the elf before it kills you.*"

Jerry grinned. "*'It'?* It's *almost* as if your teachers wanted to prevent you from talking to us."

"That's exactly what they wanted," Jackson said. "They're terrified of you."

Jerry nodded and started walking slowly again. "It's a sad business," he said. "Nobody has to be afraid of the next world over or fear anyone who lives there..." He broke off, not wanting to sound like a salesman.

Jackson caught up with Jerry and walked alongside him.

"Look," Jerry said, "I've got a lot of questions, but I don't want you to think I'm *interrogating* you." Jackson looked his question at Jerry, who continued, "Oh, I'm curious about all the stuff you'd expect: who taught you magic, what they taught you, what happened during your initiations."

Jackson made a face. "I can tell you all of that," he said. "My masters broke faith with me by threatening to kill me. But because of operations security, I don't know much about the rest of the Order or what they're up to."

Jerry looked closely at Jackson, then nodded his approval. That had been an honest answer. "I have a personal question to ask you, sir. What are your intentions toward Janjan?"

An absurdly archaic question. Jackson would have laughed, but he saw that Jerry was serious. "She's your friend," Jackson said. "You don't want her hurt."

The two stopped walking. They stood in knee-high emerald-green grass with small blue flowers scattered here and there. Jerry looked at Jackson calmly and directly, interested in whatever he would have to say and how he would say it.

For some reason the question made Jackson sweat, although the day was only warm. "I ... want to be with her," he finally said. Such a weak-ass thing to say. He was too embarrassed to look Jerry in the face, as if caring for someone was shameful. It certainly was among the Materialist Magicians.

Jerry wouldn't let up. "You know she also likes girls, right?"

"*So?*" Jackson found the question insulting, but he wasn't stupid enough to start a fight with an elf warrior over it. "Dude, we're *dating*. We're *exclusive* now." The words sounded childish and demeaning in his own ears.

Jackson was astonished to see Jerry smiling broadly.

Jerry clapped Jackson's arm. "Good!" he said. Then in Elvish, "*May you both have every happiness, brother.*"

Jackson had often been cursed in his life, but he had no memory of anyone blessing him before. Not with words of power that shone and beckoned.

And ironically, no one in the Brotherhood had ever called him "brother."

❋

Jerry and Jackson headed back toward the grove where they'd left the others.

"Are you and Leda coming back to the fae-path with us?" Jackson said.

Jerry shook his head. "Impossible. We can't see the Fae. The path you walk with them is mostly invisible to us. Haven't you and Janjan talked about this?"

Jackson looked unhappy. "The Order wanted me to send anyone who came seeking the elves to the Fae instead. I was going to make Bobby a permanent doorway from Portsmouth to the fae-road. I might have gone ahead with it if I hadn't seen Simon gathering his magic to kill me."

"How many people did you end up diverting to the Fae?"

"Hundreds for sure. Maybe a few thousand, tops? I'm not proud of it!" Jackson felt the old anger that he'd carried around since boyhood, and the despair beneath it.

"Well, except for Bobby, you offered everyone a *choice*, right?" said Jerry. "How'd you like to be able to give them—and the rest of the Fae, too—a chance to choose again, to return to Earth, if they want?"

That brought Jackson up short. "Really? What would I have to do?" He was ashamed of how much hope he felt. He'd been taught there was no hope, only fear.

"If you're willing, I'll give you a *mandala* to take on the fae-path with you. Think of it as a riddle to solve, one that's painted into your flesh and bone. I won't lie, it'll hurt."

Jackson shrugged. He couldn't imagine Jerry would give his body more pain than Simon and the Fallen had given his mind and spirit. "Let's do it," he said.

Moving slow enough not to startle him, Jerry placed his hand flat on Jackson's sternum. In his mind, Jackson heard the elf's voice: *Will you trust me in your thoughts?*

43

The Catcher in the Fae

The sun was low in the sky when Jerry and Jackson got back to the grove. Time for the earthlings to return to the Fae.

Bobby and Beth were unhappy. I was scared. Leda was concerned for us, but not upset. Bitch that I am, I resented her for that. Jerry was also at peace, a man who'd done what he came here to do. I resented him, too. The elves were pissing me off just by being themselves.

And Jackson? He looked *happy*, a man who'd been given a second chance. I thought, *Is he going to leave me now?* Yes, I was ashamed of the thought.

I was glad we were going back. Jackson and I needed to talk, and I didn't want to do it where Jerry and Leda could hear our voices—or our thoughts. Is it so wrong that I wanted them to think well of me? Is it so wrong that I didn't want to be *accountable* to them, even though they'd just saved my life?

We left the grove as three very different couples. Jerry and Leda went first, side by side, unafraid, relying on each other. *Oh yeah, that's right*, I thought, *they're married*. They were alert for anything that might pose a threat—not to themselves, but to us. And they both knew everything that had happened while they were apart. I saw information flying between them like flocks of invisible birds. Some new sense had sprung from the symbol Leda had burned into my chest.

Then came Beth and Bobby, sad and confused. They walked with one arm wrapped around each other's waists.

Jackson and I brought up the rear. He slowed me down with a hand on my arm. He held his other hand on his chest, as if it hurt. He made a face and nodded at me: *You, too?*

I nodded back: *Yeah, me, too.*

"Jerry called it a *mandala*," Jackson said.

"Can we wait to talk about this?" I meant till we got back among the Fae.

"Fair point," Jackson said. He was bursting with news. Unusual for him, my secretive bad boy.

Or was he a devious, manipulative *evil* boy—and not mine at all?

We moved fast through the dusk. Jackson remembered exactly how we'd walked to the grove from the fae-road, the path Jerry and Leda couldn't see.

"I want to go *home*," Beth said. She sounded tired and frightened, like a little girl. "I want to go back to *Portsmouth*."

Leda said, "You can't *get* there from here, sweetie." The old New England joke was literally true in this world. Leda was being kind. *She* could get back to Portsmouth from here, but only because of what she'd learned in the next world over—where Beth refused to go. The only way Beth was going to get home was if I led her there on the fae-road.

"We have to go back to the Fae for a while, Beth," I said. I was feeling panicky, because I knew my ordinary breathing was going to slow almost to a stop as soon as I stepped off this empty world.

Jackson took my hand and led me across the little stream. I took Beth by the hand and led her. Bobby held onto Beth's other hand, not wanting to go back to the Fae, but unwilling to let her go and have to stay here alone.

Before the four of us stepped onto the path (shining to us now, but invisible to Jerry and Leda), I turned my head around and said, stupidly, "Bye." I meant something like *thank you* and something like *help me* and something like *let this cup pass from me.*

Leda, who read my mind, knew what I meant. She said, "You know what to do, Janjan. Go with God." She was totally sincere and totally serious. Nothing like *that* ever came out of Leda's sarcastic mouth before. She'd moved on and I hadn't. I felt the great gulf between what I was and what Leda had become.

Jerry said in Elvish, *"Jackson my brother, Janjan my sister, we thank you for going where we cannot to do what we cannot."* Obviously nothing like *that* ever came out of Jerry's mouth before, either.

All this pressure on me was pretty fucking scary, if you want to know. Call me the Catcher in the Fae.

44

Weary, Stale, Flat, and Unprofitable

With the Elvish blessing still shining in the dusk behind us, Jackson and I gently pushed Beth and Bobby ahead of us onto the fae-road. They needed someone to tell them what to do.

This time I noticed when my mode of breathing changed. I managed not to fight for more air as Jackson and I joined Beth and Bobby on the path. People needed my help, and I didn't have time to panic just because I'd started to breathe with...such...excruciating ... *slowness*. Nobody *knew* they needed my help, but still.

One step onto the road and already the scenery on either side of it had changed. It had been twilight in the fields of the world we'd stepped out of. What we saw two steps later was daylight on mountains. I was less awed and thrilled this time. Too much TV had probably eroded my sense of wonder about the magical fae condition of being. I wondered if I would live to read another book. Suddenly I wanted nothing more than a quiet afternoon alone on the couch with one of Lee Child's Reacher novels and a cup of hot chocolate.

Standing on the fae-road again bucked Bobby up considerably; at least it was a place he knew. He smiled at Beth and rubbed her back affectionately with one big hand. This, in turn, made Beth pull herself mostly together. She put one arm around his waist and smiled back at him

Bobby glowed with greenish fae-light that no longer shone in Jackson. Huh.

As Maeve had said, the wind was always at the back of the Fae. So we, too, walked with the wind at our back, hoping we'd catch up to Coran and Maeve and all the rest somehow.

Jackson and I lagged behind our friends so we could talk privately.

"We don't seem to be heading back toward Portsmouth," Jackson said.

"I don't know what else to do right now," I said. "Getting home is going to be kind of a problem, isn't it?"

"I think we'll be able to find our way back." He tapped his breastbone and winced. "Jerry August gave me what he called a *mandala*. Burned into my chest. Hurt like hell. I can still feel it."

"Leda gave me one, too, before we all first came here. She said it was some sort of riddle I had to solve. I hadn't thought it might also be, like, a *homing device* until I called her with it."

Jackson looked at me, considering. "We can't wait for the Fae to stroll around the entire World Mountain to get back to Portsmouth again," he said. "Bobby was with them for eighty years between the Civil War and World War II, then for maybe another seventy years until you found him."

Bobby turned, grinned at us, and waved. He was happy to see we were still there. The man had no guile. Jackson and I waved back. We all kept walking and the road rose to meet our feet as if grateful for our presence.

"Why the ten year difference?" I said.

Jackson shrugged. "The Fae set their own pace. They have forever to get wherever they want to go and no particular destination to reach. They're happy wherever they end up." He paused. "I'm just speculating here. I mean, night after night they kept showing up in Great Bog for me and Bobby. Dunno *where* they went in the meantime."

We fell silent for a few long minutes. The scope of the problem struck me. It was impossible. Why, I wondered, had I not just left Bobby to freeze in the bushes back in Great Bog? Why didn't I listen to my girly-sense when it told me to drive my big white ass out of scary, precarious Portsmouth and back to safe, boring Buffalo? Why had I not told Jackson *It's not you, it's me* and extricated myself from this situation he'd gotten me into with those Very Bad Guys, the Materialist Magicians? I mean, hadn't Leda *warned* me?

I was the first to break our pleasant silence, of course I was. "I notice that Jerry didn't kill you," I said. Then to salve Jackson's ego, I added. "And you didn't kill him, either."

He gave me a wry look. "Like I *could* kill an elf. Those people got mad skills, yo. Are you wondering if I'm still part of the Order of Materialist Magicians?"

"Well, Scary Simon did say you weren't allowed to quit..."

Jackson stopped walking. He held me at arm's length and did something that surprised us both.

"*Look at me,*" he said.

And he opened his heart.

45

Hedged In

Why is light given to a man whose way is hid, and whom God hath hedged in?
The Book of Job

You think you *might* want something. Then you get it and it's kind of, well, *weird*. Like life itself, maybe, or at least like life in Portsmouth. Jackson opened his heart to me very literally. No, he didn't crack open his chest like a painting of Jesus revealing the Sacred Heart. Nothing much happened on the physical level.

I didn't know what to expect or what to do. Nobody had ever trusted me so completely before. How could I back away from him or do less than he did? His act of pure courage shamed my reluctance away.

There on the fae-path Jackson and I confronted each other. From forty paces away, Beth and Bobby sensed something happening behind them, stopped walking, and turned to watch. They wouldn't have seen much. All the action was happening inside us.

With our hearts open, I saw Jackson's light reflected in my own. I saw him see me within him. *Then shall I know even as also I am known:* I guess it was like that. There was only *knowing*, not of images in a mirror, but of real things. Realer-than-real things.

Once I'd seen a stain in Jackson from the same kind of shadow that wrapped Simon like a filthy blanket. All trace of that shadow-stain was gone. *That* was real enough.

Once I'd seen the fae-light in Jackson, dancing green and inconstant in the corner of my mind's eye. No more. Now in the center of his chest I saw a moving, changing symbol of three dimensions, maybe more. It was etched in clear elf-light and in his pain as my symbol had been etched in light and in my own hurt. Both symbols whirled and changed in my inner vision.

I saw Jackson's symbol and I saw him see mine. His *mandala* was as much a riddle to him as mine was to me. The symbols interpenetrated the realm of dreams. Their roots extended into the deep mind where all desire comes from, where reason can't go.

So much wisdom flowed through us that it was like trying to drink from a fire hose.

I did what I knew to do. I hugged him hard, put my incomprehensible symbol up against his, or as close as I could get since he was taller than me. Seeing what I wanted and wanting the same thing, my lover bent his knees and half lifted me off the ground. Woof.

And together we *saw* things. Fragments of lives, ours and others'. Fantasies, dreams, current realities? Neither of us knew what they meant; they moved too fast. Then:

A life on the Dark Path. Deep within a mile-square mill or factory on some world, not Earth, a muscular shaven-headed man with stunned eyes and a lobotomy scar is controlled by a snakelike electrical leash around his head. Holding the semi-sentient leash is an elaborately-dressed woman with cold cruel eyes. She is his mistress. He is her devoted bodyguard and selfless sexual plaything.

A life on the Other World. Deep within a pregnant woman's womb, an embryo is touched by a winged sky god and his earth goddess. The child grows to vigorous maturity and is trained to serve the Old Gods as a Myrmidon warrior. Though barren, the Myrmidon will have great physical strength and both male and female sexual organs.

Those flashes of vision shocked us apart; we let go of each other. We were part of something larger than ourselves, something that resisted understanding. What did the Dark Path have to do with Jackson? What did the Myrmidons have to do with me? It wasn't just weird, it was terrifying.

That all happened in a few long seconds. Holding on to each other for balance, we walked toward Beth and Bobby on shaky legs.

Seeing that we'd resumed walking, they smiled at whatever they'd seen on the surface of us. *Look how cute Janjan and Jackson are, they have to stop walking to hug, can't get enough of each other.* Beth and Bobby walked ahead of us. They were bound together by something intimately human but also strange, nonhuman, unearthly.

Jackson and I were a couple, too, bound together by something intimate and strange, but completely human. Except maybe for that last nightmare part.

"Are you thinking what I'm thinking?" Jackson said.

"I think I am," I said. "Sort of, anyway. Assuming what I see of you in here (I pointed to my chest) is anything like how you really are—and I'm not just making it all up."

"It's ... a lot to take in," he said. He sounded sad.

I rubbed one hand up and down his warm, hard back. "I don't know whether I'm happy or sad."

"We're in the right place for that," he said. "I feel bad for the Fae, stuck with the bitter, always chasing the sweet."

"You feel bad for yourself," I said. He looked like I'd sucker-punched him. "Hey, I feel bad for *my*self, too," I hastened to add. "Nothing—and I mean *nothing*—is going to work out the way we thought it would."

"What do you mean?"

"Look at Jerry and Leda. All they wanted was to live in Portsmouth, keep their jobs, get married, have kids. You know—have regular lives?"

"So why couldn't they just *do* that?" Was he being deliberately obtuse? He'd been pretty sweet to me through most of our time together. Was he about to reveal the inner asshole, the darker personal side, all the ugly male behavior he'd been hiding that would make me hate him?

I gave him *the look*. "Think about it. *You guys* kept coming after them. Would they have been safe from the Materialist Magicians anywhere on Earth? Ever?"

Jackson's expression was somewhere between amused and sour. "They were safe enough from *me*—after the elves kicked my ass, I mean." He saw in my face that I wanted a real answer. "Nah, you're right. The Order would've hunted them down however long it took—because we thought Quincy August and the Old Gods needed them. Plus they were friends of the elves. We were all taught to kill elves on sight, to prevent people from going home with the elves, and to eliminate all known elf assets on Earth. It's so *stupid*. We—I mean *they* can't win. It's impossible."

He was getting there, but slowly. "Jackson," I said, "at some point you and I will be going back to Earth, back to Portsmouth. When we get there, what are we going to *do*?"

"Whatever we do, I don't think we'll be living regular lives, Janjan. I'm not sure how to keep the Order from killing us."

Finally he'd gotten there. Jesus, men can be dense. "We'll do whatever we have to do," I said. "Will you stay with me while we do it?"

He looked at me and I looked back. "It's still you I want," he said. "I still can't explain it."

"*Do not inquire within*," I said. I guess he'd seen those real estate signs, too. We laughed together, or did what the Fae do in place of laughter, given the imperceptible slowness of their breathing. The amusement went on and on inside both of us the same way both men and women had orgasms here, in waves.

Whatever kind of lives we ended up living, I didn't think we'd be calling a real estate agent and buying our dream house together anytime soon.

But I still wanted Jackson the way he wanted me. It wasn't just my *mandala* and my girly-sense that were tingling.

46

A Long, Long Trail A-Winding

There's a long, long trail a-winding
Into the land of my dreams,
Where the nightingales are singing
And a white moon beams...

Stoddard King, "There's a Long, Long Trail"

"I want *you*," I said. I really did. Elf and fae magic hadn't hurt my libido a bit.

Jackson, it quickly became clear, wanted me right then and there. He grinned at me. Such a look. Talk about bedroom eyes. Not to mention. Woof.

We walked on slowly, looking around for a place where we might find a bit of privacy and enjoy each other. Was that perhaps a fae castle looming up in the dusk ahead? In fact it was, and there were two more at the side of the road, the second castle only a mile past the first, and the third a mile or two beyond the second.

Bobby was thinking like us. He turned back to us and pointed emphatically at the first castle. Beth had been through a lot; they both needed a night's rest. I wasn't surprised they wanted to find shelter now, wherever the rest of the Fae might be.

The castle looked like the one where we'd spent our first night among the Fae. Turrets and towers and walls and battlements. No moat around the outside, and a sweetwater well inside the walls. Who were their enemies that they built castles? I wondered. On the other hand, the castle looked more like decoration than protection, so maybe long ago they'd built places that reminded them of home, all based on the same design. Beth and Bobby waved to us and walked through the castle gate out of our sight.

I had lurid fantasies of a lovely, sleepless night in which Jackson would take his pleasure alone with me in every room of the castle. I might take a bit of pleasure for myself along the way. Oh, who am I kidding, a lot of pleasure, in every possible way.

Ugh, we have no birth control, I remembered. Before I could recalibrate my fantasies, a troop of Fae on horseback came trotting up to the castle. They came from *behind us*, from the direction of the wind that was always at our back. Riding at the head of the troop were Coran and Maeve.

"Have they really traveled all the way around the World Mountain already?" I said. It upset me to think such a thing was possible.

"In a single day, it seems," Jackson said.

I glared at him, thinking he was teasing, but he side-hugged me to him. Have I mentioned he was pretty strong? "I'm thinking the fae-road itself is some kind of magic," he added. "Not, you understand, that I know exactly what kind or how it works. But my teachers always said the beginning of all magic is *knowing what you want*."

"So ... the Fae wanted to catch up to us, and they did?"

He shrugged. "I think we'll get to ask Coran and Maeve. If we're going to succeed them as king and queen, maybe they'll *want* to answer our questions."

47

Too Soon Oldt, Too Late Schmardt

Ve grow too soon oldt und too late schmardt.
Pennsylvania Dutch saying on a souvenir plate
in Janjan and Beth's Portsmouth kitchen

We followed Coran and Maeve into their castle. Beth and Bobby were waiting in the great hall to pay their respects to the royals. Funny how quickly we'd all fallen in with the local customs. Beth curtseyed and Bobby bowed; neither of them asked any questions. They were too tired and sad to care about the whys and wherefores of what had happened to them. Off they went to find a bed.

In through the wide-open doors came a happy mob of Fae. They, too, curtsied or bowed to the royal couple; it went very briskly, like a receiving line. I wondered how it was decided who slept where. I figured that Coran and Maeve had their own quarters, wherever they spent the night, and that they personally chose who would dine with them at the head table. And who would share their bed. Everyone else slept wherever they liked with whoever struck their fancy.

I figured right. Coran ordered that he and the queen would be served supper in the royal bedchamber—and that *Jackson and I* would be their guests this evening. It didn't sound like the kind of invitation we should decline. Did dinner commit us to sex? I wondered. Dancing in the great hall would go on without the four of us tonight. Affairs of state.

We were all feeling fresh as daisies now that we'd walked through the Chamber of Mists. I'd been so gobsmacked my first night among the Fae that I'd walked through the place without realizing I was being gently rained on. You have to figure that even in a world where breath scarcely stirred in our lungs, and where we didn't so much speak as seem to speak, and where we didn't so much eat as seem to have eaten, and therefore (magically?) never needed to relieve ourselves, and where we walked all day without breaking a sweat, there would still be dust settling on our mortal bodies. The mist served to clean our slightly-soiled selves and our clothes as well. More magic, I suppose.

Even the horses were led through the chamber and then off to their stables. They snorted happily, glad to be clean and cool again. Very gentle, these horses. And forgive me for getting all H.P. Lovecraft here, but the fae horses' eyes were too *knowing* for mere beasts: *eldritch* is what they were. I looked once, then looked away. *A horse walks into a bar...* I thought.

Given all the sex they had, I'm sure the Fae practiced some sort of sexual hygiene. I hadn't had any sex here yet, so I hadn't had to think about that.

I was thinking about it now, though. The four of us climbed a long staircase that led to Maeve and Coran's room above the main floor. Jackson and I lagged behind the royal couple and conferred privately, leaning our heads close together.

"They *want* something from us," I said.

"Yeah, they want us to succeed them," he said.

"I get the feeling there's gonna be a *quid pro quo* before there's any transfer of power."

"What do you mean, exactly?"

"Unless I flatter myself, I think Maeve wants, well, *me*."

"Are you talking just sex or a relationship here?" Interesting question.

"Probably just sex, but it's hard to say for sure. My girly-sense has been tingling since we left Portsmouth."

Jackson stopped on the stairs and I stopped with him. "If Coran decides he wants *me*, will you hate me if I say yes to him? And what if he wants both of us and Maeve as well?"

I couldn't answer. That was a lot to think about. I had mixed feelings about sleeping with somebody else while Jackson and I were supposedly exclusive. We were kind of new as a couple to start adding other people into the mix. And hadn't I made this mistake before? That's the trouble with thinking what you want is identical to what your lover or lovers want.

I worried that our voices might echo off the stone walls and the timbered ceiling, but ... our actual voices never quite got out of our throats, did they? Weird, but I'd gotten used to it. All my ears heard were echoes from our soft footfalls on the stone-and-timber stairway. The castle below us was filling up with the *sense* of a crowd without the usual talking, shouting, and laughter of a crowd. Some mental equipment seemed to register lots of people and the sense of distant, muffled conversations and amusement.

The royal chamber featured enough floor space for a dance floor and a DJ. Naturally there was none of that; we weren't in da club here. Instead of cocktail tables there was a sturdy wooden table, spread with a fine beige linen tablecloth, old but spotless. The table was big enough for eight, and there were eight chairs. Coran and Jackson moved four of them to one of the walls, so the four of us would have plenty of elbow room.

Hot-eyed, envious fae girls and boys waited upon the king and queen and also upon us, the royals' guests. We ate and drank well, or at least in retrospect seemed to have done so. Honestly, I felt a little intimidated by the royals, though less nervous than I'd felt when I'd had to explain some silly technical issue to an ambitious Navy officer with a short attention span.

Jackson and I let Maeve and Coran lead the conversation. Their talk, and therefore ours, was mostly gossip and trivialities. Still, we learned a lot about what fae life was like by listening to our hosts, nodding politely, and asking an occasional question. The king and queen had mastered the royal art of making us feel at ease, if not quite at home.

Things got decidedly less cordial once the servers had carried away the empty plates. (What had we dined upon? I was no longer hungry, but couldn't remember what I'd eaten.) They left us our cups and two full wine pitchers, but I couldn't tell you if I'd been drinking dry red or slightly-sweeter white. It could have been syrupy golden mead for all I knew.

And now to business. Coran said to Jackson, "You've *changed* since I last saw you, magician. What's happened?" Coming from the scowling king that sounded like an accusation.

"I'm sorry, sir," Jackson said, "I don't understand."

Coran mastered his temper. "When you came to us, I recognized Eamonn's *light of other days* shining in you. That light is now *gone* from you."

Jackson put his hand on his chest, over his invisible mandala. He was thinking about Coran's question, and he was also *inquiring within*.

"While I was off the road in that empty world," Jackson finally said, "I met a friend of Janjan's. He was one of those we on Earth call 'elves', although that's not really what they are. Do you know of these people?"

"*No!*" said Coran and Maeve in unison. They were terrible liars, even worse than Bobby. It was like the time I walked in on an old boyfriend in *my* bed, between the thighs of a girl I'd thought was *my friend*. "It's not what you think!" he'd said, which was pretty fucking hilarious. After I got over him.

Jackson looked at me mildly. I returned his mild look. We managed not to laugh.

"In any event," Jackson said, "I asked Janjan's friend to help me protect myself from the people who want to kill me. He did something to *all* the light in me that hurt badly for a while." He looked up at Coran. "Do you think the elf did something to the ... light Eamonn bequeathed to me?" It was an honest question. Jackson didn't know what Jerry had done to him any more than I knew what Leda had done to me. We both had puzzles to solve.

Coran looked at Maeve. She said nothing. She was busy looking at me.

Finally Coran said, "Ah, it may be as you say, lad, it may be. Even we who live and rule in these mysteries do not fully understand them."

Maeve finally spoke. To me. Speaking of hot eyes, hers were all over me. "We have invited you to our bedchamber to teach you ... all we *do* know so that you may become worthy to rule the Fae. Come with me. We'll let the men talk awhile."

48

The Airborne Toxic Event Sings "Sometime Around Midnight"

Things got weird outside the bedroom.

Jackson didn't want Janjan to go with Maeve, but he didn't see a way around it. Obedience to authority was the path to power with the Fae, just as it was with the Order. Obedience and sex got you a negotiated agreement with death.

Do not go gently... His magical apprenticeship taught him that nobody went gently into that good night. Materialist Magicians went into a night that was anything but good. He'd heard rumors about the Dark Path, whatever that meant. The elves *did* go gently—into mystery; nobody knew where elflords went in the highlands of clear light.

So what happened here on the fae-path where you could live forever? Jackson watched the queen lead his lover behind a curtain. Now what?

When Jackson turned back to the king, he saw Coran regarding him with obvious interest. Studying him intently, though not unkindly: watching Jackson watch Janjan walk away. Jackson wondered if his thoughts and feelings were visible to Coran.

"When you're king of the Fae," said Coran, "you may find yourself swiving with men and women both. This is but one way Maeve and I show favor to those who follow and obey us."

Jackson said, "I've pleasured both men and women. I prefer women." *Kind of an understatement*, he thought.

Coran indicated the curtain with a nod of his head. "Give them time to get acquainted with one another. We'll join the ladies in a bit. But first, let's see what kind of man you are. Strip off for me, lad." Kings needn't worry about the preferences of their subjects.

Jackson stood up. He'd done this before, but had never liked it much. The old familiar numbness filled him up as he took off shirt, pants, and boots. It was like being under anesthesia, except that a low heat began to kindle at the bottom of his belly. He knew the numbness for shame and the heat for desire.

He stood naked before Coran, as relaxed as he could make himself. Under Coran's gaze, he felt himself becoming aroused. He blushed. Being desired by a woman was one thing, but being desired by a man—and desiring him back—was a transgression in the America where he'd grown up. His Brotherhood teachers had insisted on it, trying to bend Jackson's will to theirs—as their will was bent to the Claimant's.

Coran stood up and was naked in no time. "You'll do just fine, lad," he said. Jackson saw that the king was also aroused. He could think of nothing to say that wouldn't sound stupid. Simple impersonal lust turned rational thought into intermittent bursts of static.

But Coran's body was translucent, like an aquarium filled with darting green lights instead of fish. As if sexual excitement had accelerated the process transforming his ordinary flesh into sculpture illuminated from within. The king's hands, feet, and face now became semitransparent, shining like the rest of him.

It's only sex, Jackson thought, fighting for a moment of lucidity. *It's just sex*. But he knew it was never *just* sex. It was always something else as well, sometimes need, sometimes power, sometimes affection, sometimes even love, who ever knew? He was fascinated by Coran. He wanted him and he despised this desire in himself. Irrational, perhaps. Didn't Janjan desire Maeve and other women? Stupid question. Who would *not* desire women? Earth, at least, was full of double standards.

But all that aside, here was the king of the Fae standing before him ready for ... something, all shining bone and muscle, phallus turgid with bloodlight. It was fascinating how Jackson could sometimes see it and then sometimes see through it. *Jesus wants me for a sunbeam*, he thought, remembering a children's hymn from Sunday school in some Southern city.

The relevant question was one that was always in the air whenever there was a prospect of two men having intimate relations. Who would do what to whom and in what order? He and the king were not equals, not in Coran's kingdom.

Without warning, a decision *arrived* in Jackson's heart and mind. The *mandala* in his chest thrummed with it. He was tempted to ignore the impulse, strong as it was, the way he'd ignored his own healthy impulse to flee from the caves before Simon took over his volition. The tension between free will and old habit was excruciating. But Jackson had laid the foundation for this choice when he let Jerry August paint the *mandala* into his body.

Firmly but gently, Jackson took hold of the king by his radiant member. Coran gasped, as what man would not. A drop of liquid light gathered at the tip of his thick translucent glans.

"Follow me, if you would, please," Jackson said and led Coran through the scarlet curtains that separated the men from the women.

261

49

When She Came Near

Just now when she came near I thought I heard
Other small steps beating upon the floor,
And a faint music blowing in the wind,
Invisible pipes giving her feet the time.

W.B. Yeats, *The Land of Heart's Desire*

Things also got weird inside *the bedroom.*

Beckoning me to follow with the utter certainty I would obey her, Maeve left the dining table. Gulp. The way she walked made her hips rock like a model's; her ass drew my eye. Woof.

I looked back at Jackson. For what? *Permission?* We'd only started discussing this. I wasn't sure we were on the same page, or even in the same book. There was a way we knew each other completely, but in so many other ways we were strangers.

The real inside of another human being is more otherworldly than even the fae-road, and you can quote me on that.

But after hesitating a moment, Jackson nodded as if to say *Go with her. Do what you have to do and so will I.* At least that's how I interpreted his nod. It seemed to me we were still a couple, still exclusive, but that *exigent circumstances*, as they say in the Navy, were about to modify the terms of our romantic agreement.

It broke my heart a little that Jackson went along with me on this. Did I want him to save me from my slooty self? Be all, like, *Unhand my ladylove, thou Sapphic villainess*?

And if Jackson turned out to be my slooty soulmate and as bisexual as I was, would I still respect him in the morning? Or did I want him to be some kind of clueless, possessive, exclusively-straight dude, all dick and no brain, with eyes only for me? I'm kind of a bitch, but I'd always thought I was free of sexual double standards.

We'd see, right?

Maeve disappeared behind scarlet curtains that divided the dining area of the bedchamber from the sleeping area. I followed her, feeling the old familiar signs of physical excitement. If my coma-patient-suspended-animation breathing speeded up at all, I couldn't tell.

The queen stood at the foot of the bed, her hands on her hips, watching me with those hot, dark eyes of hers.

She held out one long-fingered hand to me. I could almost feel her touch on my skin. "You may disrobe for me, child." Her voice, or my impression of it, was as gentle as her manner.

Oh, *may* I? And *child*, was it? I smiled inside. Maeve seemed to want to take charge of the proceedings and teach me things. We'd see who ended up teaching who. She might have been older than anyone on Earth, but I'd had many different kinds of sex in my short life.

But oh lucky me, I was happy to undress for her! It excited me. For a little fat girl from Buffalo, I was something of an exhibitionist. I never got the memo about the requirement for female physical perfection. You never know when you'll encounter someone who is delighted with everything he (or she) sees. If you don't get naked whenever you can, you never find out who was looking for you all along but didn't know it. I'd never regretted taking Jackson to bed the first night we ever met, for example, and *he* seemed to find my body very much to his liking.

So I laid my lacy fae garments across a chair, left my thin shoes under it, and barefoot I walked up to Maeve, all the while holding her gaze.

If there's such a thing as a Moment, I'm pretty sure we were having one. Her hands dropped to her sides. Her expression said she wanted me. She was half a head taller than me. I went up on tiptoe, rested my hands gently on her slender hips, and slowly, slowly kissed her neck.

I whispered in her ear "May I disrobe *you*, Maeve?"

Older women are easy. Her lips parted in a subvocal *Oh*. She began to tremble; I could feel it through my hands at her waist. But her answer surprised me.

"Ah, so young and beautiful you are, I feel quite a hag next to you." She sounded so sad and weary it broke my heart. But she was excited, too. Would she try to deny it? "Turn around," she said. "I'll undress meself and then we'll see who still wants who."

Tingling, I turned away. Maeve really knew how to build sexual suspense. Was I really feeling her gaze on my thick ass? The only thing that would have made me hotter right now would be if Jackson could join us. And what the hell, Coran too, now that my blood was up.

I heard her moving close behind me, heard the sounds of cloth against skin. I was thinking that although I'd nuzzled her neck and hair, I still didn't know what she *smelled* like. Yeah, I know that's a silly thing to focus on, given that I was naked here in a world that wasn't Earth in front of a woman who was probably older than Jesus. It was like the way I *had a sense* of what people had said or meant to say. And I *had a sense* of what the fine food and wine had tasted like. But breathing as the Fae did eliminated the sense of smell the way we know it on Earth, direct and primitive. Men smell wonderful. Women smell a different kind of wonderful, as those of us who appreciate both genders can attest.

Finally Maeve said, "Turn and look at me, child." It sounded like she dreaded the moment I would see her.

I turned.

She held her naked arms out to the side, palms toward me. And now I saw that her body was partly transparent and filled with light. That light shone down into her hands and feet. All of the queen was darting green light within. I saw her limned by moving energy, lit by sparklers.

For all that strangeness, though, she was beautiful. There was a way I could both see and not see her, but everything I saw was lovely. The hair on her head had become a clear rainbow, lit from within. Her shining breasts were as high and firm as any girl's. There was no slack flesh on her strong and shining legs and no fat on her illuminated belly. The hair on her mound glowed like filaments of light. And although I could not smell her desire and had not yet felt it, I saw her inner heat burning with the queen's own inner fire.

"So beautiful," I said, holding her gaze so she'd know I meant it.

"I have wanted you since first I saw you," Maeve said. "Since I was a girl at the dawn of time I have had few liaisons with girls. I preferred men and swived with them almost exclusively, although sometimes Coran and I have taken a boy *and* a girl into our bed together. Coran, you see, prefers me to all others, but sometimes enjoys a young man." She nodded toward the curtain; I got the idea. Coran was enjoying Jackson. I found the idea less exciting than a liberated American girl really should. Was I jealous?

I spoke gently. "What is it that you want from me?" I know it was cruel and coquettish, but I wanted to demonstrate my mastery of her by making her ask for what she wanted. In detail.

Slowly, Maeve dropped to her knees in front of me. On the way down, she managed to touch her face to both of my breasts, not by accident, and stroked my belly with first one cheek and then the other.

Honestly, I practically came to climax right there.

The queen looked up into my eyes from where she knelt, not quite smiling, her face full of need. If her position implied supplication, there was no humility in it.

"I want…to put my mouth on you," she said. Okay, now she sounded ashamed of her own desire. Good, that's what I wanted, not the humiliation, but the honesty. If we were going to be lovers, even for a night, I wanted her to tell me everything. Some people like to make you guess what they want; I don't play that.

"What will you do *then*?" I said. This question was partly practical. If you're at all familiar with the female body, you'll understand the difficulty of attempting to use your mouth to pleasure a standing woman from the front. She tried to cast her eyes downwards, but I held her face gently with both my hands, forcing her to hold my gaze.

"May I *show* you?" Ah, she asked so humbly; that's what I'd been waiting for.

I smiled. "You may." There was a certain charm in letting her fool around down there awkwardly, knowing that before long she'd probably be begging me to spread my legs apart or scooch down or move my naughty bits onto the bed, or simply ask me to turn around so she could tongue me from the back while I bent over. I closed my eyes and let her start to show me.

But.

I felt her tongue sliding, sliding, sliding further than ought to have been possible. It felt weird. Good, but weird. Jesus, was the woman a *giraffe*, or something?

I opened my eyes and looked down at Maeve. No man is a hypocrite in his pleasures, said Samuel Johnson. Neither is a woman.

Maeve, I now saw, was not altogether a woman. And it wasn't just pleasure she was going for.

Her eyes had grown larger, relocated, and taken on an angle like no eyes I'd ever seen in a human face.

Her ears had grown tall, narrow, and pointed.

She'd been taller than me when she first kneeled in front of me. Now I couldn't fix her size clearly in my mind; she looked smaller than she ought to have been.

Her expression was clear enough, full of sharp, slippery ancient mischief, and there was nothing human in it. I remembered fairy tales about the Little People, and the Good People, how they stole children and what happened to those children.

Despite the sudden shock of fear, my excitement continued to mount. *That* was what Maeve wanted from me, the sexual crescendo. I knew bad things would come to me if I came. I trembled on the verge of it, anyway.

The *mandala* blazed a warning in my chest, but Maeve would still have gotten whatever she was after if Jackson hadn't interrupted us by walking naked through the curtains, tugging the naked king behind him by the royal penis, like a pull toy.

50

The Force That Through the Green Fuse Drives the Flower

For the thing which I greatly feared is come upon me,
and that which I was afraid of is come unto me.

The Book of Job

Speaking of Moments. One of Maeve's reconfigured eyes (now closer to the side of her newly-narrowed head) registered Jackson and Coran's arrival. Her tongue snapped (guiltily?) back into her mouth. She stood up quickly. As she did so, her burning-hot translucent nipples brushed against first my belly, then my breasts. I may have mentioned I was pretty hot myself. Again her touch almost brought me to climax, but her attention was on Coran, not on me.

Jackson released the King's penis, walked over, and threw his arms around me. And speaking of penises, Jackson's was firm against me. Right where it should be, I thought. Woof. He hugged me hard.

"I want *you*," he said softly or seemed to say. "I shouldn't have let you leave me, even for a moment. I'm sorry..."

"I want you, too," I said. "I'm so sorry I left you..."

We were shocked out of our little reconciliation, if that's what it was, by a second flare of light in the dimness of the royal bedchamber. Coran's body, also filled with darting lights, began to shift and change as he succumbed to his desire for Maeve. The king and queen became two shifting constellations of greenish energy. Their faces sharpened and the true size of their slippery bodies was impossible to see.

I know what you're thinking. Long tongues, green translucent skin, and pointy ears add up to something *reptilian* in earthly visual terms. But Coran and Maeve, as they flowed in graceful unison toward the royal bed, looked like nothing I knew of that had ever walked the Earth. Neither human nor animal; neither reptile nor insect.

They weren't repellant, whatever they were. Rather than evil and disgusting, they were weirdly beautiful.

The king and queen were filled up by their green desire, and it was way beyond anything like love or pleasure, or even mere lust, a human proclivity with which I am, ahem, intimately familiar. They were drawn together with the power of gravity, performing a dance as inevitable as Earth's seasons.

And *I was* drawn to Maeve and Coran as they clung together in a shape-shifting embrace. The things I would do to Maeve. The things I would have Coran do to me. Seeing that I wanted what they wanted, they beckoned me and Jackson to join them. I felt how deep their desire went and how piercing was the sadness that accompanied it. What bound them was the green-hued power that drove the fae-path and all the Fae upon it, ancient or newly-arrived, around and around the World Mountain forever.

Coran thrusts a thick root into the green and pouting leaves that open between Maeve's thighs. His eyes are locked with hers. They seem to whisper what might be endearments in what might be an ancient language. He withdraws savagely, bringing out a spray of verdant light that might be hers or his or both. Savagely he drives the green fuse once again into her. Now they turn like the graceful tide in flood. He drives from behind and Maeve seems to cry out.

In my body I felt faint echoes of what was happening in hers; I wanted to feel more of it and more intensely.

"We should go," Jackson said, breaking the fascination that held me to the spot.

I shook my head to clear it; that didn't work. My thoughts buzzed. My blood pooled in my loins. Seeing that I was hesitating, Jackson gathered up my clothes in one hand, threw his other arm around me, and hustled me, unresisting, away from Coran and Maeve.

Part of me very much wanted to say *Wait, wait wait*, wanted to stay and see what would happen. Another part of me very much wanted to persuade Jackson to join me on the bed with the king and queen. I knew I could do it simply by kneeling naked in front of him and, in perfect and disingenuous submission, taking as much as I could of him into my mouth and down my throat.

But the painful new intuition pulsing in my breastbone told me something else. "You're right," I told him. I told him other things, too, the kind of things lovers say to each other, things I wanted to do and have him do and why. I don't know if I was making any sense, but he knew exactly what I was talking about. His body told me how much he wanted what I wanted.

Jackson grabbed his clothes, along with mine as we hastened out of the royal bedchamber. There were no cries of sexual congress behind us now, but there were other sounds I recognized, along with noises I'd never heard before. My curiosity was mostly prurient, but not entirely. I mean, *what the hell was happening* back there? Could my eyes even perceive it?

The two of us found ourselves an empty room with an empty bed, clean and waiting—for us if we liked. Still standing up, we embraced and kissed deeply. You know how you crave each other's mouth so much that you can hardly bear to get on with what comes next?

As we held each other, I closed my eyes and accepted the fullness of whatever it was my *mandala* had been trying to tell me when we were across the hall with Coran and Maeve. I looked into myself. I saw why so many people take *Do not inquire within* as a guiding principle.

In that same flash of insight, I saw Jackson accept what his *mandala* had been saying to him. I saw him see it; he saw me see that.

Chest to chest we held each other. Heart to heart, *mandala* to *mandala,* we beheld each other. We had the same insight in the same moment. We had the same experience. We saw, impossibly, that our minds were, not two, but one.

We moved apart, but still held each other's hands, unwilling to be any further apart than that, needing to hold on to each other. The movement mirrored a step in the graceful fae-dance. On Earth we would have been breathing hard, but not here where we were still *breathing in for half of eternity.* We looked at each other wordlessly, thinking all the stupid things you think when something impossible happens.

Did you see what I saw? Did you see me see you see it? How is that possible? And so on. So many layers of questions we were afraid to admit we already had answers to.

We were shaken all the way to our unsuspected depths. *The elves left their mark on us and did it with our consent,* I thought. *Our lives will never be the same again,* I thought. *We'll never be the same again.*

Was I bitter? Yeah, maybe a little. Hope tastes bitter when you think you're entitled to whatever you want in life with no more effort than it takes to be your own sweet self. But at least the confusion was gone. I knew what had to be done next.

Was Jackson bitter? Not even a little. What he'd been before was nothing he wanted to go back to. For him, hope and purpose were enough.

51

To See Ourselves as Others See Us

Standing naked, embracing naked Janjan, then holding her hands at arm's length, Jackson was filled up with the joy of looking at her. She took the same kind pleasure in the sight of him. They saw together and everything they beheld was good. Janjan was dazzled, wondering how such a thing could be.

Jackson had been pulled unwillingly into shared perception before; he knew there was no ordinary sense to be made of it. Having Simon overpower his will was horrible. Instant demon-powered travel with Simon was worse. These initiations wounded Jackson's mind and spirit, sent something wrong within him.

When the Walloon sent him back to Portsmouth, Jackson was relieved to be with normal people like Beth, Bobby, and Janjan. They accepted him for what he seemed to be. Even after they learned he wasn't a good guy, they *still* hadn't shunned him, Jackson thought, because they couldn't see what he was like inside. They couldn't see what Jackson had become as a result of what he'd chosen and what had then been done to him.

Now, standing barefoot on the cool wooden floor of the fae castle, Janjan saw all of that in him. They swam together, as it seemed, in a great pillar of light, the clear light of vision. Janjan saw what he was inside and didn't run from him. *He saw her see these things in him:*

Fragments of his boyhood in military bases and small towns across the South and West. All the schools he'd attended because the family moved so often. A few friendships, eventually discarded. A few sexual partners, unsatisfactory. The college where he'd failed to find himself. How he'd gone looking for someone who would accept and approve of him; how he'd found the illusion of that with a Materialist Magician recruiter.

His ordination into the false priesthood of the Brotherhood. His magical education and discipleship. The promise of real power. The hideous reality of *whose* power it was: the essential fact Jackson had tried to deny, because it required the defilement of free will. In the Fallen he saw fear's face unmasked.

His work for Jerry's uncle Quincy August. His timeless time in the company of the Other World god and goddess, speaking the Old Gods' language. How the language of dreams gave him temporary advantage over even the elves, because it came out of the elves' blind spot. The elves who saw so much in all the human worlds found the Other World screened off from them by ancient magic that erased the barrier between the perceiver and the object of perception.

Things he saw (and she saw him see them):

Flashes of Janjan's sheltered Catholic childhood in Buffalo. Her realization that people lied and told stories to make themselves feel better. Her religious indoctrination, ethics mostly accepted, dogma mostly rejected, calls to chastity or marriage quickly dismissed. Her compassion for others. Her stubbornness. Her curiosity. Her sensuality.

Her troubled high school years. Her sexual exploration. Her romantic disappointments. Her need *to get out of Buffalo* at all costs. The certainty that there had to be more than marriage, children, church, and working the same shift at Target with Mom. Her happy college years. Her intellectual opening and sensual blossoming. The learning she'd kept and the men she'd left or who'd foolishly left her.

Her friendships. Her loyalty and kindness. Her work and her commitment to it. Her doubts about relationships, work, marriage—and even her own worth.

Jackson saw Janjan face to face. He knew her as he was known. Janjan saw him abandon the magical attempt to control perception. He accepted a new perception that shone through both their minds and through their bodies, too.

The elves had the same kindness and sensuality Jackson found so compelling in Janjan. They swam in the sea of life, sporting like dolphins, helping others for the joy of it. The elves accepted the clear light that shone through them: *that* was the source of their power.

Using that power, employing the natural law that manifested it, Jerry August had taken Jackson's single silver earring and etched a mysterious invisible *mandala* into Jackson's chest. The elf who wasn't really an elf did this with Jackson's consent.

What the *mandala* meant was still a puzzle to Jackson. Standing in the light with Janjan he realized what *kind* of thing his symbol was. Every human being has unique value and, simply by living in the body, plays an essential note in the eternal music: light passes through the body like breeze through a wind chime.

So Jackson saw and heard Janjan's note and loved it. He saw her see and hear and love the single note of his own being.

Whatever wrongs he'd done, whatever mistakes he'd made, she loved him anyway.

As he loved her.

52

Sentimental Journey

O dear, what can the matter be?
Johnny's so long at the fair.

Traditional

Jackson and I looked at each other with a wild surmise, as the poet says.

Love? I thought. *Huh. Really?*

A fierce current of desire thrummed through us and through the whole fae castle. Desire was bewildering enough here on the fae-road. Love complicated everything further. I guess it always does.

I thought about how badly Maeve had wanted my orgasm—for reasons that had nothing to do with our pleasure. Jackson and I had stood in the green light of Maeve and Coran's erotic cyclone; had *we* almost gotten sucked into *that*? Would we have been changed like them? Consummating our desire tonight seemed like a bad idea. Could I end up pointlessly pregnant here like Beth had? Or would I end up like Maeve, no longer human? Sex was somehow implicated in the everlasting prison where the Fae were their own guards. And I liked my chubby human body as it was, thanks.

"We really need to get everybody out of here," I said. I meant everybody who'd come over through Portsmouth, courtesy of Jackson and Bobby. The task seemed urgent and overwhelming. I picked up my clothes from where he'd dropped them and started dressing. Not at all what I wanted to be doing, but welcome to adult life, Janjan, you've stayed too long at the fair.

Jackson knew what I meant. He put his clothes back on. "*Everybody* is not going to want to go back to Portsmouth—or anywhere else on Earth."

"You and I will talk to them *together*," I said. I stroked his chest where I'd seen his shining *mandala*, now covered by his shirt, such a shame.

He put his hand between my breasts where my *mandala* pulsed from all the light that shone through it. It was pushing me toward what had to be done next.

"So much *power* there," he said. He meant in and around our hearts. "I had no idea. Look, we'll take as many people back as we can. The Fae won't fight us about it. But I *am* expecting a fight when we step back onto Earth. You ready for that?"

I'd never had a fight outside the schoolyard. I shrugged. "We'll do the best we can. What else can we do?" Yes, I was scared.

"We can ask the elves for help when we get there," he said. He patted my *mandala*. "I'm not going to let the Order just fucking *kill* us." He hated having to swallow his pride, but welcome to adult life, Jackson.

We went downstairs into another great hall where once again people were dancing and drinking as it seemed the Fae did every evening in all of their castles.

The Fae sang along with the musicians. The song was happy on top and sad underneath, like all their songs. Like the Fae themselves. Well, I should say that it was *as if* they sang and the ancient words arrived in our minds, colored and distorted by accents and experiences that were alien to us. For them, as for the inhabitants of ancient Earth, there was no difference between myth, legend, and history. What really happened? Something like tonight's song, I guess:

A lad and a lass
They took to the road
The road took them
Wherever it would
Wherever they would
They walked the road
And castles built
Along the path
They called to all
In every world
Come join the Fae
And live for aye
Come join the Fae
We never die
The Messengers came
And said Now choose
And all did choose
Except the Fae
(The Morrigna said nay
The hags went away
Lo many a day)
And none walk the path
Except the Fae

It went on like that for a long time. The story was in the words, which repeated and wove in and out of themselves like dancers repeating steps.

And the story was also in the music where themes wove together, but meaning remained elusive. The facts of history didn't matter much to the Fae, the stories mattered more. Like everyone on Earth they told stories to make sense of the world they saw around them. Their stories changed with every telling, like the constantly-changing worlds on either side of the fae-path.

We saw Beth and Bobby sitting, watching the dancers, sipping wine and looking tired and bemused. They also looked rumpled, satiated, and numb. Had they *really* just had sex so soon after what had happened to Beth today? They smiled when they saw us, friendly but *vague*.

They weren't sure who we were.

Jackson and I exchanged a look: *That's not good.*

So we sat down and talked gently with Beth and Bobby. Bit by bit they remembered who they were—in addition to being happy followers of the fae-road and loyal subjects of Coran and Maeve. And finally they remembered who Jackson and I were.

It was hard for Bobby because he'd been among the Fae for years—twice before. But as we talked, he remembered who Beth was and why he loved her. And Beth remembered what she wanted: a real life on Earth with a man who loved her and wanted to father human children with her.

Look, we said or seemed to say, *we're going back to Portsmouth. Tell everyone you know that's come over recently. Tell everyone who's even a bit interested that we're going. If they don't like it over there, they can always come back. Really, there's nothing to keep anyone here. Just endless wandering from one place to another. Just sex and not enough tenderness. No real air to breathe, no way to breathe it. No smell, nothing to savor. Nothing to achieve. No way to make the world better by your living in it. No real eternal life, just a long-delayed, inevitable decay.*

A regular human life is better than this. At least what you do matters.

We gave Beth and Bobby a task; they found they *wanted* to do it. I didn't know how long their new-found homesickness would last. Something bizarre and inexplicable had happened to Beth, something unnatural by earthly standards. But by the time Jackson and I came downstairs to talk to her, she'd forgotten giving birth in the grove in an empty world that wasn't Earth. *Cain's world*, Coran called it. Bobby's mind had been newly stunned by rejoining the Fae and by the loss of what he'd thought would be his child. His son.

We warned them not to take comfort in sex here on the fae-road; we didn't explain why. Coming from me that was especially ironic.

Forgetting was almost a mercy, and we'd taken it away from them.

They agreed they couldn't stay here. Existence was pleasant enough, a constant procession of distracting minor pleasures, but it quenched no deep human thirst.

Off went Beth and Bobby to talk to the recent émigrés from Portsmouth and from elsewhere.

Off went Jackson and I to do likewise.

You might call what we did missionary work, except that our message was: *Have you heard the bad news?* Or: *Have you heard the uncomfortable good news?* For the first time, I felt a bit of sympathy for the quietly-dressed men and women who go door to door trying to get somebody, anybody, to listen to their annoying religious spiel.

But Jackson and I weren't offering pie in the sky bye and bye. We told people that tonight *we* would be going back where we came from and that *they* could go with us. We said we were absolutely certain we could do it. *(Slight exaggeration.)* We said it was a limited-time offer, because they might not be able to go home anytime soon without our help. *(They'd forget where home was.)* We said that we didn't know what would happen to us or to them after we all returned to Earth. *(True in part.)*

We stuck to the facts and tried not to oversell. Jackson and I knew a lot of things that we couldn't tell anyone. Unlikely-sounding things we knew were true, but couldn't prove. I saw why Jerry and Leda restrained themselves from telling me over and over again how very much they wanted me to visit them in the next world over—so I could see for myself what all the fuss was about.

Mabel was a tough sell.

"Janjan," she said, "I had two Fae boys with me last night. *Two! Minimum!* And they *stayed with me* all night long, if you catch my drift."

"One for each boob?" I said. This was how we teased each other during our Shipyard lunchtimes at the Sloots' Table. Mabel was pretty well-endowed.

The Shipyard could not possibly have seemed further away to us at that moment. Mabel smiled lasciviously. "I had one boy knocking at my front door and one knocking at the rear. That's *in addition* to the other two who stopped by to lavish attention upon my *tittays*. They weren't shy about pleasuring each other, either, which was pretty hot. Do you have any idea how hard that kind of event is to arrange back on Earth?"

"You want that every night?" I said. "And how are you feeling today, if you don't mind my asking?" After all that, um, *attention*, I was kind of surprised she was able to walk and sit down without pain. I wondered if her throat was sore.

Mabel made a face. I wasn't sure what it meant. Doubt? Discouragement? Discomfort with my question?

"How do I *feel* today?" This was the first time she'd thought about it. "I guess it's like how I feel after I eat and drink here. I sort of know it happened, but it didn't leave much of a mark on me, you know? The memory's kinda fuzzy."

I nodded. She understood what I'd been hinting at. "You're coming back with us, aren't you?"

"Yeah. I *guess*," she said, or seemed to say. There was something like a sigh in her words, although sighing was as impossible here as normal breathing. "I don't think all my erotic exertions made much of an impression on anybody I was exerting myself with. Shame. I really brought my A-game, too."

"It'll be a great story to tell back at the Sloots' Table," I said.

Mabel shook her head emphatically. "*Nobody* wants to hear about this weird-ass stuff back in Portsmouth. We'll be lucky if the Shipyard gives us our jobs back."

❋

A big cluster of formerly-homeless people heard what Jackson and I had to say, but remained unconvinced.

"I'll just stay with the Fae, if it's all the same to you, Miss," said one old guy. (He didn't look so old anymore. He hadn't been here long, but his white hair was already streaked with dark.) He patted his stomach. "I don't feel hungry over here. I'm not cold and sick anymore. The fae wine holds me from one night to the next. I don't even miss the drugs."

"He's right, you know," said a middle-aged woman. She now looked svelte in the fae fashion, not gaunt and bloated from poor nutrition. "*Nobody wants us* back on Earth. No jobs, no money, living in a tent, begging for welfare or scrounging like animals. Getting robbed, raped, or killed. We're a burden to the rest of yez. Fuck a whole bunch of that."

Neither Jackson nor I had earned the right to talk about spiritual matters with the forgotten of the Earth.

Jackson looked around him and then back at the ex-hobos. "It's not too bad living here," he said, "but it's not what it seems, either."

The not-quite-so-old man laughed a silent laugh. "*It is what it is* on Earth, or so they say. Here *it is what it isn't*. No, I've had a shitty life these last seven lean years. Whatever this is or isn't, it's enough for me."

❋

The club kids were easier to sell on going back to Portsmouth.

"It's, like, so *weird* here," one skinny girl said disdainfully.

"The music is, like, *lame*," said a guy with stripes shaved into the side

285

of his hair. The Fae had taken a liking to that look and let him keep it.

"And what *is* it with these *clothes*?" said another girl. "*Flats, really?* I miss my high heels."

"I miss my mom and dad," striped-hair guy said. "It's not like I can just go visit them, you know?"

The other kids teased him a little, but their hearts weren't in it. They were homesick, too.

❋

Many of the adults who'd come to Portsmouth seeking the fae-path told us No thanks. Those who'd fled the law wanted to stay and make the best of things—until everyone who remembered their crimes was dead. But a surprising number decided to go back and play the hands they'd dealt themselves. To pay their debts, taxes, and child support. To ask wives, husbands, children, and employers for forgiveness. To let houses with underwater mortgages go into foreclosure; to find more modest places to live. In one case, even to complete a grueling course of chemotherapy. And my fellow Shipyarders worried how the Navy would stay afloat without their peerless technical skills.

We didn't find and talk to everybody, but everybody who'd recently come over from Portsmouth was going to get the word. *You are cordially invited to join Janjan and Jackson on a sentimental journey.*

It was a big world, this road that wound around the World Mountain, but there weren't many people on it. Any news traveled fast from person to person, from castle to castle.

We all knew we'd stayed too long at the fair.

53

Moira Meets the Walloon

Thus do the spirits of evil snatch their prey
Almost out of the very hand of God;
And day by day their power is more and more,
And men and women leave old paths, for pride
Comes knocking with thin knuckles on the heart.

W.B. Yeats, *The Land of Heart's Desire*

The Materialists believed money insulated them from weirdness.

Moira's workday got off to a good start. She greeted her secretary, hung up her coat, accepted and sipped her morning latte. So far, so good. It was an excellent thing indeed to be a senior vice president in a closely-held Washington financial concern. Her duties were light, her responsibilities heavy. Management of appearances was vital. She believed the latte portrayed her as a high achiever, but very much a lady.

The secretary served Moira's espresso and steamed milk with a flight attendant smile. She had been hired for her looks, her willingness to make coffee and run errands, and her absolute discretion about company business. She thought of Moira as *Da Biznatch*, but smiled winningly, did whatever was asked of her, and kept her mouth shut. Whenever she thought about getting a normal job far away from all these weirdos, she remembered how much the weirdos paid her—for a thirty-hour week.

The company's first guiding principle was *Perception Is Reality*. Moira occupied a prestigious corner office. Quiet good taste prevailed throughout the building, but Moira's office reflected *her* taste and no one else's. She'd been given an obscene amount of money to decorate it. The office featured handmade window treatments and quiet, expensively-framed reproductions of Mary Cassatt mother-and-child prints. As if her firm represented traditional American family values. Moira was bright enough, but irony had always escaped her.

Most of her workday involved talking to people on the telephone and in person. The company excelled at the old-fashioned politics of interpersonal influence. Their web presence was minimal; they avoided social media. Great circumspection was required of the successor to the late, lamented August Association. The people Moira schmoozed at lunch and on the Washington cocktail party circuit knew the company's history, though few others did.

Moira was divorced. Her husband had traded up to a younger model. Now that she'd recovered from the initial hurt and anger, she wished him well—as long as he continued paying his half of their sons' hefty tuition payments. Again, so far, so good. The Ivies weren't cheap, not for the moneyed class. Moira had had a few brief affairs, but had found no one to love among the ranks of appropriate available men. Menopause had begun to blunt her physical desire, and she felt no social pressure to remarry.

Her sons called her every week or so. She kept up with them on Facebook, or thought she did. She saw them most holidays. The boys always had girlfriends, none serious and not for long, nobody who'd break their hearts and hurt their grades. She hoped to see her sons married, but hoped they'd wait until they graduated. She hoped they'd marry other Ivy League graduates who'd do their part to perpetuate the American ruling class that had spawned Moira and her ex.

The company's second guiding principle was *Business as Usual.* The ruling-class work life took most of her time and energy. Most days were sufficiently routine that she forgot who the company actually worked *for*. It would go on that way for months on end, one normal day after another, as Moira fostered relationships with those who could be trusted to safeguard or invest tranches of the firm's assets. Moira saw to it that the money never slept for long.

Something unusual would eventually remind her who paid her salary. On those days the company president would slide past her secretary, close Moira's office door behind him, and lean against it, gasping like he'd sprinted down the hall. He was hilariously predictable, but she never let her amusement show.

Moira looked up from her desk when the door clicked shut. Her boss stood there looking panicky. He'd snuck in on his little cat feet without her even hearing him. The day which had started off so routinely was taking an unexpected turn.

Moira, who understood the male ego, knew the man couldn't admit to himself how frightened he was. She pretended not to notice that he was freaking out.

"Good morning, Stephen." She smiled and put all her natural warmth into the words. People trusted her instinctively; that was part of her gift. She was as good with her CEO as she was with the firm's stakeholders.

"Good morning, Moira," he said. He was already breathing easier; her manner calmed him. "If you wouldn't mind too much, could you drive over to, er, *McLean* this afternoon? Our, er, *principal client* has an urgent concern he prefers not to discuss on the telephone."

Moira understood perfectly. "I'll be happy to meet with the client," she said. "Have I met him or been to his office before?"

Stephen shook his head. He handed Moira a folded piece of paper; the poor man's hand trembled. "It's the client's *home*," he said. "I doubt you've been there. *I've* only been there once, I mean to say." He repressed a shiver.

She read the address. Although she knew any number of very rich people in and around the District, this client didn't live on a road she remembered. Thank God for the GPS, she thought. Moira opened her desk drawer, aiming to put the slip of paper with the address into her purse for later.

Alarmed again, Stephen said, "Please don't keep that address in writing *anywhere*. I'm sorry, I should have told you. Operations security. *OpSec*, the client's security manager calls it."

Moira nodded her agreement. This was not her first foolish, clandestine assignment for a paranoid client. She reread the address to fix it in her memory and fed the piece of paper into the shredder next to her desk.

With his message received, Stephen relaxed a little and sat down in one of the client chairs. He looked at Moira and shook his head. "If you think I'm a fool, I don't blame you. The *other side* of our house really throws me off my game."

Moira had to agree. "The Magicians *can* be scary." She didn't mention that being frightened excited her in every possible way. Some things a sexually-aroused lady is best advised not to discuss with a frightened gentleman. Her mind flashed to Jackson, the handsome, insolent, dangerous magician who'd sat across from her at their law firm's conference table. Young enough to be her son, but old enough to be her lover. *Oh, my goodness*, she thought, and crossed her legs.

"You know," Stephen said, "I was a first-rate chief financial officer, one of the best in the country. I had enough money, if there is such a thing.

I was happily married. Our winter and summer houses were paid for. My daughters were already out of college and settled down. I never really *wanted* to be head of this firm." He studied the thick carpet as if it held the answer to the riddle of himself.

"Why *did* you take the job?" Moira said, not terribly interested in the answer. She hated that men felt *entitled* to unload their feelings on her. It didn't help that her boss was a thin little fellow with a little thin hair and a weak chin, very much not her type.

Startled, Stephen looked up at her. "I thought you already knew. Well, two reasons, really. First, they practically unloaded a dump truck full of money in my driveway. And second, they threatened my family. Of course they know where I live, but they also showed me surveillance photographs of my daughters on the other side of the country. They even showed me a picture they'd taken of my wife going into her gym. The point was pretty damn clear, Moira. *Of course* I took the job; I was afraid not to."

"That's *terrible*, Stephen," she said. She spoke with perfect sincerity. Living and working in Washington had given her the illusion that it was possible to work for villains without suffering their villainy—or becoming a villain yourself. Remoras don't expect to be devoured by sharks.

"Yes, well, for the most part they give us a free hand to manage their money as we see fit. For this service they pay us handsomely. The Magicians really don't care about money, except as it gives them power to act on Earth as *they* see fit. But we shouldn't deceive ourselves. You and I work for bad guys, Moira. Very bad guys." He got to his feet and turned to leave the office.

Today was going be even more unusual than usual. Moira had learned things she would have been happier not knowing. Stephen, who had hired her, had thought she was spying on him for their principal client. Wheels within wheels. Was someone spying on *her*?

"Before you go, I have a silly question," she said. The CEO had opened the door to the outer office. He shut the door so the secretary wouldn't overhear. *OpSec*, thought Moira; she felt another frisson of arousal. The Magicians were so fanatical about Operations Security that their paranoia trickled down to financial functionaries like the CEO. "Why *me*, Stephen?"

"The Walloon asked for *you* specifically," he said. "Er, don't call him that, though. Address him as 'Master Louis'."

❈

Moira had her secretary reschedule her afternoon appointments. She left the office just before noon. The GPS device reliably got her to McLean, then lost track of where she was. As if, she thought, the Walloon's exact location had been made invisible to orbiting satellites and to their robot slaves on Earth. Fortunately she kept an old-fashioned Rand McNally road atlas in the car. You never know where the very rich might hide their lairs.

She found the Walloon's road by sheer persistence; it wasn't on the map. She wasn't entirely sure she was still in McLean. Eventually she found the correct address, marked only by faded black numbers on one of the gray stone pillars that bracketed the driveway. The pillars were attached to a thoroughly-weathered black iron fence. Trees grew close to the fence and hung over it in places. There was no gate. Tree branches had almost overgrown the narrow paved road. Was the Walloon a wealthy recluse like Howard Hughes?

She drove slowly up the driveway. Evergreen boughs brushed against the roof of her car. Bare branches ticked against the side mirrors. The trees opened up a bit as she drove further into the estate.

A quarter of a mile in she saw a small building that could only be a guardhouse. A thick-bodied man in gray winter camouflage and boots came out of the building and held up one hand. His other hand never strayed from some sort of ugly little automatic weapon slung around his neck. Moira knew the drill. She'd visited high-ranking officers on military bases around the District.

She stopped the car, put the transmission in Park, ran the driver's side window down, and kept both hands on the steering wheel where the guard could see them. Another guard watched from inside the guardhouse.

Moira smiled. "Hello," she said. Her natural feminine warmth was usually enough to defrost the frostiest man, but this guy didn't even smile back.

"May I help you, ma'am?" he said. He glanced at the empty back seat, then looked intently at Moira.

I must be losing my mojo, she thought. *Or maybe he's gay.* She gave the guard her name and the name of her firm. "Master Louis has asked to see me," she said. "Have I found the right address?"

The guard nodded impassively, but at least he nodded. He signaled to the other man in the guardhouse; that man picked up a phone. "Yes, ma'am, you're expected. If you wouldn't mind, park in that little turnout over there. Somebody will drive down from the house and pick you up."

Moira waited in the car for five minutes with the engine running to keep her warm. In town it was easy to forget that it was winter, unless it snowed and paralyzed the whole District. She found the quiet unsettling out here in what had turned out to be country, not exurbs. She was too nervous to distract herself with the radio, too nervous even to review the notes she'd made for this meeting.

A big bright-yellow SUV pulled up next to her. Another camouflage-uniformed man got out and opened the passenger door of his vehicle, presumably for her. She got out of her car and locked it with the smart key.

As she was putting the key in her purse, the driver said, "Ma'am, I need you to leave your keys and your phone in the car, please. Also your camera if you have one. The boys in the guard shack will watch your vehicle; you can leave it unlocked."

What an odd request, she thought. But she nodded agreement, put the key in the ignition, dug the smartphone out of her purse and left it on the seat.

The driver closed the SUV's passenger door behind her. He got behind the wheel and drove them through woods, deeper into the estate.

The house, when they reached it five minutes later, looked more like a castle. Gilded Age architecture, with newer wings and outbuildings.

The driver opened the SUV's door for her at the foot of stone steps that led up to the front door. The house door opened before she reached the top step. Another rugged military-looking man, this one wearing a gray suit, not fatigues. He held the door and politely gestured her in. She looked at him, then quickly looked away. The man's eyes were empty of anything like human feeling.

"Thank you," she said, just to have something to say.

"Master Louis invites you to join him for tea," the man said. "If you'd care to freshen up?" He pointed to a door off the entryway. At least his manners were impeccable.

Moira thanked the man and used the powder room. The toilet and sink looked to have been installed before the Second World War, but everything gleamed and worked smoothly. The hand towels were clean and thick. She was glad she'd just had her hair cut and had the original red color artfully restored; she looked pretty good in the antique mirror over the sink. When she emerged, she followed the man (assistant, butler, bodyguard, majordomo?) into a room with floor-to-ceiling windows.

A dining table occupied the center of the sunroom. At the center of the table, surrounded by plates of finger sandwiches, little cakes, and pastries, sat an antique samovar. She smelled strong black tea.

At the head of the table sat a thin man wearing what Moira recognized as a very expensive black suit, of European cut.

The younger man said the words "Master Louis" to Moira in low tones of respect. Her escort left the room, closing the door behind him.

"Master Louis?" Moira said. "I'm happy to be invited to your home. It's beautiful."

"Please, sit," said the Walloon, gesturing to the seat to his right. "And thank you for your kind words. May I call you Moira?"

"Of course...Master Louis."

He smiled faintly. She'd gotten the protocol right.

At his invitation, she helped herself to tea from the samovar and a finger sandwich or two. She ate less than she wanted, thinking the hunger would keep her alert.

The Walloon ate a bit of cake and drank some tea. He led the conversation, inquiring about the disposition of the assets the Order had entrusted to Moira's firm. She had notes on a stack of index cards in her purse, but found she didn't need them. The Walloon wasn't interested in the details—as long as she could explain how the Order's holdings were safe, diversified, and growing. *Stephen's right*, she thought, *the Magicians really don't care about money.*

She said nothing about the aftermath of the August Association's untimely demise and the loss of half its assets. The Walloon surely knew that the catastrophe had happened before she and Stephen were hired, on somebody else's watch. *The previous CEO, may he rest in peace*, Moira thought. The poor man's heart had just stopped beating.

As they talked, the Walloon used his obvious intelligence and old-world charm to assess what sort of person Moira was and whether she was telling the truth. He watched her with great attention; men often looked at Moira that way. And she was young enough that he might well have been interested in her as a woman; older men often were.

Something about the way he was looking at her (he also sometimes stared into the air around her) put her off balance. She didn't think he was interested in her middle-aged body, fit and trim though it was. No, he wanted something else from her. She was too old to play guessing games.

She decided just to ask.

"Stephen said you wanted *me* to drive out here and bring you up to date. I'm honored to be invited, of course, but I can't help wondering why you asked for me."

Moira had overseen the disbursements for Jackson's Portsmouth assignment, part of her job. What was not part of her job was arranging that impromptu meeting with Jackson on behalf of her fellow Materialists. It seemed she'd overstepped and someone had tattled. Was this summons to the Walloon's mansion an unintended consequence?

The Walloon looked at her out of one dark eye. He tilted his head to one side like a curious bird. His fingers tapped on the table arrhythmically.

It was an odd look. More than odd, really; there was something *awful* about it. Between the magician's glazed stare and the table tapping, Moira's stomach did something unwonted that made her wish she'd eaten even less.

Something bad is going on here, Moira thought. *That thing he's doing makes him look crazy, but it's worse than insanity. Evil itself is sitting right here next to me.* She began to sweat a cold winter sweat. She felt the kind of horror that left no room for arousal.

The Walloon stopped staring and tapping. Whatever had been going on and going wrong in his affect ceased. Finally. "Well, *you* wouldn't know, of course, but our disciples are taught that questioning a superior's orders is a breach of discipline."

"You're right, I *didn't* know," she said. "Please allow me to apologize."

The Walloon waved a hand, accepting her apology. "Really, think no more about it. Perhaps we on the magical side of the Order have become too insular. Overly *hermetic*, if you like." He smiled at his own wordplay. Moira didn't get the joke. Her nerves were still jangling. She felt like she'd almost fallen onto the Metro tracks in front of an oncoming train. "To answer your question, I asked for *you* because I have an assignment that needs…a *woman's* touch."

❈

It wasn't like I could have said no, thought Moira. She drove her cold car out of the Walloon's driveway. The heater was blasting; she was chilled to the core. *He showed me pictures of the boys*, she thought. The Walloon hadn't needed to make the threat more explicit. He'd had the dead-eyed man in the gray suit spread the pictures in front of her. Recent pictures of her sons, digital dates in the corners, taken with a telephoto lens. She wanted to cry, but she sensed that would have given the Walloon pleasure.

It hadn't occurred to Moira that she, a mere Materialist financial functionary, might be coerced in the same way Stephen had been. Why would the Magicians bother?

The Walloon had bothered, Moira thought, because it mattered to "the Order's allies" in this operation that she came from an old Irish family (she feared to inquire further). And because she was one of those who'd had the effrontery to call Jackson to account before his latest Portsmouth assignment. And because, like Jackson, she was in the Walloon's chain of command. She was needed and therefore she would serve the Order, willingly or not.

Well, that wasn't quite right. For best results, it seemed her will had to assent freely. The Walloon had been quite clear about that.

The car warmed up quickly, plenty of heat coming off the big engine. Moira turned the heater fan down a click. Halogen headlights made the narrow country road a bright tunnel fading to obscurity on either side. The road behind her was dark in her mirror, nothing to see there. Her thoughts turned to how she'd spend the evening before she left for Massachusetts in the morning. She hated dining alone in restaurants. Should she heat up something from the freezer or have something delivered?

A sound from behind her. Fabric slid across the leather rear seat. Her

297

eye was drawn by a movement in the mirror. Two women had been draped across each other like bundles of cloth. They sat up. Their faces appeared in the rear view mirror darkly.

Moira managed not to scream, but the car drifted toward the opposite side of the road. She felt faint. Worse than faint.

"Keep us on the road, lass," said a very old voice.

"We'd as soon be off to New England *tonight*, if it's all the same to you, Miss Moira," said another old, dry voice.

How had two old women managed to hide from her in her own back seat? Moira wondered. Sure, she'd been distracted by the assignment the Walloon had given her, but...

She lost track of that thought as another crowded it out of her mind. An odd thought she could neither confirm nor dismiss. Here she was, driving the car, keeping it between the lines like a good girl, okay. And behind her in the back seat were two crones, surely the Order's mysterious *allies*, both indecently pleased at having tricked her. Granted, this was a most unusual day and Moira was a long way from her normal mental state. In fact, she wasn't far from panic.

But why did it seem there was a *third* old woman in the vehicle, one Moira could not see?

54

Descent of the King and Queen

A low rumble shook the castle. In the great room, chandeliers swayed above our heads and candle flames flickered.

All of us new arrivals looked puzzled. Earthquake? Sonic boom? Volcano? The longtime Fae exchanged glances and shared a happy silent laugh.

"'Tis but Coran and Maeve, lass," a handsome Fae man told me. "When the king and queen of the Fae come to the peak of their pleasure together, it shakes the whole of the fae-road."

I'd had some earthshaking orgasms in my time, but nobody beyond the sound of my voice knew anything about them. Jackson just shrugged; not his kind of magic. Really, who knew what was possible here or even what the physical laws were?

A short time later, Coran and Maeve came down the stairs wearing their casual royal garb, holding hands, apparently solid again at least in hands, hair, and face, normal humans in size, and wrapped in the bright green fae-light of fulfillment.

The Fae raised their wine cups in a toast to the erotic power of their king and queen. Maeve and Coran acknowledged the salute with smiles, waves, and eye contact. Jackson and I raised a cup to the royals. For *us* they had only a reserved nod.

Oh, dear. We'd disappointed them badly by declining to join them in bed. Had we committed *lèse-majesté* by refusing sex?

Jackson leaned in close to me and said, "I think we missed the first initiation we would have needed to ascend the throne after Coran and Maeve, um, abdicate."

"Initiation?" That was more his sort of experience than mine.

"A sharing of power," he said. "You give something up to get it. Initiation is an exchange." He sounded sad. "Well, except maybe among the elves," he added.

I started getting weirded out. The more I learned, the less I liked the fae-road. I couldn't think of any power I wanted enough to sacrifice part of myself for. "I really need to get out of here. I don't want to wait for morning."

He thumped the *mandala* in the center of his chest. "Yeah, my heart's telling me the same thing. Now's the right time."

We made our way out of the great hall, making brief eye contact with everybody we'd talked to already. You know that head movement you make in a bar that means *We're leaving, c'mon, let's go?* Jackson and I tilted our heads at the door any number of times. So did those we'd persuaded to return with us.

Some people who'd previously declined our invitation came along with the group anyway. Peer pressure, the same reason they'd come to the Fae in the first place. Who wants to miss out on what everybody else is doing?

Who wants to miss out on the life they were meant to have?

55

Moira Meets Michael

Badb and Macha were their names. They sat in the back seat of Moira's car like they were royalty and she was their chauffeur. One hag (the only word Moira could think of that did them justice) watched the world pass by outside the car like she could see into the darkness. The other hag kept her dark eyes aimed at the back of Moira's head like she could see inside it. Beyond telling Moira to drive and telling her their names, the two said little else in English.

The Walloon had given Moira to understand that, along with a third sister *Anann,* the sisters were known as the *Morrígna.* The first surviving written record of them came from the ninth century of the Common Era, though the Morrígna were far older than that.

Not quite Old Gods, the Walloon explained, but nearly immortal magical beings who still could wield a powerful spell. The Fae had no defense against magic that came from the time they took to the road around the human worlds and divorced the rest of the human race.

Moira had thought the Walloon was making charming teatime conversation, telling her folktales of the Auld Sod, her ancestors' homeland. In fact the scary, literal little man had been *briefing* her. She remembered what she'd said to Jackson before he left for Portsmouth: *What we want is for people who go seeking the elves to find something else instead.* The Order still wanted that. Badly.

Jackson, Magician though he was, had not opened a permanent pathway to the Fae. Was he alive or dead? The Walloon had not said: *OpSec.*

Moira, mere Materialist though she was, was being sent to do the Walloon's bidding where Jackson had failed. Master Louis said the ancient sisters would join her in Portsmouth to provide the magical help she'd need; he didn't say she'd be driving them there. Moira managed to smile winningly and *say* she understood her assignment, but she hadn't really believed or understood. She still didn't understand, but she believed the Walloon now.

Her thoughts went frayed and fragmentary with fear. *All I want is...* she thought. *All I want...* She couldn't complete the thought because it set her whole life back to zero.

She meant to think: *All I want is to see my sons again—alive. All I want is to live.*

※

The drive north was grueling. The hags made her take I-95 and its offspring along the coast. How much did they know about American roads? Were they making her follow a longer route because they knew the road, or did they just enjoy tormenting her? It was useless to protest against the Morrigna. The two she could see just hissed at her dismissively. They held intermittent hissing converse with the invisible Anann in a language Moira had never heard and didn't speak.

When she sought to deviate from their orders, Moira felt Anann, the sister she could not see, *pushing* at her thoughts. It was not a good feeling. The psychic pressure sparked a hot flash. Those had been generally absent from her transition out of fertility, but when the flashes came, they swamped Moira with flu-like fever.

Badb and Macha only laughed at Moira's menopausal discomfort. When she stopped to refuel, get coffee, and use the bathroom, she wanted to leave the two—or was it three?—old creatures in the car and run away. But where would she run? What would she do when she got there? More to the point, would the Walloon have his dead-eyed servant kill her sons? Or worse, *recruit them?* There was something worse than death in the world. Something that lurked behind the Walloon's demented birdlike gaze and made him tap the table fitfully. She returned to the car and to the hags' scornful laughter.

Listening to sibilant discourse from the back seat, feeling intrusions into her private thoughts from the air around her, Moira understood that she had accepted employment from people who would do anything to accomplish their aims. *Anything at all.* Not everyone in the magical faction of the Materialist Magician confederacy was entirely human. Some of them only looked like people.

❉

It snowed off and on for hours and hours. Visibility was bad. Her head ached and her eyes burned. There were accidents, which the hags helped Moira avoid. Traffic was snarled and slow-moving in every city she passed through. The traffic didn't thin until the car reached the first stop, a suburb west of Boston.

Streetlights sparkled off a steady, light fall of snow. Most of the office buildings on this road sat dark and empty in the middle of the night. At her destination lights shone out of the ground floor windows. One other car sat in the front parking lot. Snow melted off its still-warm hood. Moira parked next to it and switched off her engine.

To Moira's surprise, Badb and Macha got out of the car and entered the building's foyer with her. Snow didn't cling to their flowing black garments.

Moira felt the invisible third presence that had probed her mind all the way from Virginia. It swirled through the glass front door into the lobby in the cold north wind.

A heavy-bodied man with thick eyebrows waited, holding his office door open for them. He glanced at the hags in resigned dismay. He looked at Moira with interest and rough sympathy. The man looked as tired as Moira felt. He needed a shave. His suit was rumpled and his tie was askew, as if he'd just been summoned and dressed quickly in yesterday's clothes to meet them here.

The man waved the visitors to the guest chairs and sat down heavily behind his desk.

"Looks like Jackson screwed up his assignment in New Hampshire," he said to Moira. "I can imagine why *they're* here." He indicated the Morrigna with a nod of his head. "But why'd the Walloon send *you*? And why does he want *me* to go up to Portsmouth with you?"

One hag sat silent, watching with malign amusement. The other stood stone-faced at her side with a crooked hand on her sister's black-clad shoulder.

"I'm in *finance*," Moira said. "I'm not quite sure why *I'm* here, either. I drove up at Master Louis' personal request. He's my firm's *principal client*, you know." Trying to salvage her dignity with an explanation that sounded stupid once she'd said it.

Something stirred in the hot, stale office air. Mr. Eyebrows (who still hadn't troubled to introduce himself) began to look ashen. Perhaps Anann was *pushing* at his mind the way she'd invaded Moira's.

The Morrigna resumed their hissing conversation, ignoring Eyebrows and Moira. Sometimes they talked to each other in their native tongue;

other times they spoke alternately into the air and listened to responses they heard clearly…and which Moira could almost hear.

Finally one of the hags pointed a bony finger at Eyebrows and spoke from her chair. "Our sister assures us that you will serve our purpose. You have weapons?"

Not trusting himself to speak, Eyebrows nodded.

"Bring them," said the hag.

The other hag pointed at Moira. "*You* will take us all to Portsmouth. Before this day is done, the fae-path will touch again upon Earth. Jackson will return, along with many others who left this world to travel with the Fae. They will be dealt with."

"You're forgetting something," Eyebrows told her. "Jackson is a *Magician*. I'd be happy to shoot him, but you shouldn't count on it."

Badb said, "The Order will send someone else to deal with Jackson, that stupid man who could have left the magicians and been king of the Fae forever. And yet Anann tells us the old king sits on the throne still! He and the old queen will not *force* their subjects to remain on the fae-road."

Eyebrows only understood part of what she told him. *Whatever*, he thought. *Fucking Magicians.* "Okay," he said, "so what do you want from me?"

Macha said, "All those with *the light of other days* in them are subject to our magic. *You* will stand guard with your weapons and kill anyone who tries to interfere with us."

"I can do that," Eyebrows said. "But how do you plan to keep me out of prison for murder?"

A voice spoke from the air, or seemed to speak. The words echoed in Moira's mind, and Eyebrows heard them, too. The voice was clear, distant, and colder than any earthly winter, cold as the interstellar void. *You Materialists worry about all the wrong things*, Anann seemed to say.

✳

Eyebrows drove his car back to his house. The Morrigna sat in the back seat as Moira followed behind him. Moira's nightmare resumed. She was loopy with fatigue and Eyebrows was a terrible driver, fast and erratic, sliding sideways around corners on the slushy roads. At least his house was near the office. He ran his garage door up, drove the car inside, and in a few minutes was back out, dressed in winter clothes. He transferred what looked like an athletic gear bag from the garage into Moira's trunk.

He closed the trunk and got in next to Moira on the passenger's side.

"Let's go get some breakfast," he said. "Sorry for not inviting you in, but I didn't want to wake the wife. She's okay with *my* sudden comings and goings, but she wouldn't think much of me running off without a word in the company of a beautiful Irish lady—even with her lovely Irish aunties as chaperones."

The Morrigna tittered at that ridiculous flattery like ancient schoolgirls. Moira smiled uncomfortably.

Eyebrows directed Moira to an all-day breakfast chain restaurant. Again the Morrigna stayed in the car, apparently not needing to eat or to relieve themselves.

Eyebrows finally introduced himself. His name was Michael but he preferred to be called Mike. Moira resisted the temptation to call him Michael anyway, as was the custom among people she knew. Mike said her name in his hilarious Massachusetts accent: *MOI-rer*. "So, MOI-rer, what exactly do you do for the Walloon? Want some more coffee, MOI-rer?"

By the end of the meal, she'd begun to find him charming. Mike might be a thug and a murderer, but he treated *her* with solicitous courtesy, like the well-brought-up Catholic schoolboy he'd been. That he'd kill her if ordered was something she managed not to think about.

He insisted on driving the rest of the way up to Portsmouth. Moira knew it was stupid, but she found it a great relief to have him take charge of things. She hadn't had a real man in her life for far too long, someone to flatter her and show interest in her and protect her. And pleasure her. That Mike was married and would never leave his young second wife and little children was another thing she managed not to think about.

Reading Moira's mood and her thoughts, the witches spent the drive north trading whispers and cackling their evil cackles. She managed not to let them spoil her mood.

Somewhere there's a man who'll save me, she thought. I'm no girl, but I'm still attractive enough. Surely someone will want me.

56

On the Fae-path After Dark

"Weird" also means "destiny." (Sigh.)

Among the Fae you can pretty much do as you please; that's one of the main attractions. Nobody cared when Jackson and I left the castle with Beth and Bobby. The evening's festivities were in full swing. Nobody noticed other pairs and groups of recent Earth-dwellers waving to their friends and leaving the party. Hot outdoor trysts in the cool darkness were common enough. So was walking down the road to find someone in another castle. But people weren't heading for an upstairs bedroom or looking to hook up, they were walking casually out the door and joining us. Like I said, the word had gone out.

The wind was at our backs when we first started walking, but the road seemed disinclined to rise to meet our steps. As more and more of our people spilled out of the other castles we passed, the fae-path began to accommodate itself to us. As if, I thought, the road *knew* we intended to return to Earth.

"This road's just something *inanimate*, right?" I said, hoping Jackson could talk me out of my uneasiness.

He stared at me in the starlight for a long moment to see if I was serious. "It's *not*," he said. "Not at all. Remember Beth's, um, *baby*?"

I'd already forgotten the newborn made of light. It wasn't just Beth and Bobby who'd fallen into the fae condition. Memory crumbled here, like the memory of dreams. "I *thought* I saw the baby disappear into the road. That can't have been what really happened, can it?"

"There's a lot we don't know about this place," he said. "We don't know much of anything about the Fae. It's all guesswork."

"We could have learned more from Coran and Maeve. I'm not sure we'd have been any happier for learning it."

"*They* don't seem happy, do they? There *has to* be a better way."

He sounded kind of desperate; was he talking about his whole life? I slid my arm around his waist and hugged him. "You and me, babe," I said. "That's all the better way I need."

Jackson hugged me back. "If this burning in my chest is any indication, I'm doing the right thing," he said. "First time for everything. I don't know whether to thank you or call you nasty names."

"The nasty name-calling can wait till we're home in bed," I teased him. The man was famously silent during our intimate moments, while I was famously vocal.

"Wherever *home* might be," he said. Mr. Buzzkill.

❋

Once again, Jackson and I walked along and walked along the shining green fae-path, under unfamiliar stars with no artificial light or pollution haze to dull them. The starlight was bright enough to see by, and it would have been hard to stray off a road so congenial to our feet. I say *unfamiliar* stars because I recognized none of the constellations above us. And where was the moon? I imagined myself as Jadwiga, the foreign-born Monarch of Poland. I saw myself not as a ruler whose reign was paralyzed by politics, religion, and custom, but instead leading my happy subjects onward to some unspecified glory.

I said to Jackson, "When I first met Maeve, she went into a trance. She called me *the queen who is also a king*. Then later she tried to seduce me..."

"Psh, like *that's* hard," Jackson said. He was smiling when he said it.

I whacked him on the shoulder, which hurt me more than it did him. "What I'm *getting* at is this. I wonder if she foresaw what's happening now."

Jackson stroked the back of my neck. "I have heard people say that the party doesn't start till Janjan shows up."

I glared at him. Even in the starlight he could see that I was in no mood for kidding around.

But he wasn't kidding. "Most of them wouldn't have followed *me* back to Portsmouth. Not without you. I mean, take a look. There must be a thousand people back there."

I looked. I couldn't see clearly in the starlit greenish darkness, but there were rows and rows of people walking along behind us, talking quietly, expectantly looking to *me* for guidance, for God's sake. Quite a responsibility.

Scary. This was not what I expected to grow up to be. I suppose everybody says that.

57

The Proposition That All Men Are Created Equal

The world will little note, nor long remember what we say here,
but it can never forget what they did here.

Abraham Lincoln, Gettysburg, 1863

What's my motivation here?

I thought about that as I walked the fae-road toward my fate. Hundreds of people followed along behind Jackson and me; whatever happened to us would happen to them, too.

If I believed what Jerry and Leda told me (I did), the elves were caught up in a war against the Materialist Magicians. It didn't matter that the elves hadn't sought the war, refused to escalate it, and won every major battle the MMs forced on them. The war went on and on because the bad guys couldn't admit they'd lost.

Like the American Civil War, the Portsmouth Wars were about slavery. What would Earth be like if the bad guys closed the way to the elves? We'd be living in a nightmare we couldn't escape—with no elves to wake us up.

Besides hating the elves, the Magicians carried a grudge against the United States. They tried to undermine Western democracy politically and economically. The Order wanted an Earth where everyone struggled just to survive. The few would govern the many. The many would have trouble believing that there was a better way to live. No place on Earth would be better than any other thanks to war, famine, and disease.

After suffering one defeat after another in the U.S., the MMs aimed magic and money at the East and the Middle East. The result? A plague of religious extremists who hated the idea of equal, free, and self-governing people. They wielded ignorance like a sword. Men had few rights in their benighted fundamentalist creed, and women had none. Extremism spread to Europe, carried by refugees from the Levant.

Russia was still a totalitarian state after the collapse of the old Soviet Union. This time the country was powered less by ideology than by stolen wealth and *Realpolitik*, if that's the right word for stealing other people's countries. MMs worked in the background there as they always had.

China was getting rich from international trade and watching the other superpowers to see who'd come out on top. The government never stopped collecting economic and military intelligence abroad. China was no democracy. The MMs had always sponsored dictators, whether they called themselves communists, capitalists, or fascists.

Religion and politics were the same thing to the MMs. In the name of "religious freedom," they tried to erase any distinction enshrined in American law. The Order used fundamentalist religions to achieve political goals. The elite would rule, ostensibly in the name of God, but actually in the name of God's adversary. Those who tried to join the elves would be brought into the MM ranks, diverted to the Fae, or simply killed. Easy peasy.

Using religion as a weapon made this uncivil war especially ironic. The Materialist Magicians served the Fallen Archangel. The Claimant's followers seceded from the first Union, so to speak, and then declared war on all Creation. They attacked personal and political freedom because they wanted to abolish free will.

Why would a girl like me take all that religious and political stuff personally? Because the MMs *hated* the idea that a woman should have ownership of her body and her life. No sex outside marriage. No birth control. No choice about how many children to have and when to have them. No meaningful work outside the family. The bad guys were all about the bad old days. They spent billions trying to turn back the clock in the United States. Elsewhere in the world, the clock was stuck in the Middle Ages. The MMs spent billions to make things worse.

Had the bad guys really declared war on me? When I asked Jackson, he just nodded sadly.

I could try to run away, but I couldn't deny the truth. This was my war now.

❋

We all walked without tiring, stopping occasionally to drink a handful of water from a stream. The wind was at our backs and the fae-path itself urged us onward toward the destination we'd fixed our minds on. I didn't know how it worked, but I could tell it was working.

Jackson and I set the pace. Everybody else hiked along behind us, relieved to be headed home to Earth. Time passed; I can't tell you how much. Finally the fae-road began a long downhill stretch. We found ourselves walking through the air above Portsmouth.

To our left was a world that must have been warm and tropical, judging by the trees that looked like palms, and the light surf that broke on a distant moonlit beach. I'd never seen the place before. I was tempted to go exploring.

But there to our right were the snow-buried marshes, gentle hills, high-tension power lines, and winter-blasted trees of Great Bog. The place looked unnaturally quiet, shining with faint reflected light. As if it was the Earth (the world I loved so much it hurt my heart) instead of me that was *breathing in for half of eternity.*

Beth and Bobby stopped beside us, waiting for guidance. The rest of the crowd straggled to a halt behind us. We all stood looking at frozen Portsmouth for a long moment. I looked at Jackson. He looked at me.

We nodded to each other: *Okay, let's go.*

We stepped off the fae-road and kept moving forward so nobody stepped on our heels. From a springy surface that rose to meet us, our feet encountered three inches of slippery dry powder snow atop a packed, frozen base. My breathing started up again with a big inhale: *Oh!* The air hurt my lungs.

As I started breathing, I could feel myself starting to age again, walking onward toward death. And what is the point of *that?*

Here we were at last, Jackson, Beth, Bobby, and me, with hundreds of other people coming along behind us, not in Gettysburg, but in another field further north, covered by five feet of ice and snow.

Jesus, it was cold. How quickly my body remembered. My skimpy outfit was no protection at all. Nobody was here to exchange fae-style clothes for Earth-style. Portsmouth had no queen and no ladies in waiting who cared about what their new playmates wore. Nobody here even cared if you lived or died; ask the hobos who stayed with the Fae.

Cold wind out of the north made my eyes water. My face hurt. My hands and feet burned. Spring in Portsmouth seemed as unlikely as a fairy tale.

58

Foreigner Sings "Double Vision"

The head Sublime, the heart Pathos, the genitals Beauty, the hands & feet Proportion.

William Blake, "Proverbs of Hell"

Weirdness unfolded around me in less time than it takes to tell it.

It's not often you have all the information you need to make a good decision. I'd always gone with my instincts, carnal and otherwise, and done okay. More or less, I mean. Never pregnant. Well, except maybe that once. (Thanks, emergency contraception.) Still free of infection. Well, except maybe for that one scare that tested out okay. (Phew.)

My point is that I'd always had to make assumptions about the other people in my life, because I couldn't read their minds. I still couldn't see thoughts, but I could see a lot about the people—and other beings—I saw around me in Great Bog. I saw *light* shining around them. The *mandala* over my heart had awakened my vision, doubled it, speeded it up.

Both eyesight and inner vision said we were all in big trouble.

Except for Jackson and me, the people pouring off the fae-path into Portsmouth were lit with a greenish light that shone brighter the longer they'd been among the Fae.

I saw people waiting for us in the field. They had light in the normal human spectrum shining in and around their bodies. Depending on the state of their, um, *spirits*, I guess?

My eyes revealed that most of these people were armed. Their weapons were pointed at the ground.

Why were they armed? What the hell? Were they soldiers? Police? They didn't seem to want to shoot us, but might that change. Shocked faces said they were scared that a whole bunch of us had just *appeared* out of nowhere. Their fear was a danger to us.

Why were they out here in the freezing cold? Had some critical mass of people disappeared from Portsmouth so the authorities were finally compelled to act? Organize search parties? Release the hounds?

What was a Materialist Magician doing here? I recognized the guy. I'd met scary Simon in the world where Beth birthed her fae-child.

What the hell were those shadow-things? An inhuman being from outside the world overshadowed Jackson's old teacher. The old man's lips began to move and the air went blacker around him like he was channeling the shadow. Standing next to Simon was an ordinary man I didn't know; his energy was stained by another shadow, one that watched him from an almost-infinite distance.

A third distant shadow tried to connect with Jackson. Jackson touched his *mandala*, and the shadow recoiled.

What looks like an old woman, but isn't? I saw two other beings standing in the field. They wore black dresses and black cloaks that swirled about them in the raw wind. They were lit with a *blackish* green the color of that salad you left to rot in the back of your refrigerator. Around them eddied the black-green shape of a being no longer confined to the body.

None of these three were human. This scared me less than it should have; I was pretty cold and getting colder. Sometimes the physical beats the metaphysical.

Jackson's inner vision was also awake. "Those two are the old women who trapped Eamonn the Fae in the cave," he whispered to me. The vapor of his breath condensed when he spoke. "Until now I never knew there was a third. I *thought* they were old women, but now I'm not sure. They're related to the Fae, maybe even older."

The creatures in the shape of old women stood on the frozen ground of Portsmouth next to the fae-path. With them stood a human woman with an expensive haircut. She wore an expensive dress coat over what looked like a classic business suit. She was probably in her late forties and definitely badly frightened. She wore a pair of those stupid high-heeled boots, also expensive.

Thinking I knew her type, I wanted to hate the woman at first sight. Crisp, brisk, officious, ambitious, driven, she could have been Estelle's older, more-successful sister. The titanium magnolia model of Southern woman.

Standing next to the woman, with one big gloved hand on her arm to keep her upright on the icy snow, was an older man, not a soldier. He had a rifle slung barrel-down behind one shoulder. When he spotted Jackson, the man scowled, ungloved his other hand and stuck it into the pocket of his cold-weather hunting clothes. Probably going for a pistol; what's one more gun among enemies?

The snow stopped falling. The full moon lit the field up and painted black tree shadows onto white ground. We who walked off the fae-road and milled around in the snow like theatergoers at intermission were further illuminated. Another larger group of travelers had showed up on the ancient path and remained on it. Their *light of other days* shone into the field and onto the rest of us. Everybody in Great Bog saw everybody else clearly.

Well, let me amend that. Another group of people at the edge of the field could see some of us, but not all of us. The elves saw Jackson and me from where they stood in front of a kind of fog bank. The elves were invisible to everybody else. We saw them because of the *mandalas* Leda and Jerry had given us. The elves, of course, could see the other ordinary people who saw us arrive from...wherever the fae-path was. I figured the elves could see the Materialist Magicians without being seen themselves.

But the elves couldn't see the Fae and were likewise invisible to them— and to the two old women cloaked in rotten fae-light. You can tell a lot from where people focus their eyes and from what their eyes pass over like it isn't there.

Why weren't the elves protecting us? The elves stood not upon Earth, but in the next world over from it. It was always spring or early summer there. They hid nothing from us. By which I also mean that they were naked. Even as cold and scared as I was, I had an instant erotic response to them: *Oh!* The revelation of their bare physical being was *telling* me something, if I could just accept it.

Leda stood there with Jerry. If possible she was even more beautiful than the last time I saw her. And Jerry was beautiful, too. I saw what she saw in him. They shone with love for each other and with love for everyone else. I saw it, and I saw Jerry through Leda's eyes and loved him. I saw Leda through Jerry's eyes and loved her more deeply. *Oh!*

Other couples—mostly man-woman, but a few same-sex—stood with arms around each other's waists. Actually, all the elves weren't men and women as I understand the genders on Earth. Some, I saw, were or had been the Myrmidons who'd helped Jerry and Leda, first in their world and later on Earth. The Myrmidon-elves were muscular like men, but had hips and breasts; had penises, but also had vulvas. *Interesting*, I thought. But I really had more pressing things to think about than who was equipped with what kind of plumbing. Jesus, Janjan...

Leda and Jerry held out their arms to us: *C'mon, it's great here. We love you.* The elves all watched Jackson and me to see what we'd decide to do with the gifts Jerry and Leda had given us. *Forever wilt thou love and she be fair,* the poet said. My friends had told me that love was certainly forever or near enough in the next world over, as were beauty and youth. Marriages, though, were not forever, same as on Earth, I guess...

Dammit, why was I thinking about *marriage* now? I shook my head. I was *so* not ready to settle down, but the appeal of what the elves were offering could not have been more obvious. So obvious, in fact, that Jackson was staring at our naked friends and *their* naked friends with naked longing.

Jackson wasn't yearning for sex with the elves or even for their happy marriages. I knew this about my lover with undeniable clarity. The meaning of his ever-moving *mandala*, which I could see and he could not, was: *Where is my deepest, truest power?*

Were our minds in synch or did Jackson catch my thought? He turned and touched me between my breasts with his palm. Compared to the north wind, his hand felt like a steam iron on my *mandala.*

"You know what *this* says, right?" he said. "It says *Where is my deepest, truest pleasure?* Your pleasure is in the next world over with the elves, not with the Fae, not even here on Earth."

"I guess that's where your *power* is, too," I said. Fear made me bitchy. I was glad at how shocked he looked. I mean, how dare he want *anything* more than he wanted little me?

He recovered quickly. "Speaking of power," he said, ignoring my fit of pique, "I recognize the lady with the two old women from the cave. She's one of the Order's Materialist business partners down in Washington. The big guy? He's from Massachusetts. He was supposed to be my handler. That's a gun in his pocket and he is *not* happy to see me."

Keeping a wary eye on Jackson, the two old crones busied themselves around the businesswoman, lips moving. We couldn't hear anything from where we stood, but we could see the smoky greenish light that flowed through the frightened woman as if her body was no obstacle to it.

The big guy raised his pistol and leveled it at Jackson. The barrel shook.

Jackson ignored the shaking gun. "*I know what they're doing to her,*" he said. "They're making her a gateway to the Fae—a permanent one. All it costs is one or two human lives." I'd never heard him sound so bitter.

"How do you know?" I said. Stupid question; I already knew the answer.

Jackson gave me a look. "I was planning to do that to Bobby."

There wasn't anything I could say. Whatever was wrong with Jackson was between him and his conscience.

"I have to put this right," Jackson said. He put both hands on his *mandala*, one atop the other. His shoulder muscles stretched his flimsy fae shirt open. Woof.

Then my lover inquired deep within his mind and ... just disappeared.

59

Do Not Inquire Within

The Authorities hate weirdness of every sort.

Jackson vanished in a release of energy. A silent, invisible shock wave of clear light spread out from the spot he'd stood on. I saw that light because my *mandala* did what Leda had meant it to do.

Armed men had been moving to surround us; they backed away. They didn't see the light, but they felt it. They'd been watching Jackson: where could he have gone? I thought, *Welcome to the weirdness, people.*

Jackson reappeared on the other side of the invisible wall that separated us mere mortals from the elves. Naked, smiling people crowded around to welcome him like he was a long-lost friend. I felt the sudden loss of him right in the middle of my body. Then I felt bad about feeling bad. Jesus, Janjan. Shouldn't a woman of the world like me be *above* petty jealousy? Jackson kept *his* clothes on, but still.

The big guy with the gun did a double-take. I knew how he felt. Seeing people vanish kinda shakes you up. The muzzle of his pistol wandered over in my direction, but he was too shaky to aim it. God knows *I* was no threat. He stuffed the weapon back in his pocket and used two hands to keep the older woman on her feet. Jackson's Materialist associate swayed like she was swooning away.

Old Simon's lips stopped moving. *He* wasn't surprised to see Jackson disappear. Vanishing people were all in a day's work for the MMs. Simon sent his confederate in my direction with a lordly gesture: *Bring me the fat girl.* The man wore an FBI balaclava that covered his nose and mouth. Great, the MMs had made a federal case of me.

The old women in black motioned the big man away from their prisoner. Their light wrapped her around; faster and faster it whirled, a thick, coarse fabric of flame the sickly color of mucus.

The woman stopped swaying. The bilious green light pulled her up straight and steady like an iron filing under a magnet. Slowly she raised her arms, one closer to the vertical than the other.

My eyes ran with tears from the cold. I blinked. Where the woman had been standing I now saw a *tree.*

Reluctantly, I used my inner vision. Instead of a tree, I saw a middle-aged woman holding her arms above her head like a dancer. Her eyes had rolled up, showing only the whites. *That* was scarier than seeing her turn into a tree. Her human energy was banked deep inside. Green fae-light burned through her trunk and limbs without consuming her.

Everything was happening at once. I suppose it always does.

I was alone in the midst of chaos. I suppose I always have been.

The ring of armed men around the field drew in tighter around the fae-road refugees. The FBI man advanced on me with his pistol drawn.

Mama didn't raise no fool. I saw how this was going to go. The Authorities would contain and control the weirdness that was pouring into Great Bog tonight. A scapegoat would be found. Perhaps a low-level federal employee who'd abandoned her Defense Department responsibilities to make big bucks smuggling illegal aliens into the United States. *Me,* allegedly. I'd be taken into federal custody and tied up in legal knots for years. Guantánamo was not out of the question. You hear things about the Patriot Act.

It would be the same way the government had always dealt with Portsmouth's embarrassing metaphysical weirdness. Find a superficially plausible explanation the public will gratefully accept. The ideal explanation completely ignores everything the Materialist Magicians do. The ideal explanation pretends the MMs in this world and the elves in the next world over don't really exist. "Magic" is just illusion, right? After all, "the elves" aren't *really* elves, are they? *How could there be other worlds you can just walk into without dying first?*

And if the walls between the worlds *are* thinner in Portsmouth, what could be better for the Authorities than a permanent gateway to shunt seekers away from the elves? Now that the Supreme Court has handed the American political process over to Big Money, why *not* let the fabulously wealthy Materialist Magicians (whose existence no one admits) have their way? One hand washes the other, strange bedfellows, art of the possible, and so forth. Follow the money if you dare.

Do Not Inquire Within. The city fathers should put that on signs at the city limits in place of "Welcome to Portsmouth." Do I sound bitter? I hated the idea of being imprisoned for life in the service of cowardly rationalization.

And speaking of weirdness, here came Coran and Maeve. They shouldered their way through a crowd of the former subjects they disdained as foolish defectors. The king and queen stepped off their fae-road and into our snow. They gasped as they started breathing at normal human speed again and their lungs filled up with freezing air. *Welcome to New Hampshire, bitches*, I thought. *Can I interest you in a side trip to Buffalo?* It stopped being funny when I saw they'd come to Portsmouth to die.

Two hags (or was it three?) turned their attention from the poor woman they'd magicked into a gateway. The old women snared the king and queen in bands of light the color of toxic algae. Coran and Maeve, so full of life and strength, flinched and faltered, like they were breathing lungfuls of Sarin nerve gas.

Coran and Maeve, so ancient, so beautiful, clasped hands and seated themselves with great dignity upon packed snow next to an old tree. With his impossible, ages-long life coming to an end, Coran put one big arm around his consort. That's what my eyes saw. But my inner vision saw what was about to happen to their *spirits*, if that's the right word. I was learning a lot of weird stuff tonight and none of it made me any happier.

Remember Beth's fae child made of light? As soon as it was born, the baby immediately slipped back into the fae-path. I couldn't deny what my eyes had seen. Instead of going wherever the rest of us go when our lives end, the hags' magic would send Coran and Maeve *back into the fae-road*. It was worse than a death sentence. What could the king and queen have done to deserve that? I was ignorant of their history; the fae folk cared more about songs and stories. Mere facts were of no concern to those who traveled the fae-path endlessly, wrapped in green light.

I had no help for Coran and Maeve. I had no help for myself. I had no help for all the people who'd followed Jackson and me out of virtual immortality and into Great Bog in winter, followed *me* in hopes that they'd be leaving a hopeless, unreal existence for a real life where hope was at least possible.

Despair was equally possible. I had a hopeless moment as bitter as the cold.

But despair only finds a foothold in the world of seasons and appearances. Within me, within the *mandala* Leda had burned into my body, I felt the contact of a mind from another world. A mind I recognized at first touch.

Janjan, Jackson thought, *come to me, come to the next world over. And tell everybody else to come to the elves with you. Everybody loves you. They'll follow you.*

Everybody? I thought back to him. *When I look within, what I see is pretty much all bitch.* I was deeply, deeply afraid to hope. Can you blame me?

I love you, Janjan, came his thought in Elvish, the Unfallen Tongue in which no one can lie. *I need you. Now hurry—before our enemies capture you—or kill you.*

60

Quantum Entanglement

And Crispin Crispian shall ne'er go by,
From this day to the ending of the world,
But we in it shall be remembered-
We few, we happy few, we band of brothers;
For he to-day that sheds his blood with me
Shall be my brother; be he ne'er so vile,
This day shall gentle his condition;
And gentlemen in England now-a-bed
Shall think themselves accurs'd they were not here,
And hold their manhoods cheap whiles any speaks
That fought with us upon Saint Crispin's day.

Shakespeare, *Henry V*, Act I

I've mentioned my mom in passing, but I haven't said much about my dad.
My father, may he rest in peace, made me learn the Saint Crispin's Day
speech from Shakespeare's *Henry V* when I was just a small, stubborn girl.
He died before I hit puberty and it hit me. His heart killed the quiet man

who saw something in me, even when I was a kid, that was invisible to my mother. In making me learn the speech, my father gave me a glimpse of his own secret heart, a part of him my mother never saw.

Anyway. I carried Shakespeare's words in my mind, along with the memory of my father. Is it possible he foresaw something like this moment: me in the midst of a motley crowd in the middle of frozen Great Bog? Who on Earth knows what's possible? I guess the elves know, but they only visit, they don't live here anymore. The tears in my eyes weren't all from the icy wind whipping into my face. I missed my father in a way I hadn't thought to do for years, a piercing, bitter, painful sense of loss in my heart. Fucking mortality, anyway.

I opened my mouth with no clear idea of what I was going to say. Hardly the first time for that. All the while I was projecting my voice to all the people that had followed Jackson and me off the fae-road, I was also talking to myself. Each word I spoke took my mind deeper *within*, deeper into an altered state of consciousness. I don't recall what I said exactly, but here's the gist:

We all went off to walk with the Fae because it looked like the best party ever. All the food, wine, and sex you want, dancing nightly, never get sick, never die.

Then when we got on the fae-path, we saw it was empty and sterile. No risk, no danger, no wisdom, no compassion. Just endless duration.

No real breath. No real love. No real babies. No real eternity.

We were all just hiding out, putting off the inevitable, holding our breath.

We're back on Earth now, surrounded by people paid by those who hate our real lives, hate where those lives come from, even hate where our real lives go.

But now, right this minute, we can choose a better way. I've got the map to a better place tattooed into my heart. Take my hand and join me, people.

Let's leave the bad guys and their employees behind. Let's go somewhere that is truly fucking awesome.

As I spoke, I saw Mabel nodding in agreemen. She was shivering and laughing and crying all at once. I figured it had to be from the cold, not from whatever was coming out of my mouth.

I read her lips. *She's right, there has to be a better way* she said to the people around her. *There has to be.* Because everyone was cold and scared, the idea spread quickly. There was death and worse than death in the air tonight.

People chose; I felt it. Around me, through me, resonant in my *mandala*, beating a soundless note out of it like my body was a gong, came a second release of clear light energy.

I was a single match. I caught fire. The close-packed refugees around me began to burn like the rest of the matches in the matchbook. Some joined me. They went where I went.

As best I could I, or the wind that blew through me, watched my physical self follow that burst of light far *within*, where we're all discouraged from inquiring. The clear light turned the *mandala* in my body into something like plasma; it aimed me in the direction I needed to go.

My eyes rolled up in my head. My thoughts ceased.

Yes, it was exactly like the little death of orgasm, thanks for asking.

It was exactly like an embrace.

61

Forever Wilt Thou Love *(Nonlinear Time)*

"Weird" also means "supernatural."

Someone's strong arms around me. I couldn't remember Jackson's name—or mine. For a long moment, we held each other tight. There was nothing else to cling to in the borderlands of the next world over.

He took my hand and led me somewhere. I couldn't see; I needed the reassurance of touch. *Where am I, anyway?* I tried to think. My eyes registered nothing but static. My ears heard only the current of my own blood. *Why can't I see here?* I tried to wonder. I didn't speak, I had no words. All ordinary thought was suspended. My small thinking self was in abeyance; I didn't go looking for it.

Whatever was happening in this featureless place didn't scare me. It had to be safer than what I'd left behind.

Blindly, step by step, we walked deeper into the cloud of unknowing on a surface that yielded under our feet. It felt different from the fae-road.

Holding Jackson's hand, I entered into the presence of the being who guards the next world over from all harm. The word we use on Earth for such beings is *angel*, which only means *messenger*. The message was in his being, and that being was more than I could take in. Eternal. Non-physical. Good—by his own choice.

I say "his," but that's only my limitation speaking through my limited language. The angel had no need of gender.

Again my eyes told me nothing useful. Huge as he was to my boggled mind, his compassion was larger still. It flowed through his heart like a river.

Hello, Daughter of Eve, his mind said in mine. His smile lit me up like the sun, although I couldn't exactly see his face. I knew he spoke the truth because I received his thoughts in the Unfallen Tongue, the language earthlings call Elvish.

Thought and speech came back to me. *Hello, Angel*, I said. I couldn't think what else to call him, and he didn't correct me. I did a curtsey like I had when Jackson and I danced with Coran and Maeve. It was a silly thing to do, but it seemed only polite. *Is it all true, then?* I asked him, *Eve, Adam, the Fall, the Crucifixion, the Resurrection?*

I felt the angel's smile grow broader, if that's possible in a being who has no proper face for eyes to fix on. He smiled because he was happy for me. *It's all true, Little One*, he said. *All that and more besides. All the deepest teachings of Earth. You were only ill-taught because of human self-interest and the limitations of your teachers. But now you will see the truth for yourself, spread out before you, the banquet our Creator sets before his creatures—and within us all.*

I curtseyed again to the angel who saw all the way into me and loved what he saw. Perhaps he inclined his head. *Welcome home, dear child*, he said. *Remember, Love and Light.* His words struck me and I vibrated with the meaning like a bell.

My ordinary thinking self started coming back to me, or me to it. I was wondering about the angel's message as Jackson and I walked out of fog and into...*grasslands*. That word hardly does the place justice. It was beautiful in every detail in ways I have no words for. The sky was a deeper blue than I'd ever seen on Earth or any other world, and the grass was green and lush and lovely; both went on and on and I could see no end to them. The sun warmed me without burning my skin. This, finally, was the place I was supposed to be. The world embraced me like a lover.

Waiting to welcome me to the next world over were my friends Leda and Jerry. There were others with them whose stories I knew, but who I hadn't met. Everybody smiled because they were as happy for me as the angel.

A lot of new information came at me all at once. First, there was the timestream difference between this world and Earth. It felt like Jackson and I had only been separated for a few minutes, but he said he'd been over here for months. I saw that his skin had a light tan, the first of the physical changes that happen in those who go to live with the elves. I wondered if that would happen to me.

I had to get used to speaking mind-to-mind with people I'd just met who knew more about me than anyone on Earth. It's banal to *say* we're all brothers and sisters, but it's also a fact. And by the way, in addition to communicating in flashes of thought and image, the only language I could use here either mentally or aloud was Elvish. Just try telling the truth all day on Earth, I dare you. Try *thinking* the truth all day without evasion. At least here everybody loved me. I loved them back, couldn't help it. My new family deserved the best I had to give.

Speaking of love, it surprised nobody but me to learn that I loved Jackson, loved him wholly and completely, the way he loved me. We'd seen it before, but we hadn't taken it in or risked talking about it. Now I accepted what I hadn't dared to think about. We hid nothing from each other and held nothing back.

"Once I saw you two together in that world off the fae-road, I knew you were *spoken for*," Jerry said.

"May you and Jackson be as happy as we are, my sister," Leda said. Here among her people—*our* people—her speech reflected the wisdom and dignity the years in the next world over had given her. I'd been wrong, I hadn't lost her. She was still my friend. We were *family* now.

And Leda and Jerry were my teachers.

—

Jackson had only gotten a slight head start on me in learning the things elves need to know. He'd spent time in the Groves of Healing repairing the damage done by using Materialist Magic. He was the same man he'd been in Portsmouth, but all his anger had turned into determination.

"I was wrong," he said calmly. "I know better now. I *did* wrong. I'll go back and undo as much as I can."

In my first days in the next world over I learned unsettling things about myself. I learned them from being intimate with Jackson. The body, of course, is the instrument, but the spirit plays the melody. We learned to have sex that happened entirely inside us as we shared a look and a touch. It was lovely. It was *powerful*. It was a lot more than just sex. I'd politely managed not to gag when Jerry and Leda talked about "making love" as they told me their story. But *lovemaking* was what I'd been missing during all my slooting around. I never felt anything deeply or thought anything through. I'd been using strong physical sensation to avoid *inquiring within*. Here in the only safe place in all the human worlds, my own true home, those mistakes were corrected.

Back in my Portsmouth kitchen, I'd asked Leda what the point of a woman's existence was. I mean, birth, copulation, children, work, and death, *really*, is that all there is? She'd told me there *was* more and that I could come see for myself. I'd resisted learning what that "more" might be. Hell, I'd kind of haphazardly fallen among the Fae, and I'd *still* fought coming here until I couldn't see another way to go. Leda said she and Jerry had to get past the same resistance. They'd been frightened of getting what they wanted most.

There were other alternatives I could have chosen. I could have joined the bad guys. Ugh. I could have held tight to what the Church had taught me, made a good Act of Contrition, lain down and died in that frozen field. Ugh, again. If you're going to surrender, at least pick something worth surrendering to. *Be a good girl, obey, and don't make waves* isn't enough to sustain a lady. Neither is Shakespeare's *Be not self-will'd, for thou art much too fair.* More bullshit from people who don't understand women, see us as lesser beings, or want to use and discard us.

During the Second World War, the Church—certain key churchmen—had collaborated with the Materialist Magicians and surrendered to the dark magic that cloaked all memory of the elves. It was partly human reluctance to give up the ordinary world we're born into. It was also unwillingness to give up the temporal power the Church got from taking the imaginary moral high ground and defending it against all comers.

If you can learn the truth for yourself simply by walking into the next world over, why would you need a priest to explain your experience away and dismiss it? Bad enough that the Church had made a mistake, worse that they knowingly clung to the error.

Anyway. I learned not to carry a grudge. Even an eternal life is too short for that.

Like Jackson, I had some healing to do. Mine was mostly physical. Things that were in the earliest stages of going wrong in my body were healed as I *inquired within* and watched them be put right.

I ended up with a different relation to my body than I started with. I wasn't exactly who I'd thought I was.

✻

Ironic that I'd always worried how a woman's story ends at the altar.

Once you enter the next world over, your story is also over. But only the story of your small, illusory self comes to an end. You learn the whole story, the story of your real self that began ages before your most recent human birth.

For most of us, being born on Earth is being *re*born. It's like walking into the theater partway through a movie. Once you see the beginning, the movie finally makes sense.

Living with those who are miscalled elves—and becoming one of them—removes any need or desire to lie. You see clearly who you are, so you don't need anyone to prop up your illusions. You don't prop up others' illusions, either. Life back on Earth quickly starts to seem like a dream. Row row row your boat.

But life on Earth still called to me. My peace here in the grasslands with Jackson remained incomplete. We felt an obligation to the people who'd followed us off the fae-path.

Some people, my teachers told me, came to the next world over with all their business complete. They spent a little time among the elves who lived in the borderlands and in the city I had yet to visit, Nextworld Portsmouth. Then they answered the call. (I felt it within me as a whisper.) They walked upcountry into who knows what and were often heard of no more. None of my new brothers and sisters would answer any questions about them.

"Go see for yourself," they said with I-dare-you grins.

I wasn't ready for the high country yet. I had things I needed to learn first. One of my stories might have ended, but that was just the story of my girlhood and adolescence. Even on Earth you can't help observing the great mystery of how things change, how people change: baby, girl, woman, wife, mother, widow, crone, corpse. Americans resist this inevitable mystery; I sure had.

Things were different here, kind of an understatement. I'd exchanged one mystery for another, given up one kind of inevitable change for something even more mysterious, a life where everything's freely given and I didn't need to cling to anything. You know how your earthly friends change when they marry or become parents? Leda and Jerry hadn't become parents (that's a bigger deal among the elves than it is on Earth), but they were thoroughly married. They loved each other. They were *spoken for*, as the elves say. It was a big change.

So I wasn't surprised when Jackson told me mind-to-mind: *We seem to be spoken for.*

We do, I thought back. *I seem to love you.* I smiled when I thought it, and there was no fear left in my mind.

"No, you really do," he said aloud. "I can see it as clearly as I can see that I love you. Before we go back to Earth to do what we signed up for, will you marry me?"

"That does seem to be the custom over here, doesn't it?" I said. I'd begun learning the elvish art of understatement. "If we're going to be husband and wife, shouldn't you at least tell me your first name, *M*. Jackson?" I'd never seen his first name in his thoughts because he thought of himself only as *Jackson*.

He shook his head and smiled. "It's *Merlin*, dear *Jadwiga*."

"Oh, *honey*," I laughed. We were both members of the Ironically-Dorky Name Club.

Jerry and Leda conducted the ceremony for us, as all the elves are empowered to do. In the next world over, where everyone is priest and doctor and warrior and statesman and lover, no one is confused about where wisdom, power, healing, and pleasure come from.

We postponed the honeymoon. Or you could say we took a working honeymoon back in frozen Great Bog.

62

Things to Do, Places to Go, People to See *(Nonlinear Time)*

Let me back up a bit.

The elves had been expecting company. I mean, a bunch of them took the trouble to get naked for little me. While I was standing in Great Bog dithering, all those bare elf bodies were *telling* me something, a message written in their beautiful golden skin, wise dark eyes, and compassionate hearts. They weren't surprised when *I* took the bait, so to speak, and came to learn everything they promised to teach me about my deepest pleasure.

But what *did* surprise the elves was all the other refugees from the fae-path who followed me to the next world over in an explosion of clear light. So many dazzled new arrivals at once and we all needed individual attention. The elves set up little encampments to train my fellow immigrants, not far from where Jackson and I were living and working. It's not like a handful of newbies overwhelmed the elves' capacities or anything. They're the last people in any world who'd want to run some kind of highly-efficient military boot camp where everybody has to dress alike, live together in a barracks, and share the ordeal.

It wasn't anything like an ordeal, and we didn't have to dress alike. Male elves are manly without being super-macho. Female elves are womanly without being super-girly. And the elves who once were Myrmidon warriors, being both manly and womanly, have a dignity all their own.

Four of those who came over when I did went back to Great Bog with Jackson and me. When you all speak the same language, never lie, and share thoughts instantly, it's pretty easy to synchronize your watches, as they say in the war movies. You don't even need watches.

Mabel was one of the four.

"What did you *think* I'd do after walking with the Fae?" she said. "Beg the Shipyard for my job back? Get a sailor to marry me and have his Navy babies? Enter a convent?"

Thus weirdness does make allies of us all, I thought. Or maybe it should be, *How ya gonna keep 'em on the Shipyard after they've seen the Fae?*

We left the next world over together. One of the Myrmidon-elves came to see Mabel off. She and Mabel weren't *spoken for* yet, but who knew what would happen if we all survived this battle and returned home? It was clear that they had things to say to each other. There's plenty of time for everything that needs to be done, or so the elves say.

I had a million questions for Mabel, of course I did, but I didn't ask them.

Priorities. We had things to do.

63

The Battle of the Bog Is Joined *(This February)*

We kill people based on metadata.
Gen. Michael Hayden, former NSA and CIA director

A few seconds of Earth time after we left Great Bog separately, Jackson and I reappeared there together. Four other newbies popped up elsewhere in the frozen field. They quickly went about their assignments, seeking out the leaders of the armed men. Did I mention that all four were women? My smiling soft-spoken dark-clad sisters went empty-handed among armed soldiers and police, calming their fears. Rifle barrels were lowered. Information was exchanged.

There was a bit of cleavage on display in those cold fields, with Mabel's leading all the rest. Like me, she was a furnace inside and she had no shame.

Jackson and I bypassed the woman disguised as a tree. We moved smoothly, deflecting attention away from ourselves. We avoided the two (or was it three?) old women who surrounded her. We avoided the man who guarded the woman, the frightened thug who thought he was Jackson's handler. Priorities.

We concentrated on the two men whose shadow creatures watched them like jealous lovers. Simon the old Magician could kill us with dark magic. Burke, the Materialist agent of influence with the FBI, had authority to shoot us. They were the primary threat.

Even clad in black pants and shirt and wearing soft-soled boots, I still looked like the little fat ginger girl who used to go clubbing with her friends in Portsmouth. I smiled shyly at Burke, who was aiming a handgun at the center mass of my body.

"You're not going to shoot *me*, are you?" I said. I did a thing I knew how to do before I joined the elves, moving my torso so as to *point* at the pistol not with my hand, but with my breasts. Women are kind of awful, or at least I am. The interesting thing about this move is that a girl doesn't even have to have big boobs to pull it off. It seems to start men contemplating what you might have under your shirt and how your chestal area would feel under their hands.

During the split second Burke's thoughts turned to boobage, I stripped the pistol out of his hand, put him on the ground, tampered with his body's energy, and put him to sleep with a whispered Elvish spell in his ear. It was my first real fight. I felt like doing a sack dance.

But I didn't want to distract Jackson who was busy with Master Simon. They spoke in low voices. Simon was furious. Seeing that Jackson had joined the enemy, the magician wrapped thick darkness around himself and prepared to strike Jackson with it. *(Oh, my God, did I see eyes in the midst of that darkness?)* Jackson moved in close and, fast as thought, struck through the massing darkness and hit the old man in the head. Hard.

The devastating blow to the temple should have killed Simon. Instead, the serpent of sentient darkness turned his body into fine smoke particles and whirled it away. Simon's spirit flew into the night with the demon. His terrified psychic screams echoed in my mind.

I saw the nausea in Jackson's spirit.

You had no choice, I thought to Jackson. *Simon was old, powerful, and bent. There was no time to show him the way off the Dark Path.*

Jackson looked at me and nodded. *Simon needed killing,* he thought, *but I enjoyed killing him too much.*

There are hundreds of lives at risk here tonight, I thought. *Let's get on with it. We'll have time to take comfort together soon enough, my love.*

Jackson's expression softened. *My love. How could I ever live long enough to get tired of hearing that?*

Are you as horny as I am?

Jesus, Janjan, who is?

He was, though. Just thinking about it made him want me. Elf couples neither hide anything from each other nor seek to. Our desire was part of our motivation here: to see things through so we could go home and drink our fill of each other, uninterrupted, for hours and days of timeless nonlinear time.

64

The Nightmare Queens

Our sister elves gently persuaded the agents of the state to fall back a bit. The distraction allowed Jackson and me time to take Simon and Burke out of action.

While that was happening, two creatures who looked like old women beckoned all who would come to come quickly out of frozen Great Bog and join them on the fae-path. The night, they said, was moving on swiftly and there was an eternal round of travel to resume. There was, they said, a specific frequency of light in which to wrap others and to be wrapped oneself.

All that was needed was to step through the doorway: a tree that was somehow also a woman.

The *light of other days* was the essence of fae magic. We saw the two embodied crones grow younger by the minute. We saw the disembodied third sister transform the blackish-green light around her into human flesh again. For now was the time of their reascension, so long delayed.

During the time the three had spent on Earth they'd been subject to the will of the prince of this world, compelled to do the bidding of the magicians who served the Claimant. Coming as they did from a fairy-tale monarchy, the three would have understood what motivated a pretender to the throne.

Why had they left the fae-road only to go all raddled with mortality as ordinary people do? And having left, why had they never died? The elves Jackson and I consulted during our nextworld training shrugged their shoulders. At different stages of being, creatures manifest different laws, like the Old Gods Jerry and Leda had encountered. Let's call the three sisters *demigoddesses*, then. The three old/young women wore the mantle of the Celtic Morrigna, the queens of nightmare. What nightmare could be worse than refusing the choice that lets you flow with the one river, the source of all life?

So the three stayed on Earth for many a year. One of them had her ancient physical body sublimed into her spirit body, but even disembodied she would not leave her sisters.

And when the Materialist Magicians asked the Morrigna to work their will on a wayward Fae who'd strayed to Earth (bored with the endless round of endless life on the endless fae-road), the Morrigna ensorcelled one of their own kind. The Fae breathed his *light of other days* into Jackson and died as men do on Earth.

Now the sisters saw their time on Earth drawing to a close. To stay longer among men and magicians was to choose the side of the Fallen by default. To take refuge in the magicians' High Enemy was to give up the power that was unique to them.

The Morrigna strove to weave a spell that would capture the powerful life energy and strong spirits of Coran and Maeve; Jackson and I would not allow it. Our original mind energy blocked the spell. *Love and light,* the angel said; we *remembered.*

We could only shield the dying king and queen because they assented. With all their remaining freedom of will, Coran and Maeve clung to us and to the help we held out to them.

65

Queen of No Angels, King of the Fae

I'd learned a lot during my time among the elves, and I'd unlearned even more. Here's the short course, as best I understand and can explain.

The elves aren't really the elves of legend any more than they're the ancient Chinese Taoist alchemist-philosophers of myth. There is no Heaven of disembodied souls, but the next world over is an actual physical Eden. It's the place we were created for, as it was created for us. Leaving our own true home was the Fall of man, caused by a thought disorder the elves call the Original Mistake. There is no Original Sin a religion can do anything about, but our mistake can be corrected—if we let it. There is no Hell outside the company of the Fallen angels. The Fall belongs only to those who continue to insist—insanely—that they have created themselves and should therefore sit on the throne of the Creator.

The Creator, source of all life, being everywhere, of course has no throne.

Free will means you can try to enter a Hell that doesn't exist or try to enter an imaginary Heaven. Reality is kinder than imagination, thank God.

What you *will* do in any fallen human world is die and be reborn again and again and again, until you learn better. When you finally choose to go home, you will be welcomed.

As to what happens to the high elves, the elflords and elfladies who are called into the highlands of the next world over, I don't know, either. Someday I'll go see for myself.

I hadn't studied hard in catechism class. Once I learned that the Church considered masturbation to be "gravely disordered," I stopped paying attention. And that was the least of the crazy quilt of fantasies and mistakes the nuns were sewing. I stopped paying attention to priests after one tried to grab my then-little ten-year-old ass. Seriously, what is *wrong* with those guys?

Anyway. Here I was in the frozen orchard with Jackson at my side. We knelt in the snow next to Coran and Maeve where they leaned up against a gnarly old apple tree. They looked older than the tree. In fact they probably *were* older than everything in Great Bog except all the local carbon atoms, born in the heart of some star after the Big Bang.

Maeve smiled at me. Her spirit began to swirl around her body. It was time for her to take a path she'd delayed walking for achingly-long ages. *Two roads diverged...*

"Ah," she said, "when I saw that you were *the queen who is also a king,* I'd no idea what the vision meant."

I held Maeve's hand. It felt colder than the snow; my warm thumb left a pale mark on her graying skin. "We're all kings and queens in the next world over," I told her. "Or none of us are." Then I remembered that, as she was, she couldn't go there. "May I help you find your way to what's next for you?"

"That would be more than kind of you." Maeve's voice was weak. We didn't have long. The queen looked frightened. I didn't blame her; I was a little frightened for her. I'd never guided anyone this way before, but the knowledge was clear as the map inside me.

Jackson held Coran's hand. Like the queen's, the king's spirit swirled around him.

"You'd have been a fine king of the Fae, lad," he said.

There were tears on Jackson's face, but he ignored them. "I'd take you home with me if I could, Coran," he said. "But the angel who guards the next world over says you've been too long away from humankind."

Coran shook his head feebly and smiled. "An angel, is it? Well, he's right enough. Maeve and I have quite lost the art of being human. Ages of shape-shifting and making mischief, I suppose. The fae-road has become more us than we ourselves." Then, more quickly, "What'll you do about the Morrigna? You and the lass saved us from their magic, but the sisters are not fit to lead the Fae."

Jackson looked directly into the king's eyes. "There's nothing I *can* do," he said. "Those who stayed on the fae-path *chose* it. Those who go back today are *choosing* the Morrigna to lead them. They're choosing not to choose, to postpone the inevitable choice again for another age—or two or three."

"Ach, lad, I know that now and there's no help for it. Well, I choose rebirth now. Someday I'll make the choice for good or evil with my life on the line. As you've done."

Jackson and I joined our thoughts to those of Coran and Maeve. As the king and queen laid their bodies down next to the gaunt, dead-looking apple tree, their original mind energy followed the map inside us to the great blessing that is human birth. Away and beyond they went, and all trace of them was lost to us.

66

The Myth of Daphne

You have thrown your arms about a drift of leaves
Or bole of an ash-tree changed into her image.

W.B. Yeats, *The Land of Heart's Desire*

The thug stood next to the tree that had been a woman. He stared at the tree intently: nothing but a tree. Huh. The woman was gone; so were the three witches. His job was done. Time to leave all this weirdness behind.

Then he saw Jackson approaching. He tried to get the pistol out of his pocket, but forgot to take his glove off. Between the cold and his fear of Jackson, he also forgot the rifle on his shoulder.

"I told you *not* to visit here," Jackson said. With his war face on, he was very impressive. I could see why even an armed thug might be intimidated.

"My orders come from way above your paygrade, pal," the big man said. "Have you forgotten the Walloon?"

Jackson shook his head. "I'm not *in* your chain of command anymore, if you follow me."

The man looked closely at Jackson and shook his head.

"Aw, shit," he said. "What, now you're the *other* kind of magician? Fuck me till I weep." He gave up on getting the pistol out of his coat pocket. It was too cold for gunplay. He was a summer soldier, and his heart wasn't in this battle.

"Here's the deal, Michael," Jackson said. "Leave now and I'll let you go. Stay and try to interfere and you may never get home again."

Michael made up his mind in a heartbeat: *My family!* He nodded agreement and turned to walk away.

"Hold up," Jackson said. "I'll need your car keys. You can keep your handgun, but leave the rifle with me."

"Eh, they're Moira's keys, anyway." He nodded at the tree and handed Jackson the keys. "How am I gonna get home?" Michael said, not quite whining. He unslung the rifle, slowly, and handed it to Jackson by the sling.

"There's a bus station a mile west of here," Jackson pointed with the barrel of the rifle. "Start walking."

Michael's shoulders sagged. "The Walloon's gonna fucking kill me. *And* my wife and kids."

"Not if he doesn't find out what happened," said Jackson. "Can you give me three days before you report in, maybe stay home sick?"

Michael's eyebrows went up hopefully. "What about the fed?" Michael pointed to Burke, unconscious on the snow in his FBI balaclava. I was surprised to see that kind of team spirit. Or maybe Michael just didn't want Burke to rat him out to the Walloon.

"Good point," I said, catching Jackson's thought. "How about if you take him with you on the bus and keep an eye on him till things settle down?"

"I'm not taking him to my fucking *house*," Michael said. "I keep work separate from my home life. Plus, the wife would kill me. I've got a camp over by Worcester. I'll take him there."

Jackson nodded. He walked over to Burke, rolled him over, and woke him up with whispered Elvish.

"I'm surprised to see you here, Mr. Burke," Jackson said.

Burke got shakily to his hands and knees, then to his feet. He took off his balaclava and used it to brush the snow off his pants and jacket.

"Orders," Burke said. "Surely you know how *that* goes. What the hell just happened to me?"

"My wife just kicked your ass. Not to put too fine a point on it."

Burke gave me a look of raw hatred. I realized what a sheltered little life I'd led before all the weirdness started up. Burke's hatred was amplified by a shadow at infinite remove, a dark creature his conscious mind was unaware of. The evil we pray to be delivered from.

"May I have my service weapon back?" Burke said. His tone was barely civil and he asked Jackson, not me. Totes sexist, yo.

Jackson extended one hand to me. I was happy to turn over the pistol, which I'd tucked inside my hoodie, hoping not to shoot myself by accident. I held it like it was a dead raccoon. The elves taught me nothing about guns; I didn't need firearms to protect myself. Jackson removed the magazine, pocketed it, and clicked the sliding part of pistol back and forth. A single bullet fell harmlessly into the snow.

"I'll take the rest of your ammunition," Jackson said. Burke wanted to protest, but finally extracted two magazines from his coat pockets. "Thanks. Now. You'll be taking the bus south with Michael here and spending some time with him at his lakeside cottage. Think of it as a few days' vacation. I'm assuming your bosses won't worry about you?"

"They don't exactly know where I am. They don't *want* to know. They've been *spoken to*, if you know what I mean." He paused. "You do realize that the Walloon is going to kill first me and then you?"

"*You* should worry about dying," Jackson said. "One of the Fallen is circling you. The demons just took Master Simon. There's no permanent Hell, but how much time do you want to spend traveling with creatures who hate you? It would *seem* like eternity. It would scar your soul and drive you mad. Do you really *want* to be reborn on the Dark Path again and again? *Here there be monsters*—and you get to be one of them."

Burke couldn't look Jackson in the eye. He did *not* want to talk about this; he refused to think about it. Free will. Michael nodded to Jackson, put one big arm on Burke's back, and began leading him out of the field and back to the highway.

I caught a hint of murderous intention just before it turned to action. Michael had taken his glove off. He was calculating the exact point where he could get his gun out, turn, and shoot us before we could stop him. He thought the Walloon would reward him handsomely.

"Don't do it, Michael," I said in a loud voice that carried clearly through the cold air. "Do *you* want to get your ass kicked by a girl?"

Michael's shoulders went high and rigid as he thought it through: anger, fear, then resignation. Then he shook his head in disgust. He and Burke kept walking. Neither man looked back at us.

＊

An untrained eye would have seen a low-growing tree. But I saw a woman standing where the fae-path touched on Earth, her arms held toward the sky. Greenish energy blossomed around her, flowing up from the earth and down from the invisible road in the air. A few people who'd followed Jackson and me off the fae-road changed their minds again and went back to the Fae. Somehow they stepped *right through the woman* like they were walking through a cheap hollow-core interior door to another room.

We stopped them doing that. *You don't have to go home, but you can't stay here*, bartenders used to say at closing time. Wherever people were going, they weren't going to use this poor lady to get there.

This was what Jackson had tried to do to Bobby. The Morrigna's fae magic had turned a living human soul into a gateway. She might have agreed to run errands for the Materialist Magicians, but she probably hadn't wanted to spend her life as a crabapple or a dogwood. Is that too catty to say? I don't think that's how I meant it.

Jackson was doing the right thing for the woman disguised as a tree, just like when he helped my wobbly old neighbor up off the icy sidewalk. Showing his true nature.

Jackson took her right shoulder, I took her left. Together we reached into her utterly-surrendered mind. Somewhere inside was her human identity...

Okay, *there* it was.

Moira? Jackson thought to her. *Remember me? We met down in Washington in January.*

Moira? I thought. *You don't know me, but I'm here to help you if you're willing.*

We felt her consciousness stir. Self-awareness reluctantly returned.

She thought: *What...?* Her arms came down. She would have collapsed if Jackson hadn't stepped behind her and held her up. We withdrew our thoughts from her mind; she hadn't invited us in.

"Moira?" I said aloud. Her eyes blinked, then focused on me. "Hi. I'm Janjan."

"And I'm Jackson," he said gently. "Can you stand on your own now?"

Moira tried a couple of times before she found her balance. She turned around to face Jackson. I stayed at her left side to steady her. She was pretty shaky. I didn't blame her.

"Jackson?" she said. "I remember you. What happened to me, anyway?" Then, as the reality began to sink in: "Oh my God, *my sons.*

They'll be killed. Can you help me?"

"Maybe," Jackson said. Such a literal man. He was right, but this was no time for realism; she was in shock.

I gave him the stinkeye. "*Definitely*," I told Moira.

I was right, too, but I didn't say what our help would require of her.

67

Beth and Bobby Leave Town

You Can't Go Home Again
1940 Thomas Wolfe novel, published posthumously

Great Bog had turned into slow-motion chaos, like a crowded fairground. The National Guard and the police were trying to round up hundreds of shivering, bewildered fae-road wanderers without hurting anyone. Beth and Bobby avoided the sweep. My friends stood concealed in the shadows of a stand of bare trees next to the railroad tracks. They were hugging each other, shaking with cold, and waiting for me to tell them what to do.

Did they see what Jackson and I had just been doing? Did they understand what they saw? If they were wary of me, they still followed me out of the field like lost sheep. They were in no shape to drive.

I kept up a stream of small talk to bring us all back to Earth. I said nothing about my side trip to the next world over. Instead, I asked what they thought had happened on our favorite TV shows while we were gone.

(No response.) I wondered aloud if spring would ever come back to Portsmouth. (Again, nothing.) Would the Shipyard fire me for abandoning my job? Bobby rallied enough to say that he thought his boss at the warehouse would forgive him; we hadn't been gone all that long, had we? Beth kept half her attention on the conversation, but never said a word. If she noticed I wasn't wearing the flimsy fae dress I'd had on just minutes before, she didn't mention it.

My car was still where I'd parked it next to Beth's in the Catholic cemetery, but my keys had gotten lost at the start of our adventures in fae-land. Beth, who was always losing her keys, religiously kept a spare in a magnetic key holder under her fender. I found the key and started her little Ford Focus.

I cursed myself for blocking her car in. How were we going to get it out of the snow next to the access road? But Bobby pushed and rocked the car till the tires got traction. I steered and gently gave it gas. Beth sat in silence in the back seat as I drove slowly *around* my car through the icy snow. I managed not to knock over any tombstones. Finally Beth's car bumped back onto the road and Bobby climbed into the passenger seat next to me.

Getting downtown wasn't easy. Both sides of the snowy road were packed with parked cars, cop cars, tactical vehicles, and big green Army trucks. I marveled that I remembered how to drive. How long *had* I been with the Fae, three days? A week? And how much longer had I been in the next world over? Although I returned to Portsmouth a few seconds of Earth time after I left, I'd lived in nonlinear time among the elves for a year or more.

Streetlights shone on red brick facades. Dirty snow piles threw shadows. Downtown was deserted in the freezing cold. The snow-narrowed streets still *looked* familiar; so did our old house, the house I'd shared with Beth and Bobby—and once shared with Leda. The landlord had plowed, so I parked in our driveway.

Nothing *felt* familiar. Portsmouth wasn't *home* anymore. It was like the *light* was wrong here. No matter how long I stared at the furnishings of my ordinary life, there was no going back to it. I was locked out because I'd found a new home and made a new life. New, vivid memories outshone old, dimmer ones. However nostalgic I felt, I couldn't really go back to Buffalo, or return to my carefree college days. And I couldn't live in Portsmouth anymore.

I had a husband now. *There's* a thought I never expected to think; I was still getting used to the idea. I didn't tell Beth. Her mind was on overload right now and closed to new inputs. All she knew was that I was here in our house to help and protect her—and to protect Bobby, of course. Protect them from what, though? From Portsmouth itself? From the government? From the bad guys?

Beth's surface thoughts fizzed in a repetitive, anxious blur: *Gotta get out of here, gotta get home, gotta get me and Bobby out of here...* And so on. I tuned the poor girl out.

Beth scurried around changing clothes and packing what she needed to take to Providence. That took all her suitcases and both of mine. (*I* wouldn't be needing them.) Bobby changed and packed everything he'd accumulated here in Portsmouth in five minutes flat. It all fit in one big canvas duffel bag: boom, done.

He sat down with me at the kitchen table. We were all still safe here, as far as my elf perceptions could tell.

Bobby smiled a big, genuine smile at me. "You look good, Janjan. You're tan! Even your eyes look different."

He made me smile. "You're not flirting with me, are you, Bobby?"

He shook his head. "I wouldn't flirt with another girl, especially with Beth right here in the house. I think I know where you went. You went to the elves, right?"

"You know about the elves?" I said.

"Sure! When I was little, we used to leave cakes for them in the grove. We knew they wouldn't hurt us, but we were still scared of them."

I remembered. Bobby was born in the 1800s, a simpler time when everybody knew about the elves, because sacred groves were everywhere. Before the twentieth century brought nuclear weapons, human treachery, and black magic to seal Earth off from all memory of the next world over.

Sometimes you have to ask stupid questions because it's your duty. "Would you like to come back with me now, Bobby? I know you didn't want to go when Jerry asked you..."

Bobby looked at me for a long time, I mean really *looked*. It was odd, but it didn't make me uneasy. I'd moved beyond mere social awkwardness. What he was looking for was there for anyone with the will to see it. *Remember, Love and Light*, the angel told me—in Elvish so I'd never forget. Memory, compassion, and illumination, the gifts new elves accept when they *inquire within*. Bobby saw those things reflected in me.

"*I'd* like to go," he finally said, "but Beth wants to put all the other worlds behind us and just live *here*—down in Providence, I mean. If I want to marry her, I guess I have to stay."

"Between the wars you fought in and the time you spent with the Fae, you haven't had much time just to be human," I said. My way of telling him I understood what he meant.

Bobby looked at me sadly. "Neither have *you*, Janjan. You seem very young to me."

He wasn't wrong, but I laughed anyway. "It seemed like the best thing to do," I said. "We all ran to the Fae to get away from the Magicians. When we came back to Earth, we were still in danger. I went to the elves to save as many lives as I could." I held my hands out in the *what are you gonna do* gesture.

Bobby was looking at me, I realized, the way he'd look at another man who was his equal. "Sometimes you have to kill to save lives," he said. He was talking from his own war experience. "Sometimes you have to run away to live to fight another day." He *had* seen Jackson kill Simon, then. He'd seen Jackson and me sit with Coran and Maeve while they were dying. He'd seen us face down Michael and Burke and send them packing. I saw these things in his mind. In matters of life and death, Bobby never missed a thing. He saw me as a reluctant warrior, like himself.

When Beth returned to the kitchen she found Bobby and me in tears, standing up and hugging each other. I waved her in and the three of us wept and rocked and hugged. *I* knew why we were all crying. Bobby knew why he and I were crying. But Beth only knew why *she* was crying. What? I might have been an elf, but I was still a bitch.

Bobby took Beth's keys and began loading his one bag and her many bags and boxes into her car's trunk and back seat.

"You don't hate me for leaving do you?" Beth said. "I mean, the rent, and we'll need heating oil soon…" I heard the panicked thought behind her rapid speech: *Jesus Christ, gotta get out of here. Jesus, Jesus…* Her beautiful face looked haggard. Anxiety would push her into brittle, premature middle age if she didn't find her way to peace.

I left a hand on her arm. "Sweetie, can't you come with me one more time? The next world over is pretty great." It was stupid to ask, but I wanted to help her and I couldn't lie.

For the first time, Beth looked at me closely. "Whatever happened to Leda is happening to you," she said. "It looks good on you, Janjan, but it's not for me. It's all … too *weird*." *Is Bobby done loading the car? Gotta get out…*

She blamed everything on *me* and hated herself for that irrational thought.

"I'm sorry for what happened to you," I said. "I had no idea anything like that was possible…" I would have said more, but she interrupted.

"Janjan, I had a baby that wasn't a baby. I mean, I carried that child in my body. Where is it now? What the hell am I going to tell the priest when I go back to church? What happened to my son? I don't even know what happened to *me. Other worlds?* Fuck that. I am so out of here, Janjan, I can't even." Now she was sobbing. "I just want a *normal life.*"

"Go with God, my sister," I said. I spoke quietly in English, not Elvish, so as not to rattle her further. She was my friend, not some kind of elf-science project, and she was incapable of hearing anything else I had to tell her.

Beth drove Bobby south in her car. I didn't know if I'd ever see them again. Life on Earth kinda sucks sometimes, and you can quote me on that.

Traveling as the elves do, I left the empty house. I'd ask the Elf Friends to square things with the landlord later.

68

Jackson and Moira Drive South

Jackson drove Moira's car out of Portsmouth on I-95. He drove smoothly, just above the speed limit. He'd already spent too much time talking to the police today.

With the radio off and the heat on, Moira fell into uneasy, exhausted sleep, only to wake up staring at him in a panic. Once she remembered who he was, where she was, and how they'd gotten here, she nodded off until unease woke her again.

Jackson could empathize. At their first meeting, Moira had been at the top of her game, while he'd been assigned a mission where failure meant death. It gave him no joy that they'd reversed positions.

Darkness alternated with light from the highway. The instrument panel glowed blue. Her eyes moved rapidly under the lids. Jackson read bad dreams in her thoughts. He whispered an Elvish blessing: *Rest in God, my sister.* The eyes stopped their restless movement. Moira drifted into deeper sleep, smiling like a little girl.

She's been through a lot, Jackson thought. *She has no safe place to go.*

Jackson wondered what he should do for her. He knew what he *could* do for her, but would she accept it?

Seeing that the big car was low on fuel, Jackson pulled into a rest stop. Moira blinked her eyes a couple of times as the deceleration woke her up. This time she knew where she was and remembered who Jackson was.

"I'm glad you're awake," Jackson said. "We need gas and I haven't got any money."

Moira smiled at him. "Thanks for driving. I feel like I've been out for hours." She opened her purse. "Huh, my wallet, credit cards and cash are all still here. I guess witches don't need money."

"Honor among thieves?" Jackson said. He regretted the joke when he saw that it hurt her feelings.

"I suppose so," she said. No smile.

She thought he was calling *her* a thief because of who she worked for. He dropped the subject. You can't talk somebody out of a bad conscience.

Jackson pumped the tank full and Moira paid with a credit card. He parked the car and they went into the restaurant, such as it was, to use the bathrooms and order coffee and food.

Jerry had warned Jackson that living in the next world over made it hard to enjoy Earth food. The rest stop menu magnified his problem. He chose a grilled cheese sandwich and hot tea with a splash of milk. The sandwich tasted bland, greasy but tolerable. The tea was hot and tasted strongly of cardboard take-out cup. The trick, Jackson found, was being grateful for the nutrition in front of him. He gave thanks silently.

Moira ordered the same thing Jackson did along with a liter bottle of water. She was hungry and thirsty, but took no enjoyment from her food and drink.

From her body language and the blur of her surface thoughts, Jackson could see she was preoccupied. "May I ask what's wrong?"

She forced herself not to cry. "The Walloon showed me pictures of my sons at college. To get me to go up to Portsmouth with the Morrigna, whatever *they* are. *He threatened my kids.*"

Jackson nodded. "The Walloon is the head bad guy. I used to work for him. But of course you know that."

Moira examined Jackson's eyes closely. She inspected what she could see of his face and hands that looked lightly tanned here in the dead of winter. "Oh, my God," she finally said, "are you an *elf?*" She whispered the question, although no one was near enough to overhear.

Jackson thought, *Huh, she's forgotten how Janjan and I talked to her mind-to-mind to remind her she wasn't a tree.* "People here *call* us elves," he said. "It's not what we are, but I guess that's as good a name as any."

"But you know what *I* am—or at least who I work for. Aren't you going to kill me?"

Jackson laughed. "No! MMs may try to kill us, but we don't kill anyone we don't have to." Seeing her puzzled look, he added, "I was told the same thing you were told. I was very surprised when Jerry August didn't kill me and then offered to *help* me."

"Jerry August of the *Portsmouth* Augusts? I was told he was missing."

"Moira, the Order tells us all kinds of things." Jackson spoke gently. "The truth doesn't matter to them. And I guess Jerry did go missing from Earth when he went to the next world over."

Moira reached out, gripped Jackson's forearm, and looked him in the eye. "Mr. Jackson, can *you* help me?"

It was the first false note he'd seen in her. A stronger Southern accent than usual, really quite a performance. *Moira's basically a decent person and an attractive woman*, he thought. *She thinks she needs someone to rescue her. She does. She also thinks that damsel-in-distress act will affect my judgment. It won't.*

Jackson patted her hand where it lay on his wrist. Her hand was still cold. "Like I said back in Portsmouth, the honest answer to that is *Maybe*. What kind of help do you need?"

Genuinely confused, Moira withdrew her hand. "Well, my sons," she said, as if that explained everything. "They're in danger, aren't they?"

"Probably," Jackson said. "There's only one safe place in all the human worlds. Will your sons agree to go there with me? I can take you there right now. Will *you* go with me?"

Before Jackson got all the words out, Moira was shaking her head and silently mouthing *No No No*. Denial was pretty strong in most human minds. *Do not inquire within*, like Janjan said. Jackson didn't want Moira to fall back into shock. She was scared; he didn't want to scare her to death.

"Moira, it's okay. *It's okay*. Nobody has to do anything they don't want to do. We're not about that. Really." Her eyes were wet when she looked up at him. "Go ahead," he said, "finish your sandwich, drink your tea. Watch me." He stuffed a good quarter of the gummy sandwich into his mouth all at once and said around the food, "Mmm, good!"

Moira laughed, wiped her eyes with a paper napkin and took a tiny bite of grilled cheese. "You're right. It is good. Sort of."

"Yeah," Jackson said, "like it's good to be alive. Sort of."

They talked some more. Moira agreed to drop him off close to the Walloon's mansion. She'd wait for Jackson at the Tyson's Corner mall, where she'd get a hotel room. After he paid the Walloon a visit, he'd come find her and they'd make further plans. If Jackson hadn't found her in three days, she could assume he wasn't coming back. At that point, she'd be on her own.

Jackson didn't tell Moira anything about his plans, or that Janjan would be meeting him. If the bad guys happened to find Moira before Jackson came back, she couldn't reveal what she didn't know. She'd given him no reason to trust her.

At their first meeting back in Washington Moira told Jackson, *What we want is to cut the elves off from Earth.* Was that what she still wanted?

69

Showdown at the Walloon's House

A considerable percentage of the people we meet on the street are people who are empty inside, that is, they are actually already dead. It is fortunate for us that we do not see and do not know it. If we knew what a number of people are actually dead and what a number of these dead people govern our lives, we should go mad with horror.

G.I. Gurdjieff

Okay, I didn't *immediately* go find Jackson. I knew he was still in Moira's car on the road south. Our minds touched. It's *so* hot to touch your lover's mind—once you get used to the idea. We gave each other comfort and agreed when to meet.

Then I went back to Great Bog. During my training in the next world over, Jerry August told me, *Go talk to people. Listen to what they say and what they don't say.* I've never been shy. Along with the other new elves who'd come back here with me, I talked to the officers in charge of the National Guard units and the various police organizations who'd been sent out in the cold to keep the peace. Or whatever the hell they'd been told to do with the wandering Fae of legend and the (mostly) American citizens who'd returned from walking with those fabulous creatures.

How had the Authorities all ended up in Great Bog? Because that's where all the clues pointed. That's where all the footprints led. That's where all the cars were parked. The police were here because so many solid citizens had gone missing. The local police asked for state police assistance. The governor declared an emergency and mobilized the National Guard. Most of the federal civilian law enforcement types were legitimately searching for missing federal employees or for illegal aliens crossing the (invisible) border. National security and so on.

A few of the feds were here because the Materialist Magicians had sent them.

All of the people in charge were men. I may have mentioned that I enjoy certain advantages in dealing with them. I was in great shape after my timeless time among the elves, but I was never going to be a beauty like Beth. Nevertheless, I find that men respond strongly to a woman who possesses her own sensual self in peace and power—straight men, anyway. I didn't have to manipulate anybody or use any of the magic embodied in the Unfallen Tongue to get my way.

Instead, I simply asked those men for their help.

For example: "Good evening, Major," I said to the man dressed in gray-and-white camouflage. "Or is it good morning?"

He stared at me for a long moment. Unless I flatter myself, the Major *got* me; I was having a strong impact on him. He finally managed to say, "Ma'am, aren't you *cold* standing out here in just a hoodie? Can we get you a blanket until the buses show up?" Guardsmen were distributing shiny thermal blankets to the semi-disoriented people who were now freezing and mortal out here a few steps away from where they'd been walking in the near-warmth of near-immortality. The Authorities weren't prepared for the crowd of people who'd appeared in Great Bog. As for me, my teachers would not have let me return to Earth until I mastered the art of inner heat. The elves had learned a lot from those who'd come to them in recent years. They knew what I'd be going back to and what skills I'd need. I wasn't thrilled about the extreme cold, but the temperature was only a minor discomfort to me now, not a danger.

"Major," I said, "*look* at me. Do you know who I am?" I was asking if he knew *what* I was. The signs of the next world over were there for anyone to see.

He looked me in the eye and then looked away. "I guess I do, ma'am. We were kind of briefed that you folks might be, um, involved here tonight."

"Call me Janjan. Everybody else does. And what do you mean by 'you folks'?"

He looked at me. More accurately, since he was taller, he looked down at me and back up again. "You're not exactly from *Earth*, are you?" He smiled nervously, caught himself looking at my boobs, then looked away. Men are a riot. My breasts are okay, but nothing special.

"I was born on Earth, same as you. But you're right, I don't live here anymore," I said. I was very curious about what he'd do with that piece of information.

"Ma'am... *Janjan*, I think you need to talk to the Colonel."

❋

I talked to the Colonel in his mobile command center. I talked to a bunch of high-powered Elf Friends who showed up, lawyers mostly. (Jackson had called them from the road.) Together, we talked to the local and State Police. I talked to certain representatives of Homeland Security, most honest, some not. (The dishonest ones walked away from our discussion unhappy.) I talked to the FBI and the CIA (all honest, thank goodness).

I talked to a couple of guys from the Naval Criminal Investigative Service who charmingly seemed to believe they had some claim on me because I was employed by the Navy. They also walked away unhappy when I refused to go somewhere they could interview me in private. I'm not stupid. They were honest, but I didn't know about their bosses.

I talked to elves both on Earth and in the next world over. I talked mind-to-mind with Jackson. All this talking took a while. The sun was up behind clouds before I was done.

Later that morning I borrowed a phone and called Estelle.

"Janjan," she said, "what kind of trouble are you in? I've had investigators from Navy and the three-letter organizations crawling all over me." I could read her surface thoughts over the phone. She was frightened. I tried to put her at ease.

"It's more of that old Portsmouth nonsense, Stell. Our government's busy doing damage control to hush it up right now. But I've got good news. Some of your people who, um, *disappeared* will be back at work soon—if you'll have them, I mean." I was a little surprised to see former colleagues who'd abandoned jobs and families follow me back to Earth. I understood why they hadn't gone to the elves with me. They just wanted to get back to their old lives and forget all the weirdness.

"Are you *kidding* me?" she said. "We've been a mess for weeks. Schedules are slipping. Everybody's blaming *my* office for not supporting waterfront work—like *that's* the real problem. The Pentagon is *very* unhappy with Portsmouth Naval Shipyard. If my subordinates come back, I will French kiss each and every one of those smug Maine mamas. No offense."

"None taken," I said. "I'm from Buffalo and I approve this message."

She paused. "Are *you* coming back, Janjan?" She'd already guessed: women's intuition or whatever.

"I'm sorry to leave you this way, Stell, but I kind of got *myself* pulled into the old Portsmouth weirdness. Couldn't be helped. I've got a new job now." My turn to pause. "Would you like to hear about it?"

Silence, then Estelle's habitual brittle staccato manager tone: "I really have to go, Jan. Morning meeting. Once I get this office running again, I've accepted a job down at Norfolk. I can't *wait* to get out of Portsmouth. Best of luck to you."

Click.

❋

Having accomplished as much as I could in Portsmouth, I left things in the capable hands of my fellow elves and the Elf Friends. I traveled to where Jackson was waiting for me in Virginia. Just like that. Mind touch turned into inner acceleration as I cooperated with certain natural laws that had previously been invisible to me. I found my husband standing on the side of the road in a place I'd never been and could not have found without him to home in on.

I hugged him hard like we'd been separated for years. I started crying, couldn't help it. It was such a relief just to *see* him again. Such a relief to have him share the mission with.

"It's really all over for us here, isn't it?" He knew I meant Earth.

"Oh, honey, no. *No.*" He hugged me back and rocked me. "*They're* our brothers and sisters, too. We can actually help them now—if they'll let us."

"Yeah?"

"Yeah. Um, did you just wipe snot on my shirt?"

"...No?"

Just like that we were laughing quietly. This was a dangerous place. Bad things had happened not far from here.

We walked a few hundred yards up the narrow road. It was warmer here than Portsmouth, but I felt a chill that couldn't be explained by the temperature. With minds linked, we cast our elf perceptions in wide circles around us. We walked quickly until we entered a driveway hemmed in on both sides by evergreens and by trees that wouldn't see leaves again till spring.

There's a guardhouse up ahead, Jackson thought. *I'm not picking up anything I recognize as a motion detector, but what do I know? I'm an ex-magician, not a spy. The Walloon may have some sort of passive system that's telling him visitors are here.*

We made inner adjustments to our minds and bodies. We moved more quietly than most human beings and radiated less body heat. We walked up the road silently and cautiously.

The guardhouse was empty. The door was shut. We walked on by. Poking around in there might trigger an alarm.

The road meandered through the woods. It should have been pleasant with the red sun sinking in the west and light still shining through the trees. It smelled good, dry earth and old pine needles. But the sense of threat increased with every step we took. The fine hairs on the back of my neck stood up. I began to feel sick to my stomach.

I looked a question at Jackson.

He looked sad. *Black magic leaves its mark on the fine-material part of the physical world*, he thought, reminding me what we'd been taught. *It frightens people away from a place the MMs want protected. If I'd stayed with the Order, I'd have learned how to do this. Unless of course they decided to kill me first.*

I rubbed his broad back and felt the muscles warm under my palm. *I'm glad you chose as you did*, I thought. *I love you.*

When we go home, he teased, *I'll let you wash the snot off my shirt.* A pause. *I love you, too.*

We walked on through the trees. We walked on the one-lane road or next to it. We moved the way animals walk a trail, irregular pace, always alert for danger. No outer danger appeared, but the inner sense of threat screamed at us from somewhere up ahead. We began to feel that the whole body of the Earth lay poisoned and dying.

Partly, it was the simple math of travel to the next world over. Returning to Earth felt like putting distance between ourselves and the source of all life. It felt like losing Paradise.

I'm almost sorry we came back here, I thought.

Jackson thought back, *What else could we have done?*

I knew what he meant. We'd signed up for this.

❀

The Walloon's mansion was dark and silent. No lights shone on the circular drive as we emerged from the woods.

I saw where the threat originated. That fucking house looming over us made me want to spit. It was worse than haunted.

But we walked up the steps to the big front door. Jackson hesitated, wondering if he should knock, then just grasped the handle in the center of the door. The door swung open.

Membership has its privileges, Jackson thought. *The Walloon left the door unlocked for me.*

I pushed the door mostly closed behind us. A bit of flickering light came from a door down the hall. I smelled a wood fire. Having been here before, Jackson took the lead. I focused my senses behind us and to the sides: no immediate threat. We walked silently down the hall.

At the door of the only lighted room Jackson halted. I stood behind him guarding our backs. Still no one.

A man's voice came from inside the room, "Mr. Jackson, is that you? Come in, come in. And your companion as well, of course." I heard a trace of accent, as if the man had said "*monsieur*," instead of "mister."

Jackson beckoned me into a library with floor-to-ceiling bookshelves. We took positions on either side of the door and let our eyes adjust to what light there was. Heavy curtains covered high windows. The room was lit only by a fire in the fireplace. Sitting next to the fire was an older man of medium height. He wore a suit and tie. He appeared to be unarmed, but I wasn't fooled. All the danger we'd been feeling since we entered the estate centered in the Walloon and emanated from him.

"Master Louis of the Order of Materialist Magicians," Jackson said, "allow me to present Ms. Jadwiga Javorski." For my protection, he kept our marriage out of the discussion.

The Walloon examined me with eyes that looked bronze; that color wasn't entirely a product of the firelight. "You were named for Jadwiga of Poland, the queen who was called a king?"

"And a saint of the Roman Catholic Church," I said. "My mother hoped I'd enter the convent."

The Walloon didn't even pretend to be amused by my ironic tone. "Mr. Jackson, why have you two come here stinking of elf? Have you perhaps betrayed the Brotherhood to the High Enemy?"

Anger flared in Jackson's mind, but his voice was calm enough. "The Order has twice tried to kill me. Speaking of betrayal."

The Walloon waved that off. "Tsk, Master Simon seems to have exceeded his brief. His, er, *reports* to me ceased some time ago. Has Master Simon *himself* ceased?"

Jackson didn't bother to reply. They both knew Simon was dead.

I felt a separate current of threat spill out of the dark hallway behind me. The muzzle of a handgun came around the door. I went to one knee, grasped the pistol, and pushed it firmly back toward the shooter's wrist. He let go of the pistol quickly before his hand broke.

This left me with the gun. I don't do guns. I'd never learned about firearms; elves don't need them, even new elves. What was I going to do, shoot this guy? I'd been taught to preserve life if I could.

I was much faster than the man now pushing into the library from the hallway, but he was *absolutely determined* to kill me first so he and the

Walloon could kill Jackson next. It's daunting having somebody fix his whole mind and will on taking your life for no apparent reason.

That wasn't the only daunting thing. Behind me, Jackson adjusted his spirit as something profoundly evil formed up to attack him. He needed my help. Jackson was as new to this kind of battle as I was.

The guy whose gun I held produced a knife and moved point and edge to cut me. Time slowed further. Inner vision gave me a view of the impending battle as if from above. As my eyes adjusted to the reality in the library, I saw the killer's flat, cold eyes. The deaths of others were nothing to him. His own death was a mere inconvenience. He had been on the Dark Path of the Materialist Magicians for lifetime after lifetime. I hadn't detected his mind because it was as blank and focused as a pit viper's.

Pistols aren't complicated. Hoping for the best, I held the weapon steady with two hands and squeezed the trigger. The pistol made a huge fucking noise. *Huge.* My ears rang. A small black hole appeared in the man's forehead. All the life went out of those dead eyes. He fell. He would have hit the back of his head on the floor if his skull had been intact. I managed not to throw up. Maybe later.

I made sure the hallway was empty of other bad guys, dropped the pistol on the floor, and turned to help Jackson. Guns are no use against the rulers of the darkness of this world.

What I saw made me want to turn tail and run away screaming like a little girl. I feel bad for men that they're so afraid of being called cowards. Jackson wanted to run away, too, but he stood his ground. I stood with him. Scared as I was, I wasn't going to leave him behind. I'd absorbed the elves' code along with all the practical skills they taught me.

Behind where the Walloon sat in his comfy chair stood a giant shadow. The man had given his will over to the shadow, or to the shadow behind that shadow. It was shadows all the way down in that ashen dimension. Turtles would have been better.

The shadow was no illusion. It was a creature my senses could make no sense of. A creature who hated Jackson as a traitor and hated me as a vile temptress. That would have made me laugh, but the thing's attack was making me sick.

The attack came through the Walloon, embodied itself in whatever ectoplasmic odds and ends it broke loose from the man's physical body and human psyche. The shadow formed itself into a snake made of darkness, a serpent with huge, terrible, knowing eyes on either side of its smoky head and dripping fangs in its gaping mouth. Whatever it struck would surely die of its venom. It shrouded the Walloon's torso and head like his body was on fire; the snake looked like a coherent seven-foot cylinder of smoke.

Is it all true, then? I'd asked the angel who guards the next world over from horrors like the one undulating through the air toward Jackson and me, *Adam, Eve, the Fall...?* I hadn't asked about the Serpent, but that was implied. *It's all true*, the angel said.

If you've ever wondered how people can encounter real personal preternatural evil and still not believe in God, well, evil is pretty fucking scary when it's right in front of you, coming to despoil your spirit and destroy your body. I'm just saying it's hard to think about anything else, especially if that *anything else* seems faraway and abstract to you.

I was more worried about Jackson than I was about myself. You can be the biggest little bitch in town and still put somebody else's welfare before your own. I loved him. I feared for him. He might have had his sins forgiven and his mistakes corrected, but it takes a while to heal the wounds of our deepest weaknesses. Jackson and I had not lived in the next world over long enough to do that.

New elves come back to Earth for that kind of healing. An old, old tradition that Richard Round had restarted back in the 1980s.

Jackson and I had met the elflord Richard. He taught us a lot without telling us much more than how to address him. ("Call me Dick," he said.) We'd sat in his presence and let him smile at us until we understood the smile was a blessing. Sounds weird, I know, but there it is. He demonstrated what he'd learned from all that happened to him. He showed us mind-to-mind how he'd helped his stepfather's spirit escape the Fallen—even though the man had tried to kill him.

Anyway. The Walloon, or the creature that worked him like a sock puppet, was directing a hard sell, first at Jackson, then at me. What came as communication in English words and in thought-images only partially masked its ungovernable lust to destroy the lives of beings it believed had no worth and no right to live: *us.* Its speech carried dispatches from an eternal war against all embodied life on Earth. I'll just paraphrase the surface meaning, which was bad enough.

Do you [Jackson] *not want power? Behold what power is and does.* [Visions of great wealth, slavish followers, possessions, houses, cars, yachts, world travel.] *All this can be yours!*

Would it be such a great matter if a short-term concubine [Me] *were to disappear forever? No one knows where she is. Who would come looking for her?*

Are there not more and better women who would be yours for the asking, once you become a High Adept of the Brotherhood? [Visions of tall, willowy, glamorous, and willing women appeared.]

This little Polish whore? Utterly disposable.

Or so said the hideous wracked and smoky face that emanated from the Walloon's thorax. It bobbed like a fever dream in unseen thermal currents of the shadowy library.

The *great matter* of this transaction was deciding where Jackson's loyalties lay. To ascertain this, the creature offered Jackson a false choice.

While it was busy tempting Jackson, the creature tried to block all my communication with the man I'd sworn myself to, who'd sworn himself to me. The enormous sense of threat it wielded roared in my mind like burning static. My nostrils stung with the stink of sulfur. Demons must figure they can't go wrong with the classics.

The thing offered me a false choice as well. *You can escape, little whore,* it told me. *Best do so quickly before this limited-time offer expires.*

But. I wasn't going anywhere.

Jackson wasn't buying the demon's pitch, but it threw him into conflict with himself. He fought against his own guilt, which he had lots of. I had to speak for both of us.

"You know this is bullshit, right?" I said. My spoken Elvish was more elegant than the bare English translation, but that was the exact point. I spoke to the thing that spoke through the Walloon. "You lost this war before human history began. How could you expect to win a war against your own Creator? We have no use for you. Begone, creature of God!"

The creature of shadows hated what I was saying. It hated the Unfallen Tongue I spoke even more: bad memories. The serpent began to fray and disperse like smoke.

The dispersion was only a strategic withdrawal. Louis allowed himself to be wrapped in the demon's shadow and began to disappear into it. As he faded from the room, the Walloon reached out a hand, imploring Jackson to save him from his master: *Help me, Obi-Wan Jackson!*

Jackson bought it. His thought to me was clear, hard, and determined: *I have to do this, Janjan. I have to undo the damage I've done on Earth.*

Jackson disappeared from the Walloon's library, traveling as the elves do in pursuit of Master Louis.

I found myself alone again, standing in the empty library next to a corpse. Firelight gave the dead man's face the illusion of some terrible meaning I couldn't grasp.

Poor Edgar Allen Poe, I thought. *This is like living in his brain.*

70

Mo Mountains, Mo Madness

The elves called it *the marriage of true minds* long before Shakespeare. My mind was linked to Jackson's. I knew where he'd gone. I also knew he didn't want me to follow him there.

I followed him anyway. He wasn't my boss, we were equals.

What was I going to do by myself in the Walloon's deserted bad-vibe mansion with his henchman dead in the hallway? Run away screaming? Clean up the mess I'd made? Call the police and explain how it was self-defense? Go to jail? No, thanks. *Let the dead bury the very dead,* I thought. I could have gone back to the next world over to wait for Jackson, but my place was at his side wherever he went. His place was next to me. We were *spoken for.*

I caught up with him in an instant. He was standing in the middle of a dim, foul-smelling place with rough smoke-blackened rock walls and ceiling. It felt like a cave.

I saw movement. A white-faced man stood watching us from a dark corner like a phantasm. He vanished, leaving only innocent shadow. The man who wasn't there.

The Walloon arrived here seconds before Jackson. When I showed up, Louis fled. He'd wanted to get Jackson alone to leverage his weaknesses, to win him back to the Order, or to kill him. Either the Walloon was no match for two elves, or he couldn't offer Jackson anything comparable to little me, she said modestly.

Jackson gave me the Look. Without me to worry about, Jackson *thought* he could protect himself from Louis, and maybe even help Louis escape the Fallen. I didn't *need* his protection, and I wasn't about to let him fall into a trap. I gave my husband the Look right back. Nobody puts Janjan in the corner.

We started out scowling and ended up smiling. We couldn't stay mad at each other.

Back to business. We cast our joined minds out like a net, seeking the Walloon, wherever he might have gone. It seemed to me that killing him would be the best possible use of our time. *Don't start nothing, won't be nothing*, another inelegant translation from the Elvish. The Walloon's scary employee should not have attacked me. The Walloon and the demon that ruled him should not have attacked us. My blood was up, and not in a good way.

There were nasty psychic traces for us to follow. These lingering, invisible, fine-material marks led our minds around the World Mountain from world to world until the trail grew faint and we lost it. Too far. Too many worlds. Too many arrivals and departures. We were new at this, and the Walloon was an old master who really didn't want to be found.

More to the point, the Walloon didn't want to be saved from the Fallen. Jackson began to accept that there was nothing he could have done for Louis, who'd surrendered his free will to the Claimant.

But the cave had mostly been Simon's home. Ugh, what a nasty place. The rock retained recent psychic residue from Simon's meeting with the

Walloon. A lot of emotion on Simon's side, none on his master's. How frightened the old man had been that Louis would kill him. How determined Simon had been to kill Jackson once Louis ordered it. I didn't blame Jackson for wanting to stop the Walloon, who'd set all the madness in motion.

Jackson shook his head, frustrated. I threw my arms around him, feeling what he felt, but not sure why he felt it.

Out in the wider world, we found no mind-traces of anyone else for miles and miles around. The locals wisely stayed far away.

With hot pursuit impossible, I recovered my cool. "Why are we chasing a bad guy, anyway?" I said. "We don't do that." By *we*, I meant the elves. "And where are we *now*, by the way?"

"In the Caucasus Mountains," he said. "Europe? Asia? Somewhere in there. I never asked. As to *why*, I thought maybe Louis was tired of *being* a bad guy."

I raised my eyebrows and thought, *Tell me more.*

Jackson smiled at me and kissed both my eyebrows. Dude loved my eyebrows. In his own quiet way he was as much a freak as I was. Even in this awful cave, the touch of his lips on my forehead aroused me.

"This is where Simon taught me before I came back to Portsmouth," he said. I intercepted a tight beam of the emotion he associated with these caves, none of it good. "For centuries, the Order has trained its disciples here. Only the strong survived."

"*You* survived," I pointed out.

"I did," he said. "But there's a lot I never learned because Simon purpose-trained me. The Walloon's idea was to have Simon sacrifice me so my bound spirit could keep the portal to the Fae open."

"Sounds like a waste." The MMs' intents and purposes never made much sense to me.

"The Order needs time to recruit and rebuild. They wanted the energy from my death to cement poor Bobby in place. We would have deflected people to the fae-road—and away from the next world over—until the Brotherhood could close the door to the elves forever." He sounded bitter and tired.

"Let's get out of here," I said. "I'm glad you're still alive, by the way."

He smiled, maybe a little sadly. "Me, too. Wanna go to the mall?"

71

The Mall's Got It All

Jackson had been to the Tyson's Corner Mall before, so we were there in an instant. Nobody saw us arrive.

It took one phone call from a pay phone (they *do* exist) to find Moira. She'd used a personal credit card and registered under her own name at the nearby hotel. She was still alive. The MMs had been willing to sacrifice her back in Portsmouth, but nobody had been sent to find her here yet.

We weren't far from the Walloon's empty house. Where had his guards and household staff gone? The Walloon himself was somewhere in the human worlds executing escape and evasion maneuvers. The scary guy I'd shot had been his security manager. Jackson and I had taken Simon, Burke, and Michael out of the game back in Portsmouth. Because of their fanatical information security, the bad guys had a lot of weak links in their chain of command. Had they simply lost track of Moira in the fog of war, or was someone using her as bait, watching the hotel from a distance to see who came to her door?

Jackson and I took the stairs up from the lobby. We found no sentries in the stairwell. We entered the carpeted hallway on Moira's floor. Our joined senses encountered nothing more dangerous than the strong smell of commercial carpet cleaner. Our minds scanned the entire hotel around us: only normal human beings and no threats. The hotel manager's office probably had a monitor and a digital recorder for the building's security cameras, but no one was in the office. The manager was walking around touching base with her employees, keeping things on track. We'd be gone before anybody ever bothered to review the video footage. If the MMs did that, they'd know who Moira's visitors were. What would happen to her then?

I wasn't sure why Jackson cared what happened to Moira. Didn't she still work for the bad guys? Hadn't she *earned* whatever happened to her? But she and Jackson had bonded like fellow employees do while he drove her back to Virginia. I didn't need chivalry anymore, but I guess Moira still needed his help. *Our* help.

Yes, I went into this predisposed to dislike her, thanks for asking.

We knocked on the door of her suite. She let us in all wide-eyed and panicky, shut the door quickly and locked it behind us. I thought, *Drama queen.*

"I'm so glad you found me," she said, all in a rush. Her tone was breathy, and she spoke to Jackson like I wasn't even there. I took a close look at the lady, interested in what made her tick. Clinically interested, too, in the kind of woman to whom a little fat girl (me) was invisible. She'd been beautiful once, but her beauty was fading fast, as beauty does on Earth in a woman's late maturity. That thought gave me no satisfaction. I've never been the jealous type and now I had no need to be jealous.

Jackson's manners were excellent. "Moira, allow me to introduce my wife Janjan."

Moira's gaze lighted on me briefly. "Hello, Janjan." *Hello, pissant.* Her gaze flicked back to Jackson. She didn't offer to shake hands, but some women don't. "I had no idea you were married, Mr. Jackson," she said. She *wanted* him—for reasons she refused to even think about. She wasn't going to get him; she also refused to think about that.

Jackson rested his right hand on the back of my neck. He saw my thoughts. *I love you, Janjan,* he thought. *You're right, she is a drama queen.* To Moira he said, "We're newlyweds."

❋

The three of us sat in the suite's living room. Moira sipped white wine. Jackson and I drank bottled water. It tasted flat. I'd gotten used to living in the next world over where the water really did taste like wine.

We talked. Boy, did we talk. Jackson told Moira things about the Order she'd never known. He expected that hearing those things would persuade her how bad the bad guys were, impress upon her what evil people employed her. But no, she couldn't or wouldn't believe the extent of it.

Jackson and I shared a glance and a thought: *Jesus, no wonder the elves don't try to convert or convince people on Earth that they should choose differently and live differently. It's fucking impossible.*

I saw why Jackson cared about her. She reminded him of his mother. At some deep level, he was thinking he'd been unable to save his mother from her own karma, but maybe he could save Moira. Once I realized it, he knew it, too. The elves—*we*—save whoever we can, but they have to *accept* our help. Usually they don't.

You're not wrong, he thought to me. *But there's a practical side to this.* His thought flashed to my mind in pictures and whole concepts.

❋

I figured it was time for the girls to talk. "Moira, have you thought about the Walloon's threat to hurt your sons?"

"Do *you* have any children, ...Jan?" she said. Pretending she didn't remember my name. Playing the Mommy Card. Women can be horrible to each other. Her tone implied that there was no way a childless girl like me could possibly understand the suffering she, the Blessed Mother, endured. The old Janjan would have hated her. The new Janjan didn't much like her, but I'd signed up for this.

I *growled* at her, a low, wordless sound. Jackson looked askance at me, but I was tired of the lady's bullshit. "Look, I don't know for sure if your kids are in any danger," I said. "Jackson and I have offered to take the three of you somewhere safe. I understand why you don't want to go. *I* wouldn't have gone to the elves, either, if I'd had a better choice." She started to protest again, but we'd already been over that ground. I held up a hand and spoke as gently as I could. "Let me finish."

Moira shut her mouth as if I'd slapped her. She sent a look of mute appeal to Jackson *(Look how rude she's being to me!)*, but he was watching me with admiration and affection and didn't notice her look. Finally she looked back at me, really looked at me like she was seeing *me* for the first time. She nodded.

Like I said, it was time for the girls to talk. Moira was finally willing to listen.

She hated everything I had to tell her, but she didn't interrupt. The poor woman looked pale and stressed. Even so, she agreed to my proposal.

Our proposal, really. After I told her what *I* wanted her to do, Jackson outlined what *he* wanted. He made it clear that she was free to accept my suggestion and reject his, especially given the extra danger she'd be putting herself in.

Moira smiled at him as if he was being silly. "No, I'll do what you and Janjan want," she said. "The bastards forfeited my loyalty when they threatened my family."

Steel Magnolias, I thought to Jackson. He nodded. He'd never seen the chick flick, but he'd grown up with Southern women.

72

Entr'acte *(Nonlinear Time)*

I shook Moira's hand (limp, but at least she made an effort). I hugged Jackson and kissed him goodbye (that was hard, and so was he).

They took the elevator down to the garage and Moira's car. Since I was traveling elf-style and alone, I didn't need either an elevator or a car. I left the hotel room and met Leda in the grasslands of the next world over, as we'd arranged.

We hugged hello. Leda said Jerry had just left for Earth. He'd be meeting with Jackson, Moira, and some Elf Friends outside Washington. I was encouraged not to inquire further.

Mind reading and instantaneous travel simplify the battle-planning process. No kidding, right? The Navy would be green with envy if they could bring themselves to admit those things are possible. But most of the Defense Department was busy pretending the real enemy was one crazy faction or another in the Middle East. Or was it the Russian Federation? The enemy couldn't possibly be the hidden Materialist Magicians whose vast wealth was pulling our political strings, goodness, no. Facing up to the real problem would mean an end to the status quo; none of the authorities wanted that.

Leda and I walked to Nextworld Portsmouth for our meeting. It was strange how much the great river and its surrounding geology looked like the Piscataqua I remembered; it gave me double vision. Of course the next world over had no political divisions like "New Hampshire," "Maine," or even "the United States." On Earth the U.S. government blew up Henderson's Point in 1905, because it created a menace to navigation. Here, where people could easily swim or walk across the river or levitate above it (and there were no warships or freighters, only boats crafted for play), we just called it "the point over there" and enjoyed the powerful currents.

The point of this get-together was to prepare me to do what I'd signed up for.

Everybody has gifts. Jackson's had to do with inner power and with *healing*. Mine had to do with the deep joys of sexual pleasure, duh, but also with *leadership*. It's a hell of a thing to believe you're a little fat girl who enjoys going to clubs and going to bed with men and women—and then to learn that Maeve queen of the Fae had been right, that you really are sort of a queen who is also a king.

I would not have predicted that. My own mother would not have predicted that. My friends on Earth might have predicted it, but only when they were drunk. My father would just have told me I could do anything I set my mind to. Then he would have made me recite the Saint Crispin's Day speech again.

Jadwiga of Poland, help me now, I thought. The people gathered around me smiled. They began teaching me things about energy that would help me find the Fae again.

Wherever the Fae had gone now that Coran and Maeve had entered the round of human rebirth and the Morrigna ruled in their place.

What *were* the Morrigna, exactly? Even the elflords and elfladies didn't know. If not Old Gods, the sisters were beings of an older sort than human beings. Still dangerous, though, to the Fae and to all who joined them.

Were the Morrigna dangerous to me? Would we even be able to see each other? So many unknowns. But now that we knew about the Fae, we had to offer our fellow creatures escape from the fae-road. That's what the elves do. And by "we" I mean "me."

I sat on the grassy bank of the great river with Leda, my very impressive friend. It was a warm and perfect day. The next world over smelled so good you wanted to laugh, things growing according to their perfect nature. This world felt so good to the body and mind, it was like you'd just had really good sex and would soon have more of it. Along with us sat Aimee and Daniel Ryun who'd both trained Jerry to bring Leda back from the world where devotees of the nameless god and goddess had imprisoned her.

Aimee and Daniel had been longer among the elves than Leda and they were even more impressive in the quiet way of the High Elves. Aimee looked like a beautiful young woman. Daniel might once have been too old for Aimee as Americans judge these things, but now he looked ageless. As Jerry August learned when he first met Daniel and Aimee, there was no such thing as a "May-December romance" among the elves. There were only people who found themselves *spoken for*, and there they were in each other's arms.

But maybe not forever. Because of his adventures (and his suffering) on Earth and in other worlds, Daniel had a different relationship to his physical body than Aimee had with hers. It wouldn't be long, as the elves think of duration, before Daniel would find himself called upcountry. I was still a newbie, but when I looked with my peripheral vision, I saw traces of Daniel's spirit shining around the outline of his body. That spirit wanted to go somewhere the rest of him wasn't ready to go.

Would Aimee be called upcountry with him? That's one of those rude questions the elves answer only with a joke.

Jean-Paul Herold and his wife Donita, it was said, walked naked into the high country. In seeking the deepest healing and the deepest wholeness, they'd walked right out of the body—while making love. Later they'd returned together to the joys and limitations of the flesh, *because they were needed*. Where were they today? If I asked, my teachers would smile and say, *Go and see for yourself*.

Aimee Amory-Ryun, though she was wise and kind and strong and beautiful, was still very much a creature of the body, it seemed to me. We sloots know each other. Aimee had once been married to another woman, one who punished Aimee for their mutual pleasure. She and Daniel were faithful to each other as the elves are—as Jackson and I were—but I could tell that other sexual joys sometimes called to her as they called to me.

Okay, fine, I found Aimee attractive. She found this amusing as she found me amusing. And she found me attractive, too. Elves have no need to hide their true selves and desires from each other. That's one reason they're able to remain faithful to their mates. That, and the fact that nextworld sex is both thrilling and profoundly satisfying. Your true self comes out to play with your lover's. Nevertheless, nothing was going to happen between Aimee and me, not as long as we were married to others, and we both knew it: *spoken for*.

Elves don't use people simply to gratify themselves or to achieve their ends. No decent human being does that, and the elves were honorable both in their own world and wherever they traveled outside it. Not always, but usually. People are ends in themselves, not means.

I mention my thoughts about this because Leda, Daniel, and Aimee in particular helped me think them. All three knew more about me than I knew about myself, and loved me for what I was. When I went back to

Earth this time, I'd be going alone. Jackson's mission lay elsewhere. We'd still keep our mental connection. But I was going to have to lead others—and this was the tricky part—without coercing anyone or violating anyone's free will. Certain skills of perception were required.

So Daniel sat on the riverbank in that beautiful world and centered himself. Aimee and Leda helped me see him with what might be called the eye of the spirit. I learned to identify the clear color of wisdom warmed by more-than-human compassion. Once I'd learned to see that light clearly in Daniel (as the poor man's spirit kept trying to fall out of his body), I learned to see the light in Aimee, his faithful wife. I saw the light in Leda, my friend and former housemate.

Because of the gentle hold Daniel's spirit had on his body, his mind had been able to locate Leda in the Other World of the Old Gods, a world that was opaque to the rest of the elves. Daniel showed me mind-to-mind what he did with his mind and spirit that let him see what no other elf could.

Like Aimee, I was a creature of the body. I didn't like taking my mind *out* of that body, even for a short test flight under Daniel's guidance; it gave me vertigo and made me feel lost, almost scared. *(Whose body is that below me? Is* that *what I look like?)* But stepping out of the body might be the only way for me to see the Fae and try to walk their road again.

Discernment of spirits, telling the good from the bad, is simple enough. But what about the Fae who refuse to choose?

I needed discerning wisdom to go back to Earth and work with Moira, a woman divided against herself as most people on Earth are divided.

Before I met up with Moira again, I'd be visiting Bobby, who'd first walked the fae-path long before I was born in this body. I would ask Bobby to help me return to the Fae. I'd have to persuade him to leave Beth, the woman he wanted to marry. Leave her only temporarily, I hoped. For the greater good, I guess. Anyway. It would be his decision.

And if Bobby did agree to go with me for a while, I'd have to persuade

Beth not to hate me forever. I hoped we'd all still be friends at the end of this.

As I sat on the warm grass, safely back in my body again, I looked at my hands, still my own little fingers, but much stronger now, toughened up from learning to fight, nails short and clean. My legs were solid with muscle as were my arms and the core of my body. I was, as discerning gentlemen would put it, still *thick*. There was still a bit of chub over the underlying muscles. My teachers had trained me for strength and endurance, not low body fat. I'd never felt stronger and healthier; it happened very gradually without any drama or deprivation. My skin was slightly darker than it ever could have been back when I was, ahem, a milk-white maiden.

My hair was darker, too, but still reddish. Elf gals cut each other's hair short and don't worry about it; hair grows slowly here, anyway. I looked a little different, but I was still basically the same person I'd been when all I cared about was going dancing, getting drunk occasionally, getting laid as often as possible, and getting to work on time at Portsmouth Naval Shipyard. I don't mind admitting that I kind of missed the old days. Living in Portsmouth—even wondering what I was doing there—had been easier than this new life I'd chosen. I'd chosen freely, but still.

At least now I knew what I was doing here. Wherever "here" happened to be. Many mansions, and all that.

73

You Again? *(This February)*

The day Leda got kidnapped and all the weirdness started in Portsmouth last year, Beth and I were having Thanksgiving dinner at her mother's house in Providence, Rhode Island. I knew the place. Traveling as the elves do doesn't let you go wherever you want on every world. There's no danger. If you get it wrong, you just don't go anywhere. Us newbies either need to have been to a *place* before, or we need to have a connection to a *person* there. That person needs to be moving no faster than a stroll. Aimee says trying to meet up with someone in a moving car or boat is like threading a needle in the dark while wearing mittens.

But even if I hadn't been here before, I knew Bobby. I'd shared a house with him and walked the fae-road with him and Beth. And of course I knew Beth very well, having lived with her for several years—and having spent one ecstatic night sharing her bed and teaching her my secrets. I suppose they're open secrets. Oh, well.

Having absorbed all I could about matters energetic and metaphysical,

I left the best possible world for Earth, a much worse one. I didn't have to worry about time while I was among the elves. I popped into Providence near Beth's mother's house in the Federal Hill neighborhood. Beth and Bobby were just pulling into the driveway.

That was a timestream surprise. I figured they'd have arrived yesterday in Earth time. Or maybe it wasn't a surprise. They'd both been exhausted when they left Portsmouth. Once they got safely out of town and the adrenaline wore off, they must have spent the night in a motel before driving the rest of the way south.

I saw them before they saw me. If you're short and elf-trained, it's easy to be inconspicuous. I was wearing loose black pants, soft boots, and a thin black sweater under a roomy gray hoodie. If you're visually boring and keep your attention centered within, other people's attention is deflected to more compelling sights. Neither of them noticed me.

Their unguarded faces were unhappy. They hadn't had a pleasant evening. Beth still looked strained and anxious. Bobby looked exhausted and sad, the way men look when women give them no sleep, too much talk, and not enough sex.

Bobby got out of the passenger side door and opened Beth's door like a gentleman. Beth sighed dramatically, got out of the car, and turned to finish what she was saying to him. Then she caught sight of me. Her face went through several emotional changes before it settled on ... *wonder.*

Beth ran up and hugged me. "*Janjan!* I almost didn't recognize you. You look so ... *different.*" She meant: *How is that possible?* Remember, she'd just seen me yesterday. Today she saw in me what we'd both seen in Leda when she came back—to recruit me into the Elf Friends.

I hugged her back and held her tight. My friend. My very good friend. I reminded myself that in Beth-land nothing essential had changed since I drove her back from Great Bog.

"Sweetie, I'm so sorry about this," I said, "but I need to ask Bobby to help me with something. If he says yes, he'll be coming with me for a while."

Beth was always transparent—even before I went to the next world over and started learning to read thoughts. She felt *relief,* deep and guilty, but all she said was, "Okay...?" She'd committed to Bobby too quickly in the heat of the moment back in Portsmouth. Now with no baby on the way, she was having second thoughts. I saw some of those thoughts.

Bobby was looking at me in simple wonder. I must have looked more different to him than I knew. No mirrors in elfland, just still water and the minds of others. He was wondering how I'd changed so much in only a day (as he saw it).

Bobby was a good and decent man, but this century was not his homeland, not even close. He thought Beth was going to marry him. He thought he'd bring home the bacon, she'd have his babies, and they'd all live happily ever after. Little did he know. During yesterday's drive from Portsmouth to the motel outside Boston, and during the drive to Providence today, Bobby babbled on about the happy life they'd have as husband and wife, spinning plans for the future. Beth developed reservations about bringing home this wandering, no-college-no-career time traveler to live with her and her very inquisitive, very conservative Catholic mother. Beth had been trying to tell him that she wasn't altogether ready to settle down, and shouldn't they take a break from each other to get some perspective? Bobby had been trying to talk his way back into her heart. Good luck with that, dude.

I didn't mention that Jackson and I were married. This visit wasn't about me.

"Bobby," I said, "I have to ask for your help. Could you maybe buy me a cup of tea in that coffee shop over there?"

Beth didn't mind if Bobby had tea with me. Not at all. She practically pushed him at me.

We walked across the street. He got me black tea and got himself coffee with real cream. He methodically stirred three sugars into it, way more than I would use. The homeless really load up on carbs and calories. It's a cold-weather survival thing. While he was living with us in Portsmouth, Bobby would fill the bottom third of his cup with sugar before adding the coffee. Hobo-style, I guess. Beth and I teased him into dialing back on the sugar, so three sugars was progress.

We got a table and sat looking out at the street. Providence had much smaller snowbanks than Portsmouth. The sun peeked through the clouds, the temperature inched above freezing, and the filthy city snow began to melt. I sniffed my tea. It smelled horrible; my senses had become painfully acute in the next world over. I debated whether milk would help the tea and finally decided it would. I went to the counter and poured some milk into the paper cup. The barista smiled at me, nodded in Bobby's direction. He was staring out the window looking lost. Winter light turned the sadness in his ordinary face into something … noble.

"He's cute," she whispered. She looked about twenty, probably a student.

"He is," I said, "and so are you." I smiled at her. Old habit or simple mischief?

She took in my short elf-girl haircut, no makeup, no visible jewelry, old clothes. Her surface thought was: *Asian? Lesbian? Hipster? Polyamorist? All of the above?* She gave me a flustered smile and busied herself behind the counter. Guess I wasn't her type.

I really shouldn't hit on people anymore, I thought. *I'm a married woman, for God's sake. I still haven't gotten used to the idea.*

I sat back down with Bobby.

"I been trying to think what help *I* could give *you*, Janjan," he said. "Is this about the Fae?" I saw on his face and in his thoughts that he hoped that was *not* what I wanted.

Around his body I also saw traces of the greenish energy years of walking the fae-path had left in him.

"You can say no," I told him. "I probably would if I were you."

Bobby looked out at the street again, thinking. Clouds moved back in front of the sun. There wasn't much traffic here this morning; everybody was at work or in school. Bobby sipped his coffee, made a face. It was too hot and still not sweet enough for him.

He turned back to me. His face was full of fatigue, no surprise, and full of old sorrow. "Janjan, I'm so damn *tired*. I'll help you if I can, sure, but is there somewhere I can rest? I feel like I might be dying or something."

I reached out and put a hand on his forearm. New perceptions showed that he wasn't dying, just exhausted. Spending a long time among the Fae, even in increments separated by years, was bad for people. Bobby's exhaustion went all the way down, body, mind, and spirit.

"I can help you with that," I said. "Right now. And you don't have to help me first—or even after. Just *come home with me*."

What was I saying? I didn't know how I was going to *find* the Fae again without Bobby's help. If I took him home to the next world over, all his green *light of other days* would be transformed. It's nothing human beings were created to live with or in. But the man in front of me had to come first, even before the mission.

Bobby grinned at me. He put a hand on top of the hand I'd kept on his forearm. "I know what you are," he said. "I owe you my life. I'll help you now and you can help me later, okay?"

"Okay," I said.

Bobby didn't have a phone. Neither did I. If you travel elf-style, you're lucky not to end up at your destination naked. You enter the next world over pretty much empty-handed; you depart with only the clothes on your back. The coffee shop had a pay phone, talk about retro. I called the office of an all-Elf-Friend law firm in Boston, identifying myself as Jerry August's business associate. Jerry had talked to them, and they'd been expecting my call. The woman who answered the phone said the firm would send a car for us.

Bobby and I spent an awkward hour chitchatting with Beth and her mother at her mother's kitchen table. Beth introduced Bobby, not as "my boyfriend" but as "our housemate." Bobby was hurt, but he pretended nothing was wrong, like men do. I was beginning not to like Beth very much. In my defense, I was still relatively new to this whole elf business, not at all enlightened, and I had some serious shit to do. Because I was Beth's friend and maybe a better one than she deserved, I explained to her mother that Bobby and I had "work back in Portsmouth." Beth gave me an embarrassed, grateful look. I gave her a level look that meant *Why did you lead him on? You're better than this.*

When the Elf Friends' car pulled up out front of the house, Beth walked us out to unlock the trunk of her car so Bobby could get his bag. She gave him a one-arm hug and quickly retreated into her mother's house. He watched her go, thinking, *But I love you.* Anyone, elf or earthling could have read the thought in his face.

"That's just Beth, Bobby," I said. "Better you find out who she is now than after you marry her."

Bobby made the face men make when they're fighting their feelings. "But you're her *friend*," he protested. He wasn't accusing me of disloyalty so much as asking why Beth was distancing herself from him.

"I *am* her friend," I said. "I'm also *your* friend. I want you to be happy with whoever you love and marry."

"Thanks, Janjan," he said. He shook his head and made the angry face men make when they're fighting off tears.

Bobby opened the car door for me so I could sit in the back seat. He got in front next to the driver, and off we went. He slept most of the way north.

I touched base with Jackson mind-to-mind. He was still in the preliminary stage of what he'd signed up for. We exchanged information and said *I love you*. That's not something I'd either said or heard much during my, um, sexually active years. I see now why people say it and enjoy hearing it. It's really something to hear from someone you're attracted to. *Thrilling*, is what it is.

If the driver bothered to look in his mirror at the chubby little elf girl in the back seat, he would have seen me smile.

74

Back-to-Bog

The driver dropped us off on the South Shore of Massachusetts. The house sat in the middle of a big lot; it was situated so neighbors couldn't see who was coming and going and ground surveillance would be difficult.

The housemother was a solid, smiling, middle-aged Elf Friend, retired military, with a holstered handgun on her belt. She assigned us rooms, showed us the kitchen, and told us when meals were served. Bobby thanked her and took himself off to bed. He said he'd see me at dinner. He was really tired, poor guy, and bed rest was only part of what he needed.

We'd be in this house for a day or two. Ugh, I hate waiting around. I was strongly tempted to go home—not to Portsmouth, but to the next world over. I stayed where I was. Earth was where I was needed. I'd signed up to do something nobody could do better than I could. But I didn't want to be here in this house right now; it made me restless.

If we'd had phones, the housemother would have put them in secure storage till we left. She kept the single house phone locked in her room—

disconnected. For security reasons, the house had a no-phone, no-internet rule, but the place offered TVs, DVDs, books, newspapers and magazines. I was tempted to strike up a conversation with the housemother. But instead of using someone or something to distract myself like I used to do, I sat on the floor of the sparsely-furnished little guestroom and closed my eyes. I had to synch up with the world of my birth again.

I entered meditation one breath at a time. Nobody who'd known me on Earth would have believed me capable of such a thing.

I remained in that hard-won concentration for hours of Earth time. My teachers were right: the meditation centered me in my true strength. A lot had gone wrong on Earth. Jackson and I had to fix what we could—and not worry about everything outside our control. Elves aren't reformers, missionaries, or martyrs. We can't govern the world or the people in it, so we work on ourselves.

As I came back to a more ordinary mental state, I tuned in to the minds of all my brothers and sisters both at home and here. Between the elves and the larger number of Elf Friends, there was a lot going on. It was like reading the news online, constantly updated, only this was information from people who told the truth. Also no health and diet fads, fashion tips, or celebrity gossip.

Jackson had invited Moira's boss Stephen to dinner and made a modest proposal. That proposal frightened the CEO deeply, but he agreed to think about it. Jackson, the former bad guy, was unable to threaten or coerce. Stephen agreed to meet three days later at a neutral location with representatives of the Elf Friends' Boston law firm and their asset managers. The man was terrified, but he'd been living in fear for years, a fear made more acute by the fact that Moira had never returned from the Walloon's house. Was she dead? And where was the Walloon? The phone at Louis' estate rang and rang without being answered or going to voicemail. No new orders came. Stephen was terrified not only for himself but for his family. Jackson told Stephen nothing about Moira and kept her separated from him; Stephen thought the Walloon had killed her and then fled the country. My husband still was kind of a bad boy.

Our allies interviewed Moira for hours about the accounts she'd been managing for the Order. The lady kept a lot of information in her head, an occupational requirement for those who manage money for the rich and crooked. She held nothing back.

Of course Moira's company was breaking any number of laws. The Elf Friends would give the evidence to the proper authorities, who would either take action or bury the case. The evidence would also go to the news media, even if journalism had become unreliably partisan in recent years. *The Wall Street Journal* would never be first to carry a story about another financial industry scandal, and who trusts *The New York Times* anymore?

Having set things in motion, Moira and Jackson picked up her sons at their school. At first, the boys thought their mother had succumbed to hysterics. They balked at leaving school so early in the semester.

Jackson convinced Moira's sons they were in danger where they were. The man was pretty good at making his case without exaggeration. He'd acquired gravitas, my Jackson. Even if their mother turned out to be suffering a break with reality, Jackson pointed out, wasn't it better to humor her? Plus: road trip. Couldn't they use a break? Best case: they'd survive but have to repeat a semester. Worst case: they'd be murdered at school but get posthumous credit for their courses.

So Jackson, Moira, and her sons were on the way to the South Shore safe house. They'd arrive tomorrow. I got all tingly just thinking about it.

❋

My tingles turned out to be for nothing. Jackson pulled up in the circular driveway at the wheel of Moira's car. He was wearing a business suit, courtesy of the Elf Friends. What *is* it about a strong man in a suit? I looked forward to taking it off him. Who knew what would happen then?

But Jackson got a mental communiqué from our Washington associates: *Shots fired, two Elf Friends wounded, High Aghartic deployed.* I got the same *Calling All Elves* summons, but along with it came direction from Daniel and Aimee Ryun: little Janjan was to round up Bobby, Moira, and her kids and head north straightaway. The guerrilla attack on our Washington friends was likely designed to deflect us from stealing the Walloon's wealth and from doing ... whatever the hell I was going to do up in Portsmouth.

Jackson and I shared a kiss and some hot mind-to-mind lovemaking. Woof. Then he was gone. At least we were still in touch. That may be the best thing about the next world over. You always know where your lover is, what he's doing, and what he's thinking about. He has the comfort of knowing that about you, too, even while he's conducting reconnaissance against the enemy.

✳

Moira and her sons looked a little shell-shocked. It's hard to understand seeing someone just *disappear* after you've spent hours in a car with them. They needed a hot meal and a nap, but a meal was all they were going to get.

I rousted Bobby out of bed and handled the introductions. The five of us sat down at the safe house dining room table. The housemother served us, pleased to have that many people to fuss over at once.

Then we got back on the road.

✳

Moira drove her car. She mostly kept her eyes on the road, but her glance kept touching base with the blond frat boy son who sat up front next to her and flicking toward the mirror to see the dark-haired frat boy son who sat in the back behind her. I sat in the middle between number-two son and Bobby. Everybody was frightened; they had every right to be. I'd been expecting a bit of condescending douchebaggery from these handsome, privileged young men, but Jackson had impressed upon them the seriousness of the occasion. Both sons remained wary and quiet.

I asked Moira to stop for gas, just to be on the safe side. I had no idea what was going to happen next. While one of her sons filled the tank for her, Moira and I went to the ladies' room together. There wasn't much traffic on this road tonight. We had the place to ourselves.

As we were washing our hands, I asked her, "Will your boss be meeting us in Portsmouth?" Jackson was busy right now protecting Elf Friends; he hadn't said or thought anything about hiding Stephen with the Fae. I needed to know if I'd have anybody else to shepherd. Things were complicated enough with just the five of us.

Moira shook her head and began to weep quietly. She wiped her eyes with a wet paper towel. "You can't do the work I do—excuse me, the work I *did*—without pretending not to know who you really work for," she said. "Stephen probably hopes everything will work itself out without having to *do* anything *himself.*" She put a lot of contempt into that last word. She didn't have much respect for the man.

Jackson had continued to keep Moira and Stephen apart, then, because he didn't fully trust her and because Stephen hadn't committed himself to anything yet. Her boss didn't know Moira was still alive.

I shrugged. "We've already talked about where you have to go if you want to be safe. Stephen was told the same thing. Everybody has to make up their own mind about going there." I paused, then, "Moira, traveling with the Fae isn't good for people; it's just a long vacation from the human condition. It's only a temporary solution to your problem. Are you *sure* you want to do this?"

Moira started a repetitive autism-spectrum head-shaking routine. Just *thinking* about seeking safety in the next world over weirded her out. I saw in her unguarded surface thoughts that she hoped we—the elves—would save the day and eliminate the threat against her. So she and her kids could just go back to their old lives. So her little family could just forget the weirdness and the unpleasantness—and the Walloon. The elves had worked wonders before, and life had gone on as usual for almost everybody. She was hoping everything would *work itself out without having to do anything* herself. All she had to do was step off the Earth until her troubles went away, right?

"No. No. *No*," Moira said. "Let's get out of here before the Walloon kills my whole family." She managed a grin. "If he kills my ex-husband, so be it."

❋

There's more than one way to get into Great Bog. A direct, easy approach was out of the question—given the number of federal, state, and local authorities who'd watched all the people stepping off the fae-path with me, apparently out of nowhere. Someone would certainly be guarding the main road. And whose side would they be on? Probably not my side. I didn't plan to ask permission to go where I needed to go.

We'd have to take an indirect approach to get to the spot where the fae-road touched on Earth. The bad news: that route required us to hike for miles through wetlands and rough terrain. The good news: the wetlands were frozen solid and covered with snow. We hadn't brought snowshoes, but the earthlings were all dressed for the cold and wore winter hiking boots. Nobody was going to get frostbite on this trip if I could help it.

I'd thought this out in advance; I knew the territory. I had Moira drive the car down a back road that bordered the east side of the bog. She pulled into an industrial park out of sight of the road. She backed into a shadowy corner with the car's exhaust blowing invisibly into the surrounding trees. I turned off the dome light before I got out of the car.

"I'm going to scout the area to be sure it's safe to hike in," I told Bobby, Moira, and her sons. "Don't turn on the interior lights or step on the brakes, okay? We do *not* want to talk to the police tonight."

Everybody nodded Okay. I'd made them all leave their phones back at the safe house, so there would be no screen lights to give them away, either. They'd just have to sit there and be bored till I got back. *Boredom*, what a concept. That was a part of the human condition I didn't miss.

No cars on the road. No sight, sound, or mental trace of human beings nearby. I used my heightened senses and found that we'd been lucky. Back here, the security cameras pointed at the loading docks, not at the parking lot. I walked a roundabout route to stay out of camera range and crossed the road.

As I was about to step into the frozen wetlands, Leda appeared: pop! We shared a grin, exchanged flashes of information, and entered the frozen marsh.

❈

You might think that anyone waiting for someone like us would have the advantage. You might think they'd hear us crunch crunch crunching across the snow. Nope.

Balanced just above the ground like Marty McFly on his *Back to the Future* hoverboard, Leda and I paused just inside the marsh. We joined quiet minds and extended our elf perceptions out across miles of marsh, across the thickets and abandoned orchards and snowy fields, across all of Great Bog. Sure enough, the authorities had set up a perimeter on the Portsmouth road to keep people out. No surprise there. The government had moved into nothing-to-see-here mode. That's what governments do, isn't it?

We *were* surprised to discover soldiers camouflaged and motionless on a little hillock between us and the spot where Earth intersected the ancient fae-road. We looked at each other, thinking, *A whole sniper team just for us?*

There were three men, a sniper, an armed spotter with some sort of night vision scope, and a roving flanker with a night vision headset, who guarded their blind side. I touched their minds and learned that they were

413

warm and dry on this cold night, wearing layers with snow-white camouflage on top. I learned that they were battle-tested, having fought in much hotter places than Portsmouth. I also learned that they were waiting for *me*, little Janjan, in particular. They'd been given my picture and ordered to kill me and anyone with me. Because apparently I was an enemy of the state, a traitor or spy, something of that sort, rather than a former entry-level civilian employee of the same Defense Department that employed them. There was a vein of corruption in the American government. Military officers bought by the MMs had ordered honest soldiers to do bad things.

These guys didn't like their orders. Killing unarmed women doesn't sit well with decent American men, and these three weren't bad boys. They'd heard rumors about "elves." They wondered why the Army would want us dead, not captured, especially if we really were some sort of deep-cover Islamist terrorists.

They had a secure communications net with only the three of them on it; they didn't like that, either. They were ordered to leave all cell phones behind. They thought maybe somebody had isolated them, set *them* up to get killed because they'd seen or done something overseas that threatened someone's political future. An officer they didn't know (he wore no name tape and no rank insignia on his uniform) had briefed them while their own lieutenant sat silent, staring at his boots. Military operations inside the United States were illegal; the nameless officer wanted them to pretend this mission never happened. They were way off the books, more easily available (and less traceable) than an armed high-altitude Reaper drone.

The spotter was thinking he hadn't seen a damn thing all night and didn't expect to. The sniper was thinking if he did acquire a female target, he could shoot to wound her and take her prisoner, orders be damned. The flanker was glad he got to move around, slowly, slowly, given that this whole mission was bullshit, that he didn't expect to see anyone sneaking into this godforsaken frozen clusterfuck, a year to go on his enlistment and he was so out of this business, what was the goddam point.

I thought of Bobby who'd had to kill more people than he'd wanted to in two better wars than any on offer in the twenty-first century. I thought of me who'd had to kill one implacable enemy because there was no better choice.

In two seconds, Leda and I reached a decision. I waited while she went for the flanker. I didn't hear anything, but five seconds later I heard her voice in my mind: *Got him. Your turn, kid.* She'd rendered the man unconscious.

I'd spent enough time skiing in Great Bog that I could travel instantly anywhere in it. I appeared behind the sniper and the spotter. I could smell that they'd been peeing in the snow close by. Ugh, boys. Girls, of course, only excrete rose water. Actually, my heightened senses were a bother on Earth. Even in winter, the world smelled far worse than I remembered.

The men didn't hear a thing until I was on them, whispering spells in Elvish and altering the energy of their bodies so their minds shut down.

Got 'em both, I thought to Leda.

We carried the first two men across the marsh using a fireman's lift. Little fat Janjan had gotten *strong* in the next world over, as had beautiful Leda of the hourglass figure. It would be more accurate to say the elves had shown us how to use our true strength. We left the two guys in the mostly-dark parking lot next to Moira's car. (The four people who'd been waiting for me stared, astonished, out breath-frosted windows.) Leda said I should save my strength for the busy night ahead. She went back across the marsh and soon came back with the third guy.

We got all the passengers out of Moira's car and quickly stuffed the three unconscious soldiers into it. We didn't want them to freeze to death. When the spell wore off at first light, they'd wake up naturally, wondering how they got here and where their weapons were, but otherwise feeling fine. I was glad we hadn't had to kill them. I wondered who'd ordered them to execute me—and why—until I remembered that didn't matter. The MMs and those who work for them have standing orders to kill all of us if they can. To accomplish that, they'd burn the Earth to a cinder. With them it's spite and shadows all the way down.

Getting Moira and her sons into Great Bog was more work than hauling the sniper team out of it. Bobby, who'd suffered through most of the Civil War and the Second World War, slogged along like a good soldier, willing to endure anything to keep his promise.

Moira started having misgivings about the expedition when she put one boot through a thin crust of snow into freezing water. She went into a helpless Southern Belle act. Bitch that I am, it was hard for me not to be sarcastic and obscene about that. But Moira's sons, after a nervous look at my Serious Face, each took one of their mother's arms and helped her along. They thought I might be one of those radical lesbian feminists the frat boys whisper stories about around the campfire.

Bobby stepped up, too, offering his hand to Moira at stone-wall crossings and such. Did Moira smile at Bobby with a little extra wattage? When Bobby offered to relieve Moira's sons on a narrow track, Moira leaned on Bobby's shoulder gratefully, while the boys walked up ahead of them and I walked behind.

Leda scouted way out in front of us, looking for trouble; she found none. We'd agreed not to speak Elvish aloud again, except in emergency. Using magic is like sending up a flare to those who know how to look. It wasn't men with guns we were worried about, it was men with black magic. The Walloon was still at large on one of the human worlds. Without warning, he could appear in front of us in an instant, carried by his guardian demon.

Shudder. Seriously, what is *wrong* with those people?

75

Not I, but the Wind

We approached the spot I remembered so well. The place where Coran, king of the travelers wrapped in light, had spoken to me out of the air, or seemed to speak. The place where Beth, Bobby, Jackson and I had leaped onto the fae-path—and leaped back off it again. It looked like everywhere else in Great Bog now, cold and snow-covered with perfect impartiality.

Were there shoeprints and bootprints? Sure, but they were no help in getting back onto the fae-road. Thousands of people had trampled over all of the central acreage. I knew exactly where the spot was, but I couldn't *see* anything helpful here, not with my human eyes, not even with my expanded elf perceptions.

I looked at Leda. She looked at me. She couldn't see anything, either. She shrugged, grinned, kissed my cheek, and disappeared. Whatever happened next was up to me.

Now what? I didn't want to take my mind out of my body if I didn't have to, not here in the war zone.

Moira looked amused at my predicament. I saw something in Moira I hadn't seen before. The energy around her body turned the pale green of new leaves. "Can you not see the doorway, then?" she said. Her posture and manner of speaking changed. Another act?

"I can't see it, Moira," I said. "What do you see?"

"Ah, well, the door's plain as day to me, but I haven't the strength to open it. For that, I'll need the help of *this* handsome lad." Moira removed her thick glove and held out her lily-white hand not to either of her sons, but to Bobby.

The light surrounding Bobby turned a deeper green. He blushed as he took off his own glove and grasped Moira's hand.

And there as if an invisible door had opened, I saw the fae-road.

"Are you sure you want this, Janjan?" Bobby said. Such a sweet man.

"I think we have to, Bobby," I said. Then to Moira's sons, "You first, gentlemen. Step right up."

With some hesitation, the frat boys took the first tentative steps of their fae-road trip.

I stepped through, took Bobby's hand, and pulled him and Moira in with me.

The door closed invisibly behind us. I felt a rush of air. I looked around quickly. The air went calm again. I was left with the impression that something had flown past at high speed. Something invisible I was meant to take for wind. It might have been the cold air of Earth blowing into the warmer realm of the Fae. My intuition said it wasn't.

The first time we'd stepped onto the fae-path, Jackson and I had been disoriented, our perceptions unreliable with stress and overloaded by weirdness. We'd been whirled apart by a flurry of energies I couldn't see and by Fae I couldn't see clearly. We'd been given new clothing, and welcomed among the Fae with a great and prurient interest. They were delighted to have new people join them and excited to costume and transform us into something more like themselves. New recruits were their only source of novelty, sexual and otherwise.

This time I saw only dark road under our feet and unfamiliar constellations far above our heads. The road shone faintly with a darker green than I remembered. No Fae appeared to greet us or to challenge our right to pass along their ancient way. Nobody seemed to care about our wardrobe. Except for me in dark pants, sweater, and hoodie, the others were in unsuitable winter clothes and boots. I stuffed my pockets with the knit hat and gloves I hadn't really needed back in Portsmouth. I could have gone naked and still been okay; I'd have to think about that.

Bobby, Moira, and her sons unzipped their parkas and took off hats and gloves. It wasn't winter here, more like stepping out of the freezing wind into a cool warehouse.

Bobby looked around and sniffed the air. "Something's *different*. I've been here four times now, but it's never been like this."

He was right. "We're *breathing*," I said. The air was flat and cool with a faint smell of old fires, charcoal with overtones of leaf mold; it wasn't a bad smell at all, reminded me of autumn in Portsmouth. My lungs were doing what human lungs always do on Earth, bringing in oxygen and taking out carbon dioxide at a normal human pace. I *inquired within;* the air had nothing harmful in it. "I'm *hearing* you—instead of understanding what you *seem to say*," I told Bobby.

We were hearing each other's words because of vibrations traveling through the air into our ears, same as it was on Earth. Not knowing what the fae-path used to be like, Moira and her sons didn't understand why we were so amazed at breath and speech.

The Fae were no longer *breathing in for half of eternity and breathing out for the other half*. Inside myself I saw none of the suspended aging those who walked the fae-road had enjoyed. Inside myself I saw what was there to see when I left the next world over. All the metabolic processes of mortality continued unchecked. Wherever they were on the road, the Fae had lost their contingent immortality.

What the hell had happened here? What should I do about Moira?

She'd almost flipped out even thinking about coming with Jackson and me to the next world over, the only place she'd be certain of escaping the Walloon's vengeance. As a poor second choice, we offered to help her and her sons reach the Fae, thinking they'd all be safe among the forever-young who walked the fae-road around all the human worlds. If the fae bargain with the universe had been annulled, how safe were they now?

Moira's demeanor had changed dramatically when we reached the invisible doorway that took us out of Great Bog. The Morrigna had used their ancient magic to turn Moira into a tree of green energy that made her a doorway to the Fae. Jackson had done the same kind of thing to Bobby. I wondered how the *light of other days* was harming them.

The fae-path emitted a darker shade of green than I remembered, but it still rose to meet our feet, encouraging us to walk, almost propelling us along like one of those moving airport sidewalks. There was no wind at our backs; things had changed.

I was tempted to take Bobby with me and leave the aging Southern belle and her progeny to their own devices. But I'd made a commitment, hadn't I? It looked like they still needed me. And Moira had kept her part of the bargain, working with Jackson and the Elf Friends to divert the Walloon's enormous stolen wealth to better use than bankrolling militant religionists and bribing public servants. I kept my thoughts to myself and walked along with expanded elf senses extended in a great globe around me, ready (I hoped) for anything.

Whatever else had changed on the fae-road, I was mostly isolated again while I walked it. My mind was cut off from Jackson and from all my new friends. I missed the intimate connection with my husband. I missed everyone from the next world over. My training allowed me to see into the minds of the people I'd come here with, but they couldn't see into mine.

I walked out ahead of the little group. Bobby and Moira walked behind me, talking of this and that. The frat boys, let's call them Brad and Chad, walked behind their mother, not saying much. Brad and Chad were overawed by the total weirdness of our surroundings. They pointed, drawing each other's attention to faintly-seen rivers or cliffs or deserts or forests or lakes or oceans in the darkness on either side of the road. They knew they were looking at something few human beings had ever seen. That humility made me like them better.

Everyone accepted my leadership without question. Huh. Who is Janjan, little fat sloot or mighty elf warrior princess? I guess none of us turn out to be who we thought we were.

Bobby and Moira talked easily as they walked. Sometimes their shoulders touched or their hands brushed; the beginnings of genuine attraction were springing up between them. Bobby had no defense against women and Moira was bringing her A-game. Beth had broken Bobby's heart, but Moira's flattering attention was quickly mending it.

The attraction started when Bobby helped her back in Great Bog. What sealed the deal was when they joined hands and exchanged energy to open the invisible door that brought us here. Love makes the world go round, blah blah blah. Moira needed a man and Bobby needed a woman who needed him.

I wondered what would happen to that attraction when Moira learned that her handsome young gentleman caller had fought for the Union in the American Civil War. Yes, I still have a bitchy dark side.

❋

Hours later I saw the familiar outline of a Fae roadside castle up ahead. No lights shone out. I felt the presence of other minds, old, cold ones, three of them. No, *four.* Aw, man, I was pretty sure it was the Morrigna, plus one. The owners of those minds were waiting there for us in the dark, their thoughts hidden behind dark shields.

Bobby said, "Janjan, something's *wrong* in there—I can feel it. Where *is* everybody? Coran and Maeve died back in Portsmouth—did everybody here die with them?"

Dread is what Bobby was feeling. Evil magic leaves its stain on the world. I'd felt the same irrational fear in the Walloon's mansion and in Simon's cave: *This is a bad place. Go away.*

"I think it's the witches, Bobby," I said. "The ones who sort of turned Moira into a tree in Great Bog."

"Sssaahh!" Moira made a hissing noise. Her manner changed, as if another person animated her. But it was Moira herself acting out an archetype inherited from her forebears, now bubbling up from the unconscious. Her nostrils flared and her eyes grew wide. "'Tis *Badb and Macha*," she said, "and perhaps *Anann* as well. *The Morrigna* have come back to fae-flesh to plague their own folk."

"*Mom...?*" said Brad.

"You're *scaring* us, Mom," said Chad.

Moira, though, was not entirely frightened, not anymore. If I'm any judge of woman-scent, she was *aroused*. Bobby gazed at Moira with frank admiration. He was definitely aroused. Was some sort of passionate extramarital intercourse about to erupt right here on the fae-road? Won't someone think of the children?

For once *I* wasn't aroused. When you take the lead, you have to be the grownup. Ugh.

"What's the plan here, folks?" I said. "Do we go back to Earth?"

Moira shook her head. "Nay, for the Walloon will kill us there."

Nay? I thought. I looked at Bobby. He was having a hard time tearing his gaze away from Moira. He liked what he saw. "Let's make a stand here, Janjan," he said. I heard the old soldier's determined resignation. War reveals patriotism, religion, and high ideals as mostly bullshit; only your comrades are worth dying for. *Greater love hath no man* and all that.

I remembered that prayer had put Simon the magician off his game when he came looking to kill Jackson and me in that empty world beside the fae-path.

"Bobby," I said, "we're going up against evil today. Do you have a prayer you say?"

"Not for a long time," he said. "Years." He was thinking, *Religion is stupid.* He wasn't entirely wrong.

I said, "All I can tell you is that if you say a prayer to yourself, it scares the bad guys. How about if you repeat 'God help me' over and over?"

Bobby grinned. After all, he'd been to war and I hadn't. "How about 'God help *us*'?"

"That'll do fine," I said. "How about you, Moira?"

Breathing deeply, still in Celtic warrior queen mode, staring at me with hot eyes, Moira pulled a rosary out from under her sweater like she was ready to go cattle-raiding and chain-whip her pagan foe with the silver crucifix on the end of it.

"Perfect," I said.

That left the boys. "You guys know anything about fighting?" I said. Stupid question. Don't brothers fight each other at every opportunity?

Chad shrugged. "I've boxed a little."

"Jiu-jitsu," Brad said.

I acknowledged their modesty with a nod. *They* knew they were way out of their depth here. Whatever waited for us in the dark castle couldn't be punched unconscious or grappled into submission.

"Religious beliefs?" I said. Nothing I'd ask in polite company, but you look for whatever advantage you can get in a survival situation. Things of the spirit included.

Brad and Chad exchanged an embarrassed look.

"We're *Catholic*, Janjan," Brad said, like it was a dirty secret. He reached under his sweater and pulled out the cross he wore on a chain around his neck.

When Chad saw that, he did likewise. I didn't think their fraternity brothers knew what their faith meant to them. Unless maybe they were all in a *God and Man at Yale* study group.

Once a Catholic, always a Catholic. Moira glared at them, like, *You better be wearing the crosses I gave you.*

I couldn't help smiling. "I was named for Saint Jadwiga of Poland, but I'm not as Catholic as used to be. Wear those crosses on the outside, people. We're going in."

76

This Is Why We Can't Have Nice Things

And ye shall hear of wars and rumours of wars: see that ye be not troubled: for all these things must come to pass, but the end is not yet.

Matthew's Gospel

We walked up to the wide-open doors. It felt worse than the Walloon's house in McLean, or whatever suburb of hell his mansion actually sat in.

The castle was dark, except for a greenish glow from deep inside. My senses and my spirit reached into the darkness and found no threat of ambush, no enemies to right or left. The only minds I sensed were shielded ones directly ahead. The owners of those minds were waiting for us. They were not our friends.

I paused at the threshold and held my arms out. Everyone halted behind me. I'd overlooked something vital, but what?

I turned back toward the fae-road. Above I saw masses of faraway stars shining brighter than the stars over Portsmouth. Down the road green shadows merged with darkness to right and left. I tried to imagine the road circling on and on around all the human worlds forever. I couldn't picture it.

Oh, wait. *The road.*

As we walk from place to place worrying about our little problems, we ignore what's under our feet. I'd forgotten where I was and assumed the fae-road was made of the same stuff as any Earth street or sidewalk. It looked so ordinary, like dark gray concrete with random mineral sparkles, neither smooth nor bumpy. But I'd never really *looked* at the road.

I let my awareness settle gently onto its surface.

The path Bobby and Beth's child of fae-light *sank into.*

The path that *flexed* underfoot almost imperceptibly and then *pushed* gently to urge me along the way I needed to walk.

The path that somehow helped the Fae meet those who might be persuaded to join them in their travels.

My awareness said the surface was as solid as it looked. I mean, we'd just been walking on it. I held open hands out to the fae-path and extended mind energy beneath the surface.

The top of the path was like the border between sea and air. My awareness went right through it. Ever go swimming near shore and have something from the deeper ocean brush your leg? Something that was *almost thought* brushed against my mind. It was a shock. I forced myself not to withdraw. I'd learned in the next world over that no ordinary mind could hurt me.

It wasn't just one almost-mind in the road. Thousands upon thousands of not-quite-sentient beings swam toward the surface of individual consciousness but failed to reach it. It was this unseen, unfelt following tide, slow and agonizing, that propelled us as we walked along the fae-path with the travelers wrapped in light. The path was the source of *the light of other days* that wrapped the travelers.

The path was where the travelers came from; it was where many of them returned.

Help me, the unbreathing, unsleeping swimmers seemed almost to say, *Help us. Help.* Further they said not, because they could not. Help them do *what*? Intuition ladled out a dollop of impossibility. Did the Morrigna consolidate their rule over the Fae by dissolving their subjects into the fae-road? I'd seen them try to do that to Coran and Maeve. It wasn't the blackest possible black magic, but it was dark enough.

Jackson had first met the Morrigna underground beneath the Walloon's mansion. I imagined the Walloon's offer: *Build me a permanent doorway to the fae-road and I'll help you ascend to the throne of all the Fae. Use Moira; she works for me.* But why would the nightmare queens ally themselves with the Materialist Magicians?

Maybe the Morrigna had tried to leverage evil and been poisoned by it; they wouldn't be the first. Eventually everyone has to choose between good and evil. Finally realizing that, Coran and Maeve had rejoined the human condition and chosen rebirth.

Frustrated with the choices available in my mundane Portsmouth existence, I'd asked Leda *What's the point?* Making the choice of good or evil *was* the point of all existence. Little Janjan had chosen. I was all grown up now. I'd need to be.

I made a promise to the helpless beings trapped in the fae-path: *May all creatures be free from suffering. Though you are numberless, though it takes me forever, I vow to free you all.* Then I added: *In the name of Jesus Christ, amen!* Elves are syncretists in matters of belief, because the shadow of religious belief disappears in the light of experience. That's not a metaphor.

My followers were giving me worried looks when I came back to myself. I'd been standing silent for a long thirty seconds. I smiled and made eye contact with each of them.

"Just getting my bearings," I said. "Okay, follow me."

I didn't share my new knowledge; it wouldn't have helped. The loneliness of command and all that.

✳

The great hall was empty of heavy tables and benches. Times had finally changed. No happy throngs would feast, drink, and dance here of an evening anymore. Our footsteps echoed off thick stone walls and the high timbered ceiling. No happy couples and clusters would swive here tonight, not if they were flowing thoughtless as jellyfish in the fae-road tide.

At the head of the hall, atop a low dais, sat four massive wooden thrones, elaborately carved chairs, really. The thrones were lit by the poisonous dark-green glow of the naked creatures who sat in them. *Made it, Ma! Top of the world!*

The three women were young and beautiful again, no longer hags. I recognized two of them despite their smooth white (I assumed) skin and nearly identical chest-length cascades of hilarious oiled ringlet curls: *See how very nubile I am*. Gimme a break, what a ridiculous hairstyle. They were overdoing the girly stuff. Maybe queens of the Fae were *required* to be sort of drag-queeny. Maybe gender *was* performance, although it didn't feel that way to me. Maeve had also overdone the feminine dramatics when she tried to have her way with me. Poor Maeve, I wished her well.

The third woman was clearly kin to the first two former hags. I'd watched her return to the flesh back in Great Bog.

"Good evening, ladies," I said. "You're all looking lovely tonight." I'm such a troublemaker.

The Morrigna gave me the side-eye and didn't respond. They deferred to the man who sat among them glowing slime green. A large naked man thick with muscle.

"If it isn't the little elf whore," came the Walloon's unmistakable accented English, amplified by a broader chest and a thicker throat. "Were you so unsatisfied with interfering in the Order's business on Earth that you brought my servant Moira *here* where *I* am the only law? You may address me as *Your Majesty*."

"Since I called the late Coran of the Fae by his given name, I'll just call you *Louis*," I said. "By the way, Louie, where *have* all your people gone?"

"All the fae-folk serve us as we direct them, child," said one of the women. Her tone was mild enough, but the thought behind the words was colder than Portsmouth's winter. And "child" was it? The witch seemed to believe she was talking to a lesser being, like *what the Fae have instead of children*. Oh, and she was avoiding my direct question.

One of her pale-skinned sisters, glowing rotten-seaweed green, continued the thought, "As you lot will serve us, too." She sounded pretty sure of herself. She looked a challenge at my little group. My companions looked away. Only I held her dark gaze.

Three thrones fell into shadow behind the women as they stood up and walked toward me, carrying their sickly light with them. They moved slowly so as not to startle the prey. They luxuriated in their power over all of us who'd ventured into their realm.

I gestured Bobby, Moira, and her boys to retreat back to the wall near the door. They couldn't outrun fae magic, but I wanted to give them a chance to try. I was the only one of us who had a chance against the power of the Morrigna.

Not to mention the Walloon. What powers remained to *him* in this place? Interesting question.

As they approached, the three naked women underwent subtle transformations. The closer I looked, the more I saw *exactly* the sort of women I was drawn to. Was one of them fair-haired and slender now, like Beth? *Oh, my.* A second could have been the dark-haired, hardbodied sister of the Providence barista I'd flirted with. *Oh, dear.* The third began to look like one of those curvy, submissive, indefatigable porn goddesses who offer their moist biscuits to me in dreams, if you take my meaning. *Woof.* All three held out green-glowing hands in eloquent gestures of appeal. Would I not accept the ecstasies only available in their embrace? Would I not be so gracious as to give them the ecstasies I alone could give?

From behind the submissive Morrigna the dominant Walloon also stood up, the Real Slim Shady. He, too, gave me a wide berth. He strode a long slow path, moving behind me where, if I was willing, he would give me every pleasure I'd always dreamt of as he moved me like a rag doll wherever he liked. *No, you mustn't. Stop, you brute.* Instead of the short, slender older man he'd been on Earth, Master Louis of the Materialist Magicians now appeared younger, taller, massively muscled, and equipped with a penis I would have to struggle to accommodate because it was approximately the size of a man's thick forearm. Was I up for the challenge? Because *he* certainly was.

Where had they gotten these ideas of what would appeal to me? From my own unshielded surface mind, that's where. My thoughts and desires still clashed and broke, rough as storm surf, because I was still new to the next world over and its teachings.

The four of them wanted to use my weaknesses against me, as enchanters always do. They assumed I still followed the command that underlay both the human and the fae condition: *Do not inquire within.* They didn't know that the elves taught me how to work with gentle persistence until inner alchemy turned weaknesses into strengths.

I won't say I wasn't tempted. I was. Of course I was. With people's lives depending on my choice, it didn't matter that I half-wanted to surrender to temptation and put out the flame of my life in a blaze of orgasmic glory. Much as some dark part of me once sought self-destruction, I knew there was no way to extinguish myself forever. For one horrible moment, I saw where my old Portsmouth life had been taking me, what I'd secretly hoped to get out of all the sex I'd been having, little death after little death. I felt a rolling spasm of lust and nausea that had nothing to do with my deepest, truest pleasure.

Fae-sex seemed to be about pleasure, but it was really about maintaining the fae condition unchanged, *a sleep and a forgetting*, as the poet said. Where was Beth and Bobby's child now? What would have happened if Jackson and I *had* lain with Coran and Maeve and been transfused by *the light of other days*? What would happen to me now if I returned to my old ways to enjoy (and suffer) all the sex on offer here?

It wasn't all about *me* anymore. There's nowhere to hide if you betray those you love.

I was separated from all other elves in this dark place. Fae reality reflected their original decision not to choose between good and evil, but to go their own way.

If I was out of touch with *my* people here, then the Walloon was out of touch with *his*. I had no way to call for help. He couldn't summon his followers. I didn't think he could conjure his master, either. This place was beyond the reach of the Fallen Archangel who called himself Claimant to the Throne of God.

The Morrigna were in their element, though. This was their homeland. The fae-road was a bypass around the human worlds, one the Morrigna now ruled. Or were they subject the Walloon even here?

My strategy was a big question mark, but the tactical situation was clear enough. Three naked nightmare queens stood five feet in front of me. One naked Walloon walked a semicircle around us toward my still-ample, black-clad backside. He watched the four of us with baleful interest. I felt no clear threat from any of them yet. I hadn't thought this through, but when in any world did I ever do that? I wasn't worried; I'd never been much of a worrier. And I had more options these days than fight, flee, or fuck, if you'll forgive the vulgarity.

But if I *was* going to worry, I had other people to worry about now, didn't I? And here came Moira walking briskly from the wall where I'd sent her and the others. I didn't send her back; I wanted to see how this played out. Moira stood at my side and laid a sisterly hand on my shoulder blade: *We're in this together.* Turning her head quickly, Moira saw that the Walloon was keeping his distance. She didn't seem at all afraid of him. She turned back and gave the Morrigna a searching up-and-down look, very rude, very challenging.

"So is this what the Good People have come to?" Moira said. "When did ye give yerselves over to the Fallen and choose death for all the fae-folk, then?"

The third queen lost all appearance of submissiveness. She now looked a head taller than an instant before. She looked angry and threatening, like she might be up for a big night of souring cows' milk and causing stillbirths on Earth. You know, in case I needed more evidence that nothing on the fae-road was ever what it seemed to be.

"I am Anann of the Fae," said the third sister. "I was walking the human worlds and *breathing in* long before your grandmother's grandmother took her first breath and screamed it out. I have walked the land between life and death since before you were born, Moira of Earth." She avoided answering Moira's question. Good luck getting a straight answer from the Fae.

But Moira nodded to acknowledge Anann's words. Moira seemed to know the Morrigan in a way I did not.

"I'm Janjan of the next world over," I said. "I'd still like to know what happened to your people, Anann. I mean, before you and your sisters take me off to bed, or whatever you're planning."

"We've seen the likes of you before, elf-girl," Anann said. "We know what you are, who would be neither queen nor king among the Fae." A new anxiety in her tone. She looked behind me where the Walloon walked a slow circle, massive turgid member swaying, savoring the moment before he closed in and took sweet sexual revenge on me.

Anann hadn't answered my question any more than she'd answered Moira's. Was *that* the message? Were the ancient, shapeshifting Morrigna *unable* to speak for themselves because even here they were under the Walloon's power?

I turned my back on Badb, Macha, and Anann and left Moira facing them. Whatever they'd been in the past, whatever they looked like now, however they reconfigured their outward appearance, the Morrigna had no power that threatened me. If the fae-road had been a kind of Eden, the Walloon was the serpent who'd brought the place to ruination.

I turned to face the Walloon. He'd gotten closer than I'd thought, closer than I liked. He was poised for attack—physical, psychic, spiritual, magical, who knew? Before he could act, I spoke Elvish for the first time here among the Fae.

"Did you come here to escape the shadow of the Fallen, Louis?"

On hearing the Unfallen Tongue, he took an involuntary step back. His body lost mass before my eyes, but still glowed poison green. The bones and sinews shaping his face worked in ways I'd never seen before. It was meant to frighten me and it did. I'm only human. That terrible face showed me how deep the fear had eaten into Louis. He *needed* terror; he ran on it like a car runs on gasoline. He'd been allowed to come here where the Fallen could not because Louis' master had left its imprint in the man's spirit. I saw a faint copy of the Claimant's face under the Walloon's: the serpent of intelligent darkness who'd attacked Jackson *through* Louis. It was the miserific vision, that visage from far beneath the bottom of all worlds. Its kingdom was the Ruined Realm.

Like Jackson and me, Louis had a kind of *mandala* that guided him. Unlike Jackson and me, Louis' inner guidance bypassed his free will. I didn't think I'd be able to interest him in anything an elf-girl had to offer. I didn't even think he was interested in my pale-gold, lightly-freckled body, not really, except to despoil and destroy it.

Still, I refused to quit. *"The source of all creation needs no praise and has no throne to seize,"* I told him. *"And yet God wills that we be saved from everything that hurts us—if we so will."*

The Walloon's earthly size and appearance resumed itself, though he still shone green. Not an impressive figure of a man, but I didn't underestimate him. Louis' power was more than physical.

His mouth opened and an armada of horrible, jagged, hateful sounds sailed out of it. Old High Aghartic, the language of the Claimant, echoed off the stone walls of a fae castle for the first time in all their history.

Behind me, I sensed the Morrigna withdrawing from the onslaught the Walloon aimed at me, moving back toward their thrones. I guess he *was* in charge here.

The Walloon's words embodied the Original Sin, which less grandly was merely the Original Mistake: *I will not serve you, Sam-I-Am, I will not serve you in a boat, I will oppose you as a goat.* The words depicted all physical reality as a fraud and an offense against the dignity of the high purely-spiritual being who had chosen to fall out of creation and who then had sought to pull the whole material universe down with him. It was scary, but when you looked at it closely, it was also profoundly stupid. Those who embrace evil never *inquire within.* They deceive themselves that they're enlisting in a glorious revolution. What they're really doing is joining a temper tantrum already in progress.

Here on the fae-road, the Walloon was separated from his master, and therefore also separated from his deadliest weapon, the serpent of darkness he'd used against Jackson on Earth. What the Walloon did have, and directed against me, was the conviction embodied in High Aghartic, the Fallen Tongue, that there was only One Will in all the universe, and that every being must surrender its own little will to that One Will.

Or else.

Always making threats. Always denying the right to choose. The Materialist Magicians tried to take everyone's inalienable human rights away and dared to call it a struggle against tyranny.

I was separated from my husband and from my brothers and sisters in the next world over, but I could never be separated from who I was. Once I *inquired within*, I saw my own free will shining. I was as I had been created. I gave voice to these thoughts in the Unfallen Tongue.

Remember, the angel told me, *Love and Light*.

I remembered. I spoke the words just as the angel had spoken them. I shared my memory of that high and loving intelligence with the Walloon. Who could resist that?

He didn't *want* to remember anything about his own creation. He'd been forbidden to *inquire within*. Revulsion twisted his body. I felt the surging threat as he prepared for a physical attack to reinforce his attack on my psyche.

He gathered himself to spring at me.

I heard a loud *crack*. An arrowhead popped out of the Walloon's ear.

A yard-long wooden shaft pierced his skull side to side. My friend Bobby, the time-traveling sniper, had taken an old war bow off the castle wall, strung it, and put an arrow through our enemy's head. One shot, one kill, one ancient broken bow. I nodded my thanks and swallowed my nausea. I pray I never get accustomed to the taking of life.

Being what he was, the Walloon stood there still alive, directing an ugly, ugly look my way. Something like old pond scum leaked out both his ears. Eww. His mouth opened and closed a few times, like the arrow had scattered his thoughts. An ordinary man would have fallen down dead, but Materialist Magicians have negotiated a different relationship to the physical universe. He grasped the shaft, contemplating pulling it out.

He decided against that. Green light flared out of every part the

Walloon's body and into the stone floor of the castle. An abridged edition of the man himself stood embodied in what the poet called *darkness visible* with no trace of green. The arrow that had penetrated his head fell through the coherent smoke of his body. The arrowhead made a dull *tock* against the stone.

One minute he was standing there screaming obscene lies at me in that hideous ancient language. The next minute the greasy smoke of his dark spirit was...*gone*.

My perception followed him into the fae-road. What was left of his mind and body flew away at high speed through slow-moving green-lit schools of almost-minds. The Walloon's blackened essence swam like a shark inside the fluid fae-path.

I lost track of him behind massing thousands of proto-Fae. They all turned toward my mind like they were sunflowers and I was the sun. They were looking for some kind of help I didn't have to give them.

77

The Light of Other Days

When I turned around, I found Moira deep in deliberation with the three sisters. The Morrigna now looked older—and clothed. What the hell? I just shook my head and accepted what I saw. Moira was in no danger; I felt no threat. The three still shone green, but it was a purer, lighter green now. Had the Walloon taken all the darkness away with him?

Bobby and Moira's sons walked shakily across the stone floor. Bobby looked bleak, alert and fearless. I saw his war face.

"Dude, that was a *righteous* shot," Brad told Bobby.

"Word," said Chad. He held up his fist; Bobby, seeing nothing to celebrate, didn't bump it. Embarrassed, Chad patted Bobby on the back.

The three men avoided the spot where the Walloon had disappeared into the floor. I didn't blame them. A world where green giants can shrink, turn black, and disappear might also have invisible quicksand.

Bobby came and stood next to Moira, to protect her if he could from all dangers, physical and metaphysical. She snuggled close to him until she could stand no closer. Moira gave Bobby such a look. *Mah hero*, it said. He put his arm around her shoulders and faced the Morrigna bravely.

"Are *you* planning to kill us?" I asked the three phantom queens. Elves are blunt in matters of life and death.

They didn't answer immediately. Anann's head was cocked to one side like she was listening to something nobody else could hear. She and her sisters shared a look, and Anann just disappeared. Well, that's not quite right. She turned transparent green and left the castle like the wind. It happened so fast that it took my mind a moment to realize what my eyes had seen. The elves taught me to look directly without second-guessing visual input.

"Nay, lass," Badb finally said, "there's no need for killing now."

"Our sister's gone to see that Master Louis gets back to Earth and to his own master," said Macha. "She has the gift of travel between worlds, y'see."

I guess I saw what she meant. Sort of.

Less than a minute later, the green wind that was Anann swept back into the castle. She appeared standing next to her sisters once again, looking as solid as they did. Another round of nods. Either they shared thoughts or no words were necessary.

The three Morrigna invited us to sit with them on the edge of the dais, and here's the tale they told.

❋

The Fae had left Earth and gone their own way when there was no human history, only tales told around fires and embellished by each teller. The Morrigna were less interested in events than in mood, feeling, ecstatic abandon—and power.

The Morrigna were part of the fae condition like blue is part of the condition of the sky. That condition sought to maintain its near-eternal balance. Sometimes, said the Morrigna, the sky was covered by clouds.

Sometimes, like the sky, the fae condition went dark for a time. This was such a time.

Sitting there listening to them weave their tale was a strange experience in what had already been a thoroughly weird day in the weirdest Earth-year of my life. The three, speaking in turn, tried to weave their thoughts in our minds. I watched and listened from inside the calm center of myself. I saw no threat in the Morrigna, but they were very different from human beings, elf or earthling. Their interests were not human interests. How could they be?

In times past, the Morrigna said, the Fae would arm themselves (hence the old weapons hanging on the castle walls) and fight alongside this or that tribe in what sounded like Ireland, Scotland, or the Hebrides. They'd had long memories for grudges in those days, and their sense of honor was easily offended. Moira, said Macha, was descended from a noble warrior family who'd fought alongside the Fae against a monstrous inhuman foe. Moira, now deep in her warrior princess persona, nodded along as if this unlikely narrative was common family lore. Bobby and the boys sat and listened politely.

I gave an internal shrug. The story was no weirder than everything that had happened to me since I met Coran—and Bobby—in Great Bog.

Sometimes, said Badb, allies from Earth would come to live with the Fae "forever and a day." With, I assumed, the odd suspension of normal breathing, and the endless travel along the fae-road.

Some time ago, said Anann, the people of Earth began to change. (She evaded my questions about *how much* time and *what kind* of change.) No Earth-dwellers sought military help from the Fae. The Fae ceased to ally themselves with tribes or with nations anywhere on Earth. This had been Coran's decision, one the Morrigna couldn't talk him out of. (Anann was also evasive about their falling-out.)

Still, fae folk continued to walk near Earth to *recruit* earthlings, the way

Coran tried to recruit me. People went away with them and were heard of no more.

But even if you live almost forever and live mostly unchanged, *what you are* begins to wear thin. You eventually turn transparent green like Coran and Maeve.

At that point, the Morrigna said, those who walk the fae-road may choose to step off the path and lay their bodies down, as the last king and queen of the Fae had done. To let their spirits fly onward to human rebirth as their green fae-light shines off into the cosmos.

Or those transparent green Fae might elect to let their *light of other days* take them into the fae-road, body and soul. In the fullness of time, their lives would emerge in the new bodies of newborn Fae, scrubbed of all the weariness of memory.

Under normal circumstances, it would have made no difference to the Morrigna what Coran and Maeve chose. But during the sisters' long stay on Earth, the fae-path itself fell out of balance as the Morrigna fell under the Walloon's dark, delusive magic. They would have magicked the old king and queen back into the fae-road if Jackson and I hadn't stopped them. The sisters saw abdicating the throne as both a personal affront and a loss of the power they existed to preserve.

They'd thought to forge an alliance with the Materialist Magicians to draw more earthlings to the Fae. Separated from the power of the fae-road, the phantom queens found themselves subject to the power of the Order. Worse still, while the Morrigna stayed on Earth, no newborn Fae could grow to maturity. Without the three sisters, *what the Fae have instead of children* simply drifted back into the fae-path, as Beth and Bobby's son had done.

Did the Morrigna and the Order not have common interests? To maintain their way of suspended life, the Fae needed a steady influx of people from Earth. The MMs wanted to shunt anyone seeking the elves away from the next world over and to the Fae. So win-win, right?

It hadn't worked out that way. Jackson and I prevented the Order from making either Bobby or Moira into a permanent on-ramp to the Fae. The sisters returned to a kingdom sadly diminished by the loss of Coran and Maeve.

After evading Jackson and me, the demon-cloaked Walloon kept watch on Great Bog. He was watching the door out of Portsmouth from afar when Moira and Bobby opened it. Leaving his demon's embrace, the magician blew past us, invisible in a gust of magical wind. He flew above the fae-road to the nearest castle much faster than we could walk. The Morrigna found themselves still too weak to resist his dark magic. The three, whose being was suspended in refusal to choose between good or evil, were used by evil once again.

I had challenged the Order. Jackson had deserted and rebelled against it. Moira had failed the Walloon and then betrayed his financial secrets. In Jackson's absence, Louis planned to begin his revenge banquet with the sexual defilement and agonizing death of the woman Jackson loved. Little me. Then he'd use poor Moira's murder like a sorbet to cleanse his palate. After that, who knew?

The Walloon still held power over the Morrigna, even in a realm where they were part of the life cycle. To improve his chances of defeating me, Louis tried to take over the fae-path. He thought he could claim the throne of the Fae in the name of his master, the Claimant to the throne of God. There are places the Fallen Archangel cannot come and has no direct influence. Those places can still be laid waste by the evil within his devotees.

Evil bloomed like a black and deadly fungus in the green *light of other days* that animated the Fae and the fae-path. As the Walloon's own dark terror spread, it poisoned all the people who traveled the fae-road. Instead of becoming loyal soldiers of the Order, the Fae simply died. They sank into the road they'd walked, like melting snow sinks into April earth. *Death for all the fae-folk*, just like Moira said.

Of all the people who'd roamed the path around the human worlds for all the ages as travelers wrapped in light, only the Morrigna remained embodied. And they weren't exactly people, were they?

78

So What Happens Now?

"So what happens now?" I said. I wasn't asking the three weird sisters. The decisions that mattered belonged to Bobby, Moira, and her sons.

Moira made a face. "If the Walloon has gone back to Earth, nothing's changed. I'm not safe in Washington and the boys aren't safe at school."

Ugh. I wasn't about to have *that* conversation with her again.

"Bobby," I said, "would you like to come home with me and Jackson? It's safe there and you can rest."

Bobby asked Moira, "If I go with Janjan, will you come with me?"

Moira started her compulsive head-shaking routine. "I can't," she said. "I can't, I can't, *I can't.*"

Elves offer, but don't push. There's no forcing free will. I turned to Brad and Chad. "You guys want to come to the next world over with me?"

"I can't leave my mom," Brad said. Chad nodded agreement. They were rationalizing, but it wasn't my job to question their motives.

"Moira *needs* me, Janjan," Bobby said. "I think I ought to stay here with her. I don't know much about your world, but nobody on Earth needs me. And I guess we'll be safe enough here. Together."

Moira gave Bobby the kind of look I'd often given Jackson. As in, *Your eye hath not seen, nor ear heard, neither have entered into your heart, the things I have prepared for you who love me.*

The Morrigna seemed gratified by these developments, but not surprised. If they'd been around since the Garden of Eden, I guess they'd seen almost everything, and maybe more than once.

Badb spoke to Bobby and Moira on behalf of her sisters, "How'd you like to be King Robert and Queen Moira, then?"

Macha spoke to Moira's sons, "Not to worry, me young princelings. There'll be girls aplenty for you to dally with before long." Brad and Chad didn't quite know what to make of that, but who would?

"Assuming Bobby and your ma agree to wed and, erm, be fruitful and multiply on behalf of the Fae," said Anann. She gave me a direct look out of dark, fathomless, incomprehensible eyes, and what she might have been thinking was as hidden from me as the fae condition is from the elvish. "Once the Lady Janjan leaves us, I think everything will come right as rain on the fae-path. The Walloon and his ilk will never be able to return here, and *we'll* not be inviting them."

It seemed the Morrigna were capable of learning from experience.

❋

Anann walked the fae-road with me. As ever, the wind was at our backs and the road rose to meet our feet. I saw the road with different eyes now. The path had the cold, green depths of the Atlantic Ocean, but supported only one kind of life. And the struggle below our feet was not for survival, but to rise all the way to conscious mind. Thousands of sleepers struggled to awaken, unable to open eyes they didn't yet possess.

The Morrigan and I didn't read each other's thoughts. We were opaque to each other, except as regards facial expression and demeanor. I don't flatter either of us when I say that I was fully human, while Anann was both far more than human and far less.

We walked along in oddly companionable silence. I sensed her intention, joined with my own, whirling the road beneath us, taking us to the place where the fae-path came close to Portsmouth. Where, as I'd seen for myself, the walls between the worlds are thin.

Anann spoke without preamble. "You are the queen who is also a king, as anyone can see. Why did you not accept the throne when Queen Maeve offered it?"

"Better to reign in Hell than serve in Heaven?" I said. I was at least partly serious. It seemed to me that the proto-creatures below us, though having no self-awareness, suffered a nightmarish state. And what had they done to deserve it? Oh, right. They'd chosen not to choose between the good angels and the fallen ones. *Two roads diverged...*

Anann waved that idea aside. "You know that the Fae—and we who protect them—have naught to do with that old business. We went our own way in the beginning of all beginnings. My sisters and I only lived on Earth for so long to bring more people to the fae-road. We do not understand why *anyone* would refuse to come here."

I stopped on the path and the Morrigan stopped with me. I gazed into her eyes, but saw nothing in them to show she understood the human condition. *Do not inquire within* operates in the human sphere, but the Morrigna *had* no "within" in which to inquire.

"*Mortality*," I said. "Even here, Anann, Maeve tattered and frayed as her spirit chafed against her flesh. By the end, she'd become so transparent I could see right through her body. Nothing human lasts forever of itself, even if we *breathe in for half of eternity and breathe out for the other half.*" I spoke gently. It wasn't like I could argue her out of the condition of her own being, whatever it was.

Annan didn't argue. "Even a very long life may still have an ending," she agreed. "Even we Morrigna cannot make our folk *want* to keep living forever."

We started hiking again. I thought about how much people gave up when they accepted the strictures of the fae-road, a life that was really only a kind of suspended animation. I knew what else was out there for human beings in a way that Bobby, Moira, and her sons didn't know and weren't yet willing to learn.

We all make our own decisions and then live with the consequences. Anann, whatever sort of creature she was, knew that. The law of cause and effect is baked into the human worlds and into the fae-path that touches on them all.

❋

Eventually we got to the right place. As if through gray curtains, I saw the gentle snow-covered hills of Great Bog and the black trees half buried in white on the right side of the fae-road. One step through and I'd be out of the dry cool and into the icy wind again.

Annan laid a cool hand on my shoulder. I thought, *Someone who's not a human being is touching me*, but I didn't flinch away.

"You've been a good friend to your friends," she said. She meant Bobby and Moira and her sons. "You might have been our greatest queen. Such a pity."

"You'll take good care of my friends?" I said.

"Oh, aye. That's what we're *for*, y'see. And King Robert and his Queen Moira will have many and many a fae-child until once again throngs of us walk the road from world to world and call out to others to join us."

I imagined Brad and Chad would be able to join in with all the begetting at some point. That seemed weird and icky to me, but the Fae didn't have to worry about the recessive genes and hereditary idiocy attendant upon inbreeding on Earth. Being frat boys, Moira's sons might even rationalize sex with Fae women as *The great joy of serving others.*

"Moira's *fertile*?" I asked because I'd perceived on Earth that her childbearing years were over.

"She is *now*," said Anann. "Restoring a fae woman's fertility is child's play to us."

As I stepped off the fae-path into Great Bog, I got a distinct impression of Anann, Badb, and Macha working as one mind, although I saw only Annan. For just an instant, my breath stopped in my lungs once again. The Fae condition was restored. Bobby and Moira and the boys would have found themselves breathing with glacial slowness and not aging.

Then I was standing on Earth again, with both feet on the snowy ground of Portsmouth, and breathing normally. Such a relief.

I looked up at Anann and she looked down from her light-wrapped path at me for a moment. She looked inscrutable, and maybe that's how I looked to her.

Even in the next world over, human life is about change and discovery. On the fae-road, human life is about changelessness and forgetting. I knew why people would choose such a life: fear.

I'd chosen love instead and accepted love's obligations. That's the elvish condition as far as I understand it.

Anann traveled on. She and the fae-path vanished from my sight.

79

We've Got to Live

Ours is essentially a tragic age, so we refuse to take it tragically. The cataclysm has happened, we are among the ruins, we start to build up new little habitats, to have new little hopes. It is rather hard work: there is now no smooth road into the future: but we go round, or scramble over the obstacles. We've got to live, no matter how many skies have fallen.

D.H. Lawrence, *Lady Chatterley's Lover*

My brothers blamed me for my mother's death. Like *I'd* stayed in Buffalo, forced her to keep smoking, and smoked a pack a day along with her until her heart faltered. They knew blaming me was irrational, but that's how they felt. I was *the girl*; I should have stayed home with Ma. After all, they were married men now with families of their own to support, harrumph, harrumph. Neither of them dared to say these things to me. They'd always found my loud mouth and forthright manner unladylike and intimidating. Now they found my elvish silence frightening, but didn't know why.

But they awarded me partial credit for showing up at Ma's bedside to say goodbye like a dutiful daughter. My mother wasn't able to accept passage to the next world over, but she honored me by letting me guide her spirit on to what was next for her, as Jackson and I had guided Coran and Maeve. I was grateful that she'd given birth to me and always loved and cared for me, even if she never understood or liked me. Yes, I cried. I'm only human.

Her parish priest anointed her (it used to be called extreme unction or the last rites) and stayed in the hospital room to pray with the family. When he glimpsed what I did for my mother, he knew instantly what I was; I saw it in his surface thoughts. The Church knows more about the elves than it deigns to teach the faithful. The good Father made the sign of the cross while maintaining eye contact with me. Just to be on the safe side, I guess. As if *the elves* were ever the problem in the world. As if *Do not inquire within* was a religious duty.

Anyway. I didn't stay in Buffalo for the funeral. Jesus said *Let the dead bury the dead*, which sounds harsh until you think about it. I had obligations among the living.

❋

Jackson worked with the Elf Friends to help repair the damage the Materialist Magicians had been doing in the world. Once he'd done all *he* could do, the work became a weariness and a vexation of spirit. He went home to the next world over to wait for me. Wherever I went, my love and I were always in touch.

Between his own abilities and the resources of the Elf Friends, it would have been easy enough for Jackson to find his mother and his sister. He decided any surviving family would be safer if he left them alone. The Walloon was hiding out somewhere, licking his wounds and planning a vengeance comeback tour.

❋

My second earthly task back in Portsmouth involved finishing Leda's and Jerry's story and turning it over to the Friends so they could put it on their website, *When Is an Elf Not an Elf?* A sweet little Elf Friend intern whose *nom de guerre* was Bobbi (synchronicity?) volunteered to help me. She didn't seem to be able to help *gazing* at me, scanning me up and down like I suited her right down to the ground, the same way Jackson looked at me. I could practically hear 2 Live Crew performing "Face Down, Ass Up." She made it abundantly clear that she would welcome me into her bed with great enthusiasm, but she also understood that married elves like me don't play that.

Bobbi also volunteered to impose some order on my hodgepodge of notes about what happened to me among the Fae, among the elves, and on Earth. Like so many people, she was strongly drawn to the next world over and those who live there, but also frightened. Her plan was to get as close as she could without actually making the trip. Yet.

❋

My third earthly obligation involved Beth. She might have disappointed me, but she was still my friend. We can't expect perfection of people, and I owed Beth.

I called her before I left Portsmouth. We met in the same Providence coffee shop where Bobby had agreed to help me find the Fae one last time. The place was half full when I walked in. Beth had already gotten tea for us both and had staked out a table.

I saw Beth before she saw me. She was dressed for a date in a Little Black Dress that was exactly the right length. Legs up to here and shoes with very high heels. Good thing most of Providence's snow had melted. Her blonde hair was artfully arranged in a fancy ponytail. She looked gorgeous, but I couldn't help noticing that she'd gotten long French fingernails that rendered her hands decorative but useless. *There's* a fetish I've never understood.

Oh, Beth, I thought. Then I let the thought go. We are what we are, I guess, and there's no controlling other people. Not in any world I want to live in. Free will.

Beth caught sight of me and waved me over. She'd always been transparent and now I saw conflicting thoughts and mixed feelings flowing across her face.

She stood up, towering over me on her high heels, and we hugged with real affection.

"You look beautiful," I said as we sat down, practically on the same side of the little table.

Beth waved a hand to dismiss the compliment. Part of her genuine appeal was that she didn't know how beautiful she was. "Mr. Right is picking me up for drinks and an early dinner," she said. "As I read the man-signs, he's probably going to propose tonight."

"What'll you say?"

"I'll probably say yes." She didn't sound terribly enthusiastic. I heard the Sound of Settling in her voice.

Beth told me about her life in Providence. How she'd continued living at home, much to her mother's satisfaction. How she'd met Mr. Right, an executive in a tech company that employed the accounting firm where she worked. How he'd been smitten by her, an old-fashioned girl, as he thought. How she'd refused to sleep with him until they were dating exclusively. How she'd then boinked his brains out. And how it seemed he was now addicted to her.

"*The Rules*, Janjan," she said. "That book really works!"

I just nodded to show I was following her train of thought and kept listening with an open heart. *She* knew what she was saying was bullshit, but I didn't have standing to call her on it, not anymore. Friendships change here on Earth.

"So anyway, his firm is promoting him and sending him to Texas. I'll probably be going with him, if I read the tea leaves right." She didn't sound all that excited about moving south.

"I hear the winters are milder down there," I said, just to be saying something.

Tears welled up in Beth's eyes. She fumbled some tissues out of her clutch and dabbed carefully so as not to mar her dramatic eye makeup. "*Dammit*, Janjan," she said, "why *shouldn't* I move someplace warmer? This has been the worst winter of *my whole fucking life.*"

"I know what you mean," I said. "I was there for it, remember?" I smiled at her.

She smiled back and then aimed a critical eye at me. "You look so *beautiful*," she said, like she was surprised to see it. "You're dressed down in black like some Goth chick, but you *glow.*"

"Jackson and I got married." I told her because she deserved to know.

"Oh, honey, I'm so *happy* for you," she said and dabbed the corners of her eyes again. She was absolutely sincere.

"'I'm happy for you, too, Beth. If you're happy, I'm happy."

She made a big deal of stuffing the tissues back into her clutch. "I guess I'm close enough to happy," she said. She was exaggerating, but again that wasn't for me to tell her. "Um, how's *Bobby* doing? If you happen to know, I mean."

"As far as I know he's okay, Beth. He met somebody who seems very taken with him. She has kids from a previous marriage, so Bobby will get to be a step-dad. I think he'll like that." She didn't need to know he was king of the Fae; it would just weird her out.

Beth looked down at her tea. "That's good," she said quickly. What she meant was, *I don't want to hear any more about this.* Then she looked up at me. "Janjan, am *I* in any danger still?"

I locked eyes with Beth so she'd see I was being straight with her. "The best I can say is *Maybe not.* The worst I can say is *Maybe.*"

She nodded. "I'm not *stupid.* I *know* there's only one safe place. I just don't want to go there."

Beautiful girls are tempted to think they can have everything their own way—at least while their beauty lasts.

I handed her a business card from the Elf Friends' Boston law firm. "I have to head out pretty soon," I told her. "If you ever need my help, these people will know how to get in touch with me." I was sure she wouldn't let me give her a *mandala* like the one Leda gave me. She wanted to be done with the elves.

She wanted to be done with *me*.

We finished our tea and left the coffee shop together. We hugged goodbye out on the sidewalk and went our separate ways.

There's so much sadness even in a fortunate life. If you had a wonderful time in college like I did, it might take you years afterward to get over the fact that *those days are never coming back*, no matter how many boys you sleep with. If you go to war, you'll carry that experience around with you forever like Bobby does—and I guess like Jackson and I do now.

But the thing that I didn't expect was how your old friendships can dry up and blow away. The Buddha was right, the world is a burning house. Feeling all the Earth's sadness makes it hard for me to breathe. I can understand why people walk with the Fae to stop breathing in sadness the way earthlings are forced to do. But even on the fae-road, deep human sadness colors all the happy songs.

There is now no smooth road into the future, the poet said, blessedly ignorant of the Fae. If he'd glimpsed the next world over, he would have known you could walk there. Like I did.

No one saw me step off that Providence sidewalk. As I stepped onto the eternally-warm earth of the next world over, Jackson was there to welcome me home. And there we were where we were supposed to be, in each other's arms in the only place in all the human worlds where no weirdness ever comes.

Dedication

Joining Janjan is dedicated to the young women who have become my friends on Facebook and elsewhere on the internet. I'm talking about you, Doc, DD, Froggy K, Penny, Moo, Fraggle, Sandia, Tentmaker, Toxie, and Siddal, just to name a few. Whether we've met in person or only talked online, I value your friendship. I could not have written this book without you and the stories you tell me about your lives.

Author's Note

✳

Joining Janjan *is a work of fiction. This means that it's* made up, *as are all the characters in it, except for some actual historical figures mentioned in passing. Those who care about such things may notice that I have again taken some liberties with the geography of Portsmouth and its borders and environs. Among other things.*

The book takes place shortly after the events described in Loving Leda *(the first Portsmouth Paranormal Romance, published by Piscataqua Press in 2015) and is set in the same twenty-first century universe as most of the Nextworld Trilogy.*

The Nextworld Trilogy contains all the backstory for those who would like to learn about the Portsmouth Wars and those who fought in them: the Materialist Magicians (who really are both those things) and the elves (who aren't really the elves of legend at all.)

The Next World Out *takes place only a few years after* The Next World Under, *the second book of the series, and more than twenty years after the events described in* The Next World Over, *the first book of the trilogy.*

Each of these novels stands on its own. If I've done my job properly, you don't have to read either the Trilogy or Loving Leda. *But you don't want to miss anything, do you? (You can find all my books by searching Barnes & Noble or Amazon.com for David H. Barnette.) Enjoy!*

When I finished Joining Janjan, *I learned that our heroine still had more to say. She'll be back in a third Portsmouth Paranormal Romance; I'm working on it now.*

David H. Barnette, March 2016

About the Author

David H. Barnette is a lifelong resident of Portsmouth, New Hampshire, where he lives with his wife Judy.

He is a graduate of Portsmouth High School. After graduating from Syracuse University, he served with the U.S. Navy in Vietnam. After working many years as a federal civilian employee, he now writes full time.

www.ingramcontent.com/pod-product-compliance
Lightning Source LLC
Chambersburg PA
CBHW051508250626
47156CB00001B/8